THE
NORTHFIELD
WAY

THE NORTHFIELD WAY

A NOVEL

RICK DUNN

The Northfield Way
First Edition, 2019
Copyright © 2019 by Rick Dunn

This novel is a work of fiction. Names, characters, places, and incidents either are the product of the author's imagination or are used fictitiously. Any resemblance to actual events, locales, organizations, or persons living or dead is entirely coincidental and beyond the intent of either the author or the publisher.

To order additional books:
www.amazon.com
www.northfieldway.com

ISBN: 978-1-7331186-9-9

E-book also available

Editorial and Book Packaging: Inspira Literary Solutions, Gig Harbor, WA
Cover Design: MTWdesign, Dickson, TN
Book Design: PerfecType, Nashville, TN
Printed in the USA by Ingram Spark

To all the coaches, teachers, leaders, and mentors who humbly,
and most often anonymously, change the world one young life a time.
You are my heroes.

To all our TN Fury coaches: may we always
"compete to win, coach to change lives."

To my children, now grown adults: I pray that seeing my story in this
story encourages you to dive deep into the redeeming waters of grace.

To my wife, Teresa: I am so thankful for our well-worn paths of grace
and love, paths that have led me back to you for four decades.
I love you.

*A coach will impact more people in one year
than the average person will in an entire lifetime.*

Reverend Billy Graham

EIGHT YEARS EARLIER

No one lives well who lives alone.
Coach John McKissack

errick "D" Walker guzzled the last sips of his first beer. As he lowered the empty can, gentle morning breezes gave way to swirling, surging bursts of wind. Dampened by Echo Lake's foggy surface, a sudden chill in the morning air met exposed skin. Derrick's whole body, startled by the cold from within and without, convulsed into a hard shiver.

Sitting cross-legged on the gray-weathered dock, Derrick rubbed his bare arms and legs. He reached again into the battered green cooler, yanking an icy can free from the fractured cubes holding it hostage. His personal goal was to be stone-cold drunk by the time the last Northfield senior shook Principal Davis' hand. With ten Old Milwaukees still untouched and an estimated ninety minutes remaining in the graduation ceremony, he appeared to be right on schedule. Plenty of beer. Plenty of time.

Derrick chugged his second beer, then lifted the empty can mockingly to the sky. "Here's to you, Northfield Senior Class!" he shouted.

Uncrossing his legs, he scooted himself, his cooler, and his backpack to the edge of the dock. He reached into his back pocket and pulled out a crumpled pack of Marlboro Reds. From his navy Under Armour backpack, he retrieved a yellow disposable lighter and a limp, wrinkled manila folder. He lit his cigarette, then reached into the cooler for his third can of beer.

Steadily alternating between drags and sips, Derrick surveyed the folder's loose layers of newspaper clippings. The oldest clipping read, *"Freshman Walker Nets 25 in Northfield Debut."* The *Lewis County Gazette* article hailed the arrival of Northfield's "golden boy." Derrick lifted the clipping to eye level, holding it outstretched over the water. He lit his lighter once more. Slowly, he moved the bright yellow flame into contact with the paper. His eyes followed the consuming fire's path as he raised the paper as high as he could reach. As the flame's sharp, burning edge rapidly approached his fingers, Derrick released what little remained of the clipping. The flaming fragment floated downward until fire met water. Thin strands of white smoke rose upward. The soaked, burned memory sank silently into the dark waters of Echo Lake.

Derrick repeated the process over and over, one article after another. *"Walker Named Region MVP." "Walker Fastest to 1000 Points in Northfield History." "Northfield Star D. Walker Gaining National Attention."* Each clipping met the same fiery fate, wafting gently toward its watery grave.

Seeing the pile reduced to a small collection of more recent articles, Derrick paused to review each one. *"Top-ranked Northfield Cruises Behind D. Walker's 43 Points." "Derrick "D" Walker Sets Northfield Record for Career Points."* Carried along by an alcohol-induced buzz, Derrick's thoughts drifted back to that record-setting December night. He smiled with deep satisfaction. That night, just six short months ago, had been his proudest, most memorable game in the navy and gold Northfield uniform. It had also been his last.

"What a run!" Derrick thought. He recalled the countless fans adoring him, multiple top-tier NCAA coaches recruiting him, and beautiful girls pursuing him. He raised his drink as a tribute to those brief but brilliant moments spent basking in the spotlight.

Derrick finished what little beer remained in the can and grabbed a fourth, which he drained as quickly as the first ones. Dropping his bare feet into the shadowy water, he leaned back on his elbows and recounted his stellar accomplishments. Glorious memories, aided by cold beer, temporarily took the edge off his aching, raw emotions. A welcomed, slow-moving numbness gradually overtook him, body and soul.

Derrick suddenly realized that his carefully planned ritual remained unfinished. Abruptly, he sat up, resolute in his commitment to complete his mission. He grabbed the final clipping from the shabby manila folder and read the headline in a voice that closely mimicked a village herald making a royal pronouncement. "Hear ye, hear ye," he began, *"Coach John McKissack Dismisses All-American Derrick Walker from Northfield Squad."*

Derrick raised his lighter to Northfield's most infamous story of broken dreams and wasted potential. As the flame turned from yellow to orange, Derrick watched the fire spread rapidly toward his forefinger and thumb. He held tightly to this final remnant of lost dreams. He watched and waited. The flame's searing heat began burning his skin. Gritting his teeth, he held on for two seconds longer. Then he ceremoniously released his grip. The charred testimony to the dramatic rise and fall of Derrick "D" Walker floated gently downward, disappearing forever.

As the last plume of gray smoke rose skyward, Derrick stared into Echo Lake's cold, still waters. Leaning even further, he examined himself in the lake's mirror-like surface. Expecting to see the blond-haired, blue-eyed, bronze-bodied "golden boy" who had once been the hometown hero, Derrick instead encountered a dark, swollen face with barely visible eyes. The unfamiliar image seemed as distant as it was blank.

"Gone," Derrick thought to himself, "It's all gone." Then he added, in a soft whisper, "I'm all gone."

Derrick turned sharply away from the troubling reflection. Returning to his faithful companions in the green cooler, Derrick reached for beer number five. He chugged it, and all the ones that followed, as rapidly as his shivering body could tolerate.

Somewhere around eight beers and 12:10 p.m., Derrick hovered between stupor and sleep. For a moment, he lingered in a dream of what might have been. *Leaving his left hand, just over the outstretched arm of a defender, the ball rotated in a perfect arc toward the goal. Derrick knew. The opposing team knew. The whole crowd knew. D Walker had just released the game-winning state championship three-point shot.*

Derrick groggily forced open his bloodshot eyes. He squinted, trying in vain to focus his vision. Rubbing his aching forehead, he surveyed the scattered empty beer cans and the tattered empty folder. Emptiness surrounded Derrick as every ember of hope he once possessed lay extinguished in the murky waters of Echo Lake.

At that same moment, just three miles to the west, Principal Davis heartily welcomed Derrick's former classmates "to the first day of the rest of your lives."

NOVEMBER

Life expands to the size of your "WHY."

Coach John McKissack

CHAPTER 1

Unacceptable! Completely unacceptable!" Coach Mac growled. His voice rumbled and rolled like distant thunder. His lips thinned, folding inward as clenched jaws ground molar against molar. His massive six-foot, six-inch frame stiffened into a rigid, silent stillness. Every muscle and tendon held steady, locked and loaded.

To players standing nearby, Coach Mac resembled a prowling lion stalking its prey—highly agitated on the inside, motionless on the outside, storing up energy and preserving power.

Glaring straight ahead, lips still constrained by the tension in his jaws, Coach Mac's voice growled, "What do you see, Coach Walker?"

The question startled Northfield's twenty-six-year-old first-year teacher and assistant coach. Until moments ago, he had been fully engaged, taking in every disappointing play of the poorly executed, sloppy scrimmage. Sensing his coach was nearing a breaking point, Derrick's thoughts drifted back to Coach Mac's comments earlier in the week. "We're going to lead them relentlessly," he had advised, "but we're going to love them even more."

Coach Mac repeated his question, jolting Derrick into the present.

"First of all," Derrick began, speaking as if he were actually prepared, "I don't see much effort. I mean, I guess that's obvious." Derrick's cheeks flushed. He drew a deep breath and dove back in. "And, well . . . okay, second of all, I've already counted three turnovers for Zeke. And, our defense sucks!"

Derrick panicked. He closed his eyes, painfully imagining a typical Coach Mac response. "Make a contribution, Coach D. Don't just spew words that say nothing, and mean less."

"What I meant to say is, well," Derrick added, "our defensive rotations are way too slow. And, there's a complete lack of communication. No one's competing at a high level."

Coach Mac remained silent, his gaze fixed on the increasingly wretched basketball being played on the court bearing his name. Hearing nothing, Derrick glanced over his shoulder. He quickly registered the scowl deepening on Coach Mac's face. Derrick observed tightly locked arms and a taut jaw. A scowl deepened on Coach Mac's visage.

Derrick turned back toward the court just in time to see Northfield's co-captain, all-state senior point guard Isaiah "Zeke" Styles, fail miserably. His attempt to defend against a fast break was half-hearted at best. Zeke's weak effort against the second unit led to an easy layup by the much slower freshman, Bam Bam Wells.

Derrick turned back towards Coach Mac. He watched Coach's eyes narrow and his shoulders rise. Derrick heard a long, low growl escalating from somewhere deep in Coach Mac's chest. And then, the lion pounced.

"ENOUGH! THAT'S ENOUGH Everyone STOP—NOW!" Coach Mac roared. "I don't want a single one of you to move. Stand right where you are!"

All motion immediately ceased, on the floor as well as on the sidelines. The gym floor resembled a large-bodied version of the childhood game of freeze tag. Even Northfield's head custodian, Carny, stopped in his tracks. Only a lone basketball still moved. The ball rhythmically retreated off the court in a series of diminishing bounces that echoed loudly through an otherwise still, silent arena.

Coach Mac methodically weaved his way through the maze of rigid bodies. Silently he prowled among them. Under the scrutiny of Coach Mac's stare, each player lowered his eyes, then his head. No one wanted to see his own half-hearted effort reflected in Coach Mac's piercing eyes.

"Zeke." Coach Mac summoned his senior floor leader firmly.

"Yes, sir!" Zeke responded with the tone of a marine called out by his sergeant.

"Come and stand beside me, son." Coach Mac's eyes never broke contact with Zeke's face. The senior co-captain, clearly guilty of poor energy and effort, jogged his way sheepishly to Coach Mac's side.

"Jamarcus," Coach Mac spoke resolutely, turning his gaze toward the team's recently honored *USA Today* pre-season high school All-American. Jamarcus was only the second player in the school's storied history ever to receive this lofty designation. The only other player to rise to such heights had plummeted faster and farther than he had risen. Ironically, that player, D Walker, now stood just a few feet from away from Coach Mac as well.

"Yes, sir," Jamarcus said quietly. In typical fashion, Jamarcus drew no attention to himself. He simply repositioned his six feet, eight inches of lean muscle next to Coach Mac's side.

"Coach Walker, would you please offer your assessment of our morning so far?" Raising his eyebrows, Coach Mac lowered his chin and added, "And please give us your clearest, most precise version."

Derrick moved to center court. Like a prosecuting attorney delivering a closing argument, he labored to choose each word with strategic precision. The delivery was neither as weighty nor as polished as Coach Mac's. Still, every word and movement by the rookie assistant coach was an unmistakable reflection of his legendary mentor's influence.

Coach Mac offered no response to Derrick's summation of the scrimmage. Instead, he instantly singled out Zeke and Jamarcus.

"As senior leaders and co-captains of this team, how would you describe the morning's effort?" Coach Mac stood leaning back, arms folded loosely. Silently and patiently, he glanced back and forth between his two senior leaders.

"Bad, real bad . . . lazy, Coach. Like you said, 'unacceptable.'" Zeke spoke first, as always.

Jamarcus was content to have Zeke speak for both of them. Coach Mac was not. His clenched arms and unflinching eye contact made that clear.

"Embarrassing, Coach," Jamarcus added, dropping his shoulders.

"Well said, men. Zeke, Jamarcus, the truth is you both look tired. And I understand. It's 8:30 in the morning on a Saturday. And it's cold. Plus, you know, it's been a long run over the last three years. You've both started every game since you were freshmen. Barring anything unforeseen, you will both graduate with more minutes played as Northfield players than anyone in history. What's more, if this team fulfills its potential, you will have captained more state championships than any player in Northfield history."

The co-captains turned toward each other, their faces contorted into puzzled expressions. "Is this good?" Zeke mouthed silently to Jamarcus. In response, Jamarcus closed his eyes as he hung his head. He then moved it rapidly back and forth in small, despairing arcs.

Coach Mac stretched his long arms around his leaders' strong shoulders, drawing them close. "So," he continued, "let's give you both a well-deserved break. Joey, put two chairs over by my spot on the sidelines. Zeke and Jamarcus, I'm going to have you sit on each side of me for the rest of our practice."

Joey, the team manager, unfolded two navy blue metal chairs. He hurriedly placed one on the right and one on the left of Coach Mac's designated coaching spot.

Waving them toward their specially assigned chairs, Coach Mac implored, "Have a seat, gentlemen."

"Coach, we're good. That is, you're right. Our effort was horrible. But we can get it going. You don't have to sit us," Zeke blurted frantically.

"No, Zeke, I think this will do just fine." Coach Mac responded. His tight lips relaxed as they widened ever so slightly. A twinkle sparkled in his eye.

"Everyone else on the baseline." Coach Mac stretched his extensive right hand and index finger in the direction of the arena's east end. Each player made his way, shoulders slumped and heads wagging, to the baseline. They scattered themselves along the large blue letters, "NORTHFIELD."

Coach Mac continued. "Gentleman, Coach Walker's assessment was somewhat helpful. But, in the end, he failed to address the core problem."

Derrick sighed. His eyes shut tightly. His stomach churned. Recently, any perceived criticism, even the slightest hint of someone's disapproval, triggered a rapid descent into a dark, anxious mood. At the bottom, the internal message was always the same: "You're such a screw up!"

With his right hand, Derrick began rubbing the back of his neck, skirting the base of his hairline. Tilting his head slightly back, he tried in vain to stretch and loosen muscles that had twisted themselves into angry knots. As he continued to rub his neck back and forth, Derrick leaned his head back to its full extent. His eyes raised. Then his heart sunk.

There it was. More precisely, there it wasn't. Where a championship banner should have been hanging, there was only empty space. Following Derrick's dismissal from the team in December of his senior season, the Warriors, the unanimous pre-season number one team in the state, faltered miserably. No state championship. No region championship. Not even a district championship.

Eight years removed from having been Northfield's most colossal disappointment, Derrick feared failure even more now. A bottle of Prilosec and a collection of sleeping aids lying beside his bed bore witness to his daily battles. "Stay in the present," Derrick coached himself.

The self-coaching worked, temporarily. He redirected his attention back to Coach Mac who, at the moment, was calmly holding court.

"This complete disaster of a scrimmage is, in fact, the natural result of failed leadership. Our senior co-captains selfishly failed to bring their whole hearts to this practice. That's the core of our problem." Coach Mac paused, taking a moment to look to the right and then to the left. "Zeke and Jamarcus, you are great young men. And, you are both exceptional leaders," Coach Mac continued. "But today, well . . ." Coach paused for emphasis, "you just decided it wasn't worth the effort. Am I right?"

"Yes, sir," Zeke responded uncomfortably.

"Yes, sir. Unfortunately, that's true, Coach," Jamarcus spoke softly. As a sign of respect, his eyes remained riveted in unflinching contact with Coach Mac's eyes.

"Yes, 'unfortunate' is a good word, Jamarcus. For all of us." Coach Mac turned to the remaining players. "Men, when leaders fail to lead, their teammates and friends pay a heavy price. That's what I've been watching all morning. Now, Zeke and Jamarcus, you can watch with me."

Zeke and Jamarcus sank deeply into their chairs.

To the players scattered in a crooked line along the blue-painted NORTHFIELD, Coach Mac barked, "Men, step up to the baseline. You're going to run ten suicide sprints."

A collective groan rose from all thirteen players. Rico Martinez, the team's sixth man and its most unfiltered emotional presence, threw his arms into the air. Then he squatted dramatically, to the floor, slapping his hands on its polished wooden surface.

Senior big man Ty "Thor" Thornton glared at his fellow seniors slumping in their folded chairs. When Coach Mac momentarily turned his back, Thor flashed both middle fingers in Zeke and Jamarcus' direction. The six-foot five, two-hundred-and-eighty-pound, seventeen-year-old Thornton had recently been named an all-state offensive tackle. But with the football season having ended just eight days earlier, the superb athlete was far from being in basketball shape.

"Joey," Coach Mac said loudly. The anxious freshman jumped to attention. "Please bring our weary co-captains some cold Gatorades and some nice, cool fresh towels. Let's make them completely comfortable during the festivities."

In the end, neither Zeke nor Jamarcus touched the Gatorades. Or the towels. Instead, they sat restlessly, legs bouncing up and down, heads lowered.

After much sweat, tears, and heaving, the ten sprints mercifully came to an end. After gathering the thirteen physically depleted players alongside his well-rested co-captains, Coach Mac moved toward the close of practice. His final instructions were, "Before you leave, shoot free throws until you make fifteen, then go home and hydrate. The next time I will see you is tomorrow night for the Northfield Nation banquet. And, remember, be dressed in line with our team travel dress code. Look sharp, be sharp."

To his co-captains, he added, "I fully expect that we will not experience a similar failure to lead on Monday night when we play Wautoca County. Are my expectations correct, men?"

"Yes, sir!" the pair asserted immediately, their voices thoroughly soaked in remorse.

"Coach, I just want to say . . ." Jamarcus began.

Coach Mac uncharacteristically interrupted his star leader. "Not now, Jarmacus. You and Zeke are still our leaders. As our leaders, there will be a time when we need you to lead with your words. Right now, we need you to lead with your actions. Earn the right to be heard, to be believed, to be respected."

Coach Mac then pointed toward the two seniors, using a long, thin "v" made with the forefinger and middle finger of his right hand. "We can't afford a game, a practice, or even a drill where the two of you choose not to lead."

Coach turned to leave, then quickly swung back. Appearing to have suddenly remembered something extremely urgent, he looked directly at the co-captains. "And, let's make one thing perfectly clear . . ." Coach Mac said as he pointed toward the sky with his right index finger.

Zeke and Jamarcus held their collective breath as Coach reloaded his passion, "Zeke, Jarmarcus, I love you both. I'm very proud to be your coach—even on your worst days."

"We love you, too, Coach . . ." Jamarcus replied, the whites of his eyes turning a light shade of red.

"Yeah, even on our worst days, we love you, Coach," Zeke added, his eyes rising to meet Coach Mac's intense stare.

As the players were dismissed to shoot free throws, Zeke and Jamarcus made their way to the baseline's blue NORTHFIELD lettering. "Coach Mac, sir, we need you to count. If you would, please?" Jamarcus asked.

Coach Mac responded with a very slight, but undeniably respectful downward tilt of his head.

"One," Coach Mac yelled proudly after the first completed suicide sprint. By the time he called out, "Ten," the remainder of the team had finished their free throws. They assembled themselves as one around Coach Mac and Coach Walker. Somewhere around the fourteenth sprint, the whole team began counting aloud. Not one player left their spot to get a drink or a shower or even to send a quick text to a girlfriend.

Nearing the end of sprint sixteen, Jamarcus and Zeke could no longer run or jog. They simply walked, as fast as they could still move their burning legs, through sprint number seventeen—and beyond.

As coaches, players, Joey, Carny, and even the cheerleaders gathered in the stands, yelled in unison, "Twenty!" Zeke and Jamarcus collapsed into individual heaps. Sprawled across the "N" and "T" in "NORTH-FIELD," they lay motionless except for the pronounced rising and falling of their chests. Joey hustled a pair of Gatorades to their sides. Both were in too much pain to care. All thirteen of their teammates rushed to encircle them. Thor lightheartedly jeered at his fellow seniors, taunting their faces' pained expressions. The underclassmen, recognizing their place in the team hierarchy, simply smiled silently.

As the coaches made their way over to the huddle of players, Coach Mac quizzed Derrick. "What do you see now, young Walker?"

"Leadership, Coach," Derrick responded with full confidence. "I see leadership."

"Zeke. Jamarcus," Coach Mac shouted toward his exhausted co-leaders.

"Yes, Coach?" Zeke spoke faintly, wearily panting for another breath.

"Fifteen made free throws before you leave. Got it?"

Simultaneously, each raised up to offer a weak, gasping, "Yes, sir, Coach," before returning their heads to the floor.

Extending his arm around Derrick's shoulders, Coach Mac leaned down. "High accountability and deep grace," Coach Mac reflected, "That's how leaders are made, D. That's how we build 'em the Northfield Way."

CHAPTER 2

Chris Denton carefully guided his late-model Nissan into a sharp left-hand turn, heading east onto County Road 261. Chris was less than ten minutes from entering Lewis County, but more than thirty-five minutes from entering his parents' driveway. Over the last hour, the gently floating flurries of the early Saturday evening had swelled into a heavy, wet snowfall. By now, the thick flakes were accumulating at the rate of an inch every half hour. The rural two-lane county road had quickly morphed from a dusty, dulled black asphalt pathway into a glistening, slick white carpet.

Chris rolled his head back and forth, hoping to prompt a relaxing crackling of the vertebrae in his neck. Then he raised his cell phone high toward the windshield. He held its glowing screen just to the right of his face, insuring a clear line of sight through whatever blurry visibility remained. He could almost audibly hear his mother's voice, "Chris, put that phone down and watch the road! You're going to get yourself killed before you reach your twenty-second birthday!" Closing the heart pumping playlist, "Game On!," Chris switched to the more soothing sounds of his "Chillin' Me Softly" playlist. Given his need for calm nerves and a steady hand, a little Chance the Rapper alongside vintage Lionel Richie and the timeless Otis Redding seemed a better choice than Queen and Pink Floyd.

Lowering his phone back to its rightful place in the console, Chris returned his full attention to the road. Immediately, he heard, and felt, an explosive, loud "POP!" The steering wheel jerked hard to the right, nearly wrenching itself from Chris' two-handed grip. Even with both hands,

Chris struggled with all his strength to regain control. Relying on every muscle in his upper body and every reflex he had developed in six short years of winter driving, Chris fought the Altima in what felt like hand-to-hand combat. Instinctively, he kept turning the steering wheel in the direction of the car's skid. Battling against the combined wills of the three remaining good tires, Chris pressed the brakes gradually. With a prayer of desperation added to the mix of nerves and muscles, Chris narrowly escaped both careening into a tailspin and slamming into a ditch.

When the car finally came to a full stop, the Altima was exactly in the middle of the road, and mostly headed in the right direction. Chris collapsed, sweat-soaked, into a long sigh of relief. He shuddered as he realized how close he had come to losing control of his car. That thought alone was sufficient to rattle Chris' nerves, even without the realization he had been driving on a deserted, snow-covered, two-lane road in, of all places, Bedford County.

With the flat left front tire flopping wildly in the snow, Chris eased the car onto the shoulder's thick layers of gravel and snow. Hands still shaking, he called his dad.

Martin was as reliable of a man and as good of a dad as any son could hope for. His job as a long-haul trucker, however, was extremely demanding. Much to his personal dismay, his family had learned to live in the disappointing reality of his absence. Thankfully, this was one of the few weekends he was home on a Saturday night.

"Pops, it's me, Chris. I need help," Chris spoke as calmly as possible, given his rising anxieties. He was grateful his dad was home. If he were gone, Chris' seventeen-year-old brother Jamarcus would be the default person on call.

"Chris, you okay? You don't sound too good—what's wrong, son? " Martin's anxiety matched, then exceeded, his son's.

"I'm fine . . . But I've blown a tire and I don't have a spare. I need you to come help me. And I need you to come now."

"Sure, of course. But where are you? And why don't you have a spare?"

"I'm on 261, about six miles west of the county line. Look, I've got plenty of gas to keep the engine running but, Dad, I'd really,

really like to get out of here and get home—soon. Please, I just need you to come and get me." Chris ignored Martin's question about the missing spare tire. He knew that dads were obligated to ask questions like that. He also decided that, under the circumstances, he wasn't obligated to answer.

"On my way. I'll call Jimmy Norris, too. He'll meet us there with his tow truck."

"Okay, but I just need you to hurry." The longer the father and son talked, the more aware Chris became of his isolation and vulnerability.

"I'm coming, Chris. I'm already walking out the door. Believe me, I wouldn't want you to hang out in Bedford County in a snowstorm . . ." Martin's voice trailed off as if, in mid-sentence, another thought hijacked his brain. "Hey, I'm going to call Sheriff Cooley. He may be able to get there faster than me. Don't move, Chris. Use your cell phone sparingly . . . keep it charged . . . lock your doors, your windows. Okay? I'm coming and I'll get Sheriff Cooley on his way, too?"

"Okay . . . well, whatever it takes. I just need you to come get me out of this mess as soon as you can," Chris replied in desperation.

"I'm already backing out of the driveway. I'm on my way and I'm calling Cooley right now . . . Chris, I love you, son. It's going to be okay."

"I love you, too, Pops. And, hey, let's not call Mom at work—it will only worry her."

"I agree. Call if you need anything, but save your battery, I'm on my way."

For the first time since the tire blew, Chris felt his body begin to retreat from its hyper-alert status. He knew he was in good hands. Even with snow-packed roads, Chris would be fully secure in less than forty minutes—even earlier if Cooley joined the rescue team.

With that reassuring thought in mind, Chris turned his attention to his temporary solitary confinement. First, he reached into his Northfield Under Armour backpack, the one Jamarcus had given him for Christmas. From its depths, he secured a pair of gloves and a scarf. Then he checked his cell phone battery—74%. Just in case things took longer than expected, Chris turned off the phone's wi-fi feature and dimmed the display. With the snow falling faster and faster, Chris was taking no chances.

As Chris confidently neared the final touches of his preparations, a pick-up truck pulled up, slowing early on but ultimately stopping less than a foot from Chris' bumper. The truck's honky-tonk music pierced the otherwise serene, snow-covered landscape. Its yellow-tinted KC light beams bounced off the pervasive whiteness of the landscape, creating an eerie golden glow that engulfed the stranded car and driver.

"This could be good . . . or this could be bad," Chris muttered to himself. As he watched a shadow of a man step outside the truck and head his way, the phrase "wrong place, wrong time" dominated his thoughts.

A bright spotlight mounted on the side of the truck suddenly submerged everything it its path. The spotlight's penetrating beams flooded Chris' car, blinding him as the beams reflected relentlessly off his side and rear-view mirrors. Chris shivered uncontrollably. It was anxiety, not the freezing weather, that shook him to the core.

"What's your name, son?" a voice yelled from just behind Chris' back bumper. Chris looked in his rear-view mirror and then his side mirror. Every attempt to discern the facial features of the shadowy figure proved futile. Chris repeatedly experimented with multiple lines of sight in the wake of the blinding spotlight. At each angle, he would first squint his eyes, then hold them wide open. The flood of light shining through wave after wave of wet snow rendered all recognition impossible. Having nothing to work with other than the man's deep voice, his workingman's clothing, and his side-to-side gait, all that Chris could gather was that the man appeared to be in his late thirties or early forties. Chris also surmised, even with near-zero visibility, that the man was not there to be helpful.

Chris pulled the toggle switch that rolled down his driver's side window, but only until the gap in the opening was no more than three inches. He intended to begin and end the conversation with as few words as possible. As the window cracked open, a burst of wind hurled large, heavy snowflakes and small ice pellets into Chris' face. Turning his face in the other direction, while shielding himself with his left arm against blinding gusts of snow and ice, Chris delivered his carefully chosen words.

"Thanks for stopping, but I'm okay. My dad's on his way and the sheriff's sending a deputy. There'll be a tow truck here soon, too. So, I've got it covered. . ." Chris' volume was loud, but his tone was relaxed, almost casual. He pressed the toggle switch and, as the window returned to its closed position, Chris added quickly, "Thanks for checking." Having shut the window tightly, Chris confirmed, for the third time in two minutes, that both doors were locked.

Turning his head back toward the front of the car, Chris indicated that, for his part, their exchange was complete. His face was aimed forward and he purposefully held his head motionless. Chris trained his left eye on the partially fogged-over driver's side mirror. Seeing no change in the man's posture or position, Chris stealthily extended his right hand and fingers, pulling his cell phone into his grasp.

Two more people, apparently males as well, exited the truck. Chris still could not see their faces clearly. One appeared to be carrying a baseball bat. The other strode toward the car like a boxer entering a ring, As the two approached the man standing by Chris' car, the three engaged in a muffled, animated conversation. The original shadowy spokesman of the group appeared to be much larger than his companions. He gestured wildly, repeatedly pointing toward Chris who sat unmoving in the front seat.

After a couple more minutes of heated debate, all three abruptly strode forward and a few feet to the left. Each intentionally remained submerged in the cover of the large spotlight's blinding beams. They steered clear of Chris' window, preferring their identities to remain hidden. The larger shadow took two additional steps forward, moving about six feet further, parallel with the Altima's front bumper. As he spat a heavy stream of steamy tobacco juice onto the white carpet of snow, he motioned for Chris to get out of the car.

Chris shook his head very slowly, moving it in a firm, exaggerated, side-to-side motion.

The larger, tobacco-spitting figure moved closer to the front of Chris' car, his face turned just enough to shield him from Chris' recognition. With a lower, and more threatening voice, he yelled,

"What's your name, boy?"

Chris' heart raced, his palms sweated, and his hands and feet began shaking involuntarily. "Look, I'm doing okay," Chris spoke loudly through the pane of his closed window. "I've got help coming. And I would appreciate it if you would just move on. I'll be gone as soon as my dad and the police arrive."

"Well, we would appreciate it if you would move on! NOW!" the spokesman responded angrily. "In fact, we would appreciate it," his tone increasingly mocking Chris, "if you would move on and never come back to Bedford County." Turning to his left, he spat again, then added with an upward nod of his head, "Where you from, anyway?"

Chris remained non-responsive, staring straight ahead. As the showdown unfolded, the smallest member of the trio walked to the back of the car, to examine it more closely. Spotting Jamarcus' vegas gold number 22 and the name 'Denton' on a navy magnetic basketball on the Altima's back bumper, he angrily peeled it off. Lifting it upwards to show the bulky ringleader, he then yelled, "Looky here! He's got that Denton kid's basketball number on his bumper!"

The recognition triggered a change of posture in the shadowy spokesman. His head snapped to attention. Spreading his legs slightly and arching his back, he placed his hands in the front waistband of his pants and rocked on his heels. "So you're a boy from Northfield? You got kin on the team?" he mocked. A sinister half-laugh and a steamy projectile of tobacco-filled saliva soon followed.

Recognizing the man's anger, Chris' emotions churned in a tumultuous conflict. He felt equally compelled to follow one of two very divergent paths forward. On the one hand, he could attempt the "one-down" position. He could play the part of the submissive, scared black man. That's what he knew they really wanted—to humiliate him by robbing him of his dignity as a man. At least, that's all he hoped they wanted. However, just the thought of portraying himself in a one-down role prompted bile to rise in his throat. He gagged, arresting the acidic liquid by dismissing the entire stream of thought.

He reasoned that the other path, a defiant "one-up" position in which he confronted the rage of racial prejudice with his own strength, would ultimately escalate the conflict. With the ratio being three to one, Chris knew that fighting fire with hotter fire risked real danger; he risked death. So, in the midst of agonizing emotional turmoil, Chris chose a third path. He chose the path taught to him by a mother and father whom he deeply loved and respected. Chris bowed his head and prayed.

Not getting the response he expected, the spokesman pushed harder. "Did you play ball there, too, son? Aren't you a little dark to be a Viking Warrior?" The trio laughed, with the previously silent one adding in a slurred voice, "Don't look like a Viking or a Warrior to me!"

The large spokesman, clearly pleased with himself, lowered his voice, and leaned in the direction of the car's window. "You one of those basketball-playing uppity 'Northfield Nation' niggers?"

Chris looked straight ahead, closed his eyes, slowed his breath, and once again calmly prayed for strength. Without saying a word, Chris held up the phone to the window, displaying its screen indicating that a 9-1-1 had just been dialed. Restraining himself from either opening his mouth or opening his door, Chris looked steadily into the ringleader's partially concealed face.

"Well, I sure hope those 9-1-1 folks can help you with your blown tire. Looks pretty bad," the spokesman responded sarcastically. Momentarily, he stared at the scraps of rubber still clinging to the metal rim of Chris' left front tire. Then, unzipping his pants, the spokesman walked over to the ravaged tire and urinated on it.

"9-1-1," the female operator responded with a voice that was part trained professional and part nurturing mother.

"Hello, my name's Chris Denton. I'm on County Road 261 in Bedford County, approximately six miles west of Lewis County," Chris spoke calmly, all the while looking directly at the shadow urinating on his car tire. "I'm a young black male with a blown front tire. Three men are harassing me. Their words are racist and hate-filled. I am not safe." Chris' voice began to quiver slightly. As he described his current reality, he faced for the first time the full extent of his personal vulnerability. "I know for sure that my dad and at least one Lewis County police officer are on their way," he added. His words were slightly reassuring, both himself and to the 9-1-1 operator.

"I was hoping that maybe you know a Bedford County officer who might be closer," Chris continued warily. "And, ma'am, I need one I can trust to help me. I don't mean to offend, but you understand that I don't need an officer who might take advantage of my situation. I'm a young black man—you understand what I'm saying?"

"Absolutely, Chris. First, do these men appear to have a weapon?"

"Not to my knowledge, except for a baseball bat . . . unless they have weapons in their truck."

"Okay, we are dispatching someone right now. Chris, I would feel better if you stayed on the phone until the officers arrive."

"I would feel better about that, too. But just give me a minute." Texting as fast as his thumbs could move, he responded to a text from his father, who had been urgently texting and calling. *I'm okay. On the phone with 9-1-1 operator. All good, but get here ASAP.* He had neither the time, or the desire, to bring his dad and brother into the scary details of his current situation.

"What's happening right now, Chris?" the operator asked. Chris' silence while texting appeared to unnerve her.

"Well, the loud mouthed one just finishing pissing on my blown front tire. Now, he's zipping his pants. What a freakin' idiot!" Had Chris not been guarding his words out of respect for the dispatcher, his language would have been much more graphic.

Having finished his business, the large spokesman banged his fist angrily on the car's hood. Chris flinched, but did not break eye contact.

"Are you still there?" the dispatcher spoke with rising concern.

"Yes, ma'am. Wait . . . okay, they're turning to go back to their truck. I think they're leaving—God, I hope they're leaving."

"Can you identify them? Make out their faces? Describe their truck?"

"Not very well . . . it's dark, snowy. And they have this massive floodlight."

The spokesman stopped just as he passed the back driver's side door of the Altima. Turning back toward Chris' rolled up window, he shouted in the loudest, most menacing voice Chris had heard yet, "I don't ever want to see your sorry black ass in Bedford County again, you hear? Go back to Lewis County—they can have you and all your kind! We don't want you here!"

As the driving snow amplified the luminous spotlight in white brilliance, Chris could barely see the outline of the men's shadows climbing back into the truck. They backed far away before turning off their light and turning around, leaving Chris with no way of describing them, their truck, or even identifying their license plate.

"They're gone," he informed the operator. "Thank you for your help."

"I'm so thankful," the woman sniffed, then cleared her throat. "And I'm so sorry. Look, I know this doesn't make up for what just happened. But just know that, for what it's worth, I'm a sixty-one-year-old white woman who was born and raised in Bedford County. Please know that those men do not represent all the people in this community."

"I know that, but I'm telling you, ma'am, sometimes it's hard to remember. I was scared for my life." Chris tried to keep his tone conversational but he couldn't help pounding the steering wheel with his left fist. Desperately trying to release the anxious energy sending tremors through his body, hot tears boiled over his eyelids.

"I understand, Chris," the operator spoke calmly. "And I can't imagine living through what just happened to you. But listen, I think Officer Owen should be there any minute."

"I see the blue lights in the distance." Then, in attempt to calm down, Chris added, "I'm going to be okay."

"Yes, you are. I can tell you are a mature young man—and one with high character. I know you're going to be just fine. I wish there were more of you in the world."

"Well, the world could you use more of people like you, too. Maybe one day there will be enough of us to stop all this hatred."

"I hope so. Is the officer there?"

"Yes, ma'am. All is well. Thank you, for everything. You've been a bright spot on a dark night."

As the officer approached the car, Chris recognized another set of flashing blue lights on the horizon. The lights were approaching from the west, in the direction of Lewis County. In spite of the 9-1-1 operator's best assurances that he was in good hands, Chris still felt tense in the company of the white police officer from Bedford County. Given all that he had just been through, he found it impossible not to flinch as the officer moved toward him.

Making his way slowly to Chris' window, the officer began calmly, "Chris, I'm Jonathan Owen." He neither asked Chris to roll down his window or open his door. Rather, recognizing Chris' anxiety, evidenced by his still-trembling body, Officer Owen continued reassuringly, "I'm here to ensure that you are not only safe in Bedford County but also that you are treated with the respect you deserve." Officer Owen looked up toward the flashing blue lights of a police car intersecting the eastern horizon. With a warm smile he added, "Just sit tight. Looks like the cavalry is on its way."

With the Lewis County policeman and most likely his dad in the car as a ride-along, Chris felt safe enough to let down his guard. He stiffly unlocked his door, willing his body past the paralyzing fear that had pinned him to his seat for the last several minutes—which had seemed like several hours.

Once outside, Chris stumbled awkwardly toward Officer Owen, helpless to stop his knees from buckling. Reaching out to catch him, Officer Owen steadied him on his feet, adding, "It's going to be okay. You should be proud of how you did tonight—really, really proud. That took a lot of strength and courage, Chris. And I know for sure your dad will be very proud of you, too."

Regaining the strength in his legs, Chris walked back to the back fender of the Altima, leaning back as he lowered his head. Chris vigorously massaged his eyes and forehead with the fingertips of both hands. Turning to look at the officer's face for the first time, Chris said gratefully, "Thank you for being a good man."

CHAPTER 3

The dull glow of the computer screen illuminated Nikki Cole's face. The seven-year-old laptop, a high school graduation gift, was heavier, slower, and less capable than more recent models, and its leopard-patterned computer skin was scuffed and scratched. Even so, Nikki's MacBook was an essential part of her daily life, and she considered it her only constant companion, on the road and at home.

On bitter cold Northfield winter nights, she indulged herself in the familiar comfort of her wardrobe's coziest layers. She wore her favorite gray sweater, the one that engulfed her upper body like a cocoon. The soft, thick top somehow managed to be way too big on her petite frame while at the same time fitting her just right. The neutral color palette set off Nikki's lush auburn hair, which cascaded gently off her shoulders. Falling in deep, layered waves, the dark ginger locks perfectly accented the fabric's fashionably neutral color. For added warmth, Nikki had buried herself from the waist down in the folds of a thick, earth-tone blanket she'd recently purchased from a local Native American artisan.

As Nikki added the finishing touches to a work proposal for a new client, she heard a door swing open. "D, is that you? Where've you been?" Hearing no answer, Nikki moved hurriedly toward the kitchen, then down the short hallway toward their bedroom.

"Hey, Nik. Listen, I can't talk right now," Derrick announced in a rushed tone. Being about ten steps ahead of her, he had already transitioned into the bedroom. "Coach Mac will be here any minute. I mean, any minute!" Derrick continued in a panic. "So, I'm going to shower and—"

"What are you talking about?" Nikki interrupted angrily. "And where have you been? You said you'd be home by six for dinner. D, I texted you at 5:30. No response. None. Then I called. But, again, no answer. Then, finally—thirty minutes later, mind you— you text me, 'Can't talk right now. Be home soon.' Derrick, it's 7:30! What's going on?"

Derrick, his back to Nikki, heaved a deep sigh and rolled his eyes as he stripped off the last of his clothes. Nikki heard the forced exhale and imagined with irritation Derrick's arrogant eye roll.

Nikki had already been churning with anxiety and anger. Ninety minutes of anger and anxiety, and feeling dismissed and disregarded, now spilled out. "Answer me! What the hell is going on, Derrick?" Nikki crossed her arms as she fumed with exasperation.

Both stood in silence, Derrick in the now-steamy shower and Nikki at the bathroom door entrance. It was not until Derrick twisted the knobs to end his two-minute shower that the silence was broken. "Nikki, are you kidding me? You want to have that argument again? Now?" He extended his arm from behind the curtain, taking the towel hung on the hook to his left. As he dried himself in the midst of the evaporating warmth of the shower's steam, Derrick pleaded his case further. "I've worked nine hours today. . . on a Saturday . . . a tough early morning practice, then game-film reviews, then preparing game plans." Stepping out of the shower and brushing past Nikki on the way to the closet, his voice raised to a stress-induced pitch, "And then Coach Mac calls. He says, 'We need to talk, Coach D. It's urgent.' So, I run home. I get here as fast as I can in this snowy mess . . ." As he pulled up his jeans, he looked directly into the blank stare of Nikki's eyes for the first time.

"Nikki," he said in a low voice. "Look . . . I'm sorry. I should have called—I know. But, now's just not a good time to deal with all this. It's just not," Derrick explained as he furiously dried his hair with his towel.

"Okay. Then WHEN is the time, D? You tell me when!" Nikki demanded. "After this 'busy pre-season'? That's what you keep saying— 'it will get better after the season starts.' But will it, D? Will it ever get better than this?"

"I'm doing the best I can! Dammit, Nikki," Derrick exploded. He jerked his navy Northfield Warrior hoodie over his still damp hair, then demanded, "You've got to give me a break! I'm working night and day." Snatching the towel from where he laid it on the bed, he shook it at her, "You have no idea what it's like! No idea at all!" he yelled.

Nikki swallowed her breath and her words, then sarcastically but calmly responded, "Okay, Derrick. I guess I'm just the clueless live-in girlfriend. I'm sorry to have bothered you with my lack of compassion for your hard, hard life. It won't happen again." With a steely stare, she added coldly, "I can promise you . . ." Nikki paused. Then carefully choosing and precisely articulating each word, she informed Derrick, "It will never happen again."

Before Derrick had time to respond, the doorbell rang. Nikki sighed, ran her hands through her hair, then made her way down the hall. As she moved toward the front door, Nikki caught a glimpse of herself in the full-length foyer mirror. In spite of all that churned beneath, she saw a face that was composed and, surprisingly, almost pleasant.

"Coach, please, come in. It's miserable out there!" Nikki waved Coach Mac into the condo's warmth. "D, Coach is here," she shouted down the hallway, betraying no hint of the unresolved anger between them.

Taking Coach Mac's snow-covered black fedora and damp, snow-speckled black wool overcoat, Nikki said apologetically, "He'll be here any minute. He just got in from working on film. So . . . sorry." Nikki's words fell awkwardly in spite of her attempts to hide her current disdain for Derrick. Speaking in her most gracious, hospitable tone, she asked, "In the meantime, Coach, may I get you a cup of coffee or maybe some hot chocolate?"

"No, thank you, Nikki. At my age, I can't handle even a hint of caffeine this late," Coach Mac responded warmly.

"How about a glass of water?" Nikki offered as she closed the door on the narrow coat closet.

"Yes, that would be nice. Thank you. And, no ice, please." Coach Mac made his way to the bar separating the kitchen area from the living room area. Making an attentive survey of the small but open living space,

Coach Mac added, "Nikki, this place looks great! Of course, I'm not surprised. But I am impressed." Coach Mac observed enthusiastically.

"Aw, thank you so much, Coach Mac," Nikki blushed, "that means a lot. And, it wasn't just me. D did a lot of the painting and manual labor. Until school started . . ." Nikki's voice dropped as if it had fallen off a ledge. Her lips, as well as her eyes, turned downward.

"A basketball season is long and demanding, Nikki," Coach Mac offered. "It can feel like running a double marathon. I know from experience—and I've got lots of it—it takes a real toll on a relationship."

Nikki wanted desperately to avoid going further down the path this conversation had taken. She was thankful for the task of handing Coach Mac a glass of water. After a quick, "Thank you," Coach Mac raised the glass to his lips, took a very long sip, and then finished his thoughts, "My Gracie can, unfortunately, tell you far too many stories about being a 'basketball widow.' I'm not proud of it, Nikki. And I'm not making excuses. But realistically, it's going to take time for you and D to figure this out."

Coach Mac closed his hand into a loose fist and, extending one finger at a time, he slowly listed Derrick's areas of responsibility. "He's got a full-time teaching job, a coaching job that's almost like a second full-time job, and then, of course, I know he wants to spend time with you."

Nikki took a deep breath, then as her cheeks puffed, let out a sigh. "I wish . . ." Even as the words escaped her lips, Nikki wished she could recapture them. Trying to exit the conversation graciously, she continued. "I know, it's just hard," she added dismissively. "And I know, of course, it's just his first year. Really, as far as coaching goes, it's just his first month, right? Add to that, my goodness, Coach, of all the places for Derrick Walker to start his coaching career . . . Northfield High School—who in their right mind could have imagined that?"

The more Nikki talked, the worse she felt. Coach Mac was Derrick's mentor, the closest thing he had ever had to a father figure, but, just as importantly, he was currently Derrick's boss. The lines were blurry, and messy. Nikki felt like she, too, was sinking neck deep in the mess.

"Well, I don't know what's taking D so long," Nikki diverted. "So, please make yourself at home, Coach."

At Nikki's prompting, Coach Mac moved toward the large, light-olive sectional where Nikki's blanket and computer lay. The oversized piece of furniture dominated the room, forming a semi-circle around a 55-inch television over the fireplace. Wireless surround-sound Bose speakers stood next to the faux stone hearth. Nikki's vision for creating a peaceful haven and Derrick's vision for creating an entertainment center mingled in conflicting coexistence.

Nikki heard Derrick exiting their bedroom. Hoping for a graceful exit herself, she reached for her coffee cup then headed to the kitchen for a warm refill. With Coach Mac settling into the comfort of the sectional's plush taupe cushions, Derrick bounded into the room. His skin was a light shade of pink, thanks to the hot shower. His wavy blond hair, normally meticulously gelled and styled, was damp and mussed. Even with his baggy clothing and rather unkempt wavy hair, Derrick's blue eyes and chiseled features still managed to convey a calm, cool, and collected persona.

"Sorry, Coach, it's been a long day in the film room. I just got home, like, thirty minutes ago. And, believe me, you would be thankful I took a shower!" Derrick spoke quickly, matching the frenetic pace he had been maintaining all day. "As crazy as the day was, though, I got the scouting reports ready for the next three weeks," Derrick continued, smiling broadly. "I know how important it is to get the season off to a good start, Coach."

Derrick collapsed his lean frame onto the inviting plush seat on the sectional, opposite of Coach Mac. The cushion's thick foam padding expelled a weak "psshhh" as it absorbed the impact of Derrick's fall.

"Getting a good start is important in every area of life, D."

Sitting in silence, Derrick offered no indication that Coach Mac's larger point had actually registered.

Nikki, standing slumped over a black granite counter top, turned with a quick, half-smile toward Coach Mac. She then returned to the task of attending to a small stack of unopened mail. Nikki had discovered the pile of mail while searching for her misplaced wireless ear buds. Curiously lying beneath a pile of pens and markers, the mail appeared to have been carelessly shoved into the drawer. Sandwiched among the random flyers and sheet after sheet of local coupons lay three white envelopes with plastic windows. All three dates on their respective post office stamps were at least one month old. Nikki reached for a knife to substitute as a letter opener even as she overheard D begin to question Coach Mac.

"Coach, what brings you here on a late Saturday night?" Derrick inquired anxiously. Leaning back casually, Derrick tried to fabricate the impression of a man at ease. The speed of his words and the nervous shaking of his right foot crossed over his left knee said otherwise.

"D, I need to bring you up to speed on an issue that requires our immediate attention." Coach Mac leaned forward, forearms on his knees, speaking in a serious, almost somber tone. "We've got a real challenge on our hands—for our team and our community . . ."

Coach Mac quickly interrupted himself. Leaning back, pressing his neck and shoulders against the sofa's large cushions, Coach Mac angled his face toward the kitchen. "Hey, Nikki," Coach Mac asked over his shoulder, "why don't you join us in here? I think your perspective would be a good gift to us."

Nikki remained stooped over the countertop, her head buried in her hands. Her thumbs were braced against the sides of her cheeks, while the tips of her fingers massaged her forehead. Scattered before her, the three bills were now opened. Each had turned out to be at least one week beyond its respective due date. The total penalties from the stashed bills would add over a hundred dollars to this month's expenses.

"Good grief, D, what were you thinking?" she whispered angrily to herself. Silently she added in her mind, *Do you even think, D? Do you even care?*

CHAPTER 4

oach Mac called out again from the living room, "Nikki, I would love for you to join us. Your wisdom would certainly be helpful at this point."

Caught off guard, Nikki looked across the counter from her safe vantage point in the kitchen, first at Coach Mac, then Derrick. "D, what do you want? Do you want me to sit in on your meeting?"

"I'm fine with either, I guess. I'm not sure what we're going to talk about, but if Coach wants your input, then, why not?" Derrick responded, "If it helps us deal with the problem, whatever it is, that's fine with me . . . you know, if that's what you want."

"Well, Coach Mac, since you invited me and since D doesn't seem to care," Nikki responded, her words carefully chosen, "I would love to join you." She came out from behind the kitchen counter and settled into the sectional, seating herself on Derrick's right. She maintained a distance, however, of no less than two feet.

"Earlier tonight," Coach Mac began, his voice low and weighty, "Jamarcus' brother, Chris, was on his way home from a friend's birthday party. Just a few miles west of the Lewis County line, in Bedford County, his front tire blew out."

Nikki gasped. "Oh no, Coach, is Chris okay? Was he hurt badly?"

"No . . . and yes. I mean, no, he wasn't physically injured—"

"Thank God!" Leaning forward, Nikki placed her right hand on the middle of her chest. She drew in a deep breath to stop her imagination from running wild.

Derrick remained focused on making sense of the half-told story. "If he wasn't injured, Coach, then what did you mean by 'yes'?"

Coach Mac paused, taking a sip of water before retelling the night's events. "I'm sorry, this is just going to be hard for me." As he related the story, Coach Mac paused at length, struggling to steady his emotional balance.

"We've been through a lot, Gracie and I, over these years," he continued slowly, "My Gracie, she's heard, seen, and experienced more than any wife ever ought to be put through. That's bad enough. But these boys, and their families . . . these good people like the Dentons, a family that adds so much to our community. . . it's a shame they're being treated this way." Coach Mac lowered his head as he rubbed his hands together.

The three sat in silence. Then Coach Mac raised his eyes. The energy coursing through his body transferred to his voice. "Our community, and Bedford County as well, ought to be beyond this by now. But we're not—we're still fighting these same battles. And it's not a color issue, never has been. It's a heart issue." Coach Mac's hands separated, drawing themselves unconsciously into individually clenched fists. "White, black, Latino, Native American, Asian," he added tersely, "Too many people in our community are still trapped in this cycle of hate."

"Coach, I'm so sorry." Nikki moved across to the other side of the sectional, closer to Coach Mac. "Derrick has told me a few things about what's happened in the past, that is, the racism. But I can't believe it's happening now. . . and to one of your player's families. It's just wrong!" Nikki leaned back against the sofa, her external posture signaling a call of restraint to her internal outrage.

Derrick threw his hands in the air, dropping them loudly onto his knees with a slap. "Coach, I'm sorry, too. I know this crap still goes on, but Chris? Of all people? And Jamarcus, he's got to be so pissed. And he should be."

Coach Mac leaned forward in his chair and wrapped his massive hands around the chair's thin armrests. Using his upper body strength, he applied the force necessary to overcome the resistance of arthritic knees. His long, tree-like legs unfurled, and he rose in a slow, stilted movement. As Coach Mac stood, his presence expanded. "D and Nikki, I need you to help me. We need to do together what I've been trying to do for thirty-five years. We need to show our community what it means to love and lead—the Northfield Way."

Derrick and Nikki listened intently as Coach Mac paced back and forth in front of the fireplace. When he stopped, he stood slightly stooped over, his broad shoulders seeming to be give under the weight of the moment. "Whatever it takes, we have to lead," Coach Mac asserted as he began pacing again, "For the sake of the Dentons, for the sake of the boys, for the sake of our community—we have to lead."

"Count me in, Coach!" Derrick offered earnestly. Then he leaned back, releasing the tension that had been building since Coach Mac began Chris' story. He took a moment to make a slow, sweeping study of Coach Mac, reflecting on how the figure before him was the man in whose footsteps he was now taking his first baby steps as a coach and a leader. Closing his eyes to open his memories, Derrick remembered how Coach Mac's large, relational presence had steadily drawn Derrick out of the turmoil of his youth. He recalled the impact of his coach's presence at the time of his father's sudden death. Derrick was fourteen when he was told Carl Walker had died in a fatal car crash. Though Carl had never been much of a dad on any level, the loss had still been devastating. Coach Mac had stood by Derrick, and his brother, Parker, at the graveside. He had been there in the long, dark days that followed as well. Years later, when, at nineteen, Derrick's self-destructive behavior pushed him over the edge toward an abyss of addiction, isolation, and despair, Coach Mac's persistent, loving pursuit was the lifeline that had rescued Derrick from himself. "I would follow that man anywhere," Derrick thought just as Coach Mac's pacing came to a stop.

The older man raised himself to his full stature as he positioned himself behind the recliner in the corner of the living room. Methodically, he wrapped his large fingers forcefully around the top of the chair. Derrick noted in the silence how Coach Mac's soft, puffy eyes contrasted with the definition in his taut jaw. Coach Mac spoke somberly, "I know first hand what happens when wounds are allowed to fester in hidden hurt and anger. It leads to serious infection, the kind that can destroy lives—and whole communities. The people of Lewis County, our people of all races, have come too far to let the hatred of a few take down the hope of the many."

"I agree one hundred percent, Coach. We can't let that happen." Derrick's entire body quickly shifted to the last two inches at the edge of the sofa. Like a runner putting his toe on a white chalk line, waiting for the signal to explode down the track, Derrick was fully engaged.

"Coach, you must be so proud of what you've built—and what you're building. Can I ask you a question, if it's okay, with you, " Nikki asked, her words faltering with insecurity, "just because it would help me understand?"

"Of course, Nikki. You're in this with us," Coach Mac responded reassuringly.

"Can you tell me what it was like? You know, when you first started at Northfield? D has told me some parts of the story, but I want to hear it for myself. Briefly, of course. I know it's late for all of us." Nikki shifted nervously. Tucking her hands underneath her thighs, she leaned forward, adding with uncertainty, "I hope that's appropriate to ask."

"Well, to be brief, I will just give you the basic facts." Coach Mac said. Then, in a series of pointed highlights, he presented his report while carefully guarding his emotions. "I was hired at age twenty-eight as the first African-American head coach in the entire tri-state area. The community was, at that time, predominantly white. In fact, I only had one player on my first team who was black. We experienced a little bit of everything in those first years. Some teams in the district actually attempted to boycott our games. I received death threats and the school received bomb threats. The worst part, at least for Gracie and me, was when our own Northfield locals would cheer for the boys during the games then treat Gracie and me as if we were invisible outside the gym. Honestly, when it comes to racial hatred . . ." Coach Mac paused. He looked away, then up toward the ceiling. Heaving a heavy sigh, he continued, ". . . the truth is, it's actually less painful to be mistreated by the radical fringe than to be dismissed and disregarded by your whole community." He added softly, "Especially a community that you're giving your whole heart to."

"How long did that go on, Coach?" Derrick's curiosity was peaked. For the most part, Coach Mac's past was a mystery—not just to Derrick, but to everyone else in the community. Coach Mac often proudly declared, "I live by the principle, 'Put the past in the past.'" That principle, Derrick reckoned to himself, seemed like a good idea. Still, the level of mystery surrounding Coach Mac sometimes left Derrick feeling uncomfortably distant.

"The first three years were the hardest. After that, the population and the culture in this region started changing. More people of color moved into town as well as into the surrounding counties. The school and, therefore, our teams became more racially diverse. Plus, we won our first couple of state championships. Winning, like love, covers a multitude of sins!" Coach Mac laughed, pleased with himself for having coined a new leadership phrase.

"We hit another tough stretch during your brother Parker's playing days." Coach continued. "The racial mix on the roster tipped toward more minorities than whites. Those were tough, tough years. Maybe Parker talked to you about it. Suddenly, it became tough to be white. Of course, it was still tough to be black, too . . . always has been . . ." Coach Mac's voiced trailed off. His Northfield history lesson ended abruptly. He was, on many levels, done for the night.

"I'm starting to understand, really understand, why Northfield basketball and the Northfield Way mean so much to this town," Nikki interjected. Turning toward Derrick, she added compassionately, "and to you, D." Nikki stood, then moved purposefully back toward Derrick's side of the sectional. Her posture yet remained stiff; her hands lay tightly folded in her lap. Still, she had moved significantly closer to Derrick than before.

"Coach, before we close out, I should tell you something I haven't told you before," Derrick said hesitantly. "It may be helpful . . . or maybe not. I don't know."

Coach Mac settled himself once again into the broad recliner. "Sounds like something I should hear. But before we continue, it's almost 9:00. Can we meet together tomorrow for lunch to talk about next steps?"

"That works great for us, right?" Derrick looked to Nikki for confirmation. She nodded, adding, "We don't have any plans. You should be free to meet."

"Well, I was hoping both of you would come," replied Coach Mac. "And I want to invite Gracie, and Coach Dale, too. Maybe her husband, Benson, can join as well. This will affect our women players, not just the guys. I've been trying to do a better job remembering that. Of course, if I don't, well, you can be sure that Carlene will remind me," Coach Mac said, shoulders heaving in hearty laughter. Then he continued, "She's a fine, strong leader, D. We're privileged to have her on the Northfield leadership team."

Coach Mac's energy surged as he considered Coach Dale's exceptional leadership capacity. Excitedly he continued, "By the way, next year I am going to plan the whole 'Northfield Nation Night' with Carlene so it's a combined launch of our seasons, men and women. That move is well past due."

"I agree. And, yes, she is an A-list leader," Derrick said. Nikki nodded enthusiastically.

"So, D, what were you saying?" Coach Mac redirected back to Derrick. Uncrossing his legs, he leaned back heavily into the high-back chair. As he did so, he sank more deeply into the seat cushion.

"I know it's dangerous to speculate. And I would ask that we keep this between us for now." Derrick lowered his voice as if the room had been rigged with spy equipment. "Back in the 'dark days' as I call them, after I . . . well, actually, when you kicked me off the team, or . . . well, you know . . ." Derrick stumbled sheepishly through his words. "There was a small group of folks who tried—repeatedly tried, Coach—to convince me that you were a racist. These guys would take me out for beers or to smoke weed, then they would tell me over and over again, 'The high and mighty Coach Mac wouldn't do that to a black player—you know he wouldn't!' Only they didn't call you Coach Mac. They called you, 'Black Mac.'"

Coach Mac jerked his weight forward in the chair. Now he was sitting upright, almost rigidly, instantly achieving a seated version of the power position. His shoulders were square, his elbows extended, and his jaw clenched. His cheeks puffed tightly constrained breaths.

"Coach, I'm sorry to be telling you this. I don't mean to make the night worse than it already is."

"You're not making it worse, D. But I'm not sure why you would bring it up now." Coach Mac's eyes widened. His left foot tapped in a torrid rhythm.

"The guys who were involved were the Wilson boys. I know you remember the youngest one, the one they called, 'Dub'?" Derrick said.

"How could I forget Dub? That kid had the potential to play ball at the next level, D2 or D3 at least. He could have played the three position on the wing as well as anyone we've had in fifteen years. But he had this attitude. Like he was superior to the rest of his team—and the world, for that matter. Like he was entitled." Coach Mac threw up his hands. He fell back once more into an exasperated slouch. "I did everything I could," he said adamantly, "to get him to work on his game, especially his ball handling. I tried to get him into the weight room, too, to improve his strength. I'll tell you the truth, I think the kid loved weed more than basketball, though." Coach slapped his knees with his hands, reflecting on Dub's wasted talent and, worse, wasted life.

"I know for a fact, Coach, Dub didn't just love weed more than basketball. He loved weed more than anything."

Coach Mac's eyes closed in response to the resurrection of a long-buried memory. Coach Mac muttered in a low voice, "I'm sure that's true. He was totally stoned the night he drove his car into that tree. Killed him instantly, but the Stinson girl . . . oh, what was her name?" Coach Mac looked toward the ceiling, trying unsuccessfully to retrieve a first name that matched his vivid memory of the young girl's face. Abandoning the search, he looked into the distance, mournfully adding, "She lingered for two weeks before she passed. Such a shame. So unnecessary."

Talking faster, and with more animated motions, Derrick's voice rose. "But, Coach, the Wilson brothers, and the group they hang with, blame you, not the weed, for Dub's failures." Derrick studied the slumping Coach Mac. He glanced toward Nikki who seemed to be shrinking under the weight of the moment. He chewed the inside of his mouth, his mind suspended between past and present.

"And?" Coach Mac waved his right hand impatiently. "Go on."

Derrick hesitated. He looked at Nikki, who leaned her head forward, gesturing her encouragement to continue. So he did. "They genuinely hate you, Coach. And, while they don't say it publicly, in private their story is always the same: you held Dub back because you favored black players. They blame you for ruining his future and turning him to drugs. So, as crazy it may sound, they ultimately blame you for his death."

"That's sad. On so many levels." Coach Mac clasped his hands together behind his head as he leaned back once again. Then, his face contorted with bewilderment. "D, maybe it's just because I'm tired, but I need some help here. What's the Wilsons' connection to Chris Denton?" he asked.

"Oh, sorry about that. There definitely is one. So, after Dub's death, the family moved to Bedford County," Derrick explained. "The ages of the guys who threatened Chris, their size, their words, their comments about Jamarcus' Northfield magnet on the car, even their truck, it sounds a lot like the Wilsons to me. The biggest one, Charlie, is by far the angriest, most hate-filled guy I've ever known. And, I don't know if you remember, but you cut him from the freshman team. I'm just saying that it's highly probable, in my mind, that the Wilson boys were the ones bullying Chris tonight. " Derrick wrapped up his story, nodding his head in an affirmation of his own conclusion.

"What a mess, what an absolute mess." When he spoke next it was in low, soft, thoughtful tones. "You know, on the surface, the Wilsons appeared to be hard-working, church-going people who love their kids, pay their bills, and do right by their neighbors. Well, the white ones, anyway. They do right by their white neighbors. Hatred . . . it just does bad things to otherwise seemingly decent people—no matter what their color."

Placing his hands on his knees, Coach Mac began another protracted ascent out of his chair. "Let's keep this to ourselves for now, okay?" he said as he reached a full standing position. Then he added, "Except for Sherriff Cooley. D, I think you will need to tell this story—confidentially, of course—to Cooley."

Nikki and Derrick stood in unison, matching Coach Mac's movement. Derrick quickly moved to retrieve their guest's coat and hat, and Nikki hugged Coach Mac tightly. His embrace put her at ease. She found herself feeling just the way she felt when her father hugged her good night as a little girl. In the unguarded moment, she surprised herself as a tender, "Love you," flowed naturally out of her heart.

Coach Mac gratefully received the still damp coat and shrugged it on. He then placed his left hand on Derrick's right shoulder. "D, we're a gift to each other and to this community," he declared with a broad smile. "One black, one white. Same insides."

Derrick added his own observations. "One long, thick post player and one quick, lean shooting guard. One old and wise man, one very young and inexperienced man."

Coach Mac laughed, then turned to a more serious tone. Taking his hat in both hands, he looked intently toward Derrick. "Who would have thought it? A black man who fought his way through the dangerous streets of Chicago's South Side and a white man who had to battle personal demons in the cornfields of Lewis County. Gifts, D. That's what we are to each other. 'Gifts of grace,' to be given to our school and our community."

Coach Mac sighed a deep breath of satisfaction, then turned to reach for the doorknob. Derrick interrupted. "Coach, I think you left out one more very important difference between the two of us."

"Really, what's that?" asked Coach Mac.

"One of us is only decently good-looking while the other is, well . . . incredibly, other-worldly handsome." Derrick's lips spread widely into a grin and he winked comically.

"You are absolutely correct." Coach Mac opened his arms wide, exposing the palms of his hands as if pleading his innocence. "But, D, I actually did think of that. I was simply afraid that, well, if I pointed out this obvious difference, it might cause you to feel . . . ," Coach Mac looked skyward, mimicking a search for just the right word, "it might make you feel insecure. And, son," Coach Mac locked both hands on Derrick's shoulders, flashing a grin that covered his entire face, "I simply don't want you to feel anything but proud of your decently good looks."

The boisterous laughter that followed lightened the heavy load each had borne over the last hour. For Derrick, another heaviness was lifted as Nikki drew close. She rested her head on his shoulder as he wrapped his arm tightly around her waist.

"He's a good man, D," Nikki said, as their eyes followed Coach Mac down the driveway and into his car. "And you—that is we—are lucky to have him."

Closing the door, Derrick turned his gaze fully toward Nikki. He recognized, for the first time in a long while, a warm, receptive softness in her emerald-green eyes. He turned to face her, pulling her gently into both of his arms.

"You know," Derrick said, "Coach Mac wouldn't call it 'luck.'"

"Oh, really?" Nikki teased impishly, "Well, what would he call it?"

Derrick spoke in barely more than a whisper, "He'd call it 'grace.' He'd say that we've been given a great grace, just to live our lives with each other."

"Well, whatever it is," Nikki sighed softly, drawing her face closer to Derrick's, "I think we could all use some more of it."

"Yes, Nik," Derrick nodded. "I don't think we can ever have too much grace." With an exaggerated slowness that drew Nikki's eyes deeper into his own, Derrick leaned into her face. He pressed his lips to hers, very lightly at first. Then, as his heart raced just as it had on the night of their first kiss, Nikki fully surrendered her lips to his.

Derrick pulled back slowly, smiling and closing his eyes.

"What?" Nikki insisted as she playfully patted his chest with her left hand.

Derrick opened his eyes. Breathing a hard breath through his nose, his lips opened to a half smile.

"What?" Nikki asked, arching her back slightly as she turned her head to one side.

"I don't know, Nik . . . I . . ." Derrick said. "I just—"

"Shhh," Nikki responded, placing a finger on his lips. "I don't know either, D. But, here we are. I know that."

"Yes. By grace, here we are."

With abandon, Derrick and Nikki drew into the passionate embrace of one another's bodies. As they did so, each remembered how deeply, and daily, they had once longed just to be close to one another. They also briefly forget how truly distant they had become.

CHAPTER 5

Slick rubber met slicker asphalt, sending Jimmy Thompson's Forerunner into an unsettling but thankfully temporary skid. As Jimmy maneuvered the vehicle securely onto Main Street, volatile winds pounded the cracked windshield with heavy snow and jagged ice. Limp, barely functional wiper blades offered little resistance to the fierce, relentless waves of winter fury. Jimmy peered desperately through a small, softball-sized clearing, eyes straining to make his way through the storm.

Jimmy's expectations for this evening had been dramatically altered. He had originally planned to arrive early for the annual Northfield Nation Night. Now, in a near whiteout, he simply hoped to survive the trip, accident-free. It was only three miles further to Northfield High School. It would feel more like thirty.

To ease his stress, Jimmy turned to his "Salt Life" playlist in iTunes. Kenny Chesney's "No Shoes, No Shirt, No Problem" was first up. His eyes were hyper-focused on successive ten-foot stretches of pavement as he plowed through Main Street. His mind, however, drifted like the snow piling up all around him. His thoughts meandered along a familiar, well-worn path to a sandy beach awash with the balmy coastal breezes of his native South Carolina. Tonight the images were so vivid that he could feel warm, gentle winds skimming across his chest. His favorite orange and white Clemson beach chair, along with his feet, gradually sank several inches into the warm, wet sand. Jimmy held a cold, fruity drink in one hand and Tara's warm, soft hand in the other. In this dreamscape, Tara was tanned and relaxed. Every meeting of their eyes was an instant spark of attraction. In this fantasy, there were no children. No deadlines. No Northfield. And, above all, no snow.

The scene surrounding Jimmy quickly jolted him back to his current, miserable circumstances. Driving into wall after wall of swirling white waves, Jimmy passed the mournful rows of Main Street's weather-worn, abandoned buildings. Jimmy was about as far from his dreams as he could be. Northfield reality had shoved his South Carolina beach fantasy into a deep freezer and locked the door.

"*You, my brown-eyed girl. Woo-oo, my brown-eyed girl.*" Jimmy's most familiar and favorite ringtone offered a welcomed distraction. The call was from Tara, his best friend of ten years, wife of nine years, and the mother of his three young children.

"Hey, Tara, I'm okay," he answered with a pre-emptive reassurance.

"Thank goodness! I was worried. You said you'd call when you got to the school. Are you still on the road?" Tara questioned.

Jimmy used the sleeve of his jacket to wipe away layers of fog forming inside his SUV's front windshield. At the same time, he attempted to respond to Tara in a voice that would mask the difficulty of the driving conditions. He was only partially successful in both endeavors. "I'm just being very, very cautious, honey. I'll be there soon," Jimmy said.

"Oh, okay. Well, I'm glad to hear you're being careful. Please call me when you arrive. Don't forget!"

"I won't. Okay. Will call soon. Love you—and, Tara, don't worry."

"Love you—and I will worry!" Tara giggled nervously.

"I know. Bye."

Jimmy navigated Main Street well below the posted twenty-five mile per hour speed limit. As he entered an even darker, more deserted stretch of downtown Northfield, Jimmy glanced from side to side through frosted windows. Even through formidable, thick walls of snow, Northfield's economic despair was glaringly visible.

Try as he might, Jimmy had never quite been able to visualize the "golden era" of Northfield. He replayed the oft-told story of a fateful week that forever altered Northfield's destiny. Twenty-three years ago, three expansive textile mills, the community's primary source of employment, hurriedly skipped town. The companies did not just leave Northfield. They left the country. All three companies abandoned the community in search of a work force that would require much lower wages. Almost overnight, half of Lewis County had to go looking for employment.

Once a postcard-worthy picture of America's Heartland, Northfield had devolved into a desolate shell of its former self. The community quickly became a neglected, sparsely populated outpost in the middle of nowhere—"nowhere" being known in these parts as Lewis County.

Dreaming of big cities and big plans, generations of Northfield High School graduates longed to pursue a brighter future in cities like Indianapolis, Minneapolis, or Chicago. Only a few escaped without circling back in disappointment. Those who did shared the belief that, "The best part of 'being from Northfield' is being *from* Northfield."

I just need one big break and I'm out of here, Jimmy comforted himself daily. And, on the worst days, hourly. For Jimmy, who possessed both high aspirations and an even higher education, life beyond Northfield remained a realistic option. For locally born residents, not so much. Limited backgrounds, limited experiences, and limiting beliefs made each successive generation increasingly less hopeful.

As Jimmy Buffet's "Margaritaville" poured out of the SUV's speakers, Jimmy turned off Main Street. Moving away from the direct onslaught of the icy snow and onto Norsemen Drive, Jimmy sang at the top of his lungs, "wasting away again here in Northfield."

Pulling into the Northfield High School parking lot, Jimmy's carpool karaoke was interrupted by the chirping sound of an incoming text. The sound of crickets identified the sender as outside of Jimmy's contact list. He pulled into a parking spot before glancing at his phone.

Need to talk. Something you need to know. Something I need help with. Coach Mac needs to deal with it too. I know people who want to bring him down! Text me back later tonight."

Jimmy texted back, *Who is this?"*

The anonymous texter replied, *Tell you later. I don't want to be texting here, not now. It's too crowded in this gym. Someone might see me texting. Can't take a chance.*

Jimmy sat motionless and dumbfounded. Even his breath was temporarily suspended. Internally, his stomach tossed. In a generation of awful scandals, including unspeakable moral tragedies at such revered institutions as Penn State, Baylor, and Michigan State, this could be really bad. Jimmy could not escape the stab of pain that shot through the pit of his stomach.

Who in the world would want to "bring Coach Mac down"? And, why? Jimmy shuddered as his mind raced. What he knew collided head-on with what he feared.

One thing he knew for sure. A scandal surrounding Coach Mac would be the worst thing he could imagine for Northfield. Racial tensions and economic uncertainties—often fueled by endless news cycles of angry voices—already placed communities like Northfield in peril. Last night's reported racist bullying of Chris Denton intensified the threat. The incident, though it had occurred in neighboring Bedford County, added another heavy weight on the already strained relational bridges holding Northfield together. By far the strongest bridge, and the one carrying the greatest weight, was Coach John McKissack.

In the wake of undeniably dim realities and bad news, the Northfield community had discovered one notable exception to its dreary existence. Year after year, decade after decade, the locals had poured their frail remaining hopes into the most successful endeavor the community had ever undertaken: to birth, raise, coach, and support championship basketball teams. For more than three decades, the teams rarely disappointed. And during those three decades of Northfield players, families, and fans, Coach John McKissack was the only coach they had ever known.

For Jimmy, like the majority of local residents, the Northfield teams provided a proverbial "light shining in the darkness." Coach Mac's unprecedented success had, in fact, been the primary reason Jimmy, a Clemson grad with a master's degree in sports journalism, had accepted the position of Managing Editor of the Lewis County Gazette.

Sitting nearly frozen now in the Northfield High School parking lot, Jimmy recalled the dream that had lured him to this unlikely destination. *With Coach Mac's reputation growing in the region, and in the nation, who knows how far the Gazette's coverage of Northfield's record-setting run could reach?* the young, idealistic twenty-four-year-old had reasoned. Looking forward to his "big break," Jimmy fully expected to publish an article in *ESPN the Magazine* or *Sports Illustrated* within the first year or two of covering Coach Mac and his team. Just one article, he supposed, could propel him onto the national scene.

Tara, pregnant with their second child, had been skeptical of Jimmy's lofty plan. She was a woman of Cajun descent from the warm backwaters of southern Louisiana. Reluctantly she had followed him north. Faithfully she had supported him. So far, however, the "one article" had eluded him. As a result, the bar on Jimmy's vision continued to descend. Five years ago Jimmy had wanted to be catapulted onto the national scene. Tonight, especially now, he just wanted to get out of Northfield—forever.

As "Sweet Home Alabama" broke into the cab of his chilled SUV, Jimmy sent a hurried text to the anonymous sender. "When can we talk? You can't just leave me hanging like this!"

No answer. After waiting five minutes, Jimmy turned off the loud vibrating engine, pulled on his gloves and his beanie, and closed his phone. *Maybe,* he hoped against hope, *it was just a prank.*

Before exiting the Forerunner, however, Jimmy committed to wait exactly two more minutes. As he did, the memory of last year's Northfield Nation Night wedged its way into his thoughts. The amusing memory of last year's drama provided a welcomed distraction.

The previous Northfield Nation Night had been preceded by a controversial student petition. The students had sought, for the fourth year in a row, to change the nickname of the school's athletic teams from the traditional "Norsemen" to the more contemporary "Warriors." The controversy had nearly split the community in two, with opposing sides falling almost exclusively along the generational lines.

"Small town drama, it's the best! You can't make this stuff up!" Jimmy laughed aloud as he replayed the tension-filled scene in Town Hall. Melissa Fairbanks, the President of Northfield's senior class and the captain of the women's basketball team, had been the most eloquent student voice. "How can you ask us, as the current student body of Northfield High School, to join together as 'Norsemen'? Where does that leave half our school's population? Are we to be 'Lady Norsemen'? Or are we to be proud 'Norsewomen'? Do we matter, or is tradition more important than our own identity?

"And, how many of our peers feel left out when we use a word that refers specifically to people of Scandinavian descent? Do we all look Scandinavian? Do our teachers all look Scandinavian? Do I look at all like I'm Scandinavian?" The articulate young native American woman had drawn laughter from the entire audience, including her opponents. Her next question, however, sparked a round of hushed gasps. "And how about Coach Mac or Mrs. Gracie Mac—do they look Scandinavian to you?"

All eyes had immediately shifted toward Coach Mac. He acknowledged their attention with a slight nod accompanied with an approving chuckle.

Lars Anderson, a four-decade member of the school board, represented the voice of the town's establishment. "The founding families of Northfield were 'Norsemen.' Men and women, boys and girls, all were known as Norsemen. All we ask is that we continue to honor their courage and sacrifice in building our community. We are here because of Norsemen—and many of us still consider ourselves to be Norsemen. We are the proud descendants of our Viking forefathers. I simply cannot turn my back on this community's proud heritage."

"Coach Mac," Mayor Johannsen had then said, "I think it's time we heard from you."

Rising from his seat, Coach Mac surveyed the room with a non-anxious, welcoming smile. The smile morphed into a mischievous grin as he added, "Well, Miss Fairbanks. You are correct. I want to put an end to all rumors that I am Scandinavian." The comment prompted laughter from all, accompanied by applause from the student section of the room. "My ancestors were from East Africa. And, unlike the visionary, pioneering Norwegian, Swedish, and Danish families who founded our community, my direct ancestors were forced to come to America by means of cruel injustice." The room fell silent as Coach Mac paused for several seconds.

With reverence and remembrance, he resumed, "Still, a part of who they are is in me. And they, like our town's founding families, demonstrated great courage and character. We must therefore demonstrate our deep respect for their legacy." Nodding heads and a smattering of "amen" filled the room. "We are all shaped by our ancestry," Coach Mac continued with a spiritual cadence, "but we cannot . . ." Coach Mac shook his head and waved his long right hand vigorously in the air as he made his way toward the front of the room. "No, we must not be wholly defined by or limited to our heritage." After waiting for his words to have their weight in the room, Coach Mac added with a smile, "Men and women, I am more of a traditionalist than anyone in this room. Good heavens, we still have the same pre-game warm-up drills as we did thirty-five years ago."

"I can testify to that!" Anders Mason shouted as if he were a member of a congregation following Coach Mac. Anders had played on Coach Mac's first team in Northfield, though at age fifty-three he had buried his youthful athleticism under seventy-five pounds of Julia Mason's irresistible cooking.

"Thank you, Anders." Coach Mac nodded affectionately to his former player turned lifelong friend. Then he softened his voice and slowed his pace, "But, friends, there comes a time when the future has to be forged by new pioneers. And that future, if Northfield is to survive at all, will be led by men and women, white and black and brown and all colors, by athletes and artists and accountants, by the next generation who will build on our legacy as well as build their own. And, in my mind, if they want to be called 'Warriors' while they're building their legacy, I vote we support them one hundred percent."

As Coach Mac made his way back toward his seat, Lars Anderson rose unsteadily from his seat. Coach Mac stopped walking immediately as a sign of respect. "Coach Mac," Lars spoke with a halting voice, "You know how much I love and admire you."

"Yes, sir, Mr. Anderson. You've been on my side since day one—and that's saying a lot. I appreciate you—and I love you, sir. I hope you know that."

"I do, Coach. I do." Turning toward the crowd, Lars continued gently, "And Miss Fairbanks, I also respect you and your friends," Lars glanced toward Melissa as he spoke. "And, while I don't like this change, well . . ." Lars looked deep in thought as he lowered his head. Then he spoke directly to Coach Mac. "You're right, John. We need to get out of their way. It's time to let these young ones build their own legacy. Maybe they can build one that will be better, not just for them, but for all the good people of Lewis County."

Under the influence of Coach Mac's gracious leadership, "Norsegate," as Jimmy called it, ended peacefully. There was no lingering relational bloodshed, though there were more than a few bruised egos. In an article published the next day, Jimmy wrote an opening line that would be memorialized for years by the people of Lewis County:

> *"When it comes to Northfield's ancestral roots, it seems that the one heritage that binds everyone together is the heart and soul of our beloved Coach John McKissack."*

Jimmy then repeated to himself, the final line of the article, "There is, and forever can only be, one Coach Mac." As he did so, Jimmy lifted the wobbly latch on his SUV's door. He pulled a navy blue and gold Northfield scarf full across his face, leaving only his eyes exposed. Just before his left foot exited the vehicle, the cell phone's chirping sound returned. Jimmy hastily grabbed the phone as he retreated back into the Forerunner and closed the door.

I'll text tonight. After I'm home. By myself. And don't try to trace these texts.

Closing himself back in the Forerunner, Jimmy frantically tore off his gloves then feverishly typed in response. *I need to know if this is for real. Can you promise me this is not a prank or some crazy rumor?*

The response was immediate. *It's real. It's serious. They know things. Bad things. And they're going to use them all against Coach Mac. They're going to bring him down!*

An intense chill ran through Jimmy's body, one so severe that he reached once again to close the door of his Forerunner. The door, however, was still closed. The source of the chill resided inside of Jimmy.

CHAPTER 6

nside Northfield High School, Derrick rapped his knuckles softly against the slender vertical glass pane in the ancient door that was the entrance to Coach Mac's headquarters. Coach raised his eyes then motioned D to join him in the cluttered, cramped office.

"Martin, that's wonderful," Coach Mac responded into his phone as he simultaneously slapped his right palm onto the desk in celebration.

Derrick slid into a well-worn leather chair facing the head coach's desk. He surveyed the four crowded walls that framed the tiny room. Thirty-five team pictures and dozens of framed newspaper clippings covered the walls like three-dimensional wallpaper. Derrick remembered how Jimmy Thompson had recently said to the Northfield Nation Boosters Club, "The story of Northfield's enduring love for its valiant Norsemen-turned-Warriors was told on those walls."

Derrick decided to start from the beginning and follow the timeline of the love story as he waited for Coach Mac to conclude his call with Martin Denton. The first picture seemed the most unlike the others. It was the only black and white photo—and, ironically, the only photo displaying almost exculsively white athletes. Derrick tried to imagine Coach Mac, barely older than Derrick was at the moment, dealing with the stress of those early years.

Derrick's eyes continued to follow the eloquent story portrayed by the team pictures. Hairstyles transitioned from short-cropped buzz cuts to long, bushy locks and afros, then back again. He observed the evolution of basketball shorts from the era of "high and tight" to the more modern "long and baggy." Most noticeably, Derrick noted how dramatically the teams morphed from majority white players to pre-dominantly ethnic minority players. This year's Warriors, for instance, had players from African, Latino, and Native American descent. Only four players appeared to be descended from the region's more traditional Northfield Scandinavian heritage.

In the midst of constant changes, however, two things remained as reliable as the bitter cold winter nights in the northern Midwest. First, there was the towering presence of Coach John McKissack. The hair-line had receded. The remaining hair had turned much lighter. But his strength and stature remained preeminent. Second of all, the cap-tions underneath the thirty-five team pictures were remarkably consis-tent. Twenty-seven pictures were captioned with "District Champions." Twenty-one added the title "Regional Champions" underneath. Eleven were designated the highest honor, "State Champions." The most glaring exception to this pattern was the team photo from Derrick's senior year. The absence of the word "champion" drove a dagger into Derrick's heart. Seeing himself smiling in the team photo, a picture taken prior to the season's first game, twisted the dagger and plunged it deeper.

If only I hadn't been such a screw up . . . Derrick's stomach knotted painfully. He coached himself sternly, *Stay in the present, man; stay in the present.*

Coach Mac's booming voice interrupted Derrick's self-talk. "Mar-tin, I can't thank you enough for partnering with me. Together we can do this. We can make our community a better place for all our fami-lies." Coach Mac paused, obviously listening intently to Martin Denton's response and nodding approvingly. Then Coach Mac moved the conver-sation toward closure.

"Yes, sir. We absolutely are, Martin. We're doing this for everybody in this community. . . . Exactly, love creates a way . . . All right, yep. Send my love to D'Lane . . . I will. . . . Me, too, Martin. Okay, see you later tonight."

"Everything going according to plan, Coach?"

"Absolutely. That was Chris' and Jamarcus' dad, Martin. We may have some deep problems in this community, D, but we also have many men and women, of all races and backgrounds, who can help us. We will prevail. We will overcome. D, I'm a blessed man to be a part of this community."

"Me, too, Coach."

"And, personally, I think we are going to have one heck of a powerful Northfield Nation Night," Coach added as he leaned back in his chair, full of satisfaction and delight. "I really do. As long as everyone can make it through this snowy mess."

"They will, Coach. They always do. Nobody wants to be the one person who missed the launch of our first ever three-peat state championship season," Derrick said proudly.

Coach Mac turned his undersized office chair toward Derrick. Leaning forward with his forearms resting on his desk, he smiled broadly. "Well, regardless of attendance, I'm just glad to have you on board to lead with me. Like I said last night, D, we need each other."

"Well, I know I need you, for sure." Derrick cleared his throat and shuffled his weight in his chair. "In fact, that's why I wanted to catch you a moment before the crowd starts to arrive." Derrick nervously shifted in and out of eye contact. He slumped forward, a look of dread moving across his face. To Coach Mac, Derrick looked like a student showing up unprepared for a major exam.

Coach Mac's cell phone buzzed, but he ignored it. "D, what's up?"

Derrick shuffled clumsily in his chair again, this time leaning back rather than toward Coach Mac's gray metal desk. "This probably isn't the best time to bring this up . . ." Derrick's thoughts suddenly disconnected from his voice, hijacked by uncertainty.

"I assure you that there's nothing else I need to be doing, D. Tonight is set. We have plenty of time to go over final details and enjoy the evening." Coach Mac reassured him. "Oh, and by the way, I so appreciate Nikki picking up Gracie. She's not very confident driving anymore at night, especially in weather like this."

"Absolutely, Coach. Nikki's thrilled to have time with her, I'm sure." Derrick paused again. He emptied his lap of his backpack, jacket, and gloves. With no more obvious tasks to distract him, Derrick's eyes blinked rapidly as they rose to meet Coach Mac's.

"Nikki and I have been living together for less than six months, but it already seems like we're doomed. I have no idea what to do next," Derrick blurted hastily. The words came pouring out, gaining force and speed like an avalanche. "Last night, I hoped things might be taking a turn for the better. After you left, I felt closer to Nikki than I have in a long time. And. . . . well, I had reason last night to believe that, you know, things were okay . . . she . . . I'm just sayin' she didn't act like anything was wrong once you left. You know what I mean?" Derrick shifted nervously. He hoped, on one level, that Coach Mac had understood his coded reference. On another level, he kind of hoped that he had not.

Coach Mac smiled. "Yes, I understand what you mean. Don't forget, I've got four decades worth of fighting and making up, D." Coach Mac chuckled knowingly.

Derrick said nothing. Staring silently toward the ceiling for a very long time, Derrick finally let out a loud of huff a breath. "Yeah, okay," Derrick forced a quickly disappearing smile, "so . . . naturally, you know, I . . . ah . . . well, I thought things were back on track, right?" Coach Mac nodded and smiled.

"But, then, Coach," Derrick continued with a steady anger building in his voice, "this morning, she asked if we could 'work through some things.' I said, 'Sure.' God, that was a huge mistake," Derrick said, drawing out the word "huge." "Coach, I'm tellin' ya, before I left for lunch, we had one of our worst fights. Ever. At one point, she said, 'I just can't pretend anymore, D! You never listen to me, except of course, when you want something from me. You know, you'll listen if it gets you sex—that's about it.'" Derrick drew a deep breath, then blew it out again, puffing his cheeks. "I'm not going to lie, Coach, that stung. And the whole thing was over a few stupid unpaid bills and one unanswered phone call!"

Derrick looked back over his right shoulder, returning his gaze to his senior team photo. He grimaced at the fifteen adolescent faces staring back. Derrick's eyes glared with contempt at their foolish, hope-filled smiles.

Coach Mac said nothing as Derrick turned his eyes away from the wall and toward his outstretched feet on the floor. Then Derrick snapped to attention. Energized by an "aha" moment, he began speaking in animated gestures, "Okay, here's what it feels like, Coach," Derrick said. "I am playing in the biggest game of my life. Early on, our whole team is on fire. We're cruising our way to victory. Suddenly, and for no reason, we're in the fourth quarter and we've completely fallen apart. Now we're hopelessly losing the game. No matter what we do, we can't get our momentum back. You can just feel it, we're going to lose, and there's not a damn thing we can do about it . . ."

"That's a darn good analogy, D," Coach Mac observed.

Derrick caught the intent of Coach Mac's not so subtle wording. Coach Mac adamantly preached his conviction that swearing was a poor use of the English language. Derrick silently reasoned, "Okay, okay, Coach. But right now I don't give a damn about my use of the English language." He massaged the left side of his face roughly. "I don't know. Maybe if this were a game, I'd know what to do."

"If it helps, D, I've been right where you are—only worse."

"You . . . what?" Derrick leaned further into the conversation.

Coach Mac turned his whole body toward Derrick. He commented wryly, "Man, how did that woman ever stay with me? . . . D, I've made more mistakes with Gracie than you could ever imagine. To use your example, I got behind in the second quarter, got into foul trouble, made more turnovers than shots, and injured both ankles before I realized how bad things actually were." Coach Mac murmured wistfully through tightly closed lips, "Ummm . . . But, this isn't about me, D." He shifted in his chair as he shifted the conversation. "I can tell my story another time. Let's talk about what you think is your core problem with Nikki. I seriously doubt it's just about, how did you put it—'a few stupid unpaid bills and one unanswered phone call'?"

Derrick paused for a long while, offering his brain a brief moment to realign itself after Coach Mac's unexpected disclosure. "Okay, Coach. But you have got to finish that story some time."

"I will. Not today, though. Again, D, what do you think is the core problem here?"

"Me," Derrick spoke shamefully. "Yep, it's me for sure. I'm not the person Nikki really wants. At one point I was." Thinking for a moment in silence, he added with a long sigh, "Maybe I was. But not now. Every day it seems she finds some new reason to be disappointed in me. So, yeah, I think I'm the problem—and that's kind of hard to fix."

"I agree," Coach Mac began.

With those words, Derrick breathed out every molecule that remained in his lungs. He slumped forward in his chair. Raising his right hand to his forehead, Derrick swept his hand back and forth through his wavy hair. Then he ran his hand down his face, briskly rubbing his cheeks and chin.

"But not entirely," Coach Mac added.

"What does that mean?" Derrick challenged, making no attempt to mask his growing irritation.

"It means that, at the moment, I do think you are the biggest problem in the relationship. And I think you are disappointing Nikki over and over. But, I also believe—wholeheartedly—that you are actually the person Nikki wants. And loves."

Derrick rapidly retraced the storyline of photos on the walls. He then looked toward the door while reaching down for his backpack. Coach Mac interrupted his movement with a firm voice, "Derrick, I want you to listen to me on this."

Derrick released his grip on the backpack, leaving it sitting on the floor. Coach Mac continued, "I'm quite confident Nikki also carries some of the blame. Now's not the time to focus on that. And, above all, D, trying to fix yourself to please Nikki is only going to make this worse." Coach Mac moved his head down and to his left. Moving his eyes lower than the slumping Derrick's, he managed to make eye contact. "Remember, D. The key is grace. Grace under pressure. That's the foundation of the Northfield Way. You can't just perform your way out of this one. Pressuring yourself to 'try harder' or 'do better' will never work. This is a grace-sized problem."

Derrick rose from his chair. He strode to within two feet of the haunting photo that included senior team captain, D Walker. He studied eighteen-year-old D Walker's face. It looked like a Halloween mask to Derrick. The smiling happy face was no more the true Derrick Walker than if he had been wearing a Superman costume and cape. Derrick stared angrily at the space beneath the photo, and even more angrily at the teenage D. "You're a joke," he whispered. "A bad freakin' joke."

Turning back to Coach Mac, Derrick adopted a matter of fact voice. "You know, maybe this was just a bad idea, Coach. I just don't get all this grace stuff like you do. Maybe . . . maybe it just doesn't work for me, you know."

Coach Mac stood and walked toward Derrick. Derrick's body unconsciously retreated, backing up to the wall. Coach Mac stopped walking. He stared up at the senior in the photo, then looked back at the young man standing before him. "Derrick Walker, as your coach and your friend, I can assure you: you get more of 'this stuff' than you realize. Otherwise you wouldn't be here tonight. You wouldn't have come back. And, honestly, I wouldn't have asked you to."

Sensing openness, Coach Mac resumed his movement toward Derrick. He placed both hands onto Derrick's shoulders. "You may be in the fourth quarter, but you're about to make a run, Coach Derrick Walker. I can feel it. I can see it. And this comeback is going to be one for the ages."

Derrick separated himself from Coach Mac—not forcefully pushing him away, but clearly disconnecting with purpose. Returning to his seat, he put Coach Mac to the test, "And how am I supposed to do that? I don't need another pep talk, Coach," Derrick's voice rose in defiance, "I need specifics on how to solve this!"

Coach Mac returned slowly to his gray metal chair. This time he leaned back, maintaining the space that Derrick's body language demanded.

Derrick bit down on his lower lip as he tapped the fingers of both hands rapidly in rhythm on his knees. Turning toward Coach Mac, Derrick said sorrowfully, "I'm losing her, Coach. I'm losing her and I . . ."

"You're losing her and you . . . ? What were you about to say, D?"

"I love her." Derrick turned his face away. He dabbed his eyes with his sleeve. A rattling, sniffling deep breath inhaled through his nose. Clearing his throat, he repeated, "I love her . . ." His voice was low in volume but loud in fear.

"I know you do. And she loves you." And that's why I am confident you will get through this. Love always creates a way."

Derrick looked blankly at Coach Mac.

"This isn't coach-speak," Coach Mac said. "I've watched Nikki. She's reaching out to you. That's what last night was about—and, you may not believe it, but that's what this morning was about, too. She's not just reaching out to you, D, she's reaching out for you. But she can't find you. At least not the Derrick she knows, the one she loves."

Derrick's squinting eyes and pursed lips gave way to a look of profound resignation. "I have no idea what you're talking about. No idea." Derrick threw up his hands, raising them with palms upward as his shoulders shrugged. "What do I do, Coach? What?" Derrick challenged. "And, please, be practical."

"You get back to the Derrick Walker that Nikki Coles fell in love with. Back to the one coach I chose above all the two hundred applications I had in my office. The man who turned his life around and came back to slay his dragons and silence his demons."

"And . . ." Derrick inquired with raised eyebrows. Moving his hand in a circular motion, Derrick begged, ". . . c'mon, Coach. Exactly *how* do I do that?" Derrick moved his left hand in a sweeping motion toward Coach Mac. As his arm reached full motion, he exposed his palm to Coach Mac with a sarcastic, "And please. Do not tell me, 'The Northfield Way.'"

"Okay," Coach Mac responded flatly. The silence lingered as Coach Mac sat relaxed, his arms and legs in an open posture. The senior coach's breathing was slow and natural, as if he were sitting by the pool on a warm summer day reading a new favorite book.

By contrast, Derrick sat with arms and legs crossed as he repeatedly broke off then reconnected his eye contact with Coach Mac. He was determined not to speak first.

Derrick huffed a deep sigh. "Okay, okay," relenting after an unbearable thirty seconds of silence. "I'm sure 'The Northfield Way' is the answer, but I swear, Coach Mac, you're going to have to help me on this. Nothing personal, but right now this all feels like wholesale b—s— coach-speak."

Coach Mac smiled. "I'm sure it does. And, of course, the Northfield Way isn't going to fix anything, D. But it does provide a very real pathway toward regaining that lost momentum." Then he added, "It's just a pathway." Coach Mac pointed a long, straight finger toward Derrick. "You have to do the work. But the pathway will direct your steps as you do the work." Then Coach Mac turned his long finger toward himself and buried it deep into his chest, "And I'll be here to help—every step of the way."

"Coach, I get the Northfield Way, for basketball, I mean. But with Nikki? I'm clueless. That's me speaking the truth to you. Look, I'm as clueless as a first grader being told to play help-side defense. I can hear the words, but I can't grasp the concepts." By now, Derrick's arms were uncrossed. The rigidity had left his body. The look on his face, however, remained painfully strained.

"Let's get through tonight's event and tomorrow night's home opener. Once the season is underway, we can talk more about the Northfield Way as it relates to your relationship with Nikki. D, I promise you, you're going to see that much of what we do on the court is both a mirror and metaphor for your real life."

"Coach, I do have one request. And I'd like you to agree to honor it," Derrick asked firmly.

"Well, I have to hear your request before I can agree or disagree," Coach Mac answered.

"I'm asking you not to lecture me on why I should marry Nikki instead of just living with her. Look, I respect your faith and your traditional values. And, of course, I absolutely respect the great marriage you and Mrs. Gracie have. But I do not, in any way, want to feel pressured to get married. At least not now," Derrick explained adamantly.

"Hmmm . . . that's an interesting request, Coach Walker." After a lengthy period of silence, Coach Mac's eyes returned to decades of his life played out on cluttered office walls. Coach Mac then leaned in toward Derrick. A warm smile appeared on the aged man's face. The smile perfectly matched the tone that was to follow. "I think that's a fair request, D. I get why you don't want to be pressured toward marriage." Coach

Mac extended his right hand for a handshake to seal the deal, as if the two had just concluded a long day of intense negotiations.

"Thank you, Coach," Derrick replied as his hand disappeared into Coach Mac's massive grip. "That helps a lot."

"There's absolutely no sense in me beating you over the head with my convictions and my values," Coach Mac added affirmatively.

"Exactly!" Derrick nodded vigorously, his whole body relaxing into this chair.

"Besides," Coach Mac added with a smile, "By the time you finish the pathway of The Northfield Way, you'll have your own answers on Nikki and on marriage."

"What do you mean by that?" Derrick asked suspiciously.

"I meant what I said," Coach Mac responded. "You will have your own answer. Not my answer. Not Nikki's answer. You'll have Derrick Walker's answer."

"What do you think the answer will be, Coach? Will it be the same as your answer?" Derrick interrogated.

"Well, that all depends."

"On what?"

"On your answer that the first maxim of the Northfield Way forces you to answer. When you know, on a heart level, your greater purpose in this relationship, the rest will become clear. You have to answer 'Why?' with a purpose that's greater than just you. Once you do, your relationship with Nikki, and your life, will naturally expand to the size of your 'why?' That's how it works."

"Well, let's hope it works for me."

"Oh, it will. I have no doubt, D. It will." Coach Mac reached out and squeezed D's left forearm. Releasing his grip, he then stood upright. As Derrick reached a full standing position next to him, Coach Mac added with a wink, "And, by the way, don't underestimate the potential of a six-year-old. Help defense may be a tough concept to learn for a young player. But, D, I'm telling you, from my own personal experience, you should never underestimate what can happen when fear of failure loses out to grace under pressure."

CHAPTER 7

Climbing out of his Forerunner, Jimmy's boots immediately sank calf-deep into swollen heaps of wet snow. The rest of his body had it worse, absorbing blow after blow of ice-laden gusts of wind. "Miserable," Jimmy mumbled to himself.

He thought back to how the day had begun. A cloudless blue sky had gradually emerged as a bright winter sun melted away layers of dense fog. Frozen black fields, blanketed by the previous night's snow, intersected a glowing orange and red horizon. Even Jimmy had to admit that the northern Midwest could produce spectacular winter scenery. As the day advanced, however, so did a rolling edge of gray clouds. Propelled by increasingly powerful winds, a cold front plowed its way into Northfield. Waves of dark clouds consumed the western blue sky, then the sun, then the eastern horizon. The day progressively devolved from a warm, sunny morning to a cool, cloudy afternoon, then into a freezing, snowy mess of a night.

"There's at least one advantage to living on the plains," Jimmy had remarked to Tara over a quick sandwich at Sven's café. "At least you can see what's coming way before it gets here."

"True. I mean, sort of. Out here, you can see what's coming toward you. But you never know, Jimmy. You never really know what's next," Tara reflected as she leaned toward the diner's large window, peering upward at the gathering clouds.

Once inside the door of the John McKissack Arena, Jimmy stomped the slush off his boots and shook loose the snow covering his black wool beanie. The mysterious texts he had received over the last several minutes had left him feeling unsettled. Jimmy suspiciously scanned the room. A familiar rolling sea of navy and vegas gold loyalists greeted him in every direction. Everything, and everyone, seemed to be in its rightful place.

Seated near the front, as usual, was Buster Olsen. Attending his thirty-sixth consecutive Night, Buster sat next to his wife of fifty-four years, Millie. Once again, Buster had shoved himself into the faded, navy Northfield sweatshirt he had first worn thirty-three years ago. That season, Coach Mac had led Northfield to the school's first-ever district championship. Though the retired handyman's enlarged "3XL" torso could no longer be successfully contained by the threadbare "L" sweatshirt, he still wore it proudly—almost as proudly as the night he celebrated Junior Olsen's District Tourney MVP award.

Recalling Junior's MVP night once again, Buster leaned over to his beloved Millie, whispering softly in her ear, "Northfield basketball is the second-best thing that ever happened to me, Millicent Olsen." As her husband kissed her lovingly on the cheek, Millie smiled. Coming from Buster's navy-and-gold-blooded heart, the words were high praise indeed.

To the far left, near the back, sat Sheila Jordan. Sheila was a single mother who had raised three of Lewis County's finest young men, and had done so in spite of severe financial difficulties, including being the primary caretaker for her disabled mother, Miriam. Though the boys had all moved on to successful careers in other states, Sheila continued to attend Northfield Nation Nights. Tonight, she had proudly texted to her oldest, Michael, that it was twenty-four in a row and counting.

Jimmy watched as locals of all ages, ethnicities, and incomes paused to say a "hello" or offer a warm embrace to Sheila. She was, Jimmy considered, the second most widely respected woman in the whole town—behind Mrs. Gracie Mac, of course. Jimmy recalled once asking Sheila, "How did you do it? You're a single mom working sixty hours a week; how is this possible?"

"I prayed a lot—a whole lot," Sheila had responded humbly, "And, thank God, He answered my prayers. He sent Coach Mac to teach my boys how to be men." Then Sheila would add, with a slight tremble of overwhelming gratitude in her voice, "There's only so much a momma can do with boys—the rest I just had to leave in the hands of God and Coach Mac. They knew what to do."

Front and center sat Jimbo Larsen and his wife, Carla Marie. Jimbo came off the bench to score six points, including the game-winning free throw, for Coach Mac's first Northfield Norsemen state championship. Jimbo wore his standard neatly pressed white dress shirt with a broad, outdated gold tie boasting a large navy monogrammed N. His face was full and red, reflecting both his bold personality and the two Jack Daniels and Coca Colas he had consumed prior to arriving.

Jimbo's story was one of a "hometown boy made good." His was the kind of rags-to-riches tale that people in small towns love to repeat as often as someone would listen. The unsophisticated, naïve teenage farm boy had moved to Chicago, eventually working his way through the Kellogg business school at Northwestern. He then interned at, and later took a full-time role with, the Chicago Board of Trade. Before the age of 30, Jimbo had become the first—and to this date only—President of Northfield's brightest financial jewel, the exceedingly successful Northfield Community Bank. Jimbo was equally respected in the community both for his business successes and his personal generosity.

Carla Marie, on the other hand, was best known for her fashion statements. Most noteworthy—and Carla Marie was always noteworthy—she had amassed a huge collection of top-shelf, custom-made Northfield blouses, sweaters, accessories, and jewelry. The recent switch from the Norsemen logo to the Warrior identity had provided the perfect excuse for Carla Marie to replenish her Northfield wardrobe. Jimmy shook his head as he surveyed, and almost admired, Carla Marie's gaudy display of Northfield enthusiasm. She wore a large gold bow in her hair, complementing her thick, navy scarf and dangling gold N earrings. Her gold sweater had a custom-monogrammed navy blue N with "Warriors" sewn underneath. She had also pinned to the sweater a 24-carat gold N broach, outlined in diamonds.

To the less fashion-conscious among the Northfield Nation, and that would include pretty much everybody except Carla Marie, her expensive navy and gold ensembles seemed "over the top." More than a few indignant ladies in the community could be heard to remark, "The diamonds and gold may be real, but there are some parts of Carla Marie that clearly are not!"

"JT, good to see you tonight." A booming voice interrupted Jimmy's musings on Northfield's lone fashionista.

Coach Mac's large presence, more than his voice, startled Jimmy. He suddenly felt awkward, similar to the way he had felt when he first arrived in Northfield five years ago. "How do I do small talk with Coach Mac now? After those texts?" Jimmy wondered anxiously.

"JT, you okay?"

"I'm fine, Coach. I guess it's just this crazy weather," Jimmy lied. He immediately regretted it. "You know, we southern boys never get used to the cold," he deflected.

"Of course, of course," Coach Mac responded, clearly unconvinced. "Well . . ." Coach Mac searched for words to press below the surface, "Just remember, in all things—and I mean all things, JT—you're one of us. You're not just a transplanted South Carolinian anymore. You're Northfield Nation through and through." Coach Mac patted Jimmy on the shoulder and added, "And you're not the only one around here who hates this weather, believe me."

"Thanks, Coach," Jimmy laughed nervously. "And I believe you. I believe all that you said—that is, about the weather," Jimmy replied, his cheeks flushed with anxiety.

Principal Davis stepped behind an expansive, solid mahogany podium. Its impressive, hand-carved navy "N" and a gold-embossed Viking Warrior logo had been donated two seasons earlier by the families of Northfield's state championship team. During that process, Carla Marie's extravagant flamboyance and deep pockets had enjoyed full reign. Her nephew had been the captain of the team, which explained the podium's excessive dimensions and gaudy adornments.

"Tonight," Principal Davis began, "We remember the success of last year's Northfield team." For a moment, he successfully held in check the crowd's bottled up energy. He could not, however, constrain himself for very long. As soon as he gave words to the Northfield Nation's expectations of an historical record-breaking season, Principal Davis suddenly, unconsciously found himself personally swept away by his own tide of Warrior mania.

"But now, even as we recall last season's incredible run of Northfield victories, 29 straight wins to end the season with a repeat state championship . . . it is time . . . it is time to begin cheering for what we *hope and pray and dream* will be the next Northfield Basketball state championship team!" With an increasingly rapid cadence, and with his right hand raised, pointing to the sky, Principal Davis fully abandoned himself to visions of Warrior glory. "We will give our full support to these valiant young men who, starting tomorrow night, will chase history with all their might and with all their hearts, fighting night after night, game after game, with the dream of becoming the first-ever Northfield team to become three-peat state champions!"

Like a front-running candidate at his own election night rally, Principal Davis unleashed a frenzied ovation. On this painfully frigid November night, the outside air temperature would dip far below freezing. The biting wind chill would plunge several degrees below zero. Even so, Buster and Millie Olsen, Sheila Jordan, Jimbo and Carla Marie Larsen, and 1700 other Northfield family members would find warmth for their bodies and their souls. Life was as it should be for the moment. Internally, irrationally, they hoped it would always be so.

In the back, Jimmy Thompson leaned heavily against the "Wall of Fame." The dozens of plaques and jerseys lining the wall bore testimony to three-plus decades of Northfield dominance. Added to this splendor were more than two-dozen championship banners hanging in the arena's wooden rafters. The combined glory of the wall and the rafters evoked awe among the home team fans and intimidation in the hearts of visitors.

Jimmy quickly jotted down his notes, trying not to be distracted by his erratic, racing thoughts. *Who sent those texts? Where were they actually sitting in this room?* If he made eye contact with them, would he be able to tell—from the look on their faces? Had he seen anything that was worthy of his suspicion?"

The Northfield fan base's passion was just warming up as Principal Davis concluded his stirring introductory remarks. The full fury of Warrior passion was, however, yet to be unleashed. That furor was reserved, this year and every year, for the moment when their beloved Coach Mac rose to speak. The family's patriarch, as well as its priest and prophet, would once again have full command of the room, just as he had done last year, and every year for more than three decades, on this hallowed night.

Northfield Night annually ranked near or at the very top of every fan's list of treasured Northfield traditions. Over the years, a particularly sacred ritual had evolved within its context: the well-orchestrated introduction of Coach Mac. Previous introductions had been made by former players, by family members of former players, and on rare occasions, someone external to the Northfield family. The basis of selection for this high honor was singular. The "introducer" had to possess a personal, powerful story that offered an inspiring glimpse into the breadth and depth of Coach Mac's impact on the community.

To add an element of mystery and intrigue to the super-charged atmosphere, the introducer's identity remained concealed until the last possible moment. Year after year, like a Times Square crowd at 11:59 p.m. on New Year's Eve, the audience waited impatiently for the unveiling of a well-guarded secret. Once the "introducer" had been introduced, the room typically responded with a roar of universal approval. Almost without fail, the crowd's enthusiasm sparked a standing ovation.

On this night, the crowd's response was uncharacteristically underwhelming, but not because the Warrior family disapproved of the "introducer." Rather, they simply had no idea what to think. Some hadn't even recalled even hearing the man's name before. The choice of David Abernathy, therefore, puzzled the good people of Lewis County.

Abernathy, the Northfield High theater arts teacher, was surprisingly non-athletic, at least in stature and gait. Moreover, since he entered the room almost universally unknown to the Northfield family, they had no context for assessing his worthiness for the task. To their knowledge, he had never previously attended this event. Even more concerning, it seemed very possible that he may never have cheered on the boys in their sacred John McKissack Arena.

Coach Mac, seated to the audience's right, behind the imposing over-sized lectern, immediately recognized the crowd's hesitancy. Rising from his undersized and obviously uncomfortable molded plastic chair, he slowly unfolded his massive frame. Coach Mac's movements, though still imposing, were noticeably more deliberate and significantly slower than in years past. What he lacked in agility, however, he more than made up for in the remarkable dignity of his leadership presence. Taking two long strides with his towering legs, Coach Mac intercepted David Abernathy with an energetic, affectionate embrace.

To the crowd's amusement, the five-foot, eight-inch theater arts teacher appeared to be more engulfed than embraced by the towering patriarch. Coach Mac's gigantic, generous hug signaled to everyone that the proper reaction to the diminutive Abernathy would be a full-bore, high energy Northfield welcome. The crowd immediately mirrored Coach Mac's lead with a standing ovation worthy of a returning hero's welcome.

Coach Mac's bear hug had reassured the crowd of David Aberna-thy's acceptability, in spite of his appearance and their prejudices. More importantly, the mammoth embrace reassured the young teacher that not only was he welcomed, but also that he belonged in this sacred Northfield moment.

CHAPTER 8

Bolstered by Coach Mac's clear display of affirmation, David Abernathy playfully responded to the crowd's lingering doubts about his fit for the moment. "I know what you're all thinking," he said with a dramatic wave of his right hand across the whole of the arena. 'You're thinking, *For real? That's the guy who's going to introduce Coach Mac?*' Believe me, I had the same question when the Boosters first approached me. But then it occurred to me how much we all have in common." The room leaned in, sensing that there might just be more to the small in stature young man than what met the eye.

"While our Northfield Nation grows in its diversity, year by year—and for that I am truly thankful—we still hold in common at least two very, very important life experiences." Abernathy continued, the confidence in his voice building with each sentence he spoke. "These two experiences inseparably bind you and me together. So, rather than trying to explain myself, let me just tell you two stories."

"It was three years ago last spring that I first interviewed with Principal Davis," began Abernathy. "I was being considered for the first-ever theater arts faculty position at Northfield. Fresh out of grad school, I was scared to death! I'm so fortunate I wore a sports coat that day; because my dress shirt was soaked within the first half hour! What kept me going, however, was a burning desire to prove that David Abernathy 'had the goods' to build the finest theater arts program in the tri-state area."

By now, Abernathy had stepped purposefully from behind the podium, gesturing enthusiastically. He threw himself, body and soul, into his storytelling. He spoke as if he were delivering dramatic lines in a Broadway production. Every table responded with affirming smiles, approving nods, and intentional eye contact. Non-verbally, but very loudly, the crowd communicated, *Hey, kid, you're all right.* Northfield High School Athletic Director John Butler would later observe to his wife, "The Nation may not be well acquainted with musical theater, but they can recognize a competitive spirit from a country mile."

Young Abernathy moved closer to the front row of round tables, each fully wrapped in a WARRIOR-embossed navy and gold tablecloth complimented by the embroidered image of a fierce Viking warrior. The dramatic theatre teacher used each of his few short steps to decrease the distance between his story and their hearts.

"I was convinced on that very first day—and it has been confirmed to me every day since—that there exists an almost limitless potential for Northfield students to excel in the arts. But I was also convinced on that day—and quite honestly, I was *personally threatened* on that day—by the realization that Northfield basketball reigned supreme in Lewis County."

"Amen!" called out a voice from the back. "That's right!" someone called out with the spiritual tone of a true Northfield Nation believer. Laughter and scattered applause rippled through the room.

"See what I mean?" Abernathy confidently continued, riding the momentum of the crowd's passion. "I recognized the power of the Northfield basketball fan base in the first hour of my interview. And, honestly, that deeply concerned me. That's the gospel truth. I truly feared that Norsemen basketball . . . oops, sorry." The laughter was hearty, but laced with a twinge of groaning. Evidently, not all the wounds from the "Norse-gate" era had fully healed.

"I feared *Warrior* basketball," Abernathy added, "would be an overwhelming obstacle to my vision for the arts. Based on my past experiences in public schools with great sports programs, I imagined that I would be in constant, direct competition with Coach John McKissack and his basketball teams. And, in case you haven't noticed, Coach John Mac and his teams typically don't end up on the losing end of any competition."

To the left of Abernathy, from the farthest table on the front row, an almost spiritual "Aaaa-men, brother!" filled the room, prompting brief but widespread applause.

"But on my first day as a faculty member—actually, in the first hour of my first day as a faculty member—Coach John McKissack strode into my office with two cups of coffee."

Abernathy turned to face the smiling Coach Mac. "You handed me a cup with a splash of cream and two teaspoons of sugar. Just the way I like it, Coach. To this day, I still have no idea how you knew."

Returning his gaze to the Northfield Nation family, Abernathy's voice slowed as if he were ushering the room into a spirit of reverence. "Coach Mac's first words to me were, 'I am so thankful you are here.' Coach then said, 'Our school and our community are in desperate need of your vision. Let me know if there is anything I can do to support you and our Theatre Arts Department.'"

Lowering his head, as if he were looking toward an invisible tele-prompter to find his next sentence, Abernathy continued. "Honestly, folks . . . and I am not proud to admit this, but I was thinking to myself, 'What's his angle? Is he just trying to set me up?' But later that first semester, just moments before the first ever Northfield musical production, I looked from behind the curtain to see—to my absolute amazement—" Abernathy lingered on the last word as if he had been teleported back into the very moment of his memory.

"Sitting there, front and center," his voiced cracked rather sharply, prompting the young teacher to inhale sharply. Regaining self-control, Abernathy pointed to the middle of the room for emphasis, "Front and center . . . the entire Northfield basketball program was sitting front and center, all of them: players, managers, coaches, statisticians, and videog-raphers. All were gathered in support of Northfield's first-ever musical drama. It will probably be no surprise to you—given the emotion you see right now from, of course, the drama teacher—anyway, seeing the Northfield basketball team there, all in support of my cast and crew, well, it moved me to tears—lots of them, in fact." Abernathy paused, lost in the memory, smiling to himself more than to the crowd.

"That's the first of my stories that center around Coach Mac's powerful influence on my life. But it certainly is not the last. Six months later, my father died suddenly of a brain aneurysm." Abernathy hesitated just long enough to breathe then exhale a breath strong enough to settle his rising emotions. "And, of course, Coach Mac and Ms. Gracie were the first people to arrive at my home. They brought Annie and me a wonderful home-cooked meal, and oh my! As you know, Ms. Gracie can cook!" Sporadic then universal applause temporarily interrupted Abernathy. Among the Northfield Nation family, Gracie's pies were nearly as legendary as the great Coach himself.

"More importantly," and with this phrase Abernathy returned his voice to a quiet reverence, "Coach Mac and Ms. Gracie brought to us their huge hearts of compassion and love. Many of you know exactly what I'm talking about. After giving me a huge bear hug—and given what you just witnessed you can see I speak the truth about the huge bear hug—Coach Mac just sat down with us. Then, after what must have been a very long period of silence . . ." Abernathy turned toward Coach Mac. "Do you remember that conversation, Coach?"

Coach Mac nodded graciously, speaking a quiet, "Yes," that only Abernathy could hear.

"Coach, you said, 'David, could you please tell me a story about your father? I wish I had gotten to know him. He sure raised one heck of a fine son.'"

Abernathy stared once again into the floor, tossed about internally by swirling waves of emotion. Drawing upon all of his poise and skill as an experienced communicator, Abernathy willed his voice to connect personally with the crowd, which sat in rapt silence.

"Here's the crazy thing," he spoke intimately, "Coach Mac genuinely wanted to know about my father. And, after not one story, but at least ten stories . . ."

Abernathy directed his eyes toward the faces seated immediately in front of him, "Folks, I want you to know . . ." Looking up, he repeated, to the entire room, "I want all of you to know. While I was still filled with intense grief, I was also experiencing a fierce love. And I was finding hope. I had lost my father. His place in my in my life was, and still is, irreplaceable. But, somehow, and I can't explain it, the pain was easier to bear just because Coach John McKissack was with me."

The applause echoed through the house as loudly as before, but the clapping was less raucous, more gracious and soul-filled. "I have never been a religious man, well, up until that point at least . . . but on that night, Coach Mac felt like my priest or pastor, and, more importantly, my friend. And I absolutely know, that in some version, that's your Coach Mac story, too . . ." Abernathy's voiced trailed off as he scanned the room, pausing repeatedly to make eye contact with individuals along the way.

"So, if nothing else, we share together, as the Northfield Nation, in this reality: Each of us has a personal story of how Coach John McKissack's fatherly presence has made our lives better. And we all—including your non-athletic, nerdy-looking, drama king of a theatre arts teacher— have, in Coach Mac's words, 'been given the grace' to join together as the Warrior family. So, on our annual Northfield Night, we begin a season when our Coach will, with just 17 more wins, have won more games than any head coach, in any sport, in our state's history. On such a night as this, it is my undeserved privilege to introduce the man who is not a myth but is certainly a legend—and, most importantly . . ." Abernathy again paused to capture the power of the moment. "And, most importantly," he repeated, lengthening each word with dramatic flair, "my friend, Coach John McKissack."

Hands clapped. Bodies stood. Hearts were raised. Tears flowed. In fact, months later many would swear they observed a tear inching its way down the chiseled, well-worn face of the aging architect of the Northfield Way himself.

"Just sweat," Coach Mac would argue in response to any mention of the infamous Northfield Night tear.

If you asked Gracie she would simply note, with a wink and smile, "Well, you'd think that, after all these years, Coach would know his secret is out! We all know how much he 'sweats' over his boys and his community."

As Coach Mac leaned his imposing frame over the outdated microphone and stand, Jimmy wondered what the future would hold, for himself and for everyone else in the room. A pervasive sadness engulfed him
like a dark cloud. For the first time in Jimmy's five years of covering
Northfield basketball, Jimmy wanted to be anywhere but in "the house
that John McKissack built" on Northfield Nation Night.

True to form, Coach Mac's speech would be shorter, by a lot, than
his introducer's. After acknowledging his gratitude to David Abernathy,
to the administration, to the Northfield family, to his young assistant
coach, Derrick "D" Walker, and, of course, to his beloved wife, Gracie,
Coach Mac turned his attention to uniting the Northfield Nation in
vision and mission.

"I know you are proud of our young men. You should be. I know you
are excited about this next season. You should be! So, let's take a moment
and let our young men know how much we are behind them! " A standing ovation erupted, ending only as Coach Mac waved the crowd back
into their seats. He paused, gathering a deep breath for the eruption of
words that had been building in his heart for weeks. With a voice that
signaled, 'Game on,' Coach Mac commenced his paternal call to the
Northfield Way.

"While I deeply appreciate Principal Davis' generous comments, I
also want to challenge each of you to join me in moving past all the
pre-season hype. It is time, family. It is, in fact, past time . . . to put
away all the talk about an historic three-peat. To put to rest all the
chatter about individual and team records. We must discard our aspirations for trophies and personal glory." Coach Mac's words had grown
increasingly emphatic, but it was the next word that bore the heaviest
weight, "Together . . . yes, together we must all ambitiously pursue
the principles of the Northfield Way. And by together, I am not just
speaking about our very talented young players, our incredibly capable
assistant coach, Derrick Walker, or even this ancient relic of a head
coach. I'm speaking of all of us, in this school and in this community,
in our businesses and our houses of worship, in our homes and in our

neighborhoods—we must all pursue The Northfield Way that leads us to our True North!"

As applause thundered across the gym floor, Coach Mac waved feverishly toward the back of the room. Seeing the dramatic motioning of his outstretched arm and hand, the crowd turned their collective attention in the same direction. As they did so, a surge of energy electrified the room and an immediate rush of adrenaline stirred the crowd into another impromptu standing ovation.

Walking together, stride for stride, from the back of the room were Martin Denton, flanked by his son, Chris, and by two police officers in full uniform. One officer, with his shiny, white, bald head and barrel-chested, straight-as-an-arrow posture, was immediately recognizable as Lewis County Sheriff Joshua Cooley. The other officer, a young man of smaller stature but equally fit body, would later be identified as officer Jonathan Owen of the Bedford County Sheriff's Department. Following them were the entire basketball team, holding hands as one long strand of young men with varied skin tones and diverse family backgrounds.

Jimmy, like any good journalist, moved to the front of the standing throng to survey the reactions displayed on the faces of the Nation's members. The tears running down Sheila Jordan's face and those smearing Carla Marie's heavily layered makeup were unsurprising. However, the not so subtle wiping of the eyes by Jimbo Larsen was as unexpected as a warm breeze blowing through Northfield on this frigid November night.

"He's done it again," Jimmy thought with deep satisfaction.

Coach Mac finally settled the crowd down and seated them. He stood surrounded by the four men and the team who had made their way to the front. Drawing in close his beloved Gracie Mac, he motioned for Coach Derrick Walker and Nikki Coles to join them as well.

Coach Mac began again, his voice booming with passion. "We stand here together as a picture of what can be. We stand here as a picture of what will be, if," he paused to let that small two-letter word gain weight in the hearts and minds of his listeners. "If . . . we choose to commit our-selves to join together with a united vision. So, tonight, we are not going to talk about basketball anymore. We are, instead, going to go straight to our annual reading of the Northfield Way Maxims. However, we are going to add a new element to the Northfield Nation Night. Starting tonight and going forward, the Northfield Warrior women's basketball team will be joining the men's team in our Northfield Nation Night. It's way past time that we stop treating our fine women's program with less attention and support than our men's team. Let's welcome Coach Carlene Dale and last year's district championship team, the Northfield Warriors, to join us on the platform."

The applause was respectful, but subdued at first. Then Principal Davis and AD Butler stood. Millie Olsen stood next, her hands clapping furiously. Students, parents, and even the old guard traditionalists soon joined in an appreciative ovation.

"Tonight, Coach Dale, Martin Denton, officers Cooley and Owen, my Gracie, Coach Walker, and Nikki Coles will read the five maxims in unison. I'm going to ask you all to recite them with us. After we read each main word, the men and women Warrior players will read the cor-responding maxim. By doing so they will affirm who they are and who they are choosing to become."

Like a worship service at the local Episcopal church, the people all stood for the sacred Northfield liturgy. Having memorized these lines over the many years of Coach Mac's leadership, however, no one needed a printed handout or words projected onto a screen.

The chorus of adult men and women went first,

Maxim 1 : PURPOSE

"My first commitment will be to a purpose greater than myself."

The young men and women players, who had come early to rehearse as a combined chorus, boldly stated the first maxim in unison. From that point forward, everyone joined on both parts.

Maxim 2 : PASSION
"My first response to pressure will be passion."

Maxim 3 : LOVE
"My first priority will be love."

Maxim 4 : RESPONSIBILITY
"My first responsibility will be to lead myself."

Maxim 5 : HUMILITY
"My first ambition will be to serve with strength, courage, and humility."

As the chorus of maxims and declarations concluded, Coach Mac added the traditional, "Now, let's observe a moment of silence and-or prayer, depending on your personal beliefs and preferences. Let's commit ourselves, and our players, to these principles."

"Amen and thank you all," Coach Mac concluded after a few moments as the crowd whooped and yelled, releasing the energy and tension that had continued to build throughout the program.

Jimmy scribbled a rough draft of his opening line for tomorrow's lead article in the Gazette. "Coach Mac, in his incomparable wisdom and immeasurable strength, has once again redirected this community's vision toward the path of the Northfield Way." He then silently fretted to himself, *What good could come from tearing down a man like that? And tearing apart the Northfield family?* Jimmy's secret knowledge of a dark conspiracy against Coach Mac had already become an oppressive burden. In a room packed with virtually everyone he knew in Lewis County, he suddenly felt very, very alone.

Jimmy pulled out his cell phone as he hastily made his way through the frenzied crowd. He kept his head down, refraining from eye contact with anyone. As he approached the exit door, he texted Tara. *I'm coming home, babe. I need to get out of here. See you soon.*

Jimmy put in his ear buds and, preparing himself for the snowy, sloppy ride home, returned to his "Salt Life" playlist. As he reached the Forerunner, he once again joined his voice to Jimmy Buffet's. "Pour me somethin' tall an' strong, Make it a hurricane before I go insane, It's only half-past twelve but I don't care, It's five o'clock somewhere."

"'Somewhere' sounds like a good place to be right now," Jimmy mumbled as he cranked the Forerunner's reluctant engine and headed into the wintry wasteland of Northfield.

JANUARY

Love creates a way.

Coach John McKissack

CHAPTER 9

et's go, Eagles!" *Clap, clap. Clap, clap, clap.* "Let's go, Eagles!" *Clap, clap. Clap, clap, clap.* With each repetition, the Silver Lake fans grew louder. And bolder. Roving, roaring bands of green and silver clad Silver Lake students roamed up and down the steep steps of the expansive John McKissack Arena. Exaggerated high fives, gregarious hugs, and grunt-filled chest bumps transformed the already rowdy student section into a frenzied mosh pit.

A painted-up senior Eagle with a large belly hanging out of the corners of his green overalls stood in the center of the churning waves of celebration in the visitors' section. In his massive hands he carried an oversized green flag emblazoned with an embossed and attacking silver eagle in its center. Back and forth, the Silver Lake ringleader waved the victory banner.

On the opposite side of the arena, the Warrior faithful sat silent. Navy and gold shakers fell limp, mirroring the slumped posture of their handlers. The student section, known affectionately as the "Bezerkers," stared blankly into the distance. Weakening under the burden of an upset defeat, their heads rested in their hands or on nearby slumped shoulders.

"This is our third loss in a row," Jimbo Larsen despaired, speaking over his left shoulder to Sheila Jordan.

"And by far the worst," she responded. Dropping her face into both cupped hands, Sheila then mumbled a pleading prayer, "Help 'em, Lord Jesus, help 'em."

Jimbo shrugged his large shoulders, sighing with disgust, "Maybe our worst ever. What's gotten into these boys?"

On the Northfield baseline, Jimmy Thompson crouched low. He had positioned himself just in front of the dejected Warrior cheerleaders. With pom poms resting on the floor, the whole squad stood motionless, arms folded tightly. Jimmy was still moving, though his motion was barely perceptible. Like a bow hunter seeking the perfect shot, Jimmy maneuvered his body and his Nikon camera with patient precision.

Through the camera's viewfinder, Jimmy observed Coach Mac kneeling in front of the Northfield bench. The Warrior players, clad neatly in their white home uniforms, sat slightly behind their coach, and to his left, in various postures of defeat and despair.

The forefinger on Jimmy's right hand applied subtle pressure to the Nikon's shutter button. He held the button down for several seconds as the shutter responded faithfully. Opening and closing in rapid-fire succession, the lens memorialized dozens of poignant shots of the closing seconds of the ill-fated game. Jimmy hoped he had captured a rare, but enduring image of what was sure to become an infamous piece of Northfield basketball history.

Jimmy pulled his head back. He pressed the camera forward, almost at arm's length, studying each successive digitally recorded image, hoping to find his trophy shot. But before he could finish scrolling, a blaring buzzer signaled the merciful end of the game. Led by the large, overall-clad flag bearer, the Silver Lake student section spilled onto the court in a turbulent crash of adolescent hysteria, like a flash flood of green and silver flowing onto the court in relentless waves.

Jimmy scurried frantically toward the Northfield stands, shielding himself from the surging mob of Silver Lake players, cheerleaders, and students. Finding a secure spot near the home team's bench, Jimmy furiously typed with his thumbs, entering a few bullet points into the notes on his phone. *Warriors fall hard. Record falls harder. Northfield, previously number one in state, now number two in district. Coach Mac's record-setting 679th win delayed—again! From disappointment to despair, Warriors go ice cold in January.*

Jimmy admired his work. Catching himself up short, he quickly forced his face to a more appropriate joyless, stoic expression. In a small town dominated by the Northfield Nation, the local sports reporter could not afford to be seen smiling at a time like this. The buzz of an incoming text interrupted his efforts.

It's beginning.'

Jimmy texted back rapidly.

What's beginning?

The end, the text read cryptically.

Jimmy replied hastily, *Please explain.* His heart raced. Even though it had been two months since the Northfield Nation Night, his gut told him instantly that this was the same anonymous texter. The gloom of that brief text exchange in November had haunted him almost daily since. Receiving no response, Jimmy texted again. *The end of what?*

Thirty seconds passed. Then, a minute more. Still, no response. Angrily, Jimmy shoved the phone into his jacket pocket, then jerked it back out again. Disgusted with whoever was toying with him, he began typing again. *Listen, you idiot. Don't*—An incoming text abruptly cut him off.

Coach Mac's time, the message read. Then another text message, *It's over.*

Jimmy's patience had been strained like a rubber band stretched to its thinnest point. He resumed typing his unfinished text. Furiously, his thumbs roared back, *If you think you can just screw around with . . .* Fortunately, Jimmy's deeper journalistic senses sidestepped his anger. He willed the more rational processes of his mind to cut to the front of the line. Frantically, erasing his caustic rebuke, Jimmy rewrote the text with a calm, professional manner. *Please, tell me more.*

The response was curt. *That's all. For now.*

Jimmy thought caustically, *Journalistic professionalism be damned,* and shoved his rational self aside. He typed, *Look, stop playing games and get to the point. Either give me some info I can run with or shut the . . .* Jimmy paused. His professional conscience protested loudly. Weighing his options, he chose a compromise. His final text read, *Look, at some point I'm going to need more. This is not a game—so I'm not going to keep playing along. I can promise you confidentiality, BUT you have to give me more than vague warnings.*

For ten weeks, Jimmy had hoped daily for a follow-up text from the mysterious informant. As recently as yesterday, Jimmy had almost convinced himself that it was all a hoax. Try as he might, however, Jimmy could never shake a nagging, queasy feeling in the pit of his stomach.

"Trust your gut, Jimmy. God gave you a good one—don't talk your mind out of what your heart knows," Dr. Karen McCombs, his journalism adviser at Clemson, had coached Jimmy repeatedly.

As Jimmy waited for the anonymous texter to respond, he took a screen shot of tonight's thread. "I'm done," he said aloud quietly to himself. "I'm not even going to respond to the next time they text me." But he knew that wasn't true.

Jimmy slowly approached the small, somber gathering near the Northfield locker room. A handful of family members, faculty and administration, cheerleaders, and girlfriends assembled in small, silent clusters. No one made eye contact with Jimmy. Even AD Butler quickly averted his eyes, immersing himself in a low-volume conversation with a player's dad.

Occupational hazard, Jimmy chuckled to himself. After such a devastating loss, no one wanted to risk offering an unintentionally quotable line to be published in tomorrow's Gazette.

The Northfield players began filing out, exiting the locker room with all the enthusiasm of prisoners of war being transferred to a new prison. Most walked with their chins touching their chests, towels covering their faces, hiding red, swollen eyes.

Warm embraces awaited the team, though very little affection was offered in return. "I just want to go home," was the most repeated refrain from the vanquished Warriors. Trailing the rest of the team by at least thirty seconds, Jamarcus Denton lumbered in slow, heavy strides toward his mother, father, and brother, Chris. The family closed ranks, speaking intimately in hushed tones. Since Jamarcus had emerged on the national scene in December as an ESPN 100 prospect, much of their lives had been on public display. For the Dentons, however, some moments still remained sacred.

Jimmy respectfully waited for the Denton family huddle to open. "Jamarcus, can you give me just a couple of minutes before you leave with your family?" Jimmy asked cordially, reminding himself that this massive man was still only seventeen.

"Yes, sir," Jamarcus responded respectfully.

"Jamarcus," Jimmy spoke in a slow, low voice, "I know it was a tough night. Can you tell me what happened out there?"

"What can I say? We just didn't come to play. We're so inconsistent in our effort right now. And, that's on me. I have to set the tone. Tonight, I didn't get it done . . . you know, I let everyone down." Jamarcus took another look at the scoreboard, a look of disgust on his face. Wiping eyes still pooling with sweat and tears, Jamarcus spoke more to himself than to Jimmy, "Man, this hurts."

"Jamarcus, you've been struggling with injuries most of the season. I know your left ankle has been weak since before Christmas. Do you think that's affecting your game more than people know?"

"No, sir." Jamarcus straightened his posture and looked directly at Jimmy for the first time in their conversation. "There are no excuses to be made. I failed to lead. It's that simple."

"Jamarcus, one more question and I'll let you go. This was such an important night. A win would have made Coach Mac the winningest coach in state history and would have kept you well ahead of Colliersville in the district and tied in the region with the state's fourth ranked team, the West Chamberlain Bulldogs. Can you tell me the mood of the team after such a heart-breaking overtime loss?"

Jamarcus shook his head, then lowered it to his chest. "What can I say? We let Coach down. We let our families and fans down. We let each other down." Raising his eyes to renew eye contact, Jamarcus spoke directly into Jimmy's tiny digital voice recorder, "But I promise you, we'll learn from it. We will get better—I will get better. That's just the way it's gonna be. That's the Northfield Way."

"Thanks, Jamarcus. I appreciate the time," Jimmy concluded, turning off his recorder.

"Yes, sir. You have a good weekend, Mr. Thompson," Jamarcus spoke politely, reaching out his large right hand for a handshake.

"You, too." Jimmy hurriedly moved away from Jamarcus and toward Coach Mac who was surrounded by Coach Walker, a few parents, AD Butler, and Principal Davis. Jimmy moved toward Coach Mac as soon as the coach acknowledged his presence.

"I'll take a few questions, JT. Just a few. I think you understand. It's been a long night." Drenched in sweat, his shoulders drooped and his eyes puffy, Coach Mac's appearance offered a convincing argument for keeping the interview short.

"Yes, Coach. I understand." Jimmy hurriedly moved his recorder into position. "Coach, what did you tell the players in the locker room?"

"I told them the truth," Coach Mac spoke adamantly. "We got out-played and outcoached tonight. The loss was inexcusable. Their effort was inexcusable—but the blame starts with me."

"Coach, it seems like you've been struggling for a while to find an offensive rhythm. And you've given up a lot of points defensively, too. Can you point to one thing you can do to solve these problems?"

"Yes . . . and no," Coach Mac said with a deep sigh. "Yes, the problem is focus. No question in my mind. From coaches to starters to players on the bench, we lack focus. As a result, we are inconsistent in our attention and effort—on both ends of the court."

"And, the 'no' part of your answer?" Jimmy inquired cautiously.

"We have seventeen total coaches and players on this team—and therefore we have eighteen different issues to address." Coach Mac swept his left hand back toward the locker room, his extended forefinger waving up and down. "And everybody on this team has to take personal responsibility for regaining focus." Coach Mac's intensity was rising with every word, his facial expression growing more severe. "Everybody in that locker room is responsible. But, Jimmy, as I said earlier, it starts with me."

"Coach, I know this is may be too personal . . . but what do you think is . . . well, you know, personally distracting you?" Jimmy's voice pitched higher, his words stumbling across a line he felt uncertain to cross.

"Yes." Coach Mac responded with his lips and jaws barely moving.

"Yes?" Jimmy questioned.

"Yes," Coach Mac's narrowed eyes and tense jawline spoke louder than the words that followed, "that's too personal, Jimmy." The interview was over.

"Yes, sir. I respect that," Jimmy offered apologetically.

"Look, JT." Coach Mac's face softened as his massive left hand engulfed Jimmy's slender shoulder. "It's been a long night. Come back after practice on Monday and I will try to give you more to work with. But," Coach Mac spoke firmly, his hand patting Jimmy slowly on the shoulder as he spoke, "I'm going to have to ask you to respect me and our team. Some of this has to be worked out privately. Understood?"

"Yes, sir. I understand. And I'll take you up on that offer on Monday."

Jimmy packed up his equipment with a chorus of gym doors repeatedly opening and closing behind him. He paused to review his conversation with Coach Mac. His mind rapidly composed a list of questions he wished he had asked: *How does this affect your progress toward a state championship? Have you ever had a team underperform at this level before? Has the pressure of setting the state record for coaching wins and being the first team in state to three-peat negatively affected this season?*

Why didn't I ask those questions? Filled with self-recrimination, Jimmy rubbed his eyes, pinched the bridge of his nose, then stroked his scruffy brown beard thoughtfully. "I'll never get out of this wasteland if I don't get my crap together," he muttered aloud.

He zipped up his camera bag with an exaggerated jerking and considered the evening's maddening series of events. Wearily, he lifted the bag to his shoulders, only to be frozen by the recollection of an unfinished task. Moving swiftly, Jimmy lowered the bag and unzipped it as he had closed it seconds ago. Jimmy excitedly pushed the "on" button of the camera. He scrolled rapidly through the full series of images captured just before the final buzzer. About a dozen images into the scroll, Jimmy landed on what he would later refer to as "my trophy shot."

With the despairing bench just behind him, Coach Mac knelt slightly inside the boundaries of the court. His right knee on the ground, his

bony left knee was bent at more than a ninety-degree angle, thus pointing its substantial length toward the ceiling. On that knee, Coach Mac
rested his left elbow. In his left hand, he rested his head. In the photo, his
head appeared to be pressing downward into his palm. Coach Mac had
wrapped the long, bony fingers of his left hand tightly around his forehead as if to manage the tilt of his head under the weight of the moment.
His tightly squinted eyes could barely be seen. A clipboard dangled
loosely from his right hand, scraping the edge of the court below. At the
angle the photo was taken, the scoreboard appeared just above his head
and slightly to the left. It read, "NORTHFIELD 71, SILVER LAKE
75." The red lights shining out 00:04 on the digital clock remained per-
manently frozen in time.

Jimmy's smiled returned. His satisfaction growing by the second,
Jimmy studied it even closer. To Coach Mac's right, with his back turned,
stood number 22, Jamarcus Denton. Looking down toward his wearied
coach, Jamarcus had his left hand resting on Coach Mac's left shoulder.
Jimmy noted that, while Jamarcus had his back turned, he was looking
back toward Coach Mac, his face unexpectedly soft in its features. The
look on the young player's expression clearly offered compassion and concern to his beleaguered coach.

Jimmy had hoped to capture a valuable piece of Warrior lore for his
portfolio, and this was surely it. Jimmy studied the masterpiece in more
detail, and suddenly realized that he had immortalized much more than
previously imagined. While remaining on the court, Jamarcus had bent
his body awkwardly in Coach Mac's direction, his hand reaching toward
Coach Mac's shoulder. Jimmy's eyes strained to focus on the image's
finer details. He noticed that Jamarcus had spoken to Coach Mac at the
precise moment the camera's shutter was rapidly opening and closing.
Jimmy scrolled backwards to the first of the photos in the series, then
scrolled speedily forward. He repeated the process, scrolling backward
then forward.

Certain that the photo was taken at an angle where Jimmy could read Jamarcus' lips, he scrolled backward again. Then he zoomed in closer on Jamarcus' face. He scrolled forward, slowly, following the movement of Jamarcus' lips. He repeated the process much more rapidly.

Jamarcus' words were unmistakable. In the heat of the battle, in the ruins of defeat, Jamarcus had only one thing to say to the vanquished leader of the Northfield Nation, "I love you, Coach."

CHAPTER 10

At the far western edge of the Northfield campus, Coach Mac's forest green Accord exited the parking lot and sputtered its way onto County Road 69. Worn down by its nineteen Northfield winters and worn out by its 260,000 miles, the car offered little comfort to its stricken passengers, and even less warmth.

Derrick sat rigidly in the passenger seat, stiffened by a perfect storm of stress. The Warriors' embarrassing loss to the undermanned Silver Lake Eagles left them with an 18-3 record, no longer in first place in the district. As if to punctuate the futility of the night, Derrick's truck had failed to start. He had been left with no alternative but to ask Coach Mac for a lift home. Coach Mac's less than enthusiastic "Sure, let's get going," only added to Derrick's disappointing evening. Worst of all, Coach Mac had retreated into an absolute silence.

Derrick stared vacantly out the frosted passenger door window. *We shouldn't be in this mess*, he reasoned angrily to himself. *We should've just won the stupid game. What a ridiculous loss—to Silver Lake. The whole thing is such a stupid mess!* He angrily smacked his right fist against the car door. Glancing to his right, Coach Mac addressed the young coach's dejection. "You look like somebody just ran over your dog, Coach Walker." Coach Mac spoke in monotone, his eyes redirected toward the road. Hearing no response, Coach Mac turned toward Derrick, asking in a more serious tone, "You okay, D?"

Derrick turned toward Coach Mac and quipped, "I was just about to ask you the same thing. Honestly, Coach, you look more like someone just ran over your dog, then backed up to do it again."

Coach Mac offered no response. Then he smiled, followed by a shallow chuckle. "Yeah, somebody ran over it twice. Buried it. Dug it up and ran over it again."

"Sheesh! Silver Lake?" Derrick unleashed his frustration. "It's one thing to lose three games, in a row! Good grief, that's bad enough. But to lose to that bunch . . . at home . . . and, of all nights, on the night you should have set the state record! We're terrible right now, Coach. We suck—bad."

"That's an interesting analysis, Coach Walker."

Derrick rolled his head backward, looking up at the wrinkled, half-loosened fabric on the ancient Accord's interior roof. "I know, I know. That's not helpful . . ." Derrick ground his back teeth. "But it is true," Derrick argued, returning to his agitated tone, "we're horrible right now, Coach. Those players—they've got to understand. They can't just piss around in the regular season, then hope to make a run toward a three-peat. Crap, at this rate, we might not even make it out of the district!" Derrick's body shuddered at the thought.

"And if we don't?" Coach Mac pressed.

"If we don't? You mean, if we don't make it out of the district? Are you kidding me? Are you freakin' kidding me?" Derrick's attempts to restrain his emotions began to unravel like the hapless Warrior defense against Silver Lake earlier that evening. "With this kind of talent? It would be a total failure—no one would ever forgive this team for pissing away an opportunity like this." Derrick paused, then continued somberly, "The town would never forgive. And . . . and they would never forget." The words seemed suspended in mid-air, frozen in the frosty interior of the Accord. They hung there long enough for Derrick to begin to recognize how personal they were to him. "They'd always remember them as a team that had everything and accomplished nothing. . . just a bunch of losers, that's how this team would be remembered." Derrick slowly returned his gaze to the hazy, frosted passenger door window. With the thumb and forefinger of his left hand, he rubbed his eyes hard as if trying to erase a dreadful image. "The curse of D Walker, round two," Derrick muttered as he faced a terrifying vision of the ghost of Northfield's future.

"Who's to blame for this loss, D?" Coach Mac inquired.

Derrick, guarding against the brash impulsivity of his earlier comments, took a moment to think. As he did, Coach Mac slowly made the right hand turn onto Jefferson Avenue. The turn led them off of the rural darkened CR 69 and onto a road lined with modest houses and condos. Nothing but stillness surrounded them on the quiet street. Derrick stared straight ahead at the blank, black canvas of the night, projecting his thoughts against its surface.

"Who's to blame, Coach? Who's not to blame?" Derrick retorted. "Jamarcus and Zeke are inconsistent in their focus and effort. They've got their heads up their butts for some reason. Our offense is about as smooth as this car we are riding in—no offense. . . but you know what I mean. We hardly ever communicate on defense. And our bench, they're not even contributing. They're all to blame, all fifteen of them, as far as I'm concerned."

"Anybody else?"

Derrick swallowed hard as he leaned back in his seat. His rear end slid forward in the tattered, stained beige fabric of the passenger seat. His shoulders lowered and his head tilted forward. Once he reached the full measure of a slumped body and a bowed head, he added reluctantly, "I'm sure that I'm to blame, too, Coach. I'm not exactly a shining role model of how to live up to your talent and potential." He tried to coach himself internally with his regular mantra, *Stay in the present,* but it was too late. Haunted by the taunting ghosts of his Northfield past, the present lay before him shrouded in lingering, debilitating past shame.

Coach Mac made a deliberately slow left turn onto Meadowlark Avenue, and with an immediate right turn, he eased the Accord into the driveway of Derrick and Nikki's condo. He left the clanking engine running, irrationally hoping it would generate some form of warmth. Extending his right hand to Derrick's left shoulder, Coach Mac spoke firmly. "At some point, you've got to let go of this burden, D. You've got a thousand-pound weight of shame on your shoulders. It's slowing you down. Even worse, it's dragging you down." Coach Mac retrieved his hand and redirected the conversation. "We need to talk about this in depth—at another time and," Coach Mac chuckled, "in a much warmer place. For now let's stay on point in the present."

"I'm listening," Derrick replied, welcoming the shift.

Coach Mac leaned back, studying his young apprentice. He shot straight to the point. "The players are all definitely to blame. I don't disagree with you at all. And, you do have work to do as a coach and a leader. That's why I brought you onto my staff, to grow you up, as a man and a coach. And I don't regret it for one second."

Derrick didn't believe Coach Mac's words. At least, not entirely. Even so, he drank them in like a warm cup of hot chocolate.

"But the real blame, the true source of the problem, should be obvious to you."

Derrick felt himself flinch.

"The person most to blame is me. I did a horrible job coaching tonight—and not just tonight. I've been lacking in my leadership since the first of the year." Coach Mac leaned in toward Derrick, his brown steely eyes honing in with a laser focus. "I'm not getting the best effort out of these players. And that's my fault. The blame starts with me."

Derrick ran his hands over his legs, hoping to revive his thighs from the numbness creeping up his body. He pushed his thoughts awkwardly through his lips. "It's not your fault. You can't take the blame for this, Coach. It's not fair. You can't."

"Hey, it's late. We're both tired and we're going to get hypothermia sitting in this deep freeze of a car." Coach Mac leaned back, then turned his whole body back toward Derrick. "D, it's time I let you in on something. I should have done this weeks ago. It won't excuse my poor coaching, but it will hopefully help explain it. I need you to keep this information confidential. I'll tell the team soon, but for now, this is just between us."

Derrick froze, not moving a muscle. Derrick received Coach Mac's words as a signal of great danger, like a warning shot across the bow. Time and thought stood still. Derrick anxiously asked the one question that had haunted him since the day he accepted the job six months ago. "Coach, you're not going to . . ." Derrick could not say the word.

"Retire? Quit?" Coach Mac seemed stunned. "No, no way. Do I look like I'm old enough to retire?" Coach Mac smiled broadly.

Derrick shook his head side to side, sighing with intense relief. "You had me scared, Coach."

Coach Mac cut to the chase. "Gracie's cancer has returned. She has a fighting chance, but it's serious." Coach Mac turned away. His eyes slipped into an unfocused gaze. "After almost ten years of remission, it's back." Coach Mac pressed in deeper, tightly grasping the steering wheel with his left hand and bracing against the middle console with his right. "And I am . . . I am afraid, D. It's hard for me to admit, but tonight I am fighting against fear in a way unlike anything I can remember. I fear she does not have the energy or strength left to fight again. . . And I'm afraid . . . the doctors give her a decent chance of surviving but . . ." With the back of his jacket, he wiped moisture from his eyes. He leaned his head back, sniffling as he took in a deep, long breath.

Derrick's gaze fell and he brought his hands to his head in shock, rubbing his temples. Letting his breath out slowly, he replied in a low tone, "I don't know what to say. This can't be happening."

"Well, it is." Coach Mac shifted his body deliberately, returning to his normally strong, straight posture. "And I have to find a way to love Gracie well and, at the same time, I have to find a way to lead this team well. If I'm brutally honest—and in the times like this we have to be brutally honest with ourselves and others—I've allowed my personal fears to drain me and distract me."

Derrick stared blankly at Coach Mac. His mind was now as numb as his toes. All he could manage was a repetitious, helpless, "I'm so sorry, Coach. I'm just so sorry."

"I appreciate your concern. I really do. But I want you to know," Coach Mac placed a reassuring hand on Derrick's shoulder and leaned in close, "Gracie and I will make it through this. She's the strongest woman, with the strongest faith, I have ever known. And, our WHY is big enough for the battle ahead."

Pleading internally for inspiration for some way to help, Derrick responded, "Is there anything I can do, Coach? Anything at all?"

"You can pray. That's where I'm starting. And you can help me get these Warriors back on track. Starting tomorrow at practice, we are going to push the 'reset' button this season—and I do mean push!" Coach Mac nodded his head, raising his eyebrows and his voice.

"I'm not too sure how to help with the first part. The whole prayer thing is still . . . I don't know. . . But I'll try to pray for you," Then Derrick added with boldness, "On the second part, though, I'm in. Whatever it takes!"

Silence followed as both men retreated into moments of personal reflection. After a couple of minutes, Derrick turned toward Coach Mac. He opened his mouth to speak. No words came out. Turning back to stare at the front windshield, Derrick searched for words to match his thoughts.

"Coach, to be, as you say, brutally honest," Derrick reached up to pinch the bridge of his nose with his left hand. His thumb and finger slid upward, rubbing against his eyes. He turned once again to face Coach Mac. After swallowing hard, he said, "Coach, I really don't want to be the Northfield's biggest screw up twice. You know what I mean?"

"I know. I get it," Coach Mac responded as he reached to squeeze Derrick's left forearm. "There's a way out of that, D." Coach Mac said as he glanced toward Derrick. Making brief eye contact, he added, "And I'm going to walk it with you."

"The Northfield Way, right?" Derrick asked.

"Yep. The Northfield Way—grace under pressure. We've got to get that thousand-pound weight off your shoulders. So, you pray for me and Gracie, and I'll keep praying for you.

"That'll be a full-time job, Coach," Derrick said.

"I'm up for it. Are you?" Coach Mac challenged.

"I hope so." Derrick responded as he stared once again out the front windshield.

"I believe in you, D. But you have to believe, too. And not just in yourself. You can't manufacture grace for yourself. It's got to come from a bigger source than you. So," Coach Mac guarded his tone against lecturing while also speaking the sincerity of his convictions in genuine love. "It's important," he continued, "regardless of where you are on your faith journey, that you learn to pray. A man who cannot pray is a man left alone in the deepest parts of his heart. I don't want you to be left alone, D."

Derrick sniffed back the moisture dripping into his nose. He acknowledged Coach Mac's words with a rapid nodding of his head.

"No one who lives alone lives well. That's our first real battle in life, isn't it? To not be alone?"

"I guess, Coach. I mean, sure. It's been a long night. I think I need some sleep." Derrick stammered, feeling the need to end the conversation as quickly as possible. It was getting uncomfortable. He began to pull at the door handle, but his first two tries were unsuccessful.

"That's a hard lock to open. Let me see if I can help." Reaching across Derrick, Coach Mac maneuvered it open. "Give Nikki a hug for Gracie and me," Coach Mac added just before Derrick exited.

Briefly pulling the door back just short of closing again, Derrick replied, "I will, if she's home, that is. I never really know whether she'll be at home, on the road for work, or out with 'the girls,' " Derrick used the universal motion for air quotes as he spoke the words, "the girls." Then he hurriedly opened the door again, adding, "Look, Coach, this night has been hard enough already. I don't want to drag you into the dumpster fire of my relationship with Nikki."

"Are things worse, D?" Coach Mac asked with concern.

"Yeah." Derrick said as he lifted his right foot onto the snowy driveway. Leaning his head back into the car as he held the door open, Derrick said, "Going into the holidays we were good. At least I thought we were. But, man, ever since we got back to Northfield, it's been . . ." Derrick shook his head with a sad disbelief. "Good night, Coach. Thanks for the ride and for telling me about Mrs. Gracie. Please tell her that I'm . . . that I'll be thinking of her. I'll see you in the morning." Derrick was anxious to leave the cold and the conversation with haste.

"You bet," Coach Mac replied. "We've got plenty of work ahead. At least we will do it together, D." Leaning over to look Derrick directly in the eye, he added, "I wouldn't want either of us to be alone in this, you know."

"Yeah, I know." Derrick closed the door, giving it a final push at the end to insure the lock held. He stood for a moment, staring as Coach

Mac shifted into reverse. He shot a hearty wave in Coach Mac's direction and approached the garage door key pad. As he punched the code into the pad, Derrick looked back over his left shoulder. The Accord's left red taillight, the only one still working, faded into the darkness.

Derrick shuffled into the garage. As the door closed noisily behind him, he opened the service door into the kitchen. The condo was at least sixty degrees warmer than the wind chill outdoors. Still he felt a chill from beneath his skin. Entering his empty home felt like transitioning from one moment of significant loss to another.

Sadly, he could think of nowhere to go to warm up from this kind of cold.

CHAPTER 11

For precisely 154 days, Derrick Walker had walked into the Northfield campus hallways as a faculty member and assistant basketball coach. Day 155, the day after the home debacle against Silver Lake, would be his least favorite day—by far.

Derrick led his first two classes in reviews for upcoming tests, painstakingly presenting his well-prepared material to students much less enthusiastic about the subject matter than he was—most of whom sat slouched in their desks with their butts low in the seats. Their eyes closed and their minds drifted. A few sneakily checked Instagram as they feigned interest. A smaller group engaged in not so subtle flirting. Derrick imagined his students hearing his voice in the same way as the teacher's voice in Charlie Brown television specials: "Blah, blah, blah."

During his free period, Derrick facilitated a parent-teacher conference with Richard McIntosh's parents. The conversation began with an angry declaration by Richard's father, Big Rich, a predictable opening statement that went, "Let's get something straight, right off the bat, Mr. Walker. Richard has never had these kinds of problems before." From that point, things got progressively worse. Assistant Principal Clarke attended the meeting under the pretense of supporting Derrick but his body language indicated otherwise. For the first fifteen minutes of the conversation, Mr. Clarke "represented the administration" by sitting in silence. Staring straight ahead, he tucked his beefy hands firmly in the armpits of his faded, wide-lapel blue pinstripe suit coat.

Ultimately, and in Derrick's assessment, reluctantly, Mr. Clarke offered a half-hearted defense of the young teacher. "Mr. and Mrs.

McIntosh," the assistant principal droned mechanically, "it's Mr. Walker's right to hold the line on his grading requirements. My job is to back him up, whether I agree with him or not."

Derrick left the meeting fuming. "Just one word of encouragement—couldn't he give me just one single, freakin' word—" he muttered aloud as he stomped down the hallway. He stormed past the dark wooden door with "Mr. Andrew Clarke, Assistant Principal" etched in gold letters on the glass window and recalled being repeatedly kicked out of Clarke's class when he was in high school. In Mr. Clarke's words, he was "disruptive and disrespectful." Derrick still remembered Mr. Clarke's mantra, "You will reap what you sow, Mr. Walker."

"Evidently," Derrick thought angrily, "when you're Derrick Walker, you get to reap and reap and reap!"

The half day already felt like a half month when the lunch bell sounded. Derrick's lunch consisted of brownish school cafeteria "meat," waxy green beans, and a white, glue-like substance masquerading as mashed potatoes. The "fake food," as the students affectionately called cafeteria lunches, contributed generously to his already agitated stomach. It did not help that the gastro-intestinal weapon of mass destruction began to have its full effect just as he entered the hardest part of his day.

In only his second year as a teacher and his first year as a full-time faculty member, Derrick felt unprepared and unqualified to teach Honors U.S. History. For sure, there were some days when he was "feeling it," like a three-point shooter on a ridiculous hot streak. On those days, he reminded himself, "I was made for this." Those days were scarce, though, scarce as any textbooks the students considered relevant and engaging. On most days, Derrick felt more like a guy who, with no time left on the clock, missed both free throws to seal his team's defeat.

Added to the pressure, and irony, of teaching an honors class in the high school where he failed to graduate, was the presence of Alli Davis. Derrick found Principal Davis' only daughter entirely likeable. Everyone did. Why wouldn't they? Everything about Alli was entirely likeable. Unfortunately, for both of them, Alli was unmotivated by schoolwork.

From an objective point of view, Alli's academic disinterest made sense. She was an extrovert, a flirt, and a slam dunk for Homecoming Queen next fall. From Alli's perspective, academics had nothing of value to add to her already full life. In fact, the only person who ever wanted her to take an honors class was her "Daddy." Derrick monitored her grades daily, hoping she would maintain at least a C. He wanted Alli to make Daddy happy for her sake, not his.

Mercifully, at 3:15, Derrick began his daily five-minute pilgrimage toward John McKissack Arena. There he would trade his "Mr. Derrick Walker" identity for his more natural role as "Coach D Walker." First as a student and a player, now as a coach, Derrick had walked this path no less than a thousand times. He could, he supposed, have made the whole trip blindfolded without a misstep. Taking the first left after the choir room, he headed down the expansive navy blue curved hallway leading to the arena. On most days, Derrick approached this welcomed sanctuary to escape from the stress of his real world. Today was not one of those days.

A litany of thoughts fired rapidly in Derrick's head. "What would Coach Mac say? How would he respond after the loss? How would Mrs. Gracie's sickness affect his leadership today?"

After a loss, Coach Mac was even more relentless than usual in practice. He demanded from his team the excellence they had failed to produce the night before. However, after last night's conversation with Coach Mac, Derrick had no idea what to expect. Seeing Coach Mac visibly shaken was new territory for Derrick.

As Derrick approached the gray metal entry door to the gym, a familiar symphony greeted him. Basketballs pounded the floor, swished through nets, and clanked off rims. Gym shoes rhythmically squeaked on the recently waxed wood floor. Unlike every other practice Derrick could remember, however, no one spoke a word.

Coach Mac's shrill whistle interrupted the cacophony of basketball sounds. Pointing toward the door from which the players had just exited in their practice jerseys and shorts, Coach Mac's voice boomed, "We'll meet in the team room before we start practice."

The players compliantly obeyed their coach's unexpected directive. The team room was normally their haven. In this space they had bonded over game film, told exaggerated legends of their latest adolescent male adventures, bounced to the highly amplified bass beats of hip-hop music, and practiced the fine art of horseplay. The room had never been used for a pre-practice meeting.

On the way into the locker room, Derrick heard the quiet, deep voice of Thor whisper to Zeke, "Whatever's about to happen, gonna be ugly."

"Have a seat—each one of you—in front of your own locker," Coach Mac directed with a firm voice. Senior captains Jamarcus and Zeke were the first to comply.

"First, before I begin, you should know that there will be a chance for each of you to speak. Second, this practice will likely be the hardest seventy-five minutes of your lives, PERIOD." Coach Mac spoke slowly, emphasizing each word with deliberate force. Raising both arms, Coach Mac continued like a prophet naming the sins of the people. "Your lack of focus and team unity last night goes against everything we stand for. All that we've worked for was undermined by your lack of commitment to play the Northfield Way. I will not tolerate it—and neither should you. Do you understand, men?"

"Yes sir," the team mumbled unenthusiastically.

"I have two things I want to say to you about last night's game. But I must begin by speaking to you on a very personal level." The players leaned in as one. Quick, bewildered glances bounced from face to face as if a pinball had been released into the room.

"Men, I speak often about us being a family. Our heart commitment to love each other like a family is what makes Northfield basketball so special. And so powerful. Love is what creates our winning tradition." Spurred on by the receptive silence of his audience, Coach Mac paced the room, his hands folded behind his back. "And, men, when we recite the maxims of the Northfield Way—it's not just some gimmick, some routine I use to motivate you."

Coach Mac paused his words and ceased his pacing. Looking intently toward the young men entrusted to his leadership, he spoke in a measured tone. "The Maxims are how we live together as a family. They are how our team, our family, follows the path to our true north." The coach walked so close to his players that they had to lean their heads back to make eye contact. "Men, for the next few minutes, this is a family meeting."

Coach Mac knelt down to meet the eye level of his players. He paused before speaking, and his barrel chest visibly heaved and fell. Then he began, "I am in a very tough personal battle right now." Another deep inhale, another long release. "Once again, my beautiful wife of 41 years, Gracie, is in a battle for her life. That's why she wasn't at the game last night . . ." Coach Mac's voice trailed off. He cleared his throat, repressing a sob forcing its way up his throat.

To a man, the players found the wells of their eyes rapidly filling. Jamarcus and Rico already had long trails of tears flowing down both cheeks. Mrs. Mac was like a mother to the whole team—in fact, Mrs. Mac had been the team mom to 35 previous teams of Northfield players. First Norsemen, and now Warriors. Her smile, her famous "Mrs. Mac's Mac-n-Cheese" dinners, her handwritten birthday cards to "her boys"— every single one, every year, including alumni—her listening ear: all were as much a part of basketball as the navy and vegas gold Viking logo painted at the center court of the John McKissack Arena.

Looking upward, away from his tearful players, Coach Mac fought to compose himself. "She just started chemo again. She was still too weak to make it out to the game. She was planning to come to the post-game celebration, but . . . well, we all know how that went." Coach Mac braced himself against the surge of emotion rising in the room. With an unwavering resolve, he offered himself to his team. His words were unlike anything he had said in thirty-five seasons of coaching. "Men, this is serious. It's life or death stuff. And, to be honest, I'm scared."

Sensing the growing anxiety in the room, Coach Mac added reassuringly, "Now, there's every reason to have hope. We caught this recurrence early. Besides, you know how tough Mrs. Gracie is. You know how much she trusts God with every part of her life. With His help, she beat cancer once. And with His help, she will beat it again. She is the strongest woman I have ever known."

"You got that right!" Zeke blurted out like a deacon in the church choir. Every player chimed in loudly, voicing his affirmation.

Still kneeling, Coach Mac drew even closer to his family of players. "I was wrong for carrying this alone. It's foolish to shut out people who truly care about you. The truth is I have been giving into my fears."

Coach Mac scanned the room, ensuring eye contact with every person semi-circled in front of him. "Men, I am your coach and your leader. But I am also your family and friend. Fear shut me out and shut me down; but through prayer and time spent with my sweet Gracie, love has called me out. And now I'm back!"

The unity compromised during last night's loss now returned with a fury. Northfield's sense of purpose had deepened in an instant. Coach Mac now turned his words to basketball, and to their embarrassing performance the night before.

"Jamarcus and Zeke, lead us in Maxim 4 of the Northfield Way."

"**RESPONSIBILITY.** *My first responsibility will be to lead myself.*" The players' voices mirrored the unity of the commitment to follow Coach Mac's example.

"So, we begin with me." Coach Mac's words were met with a blank stare of confusion from his audience. The players were certain that the blame for last night's loss lay at their feet alone.

Jamarcus spoke for all of them. "What do you mean, Coach? We're the ones who blew it."

"I blew more than one of our chances to win last night," Coach Mac replied soberly. My poor use of timeouts and my lack of attention to detail, especially in the overtime period—all contributed to the loss. I let the pressure of my own negative emotions bury my passion," Coach Mac confessed. Then he continued with a familiar Northfield mantra, "I take full responsibility for my actions. I will learn from it and I will get better, men."

"Coach, it's okay . . ." Rico, Northfield's newest rising star, cut into Coach Mac's monologue. "You know, with Mrs. Mac and all that you had on your mind . . . like, you know, it's . . ."

Coach Mac's response was pointed—not unkind, but very direct. "Rico, I appreciate your intent. But I do not make excuses. I ask that you not make excuses for me either. It's not the Northfield Way. It's not my way. It's not our way."

"Now, it is your time, men," Coach Mac said as he stood, shifting his position and his tone. "It's time for each of you to take personal responsibility for your role in that embarrassing, unacceptable, half-hearted, miserable excuse for a basketball game."

Jamarcus and Zeke looked at each other and, with no advance planning, stood up together. "It starts with us," Jamarcus began. "We are the senior captains. The responsibility starts with us."

"Yeah. We let you down." Zeke, like the man who taught him how to be a man, took a moment to look every player in the room straight on. "We were prideful, satisfied with our past success. We—no, I am going to say 'I'—didn't care about the rest of you. I was just thinking about getting the game over with, getting my points, and moving on to the win. I made it all about me."

Jamarcus nodded. "I made it about me, too. I've grown up playing against and beating the crap out of Silver Lake teams. I knew I was better than them—all of them. So, I had a 'chill' attitude before the game. No focus. No thought of my teammates . . . and . . . I . . ." At this point Jamarcus, the best player in the state, the toughest minded and most physical player who had ever played for the mighty Northfield program, continued tearfully, "I've got to be honest, man, I never even thought about what the night meant to you, Coach Mac . . ." Jamarcus stared apologetically but intensely into Coach Mac's unblinking eyes. "I take personal responsibility for my actions. I make no excuses. I will learn; I will get better."

Zeke made eye contact with Coach Mac as well, echoing Jamarcus' words. "I take personal responsibility for my actions. I make no excuses. I will learn; I will get better."

Each player who had stepped onto the court against Silver Lake took a turn. Even the two freshman, Billy Connors and Bam Bam Wells, who each played sparingly, confessed their lack of effort.

When everything that should be said had been said, the team passionately recited all five of the Northfield Way Maxims, including their respective personal declarations.

Maxim 1 : PURPOSE
"My first commitment will be to a purpose greater than myself."

Maxim 2 : PASSION
"My first response to pressure will be passion."

Maxim 3 : LOVE
"My first priority will be love."

Maxim 4 : RESPONSIBILITY
"My first responsibility will be to lead myself."

Maxim 5 : HUMILITY
"My first ambition will be to serve with strength, courage, and humility."

Like a master artist admiring his crowning achievement, Coach Mac beamed with pride. Derrick's enthusiasm, however, was muted. He knew what was next. Earlier he had said to Joey, "Last night is going to feel like Disneyworld compared to this." The next few minutes would be one of the few times that Derrick didn't miss playing for Coach Mac. He didn't miss it at all.

Jamarcus would be the first player to "hurl"—that was about 45 minutes into the self-discipline drills. Jamarcus was followed closely by Rico and Bam Bam. Eventually half the players would be losing their lunch from the sprinting, jumping, and repeated core work.

Following practice, Jamarcus and Zeke strode side-by-side toward the east gym doors. Both were weak in the legs, but stronger than ever in their hearts. Walking by Coach Mac standing at the gym door, Zeke turned toward the leader who had pushed him to the brink of exhaustion.

"Great practice, coach," Zeke teased with a wink and very, very sly grin. "I enjoyed it."

Coach Mac smiled broadly, laughing to himself. Then he shot back, "I'm glad you did. And, if you play like you did last night against West Chamberlain, you'll have even more fun on Friday."

Jamarcus and Zeke just shook their heads. "You are relentless, Coach Mac," Jamarcus laughed.

"More like ruthless," Zeke added.

Allowing the guys to walk a few steps further, Coach Mac shouted at his senior leaders. As they pressed the long bar on the door that would release them into the frigid night air he yelled, "Hey, Captains!"

The two seniors turned to face their leader. Coach Mac nodded, then saluted them. "Great leadership by both of you. That's the kind of leadership that leads to a state championship. I was honored to take the court with both of you men today."

"Uh, yeah. Thanks, Coach Mac," Jamarcus responded.

"We're honored too, Coach. Hey Coach, you do know we're going to get you and Mrs. Gracie that win against the Bulldogs on Thursday night, right?" Zeke added.

"The win's going belong to all of us—and it's going to take the best from all of us to make it happen. Mrs. Gracie has already told me she will be there to do her part."

Jamarcus and Zeke flashed huge smiles, giving each other an enthusiastic fist bump.

"Dog meat," Jamarcus yelled, "I suddenly got a big old craving for some dog meat."

Observing their exchange from a distance, Derrick prepared to exit. As he passed by the bronze plaque that dedicated the hallowed arena to the life and leadership of Coach John McKissack, he paused to read it for the first time. Derrick noted the deeply etched italicized quote from Coach Mac: *My life is best lived in the service of others.* Derrick took a deep breath and, as best he knew how, said a brief prayer with his head bowed and eyes closed.

God, if you're listening. Please take care of Mrs. Gracie. And then he added, *If it's not too much to ask, please help me, you know, to be . . . better or something. Thanks, I guess.* Derrick opened his eyes, then shut them quickly again before adding, *And, oh yeah, Amen.*

Reopening his eyes, Derrick raised his head and shook it side to side. With a quiet laugh, he muttered out loud, "Well, that was lame." He pressed the metal bar on the door to exit the gym, then looked back over his shoulder. He hoped that no one had observed his clumsy attempt at being religious. No one was there to notice.

He doubted God was either.

CHAPTER 12

s the garage door slowly clanked open, the clear outline of Nikki's black on black Mini Cooper emerged. Entering the house, Derrick yelled out, "Nikki!! Nikki? Hey, where are you?"

At first glance, Nikki was nowhere to be found. Even when she was not there, however, Derrick could feel her presence. He could see it, too. Every square inch of their two-bedroom condo mirrored Nikki's approach to life: bright colors, one-of-a-kind objects, repurposed things as works of art. Each individual room bore its own unique expression of "Nikki chic." As Derrick walked down the narrow hallway, he entered their bedroom. Her clothes, as always, lay in neat, small piles, a testament to her "organized chaos" lifestyle.

"Nikki, are you home?" Derrick yelled again, this time impatiently.

"D?" Nikki responded with surprise as she exited the guest bedroom. "What are you doing home? I thought you had practice. You shouldn't be home until after 6!"

"It's 6:15, Nikki! And where have you been the last two days?" Derrick's words had a sharp, confrontational edge to them.

"Oh . . . I thought it was . . . Oh no!! I'm supposed to be meeting Jasmine and Ashland for drinks at 7:30. It's at least an hour drive to the club. I've got to hit the shower!" Nikki brushed by Derrick in a panic, barely acknowledging his presence.

"Nikki . . ." Derrick called gently. Hearing no response, he demanded forcefully, "Nikki!"

"What! I am in a major rush—what do you want?" Nikki called back with annoyance in her voice. Nikki's eyebrows raised, her neck stiffened, and her green eyes bore into Derrick's.

Recognizing the firestorm his demands had sparked, Derrick softened. "I just want to talk, Nikki. I *need* to talk to you right now. There's a lot going on."

"Well, I can't talk right now, D! I have 15 minutes—make that 13 now—to be showered, dressed, and head out to the club in Spencerville. So, whatever it is, it has to wait."

Nikki hastily headed into the master bathroom, then into their shared bathroom, closing the door sharply behind her.

Derrick fumed. "So, that's your answer?" Derrick yelled through the closed door. " 'Whatever it is, it has to wait.' Really?"

No answer. Derrick dropped onto the edge of the bed while he waited. He distracted himself with his phone, checking Twitter, Instagram, and Snapchat.

In less than five minutes, Nikki hastily emerged from the closed bathroom, wrapped in a towel, her long auburn hair falling in curled piles across her shoulders. She flashed a quick, irritated glance toward Derrick. She said nothing.

"Look, Nikki. I don't want to hold you up." Derrick attempted to speak with a more inviting voice. "But I do need to talk to you and you are never—"

"I am going to take one minute and say this to you," Nikki said firmly. She paused briefly, taking a deep breath. She bit her lip before continuing, "D, you have your life and I have mine. That's what we agreed to when we moved in together. In the beginning I wanted more—more time, more commitment, more of a sense of the future together—and I'm not talking about marriage, D." Nikki paused, lowering her voice and choosing her words carefully. "D, you made it very clear that you weren't ready for more. You didn't have *time* for more. You were a first-year teacher and coach. You didn't have *time* to give more. So, I've made the adjustment. And now, you're demanding time from me?" Nikki turned around, walking into the closet as she searched frantically for a pair of shoes she had just purchased.

"But Nikki, c'mon," Derrick fumed as she turned her back. "You know—"

Nikki wheeled around, raising her hand, palm facing Derrick's face. She walked slowly to within a couple of feet of where he sat. Her raised palm morphed into an adamant, accusatory pointing finger. "I've decided to believe you, Derrick. You're right," Nikki said, raising both of her hands in the air as if surrendering to an unseen opponent. "You don't have time for me. So, instead of waiting around for you to be ready for more, I have created my own life. If that's not working for you, then . . ." her voice trailed off as she turned back toward the closet.

"Then what . . . then what, Nikki?" With her back turned toward Derrick, Nikki began to get dressed in the closet.

"I asked you, *then what,* Nikki?" Derrick pressed angrily.

Nikki pulled on the chic black pencil dress over her shoulders, then her hips. Smoothing out the edges of the outfit so it fit in the most flattering manner, Nikki turned back toward Derrick. For a moment, their eyes met. Nikki studied the dazed look on Derrick's normally clear blue eyes. He looked everything like the strikingly handsome man she had fallen in love with a year ago. And yet, at the same time, he looked nothing like that Derrick.

Derrick took in the full picture of the woman standing before him. He deeply explored her green eyes, accented by her auburn hair. He noted how perfectly she filled out the dress she had first worn the night they celebrated his Northfield job offer.

A thousand memories and moments flooded both of their minds.

With exasperation, Nikki quietly broke the silence, "I don't know what, D. I don't know. But I do know neither one of us is very happy with the way things are and I . . ." Nikki's voice trailed off in sadness. "Look, I have to go. Can we talk about this later in the week?"

"Yeah, sure, Nikki. If you're leaving then so am I," Derrick retorted angrily, not wanting to watch her walk out the door. "I guess I'll see you later this week."

"Okay. Now, I've got to finish getting ready," Nikki replied flatly.

Derrick stormed out to the garage and jumped into his four-wheel-drive pickup. He pushed in the clutch, shifted the truck into neutral, and revved the engine as loudly as he could. As the garage door rose behind him, he slammed the stick shift into reverse, backed out of the garage, and drove away, tires squealing.

Within seconds, his phone buzzed. The incoming text was from Nikki. It read simply, *I'm sorry it's come to this. I just wanted you to know. I am truly sorry. It's not what I want.*

Derrick responded shortly, texting a terse, *Yeah, me neither.* Then, looking both ways again, he pulled away as quickly as possible from the intersection, and from Nikki. He wasn't sure how she would interpret his text. He didn't care.

As Derrick came to another full stop at the intersection of 4th and Main, he checked his messages again. Less than one minute ago, an incoming text had been signaled by another loud buzz. "Well, here we go," Derrick said aloud. "She probably didn't like the 'tone' of my text."

The sender's name on the screen shocked Derrick. *Coach Mac.* Coach Mac was strict about leaving his work behind. Except for game nights, his goal was to be with Mrs. Mac and away from basketball every night by 6:30 p.m. Derrick anxiously swiped his phone to open the text.

D, I was just talking with Gracie. She suggested and I agreed that we talk strategy. I think she's tired of listening! Her sister is here, so it's a good time to get away. Could we grab a beer and talk?

Derrick glanced ahead, realizing that the light had turned green—probably a long time ago. Pulling through the intersection, he eased into the right-hand lane, then turned into the empty parking lot of Northfield Community Bank. There he safely texted: *Coach Mac. I am honored you would ask. Turns out I'm also free. I haven't had dinner either. Could we meet at Del Roma's for pizza and beer?*

Coach Mac responded immediately. *Great plan! I knew I hired well when I hired you. 6:45 work for you?*

Derrick typed back: *Perfect!*

With twenty minutes to kill, Derrick sat alone in his truck in the bank parking lot. He replayed the harsh words he and Nikki had just exchanged. Less than six months ago, they were a happy couple excited to build a life together. Now, they weren't just unhappy—they were miserable.

Derrick put his forefinger to the photos on his phone. Opening the app, he searched for the first photo he had taken of Nikki. It was a selfie, taken on his first official visit to Northern Iowa. Derrick smiled. The visit, the scholarship offer that came with it, and meeting Nikki all happened in one glorious day.

An engaging, intelligent, competitive grad student, Nikki Coles had worked her way into a part-time staff position with Northern Iowa's Athletic Department. One of her roles included chaperoning recruits on their official visits. As Nikki led Derrick and two other athletes on a campus tour, Derrick could tell she was genuinely unimpressed with him. For his part, however, Derrick was immediately attracted to her natural ease with people. Moreover, he noted how Nikki energized every space she entered. The stunning combination of her cascading auburn hair and sparkling emerald eyes only added fuel to the flames of his attraction. "Those eyes," Derrick repeated to himself over and over in the days following his visit.

Derrick scrolled to the next picture he had of Nikki, a group picture that included Derrick. The snapshot had been captured during a Special Olympics event hosted by the UNI athletic department. Even though they stood with arms around each other in the line of volunteers, their relationship was still surface at best. Derrick laughed. He recalled how incredibly awkward he had been around Nikki at first. His shame over being a former high school dropout had convinced Derrick that a girl of Nikki's caliber was unlikely to fall for him.

Photos of Nikki increased in regularity as Derrick swiped rapidly forward. The next picture to arrest Derrick's attention was taken during a student beach trip just over a year ago. Derrick and Nikki were tanned, smiling, and without question moving past a surface friendship. Earlier that week, a long night of walking and talking on the beach had led to much more personal conversations. Nikki remarked at the end of one walk, "I feel like I've always known you, D. But still I want to know you so much more."

Derrick, fueled by a rush of adrenaline and testosterone, embarrassingly replied, "Yeah, I know." Quickly correcting his narcissistic phrasing, he added, "I mean, that's how I feel about you, too, Nikki." They laughed, then embraced one another with gentle strength. After a few moments of staring into one another's eyes, Derrick and Nikki had shared a long, passionate kiss. That kiss forever changed their relationship.

Derrick's smile gradually disappeared as a wave of sadness slowly washed over his heart. Fleeing from that feeling, Derrick immediately swiped through more pictures. He stopped at a photo taken just after the end of his last season at NIU. Derrick shook his head. "We were so happy," he mumbled aloud, sighing deeply. Remembering the trip, his mind settled on one particularly vivid conversation.

"I've got some baggage, Nikki. A crapload of it, actually." Derrick followed this sloppy introduction to his inner world with a full revelation of his family's carefully guarded secrets.

"Just weeks before dad's fatal car accident," he began in almost a whisper, "my brother, Parker, figured out that our mom was having an affair. We already knew—hell, half the town knew—that dad had cheated on mom. More than once. Carl Walker wasn't much of a husband or dad," Derrick huffed. "He wasn't much of a human being for that matter." Derrick had paused, burdened by the nearness of the pain that he constantly fought to keep distant. "But Mom, I mean, my mom was sleeping around on my dad?" Derrick stood up, arched his back, and looked away into the distance

Nikki stood and positioned herself directly in front of Derrick. "Oh, honey, D. I'm so sorry, really, so sorry. That's awful," Nikki gently stroked Derrick's face with her right hand.

Derrick recoiled from the touch. He sat back down and continued. "Yeah, well it got worse. By the time we were nearing Thanksgiving our family just fell apart. No one but us knew, but Dad was not even living at home the day he died."

"What happened after he died? Was that when your mom met Walter? Surely she wasn't sleeping with Walter while your dad was alive." Nikki's word rolled out of her mouth rapidly and unfiltered. Catching herself, she leaned toward Derrick, "D, I'm sorry, I'm just trying to make sense out of all this."

"Well, don't," Derrick replied with a sharp turn of his head. "No one will ever make sense of my family." Then, with a less agitated voice, Derrick continued, "But, to answer your question, Mom felt extremely guilty, like a dark, all-consuming guilt. Blamed herself for the accident— you know, like she had anything to do with my dad's drinking and driving and generally sorry-ass life." Derrick began moving restlessly again. "And Walter?" Derrick chuckled darkly, "Mom met Walter at a grief support group. He's barely an upgrade from good ol' Carl. I'm pretty sure he cheats on her, too." Derrick shook his head. "That bastard."

The two had sat in the silent, somber wake of Derrick's words. A strong gust of wind blasted them both, and leaves and dust swirled all around them. Derrick coughed, choking from the dirty air. Both wiped their eyes to free them from debris. Having cleared them, their eyes met. Derrick had reached for Nikki's hand. She accepted his gesture as a warm, compassionate smile spread across her face.

Holding Nikki's hand, Derrick added in a severe voice, "So, Nikki, I hope you understand. Marriage is just not something I'm interested in . . . at least not any time soon."

Nikki's hand had released Derrick's. He saw her face drop into a look of disappointment bordering on devastation, then she let her hands fall softly into her lap. She tugged on the ends of her sweatshirt, pulling the sleeves all the way across the tips of her fingers. Following a slight shiver, her arms tightened close to her body.

To rescue the moment, Derrick quickly added, "But, Nikki, you know I want to be with you. I want to come home to you at night. I want to share adventures in life with you. I just don't want to get all tangled up in a marriage, especially when we could be so much happier just living together."

Nikki stared blankly back at Derrick. Anxiously, he pleaded, "I want you to have your life and I want to have my life, and, you know, I just want us to keep sharing our lives like we do now. I mean, it's working right?"

Nothing was resolved that night. Nikki eventually—and reluctantly—agreed to a live-in relationship. Soon afterwards, Derrick took the astonishing offer to join Coach Mac at Northfield. Nikki then landed a dream job with a marketing firm that allowed her to combine working from home with only occasional travel. By May, they had a contract on a condo. The down payment had been funded by a small trust fund Nikki had inherited upon her graduation from college.

Derrick hastily scrolled through the next several months of photos that brought him to the present. Pictures from the weddings of one, two, and then a third set of friends appeared. Nikki and Derrick had attended or been a part of five weddings total in the last eight months. After the third wedding in June, Nikki had challenged Derrick, "D, if marriage does not become an option at some point in our future, and I mean sooner than later, then don't be surprised if I move out—and move on." In each successive picture, Derrick could not help but notice Nikki's face being less expressive, her eyes more distant.

Derrick attributed Nikki's marriage fixation to be a default product of her family's conservative religious influence. She was, in her terms, a "PK," a pastor's kid. She had been raised in what people once considered a "traditional" American family, complete with a stereotypical Midwestern work ethic and deeply ingrained conservative religious values. Derrick had consistently blamed her naïveté on her lack of understanding of how the "real" world worked.

Sitting silently in his truck in a bank parking lot, Derrick began to wonder if he knew how the "real" world worked. Nikki's words echoed loudly in his mind, "Don't be surprised if I move out—and move on."

Derrick swiped to the most recent picture he had taken of Nikki, ironically at another wedding just last month. Noting her forced smile and the weariness in her eyes, Derrick confronted himself, "How could you have been so blind? You've screwed this up—like everything else."

Derrick lamented aloud, "I've lost your heart, Nikki. And mine."

As vividly as if Coach Mac were sitting next to him, in the car, he could hear Coach Mac's constant reminder to his players: "If you lose your heart, you lose everything."

CHAPTER 13

By the time Coach Mac had ordered a large Del Roma's "Big Man's All-Meat" pizza and they had each downed one light beer each, Derrick already had tears welling up in his eyes—not sad tears, laugh-out-loud tears. Derrick had heard most of Coach Mac's stories before. Tonight—maybe because he really needed a good laugh—Coach Mac was funnier than ever. Coach Mac, who definitely needed a good laugh, was in rare form.

"Okay, hold on, Coach. So, here's what I heard, and I can't believe I'm actually asking you before we eat, but I've heard that a few years ago Chip Davis actually slipped on a projectile hurl of another player. I heard he fell right into the mess . . . and . . ." Coach Mac's dramatic facial expression ignited a chain reaction of laughter between the two of them. The repeated howls from both men made it nearly impossible for Derrick to finish his version of the story. ". . . he falls flat on his face, covered in . . . well, you know. And then, at least this is what I heard, Principal Davis called you into the office the next day to unload on you."

Coach Mac nodded, adding, "That's right. That's exactly what happened. Well . . . almost. Man, I'm telling you, on the way to his office I was already thinking about how to get a new job. We had won seven championships at that point, but I figured 70 championships wouldn't be enough to keep my job after the principal's son falls flat on his face into a puddle of . . ." Coach Mac couldn't finish. He could barely catch his breath between laughs.

Derrick somehow managed to question, "Well, what did he say? I heard that by the time you walked out of his office you looked like a man sent to death row."

Coach Mac hesitated a moment. He drew Derrick close, as if what he was about to speak a matter of national security. "Derrick, I have never told anyone what actually happened. Frank, that is, Principal Davis, and I agreed that it would be best for everyone not to know what was said. But it's been a good six years and . . ."

Coach Mac surveyed the room, checking to see who might be close enough to hear his confession. Assured it was safe, he began in a whisper, "Well, I suppose I can trust you."

"Of course, Coach . . . of course. I can keep a secret."

"Principal Davis said, 'Coach Mac, if you ever even think about having a practice like that with my son and his teammates, a practice where something as gross and disgusting as that could happen again—" Coach Mac's solemn face broke into a huge grin, "don't you even think of doing that again unless you invite me to come and watch!'" Coach Mac burst into laughter that brought more tears. Between huge outbursts, he managed to finish his thought. "Then he slapped me on the back and we both almost rolled out of our chairs from laughing so hard."

"No way!" The two leaned back in the glory of Coach Mac's best story yet. Derrick was envisioning Principal Davis slapping Coach Mac on the back as they conspired to conceal the moment.

Interrupting Derrick's daydreaming Coach Mac observed, "D, it's good that everyone knows we follow the 'Just One' rule. Otherwise they would probably think we were both stone cold drunk!" Coach was only half joking.

Coach Mac's "Just One" rule offered one more example of the man's commitment to his principles. He was not only the first man of color to coach in the tri-county area, he was known as the first high school coach to drink a beer in public. In the conservative community of Northfield, people had odd ways of dealing with the consumption of alcoholic beverages. Back in the day, some townspeople had actually demanded that

Coach Mac be fired for his public disorderliness. (The "disorderliness" being one beer while out to dinner with Mrs. Gracie.)

Most people in the community respected Coach Mac and his "Just One" rule. A few folks in the community, however, came down hard on him. At the time, it was impossible to tell whether they were angered primarily by his having a drink or by the color of his skin or by the fact that he was a man of faith who was not controlled by constant religious guilt. All three seemed particularly offensive to some of the more legalistic members of the Northfield community.

"Okay, Derrick," Coach Mac asserted, pushing his empty plate and glass to the side. "We need to talk about how we are going to beat a very talented West Chamberlain team. Let's walk through the 'Our Strengths, Their Weaknesses' process and see if there's anything we've missed."

Coach Mac approached every game with the same routine: identify and maximize the impact of Northfield's strengths, then identify and exploit the vulnerabilities of the opposing team's weaknesses. The strategy had produced 678 wins and eleven state championships. Derrick was not about to suggest anything to the contrary.

Coach Mac pulled out his tattered notebook and put the first piece of paper on the table between them. Together they compiled their lists citing the Warriors' strengths and the Bulldogs' weaknesses.

"So, Coach Walker, where does this information lead you?" Coach Mac patiently, intentionally continued to draw Derrick deeper into the processes of coaching. Derrick was honored. He was also caught off guard. His mentor was truly partnering with Derrick as the biggest game of the season loomed on the horizon.

"The obvious answer? We use our quickness to exploit their slowness at the guard position. We force them into a fast-tempo game, relying on our ability to get to the rim off the fast break. That way we neutralize their efforts to force a slow-tempo, half-court post-up game." Derrick felt confident what he had delivered was a great initial plan. Coach Mac's approving nod added to his confidence.

"Go on. Your points are logical—but what does your gut tell you?"

"Well, you may think I'm crazy . . ."

"Actually, Derrick I am absolutely confident that you are crazy, but that's not the point," the aged veteran replied mischievously.

"I would start Rico . . . I know he can be erratic and his three-point shooting is hot and cold . . . but he is so disruptive, Coach. His quickness usually gives us a boost off the bench, but I think we need to attack from the opening tipoff." Derrick waited to see Coach Mac's response. Rico had started less than five games this season. Though he was a rising star, he had not been entirely reliable.

"That's interesting. Anything else?"

"Well, I would start the game in our 'Fury press' after every made basket, falling back into our half-court, trapping man-to-man defense." Derrick waited for Coach Mac to interrupt, but he didn't. Much to Derrick's surprise, the soon-to-be winningest coach in state history seemed genuinely interested. "After a missed basket, we catch them off guard with a 1-3-1 zone trap, Jamarcus at the top and Rico on the baseline. We lose rebounding power but we add pressure against their guards."

Coach Mac's eyebrows furrowed. "To be honest, D, I don't like to make changes mid-season. I like to stick exclusively to what we've practiced over and over." Coach paused once again, for a very long time.

Derrick tried to talk himself off an anxiety ledge. *At least he's letting me down easy,* he reassured himself.

As Derrick's anxieties escalated, Coach Mac broke the silence. "And my tendency to stick to what we've been practicing, well, it's a strength of mine for sure. But a man's greatest weakness is the abuse of his strength." Coach Mac paused. "And D, I think my reluctance to change may have cost us the overtime game against Silver Lake. I have watched the film of the overtime at least five times. I ignored key opportunities to adapt to the flow of the game. I was distracted, and risk averse. That may have been my worst coaching of my entire career—and that's saying a lot, because I've stunk it up on multiple occasions."

"How did you have time to watch the overtime five times since last night's game?" Derrick marveled aloud. Internally, he observed, *That man is the man when it comes to coaching. No wonder he's won 678 games.*

Coach Mac continued, "So let's go with your strategy. In fact, I want you in charge of our defensive game plan."

If Assistant Coach Derrick Walker had written a script for a dream conversation, this would have been the storyline. Coach John McKissack had entrusted him with a significant leadership role in a pivotal game in Northfield's season. Derrick sat in disbelief, to the point that he finally muttered in a halting voice, "Wait, are you sure, Coach?"

"Yes, I'm absolutely sure. Now, I need to talk to you about what I am thinking offensively. Starting Rico works perfectly with my plans."

Coach Mac's ideas on the offensive strategy were simple, yet brilliant. Most coaches would be strategizing a way to escape with a win against the powerful West Chamberlain squad. Coach Mac strategized to bury them.

With their night nearing an end, Derrick prepared to ask Coach Mac a question that was weighing heavily on his mind. Before he could form the words, however, Jimmy Thompson stopped by their table. "Coach, when would be a good time to finish our interview from last night? I'm not letting you off the hook," Jimmy said nervously. The reporter's left hand shook slightly as he held it at arm's length to check his calendar.

"Of course, Jimmy," Coach Mac assured. "I promised you more and I'm a man of my word. I can probably give you ten minutes after practice tomorrow. Would that work?"

"Well, Coach," Jimmy offered, shifting his weight from one foot to the other while also fidgeting with his cell phone in the other. "I would actually prefer, if it works for you, to do a longer interview . . . and, I . . ." Jimmy paused and looked into the distance. "I just . . ."

"Yes, Jimmy. Is something the matter?" Coach Mac asked.

"No, not all," Jimmy answered unconvincingly. "It's just that, well, I was hoping that . . ." Jimmy paused again, then spat out his words quickly. "I was just hoping that I could share some things with you . . . you know, things that have been, kind of, on my mind."

"Okay, that's fine," Coach Mac said. "Text me some times on Friday that work for you and I'll make it work for as long as you . . ." Coach Mac paused. With concern he added, "Jimmy, are you okay?"

"Yes," Jimmy replied quickly, "Of course, Coach. I'll text you tonight." Jimmy gave a thumbs up and concluded with a strangely worded, "It will be good for us to, you know, get stuff squared away, professional-wise and all."

Jimmy retreated from the table as rapidly as possible. Upon the advice of his mentor, Dr. McCombs, he had taken the scary first step toward laying everything on the line. He would ask the hard questions, including asking about Coach Mac's past. He would disclose the anonymous texts to Coach Mac and ask for an explanation. "The sooner I get this over," Jimmy thought to himself as he walked toward the exit door with eyes and head down, "the sooner I'll be sleeping again."

"Was that as awkward as it felt to me, D?" Coach Mac inquired of Derrick.

"It wasn't just awkward. It was downright strange," Derrick observed.

"So, D, you were about to ask me a question before Jimmy interrupted. What's up?"

Derrick hesitated briefly. "Well, here comes another awkward moment," Derrick thought to himself. He breathed a long breath through his nose then forcefully exhaled through his mouth . "Coach, I want to ask a very personal question—at least for me it's personal . . ."

"Take the shot, Coach Walker."

"I want to learn to live and lead like you do, Coach," Derrick blurted out, providing no background or context for his request. Derrick fumbled for words to clarify his request. "I hope that doesn't sound weird, but I mean, not just in basketball, but you know, in life. You always talk about the maxims of the Northfield Way and how they relate to real life. Well, I still have no idea where to start. Will you help me?"

Derrick had been sitting with his elbows on the table, resting himself against them. He had now shifted his weight, leaning far back in his chair with his arms folded.

"Does this have anything to do with your relationship with Nikki?" Coach Mac asked as he shifted himself toward Derrick.

Derrick tightened his arms around his chest. His legs were crossed. He looked toward the clanging hustle and bustle in the restaurant's kitchen. "Yeah, it kind of has to do with Nikki, sort of . . . I mean not totally," he said, still looking away from Coach Mac. Backpedaling, Derrick redirected the conversation. "Hey, Coach, let's just wait until after the season. I mean, you've got enough on your plate already without . . . you know, so yeah, let's just wait." Derrick couldn't get up from his chair fast enough.

"Now hold on, Derrick." Coach Mac firmly placed his large right hand on top of Derrick's left arm, applying enough pressure to discourage him from rising. First of all, you've heard me say it a thousand times, 'No one lives well who lives alone.' You, of all people should—"

"Yes sir, I know. 'The myth of self-sufficiency,' " Derrick interrupted.

"Exactly. I would be honored to help you think through the Northfield Way. You know, D, I think God made all of us to be fierce warriors, to fight important personal battles that make a difference in the world. I would count it a great privilege to walk this out with you. D, you should know that I see you as an up-and-coming warrior. And, you have to admit, with that blond hair and those blue eyes you look much more like a Viking Warrior than I do!" Coach Mac laughed heartily.

"Thank you, Coach Mac. That means a lot to me," Derrick replied, a large smile of relief and joy spreading across his face.

"Here's is what I propose. Let's meet here for pizza and beer every other Monday night until at least the end of the semester. In preparation, start with Maxim #1. Work your way through your first thoughts about the maxim and how it relates to your current reality. After we've sat with Maxim #1 for a while, we will move on to #2—the first one will take the longest, by far."

Derrick continued to smile, nodding his head in approval. His arms relaxed and his legs uncrossed.

"I do, however, need to make two asks of you," Coach Mac added.

"Sure, whatever you want, Coach," Derrick said. "Whatever I need to do, I will do it. I'll even buy the pizza and beer every week!"

"That won't be necessary, D. But thanks for the offer. We can split the cost of the food. Here are my two 'asks.'" Coach Mac held up a long, crooked index finger on his right hand. "First, as we talk through the five maxims, I expect you to be *brutally honest* with yourself and with me. You cannot do this half-heartedly. The Northfield Way is about being wholehearted, all in. You can't fake your way through it. Will you commit to that?"

"Yes, sir," Derrick replied as he leaned his elbows onto the table.

"Wonderful! I thought you would say, 'Yes.'" Coach Mac continued, holding up his less crooked middle finger to join the index finger. "Second, I ask that you be willing to keep a journal through the process. I will give you some things to keep track of in your life and I will ask you to write a couple of reflections weekly. Now, this is nothing like honors U.S. History homework," Coach Mac assured the clearly hesitant young coach. "I'm thinking it will take less than an hour a week to do—but you must do it faithfully for the process to have its full effect."

"Yeah, sure. I'm in, Coach. When do we start?" Derrick pressed enthusiastically.

"Tonight, Derrick. We start tonight. Buy a small journal on your way home. Or just grab a small spiral notebook you have lying around the house. It doesn't need to be something fancy. Then, I want you to start tonight working on applying Maxim #1. Answer this question, 'What's the 'WHY'—the greater purpose you are living for at the moment? Specifically, what's the 'WHY' that drives your relationship with Nikki? Be brutally honest about reason or reasons behind what you are choosing in the big areas of your life." Coach Mac quietly slapped the table with both of his hands, nodded vigorously, and added, "We'll start there and move forward."

Derrick stared back at Coach Mac as he tried to take it all in. The emotions of the moment drew him back to another unforgettable moment. The memory was so vivid he could almost feel the heat of the day on his skin. It was a Saturday afternoon, just before Derrick's junior season at Northfield. The day would be remembered by even the old-timers as one of the hottest summer days ever experienced by the citizens of Lewis County. The moment began with a crossover dribble, which temporarily paralyzed Parker. As Parker tried to recover from being thrown off balance, Derrick slashed by his hip. Dribbling ferociously down the right side of the foul lane, he took a power step onto his left leg, then elevated toward the basket. Derrick had worked endlessly for months, perfecting the move in his mind and in his muscle memory. Parker used his quickness and length and recovered in time to position himself—for the thousandth time—to block Derrick's incoming layup. Only this time, for the first time, Derrick rose high above Parker's outstretched hand and slammed home a glorious, rim-rattling dunk.

Tonight, for the first time in his life—even with life staring him down like a shut-down defender—Derrick could actually envision a future where he could rise above his past failures. *Regardless of what happens next,* Derrick thought to himself as he turned the key to start his truck. Shivering as he waited for the truck to warm, Derrick committed himself to a new vision for his life. "I'm taking life to the rim," he boldly announced aloud to himself.

On the way home, however, Derrick fought to keep his hopes alive. His mind flooded with memory after memory of failure. By the time he got home, he could barely envision anything other than having his dreams hopelessly dashed. He could almost hear the footsteps chasing him down.

CHAPTER 14

As he neared home, Derrick's phone played a familiar, yet largely neglected ringtone, "Walk This Way," the Run DMC and Aerosmith version. "Walk this Way" signaled a phone call from his brother, Parker.

"Well, that fits the moment," Derrick laughed aloud. Then he spoke aloud to himself, "I don't need this right now." Derrick's chest tightened. He tossed the phone to the other side of the truck cab.

Parker's life had been more of a disaster than Derrick's. His older brother had spiraled out of control, much like Derrick had, at age 19. Parker, however, had not pulled out of his spiral until a couple of years ago. At age 27, he checked himself into an alcohol rehab center. To Parker's credit, he had been sober every day since.

Derrick loved Parker—from a distance. For most of Derrick's life, Parker had appeared to be on a singular mission to beat Derrick down; he had certainly attempted to do so in every possible way. It was true that Parker was his own brother, his flesh-and-blood relative. But it was just as true that Derrick considered his brother to be his personal enemy.

In a span of less than three minutes, Parker had called four times. *Same old Parker*, Derrick reasoned. *Relentless and annoying. But crappy brother or not, I can't ignore four calls in three minutes.* Derrick reluctantly instructed Siri, "Call 'Parker cell.'"

"Hey, little brother!" Parker answered.

Derrick recoiled. Parker always referred to him as "little" something. "Little Brother" or "Little D" or "Little Man." Derrick recovered quickly, responding cordially, "Hey, Parker. Everything okay, man?"

"Yeah, yeah, everything's great, man. Just great! Sorry, I just needed to talk to you today. Listen, everything is really going well. In fact, I have some really good news. But that's not actually why I called." Derrick was relieved, curious, and—at least for now—motivated for a short talk with Parker.

"Derrick, I want to tell you, I'm just so proud of you!" Parker exclaimed. "I know it took courage to go back to Northfield, what with your past, my past, and our whole family's past. I'm talking about real courage, Derrick."

Parker's affirmation of Derrick hit him hard, like a teammate's chest pass that he hadn't seen coming. Congratulating Derrick appeared to have been Parker's primary reason for calling. Typically, Parker's favorite subject was Parker.

"Well, thanks, Parker. That means a lot . . . it *really* means a lot," Derrick replied. His tone was sincere, his thoughts skeptical.

"I really am so proud of you, Derrick. I knew you had what it takes . . . and, as you know, obviously, well, let's just tell it like it is: I haven't done a very good job of telling you how much I believe in you. So, I want you to know that I'm not at all surprised by your success. I saw greatness in you from the time you could walk."

Derrick's mind froze. His thoughts were immobilized by distrust. Derrick had always dreamed of hearing words like this from a man in his family. Now, he pushed the words away, protecting himself from the emotional fallout that was sure to follow this fleeting fantasy.

"You there, Derrick? Can you hear me?" Parker assumed the call had been dropped.

"Yeah, yeah . . . I'm here, Parker. Again, thanks . . . I'm not sure what else to say."

"Well, if it's okay, I would like to say a couple more things. One day I will say them face to face, but they need to be said."

"Okay, sure," Derrick said.

"Derrick, I've made a lot of stupid choices and hurt a lot of people. I got lost in anger. I was pissed about how my life wasn't working out . . . and, well, I took a lot of that out on you. Part of it was I wanted you to be tougher than me, to have it better than me. But part of it, honestly, was just pure meanness and selfishness."

"That sounds about right," Derrick responded coldly. His eyes focused on the dark, empty road ahead.

"Yeah, I know." Parker's words carried a thick layer of remorse. Derrick let them hang in silence, like an impenetrable force field between them. After a long pause, Parker pleaded, "But I've changed, Derrick—really changed. With Becky's help, I've been finding a bigger 'WHY,' just like Coach Mac preaches. And with Pastor Doug's help, I've started taking personal responsibility for my stupidity. And, Derrick, Coach Mac was right. Grace is the story we should all be telling with our lives," Parker's voice cracked slightly. "By grace, Derrick . . . only by grace, man, I'm a husband and a father, and in spite of myself, I've got a really good life, D. . ." More silence, as Parker's voice disappeared. Then he added wistfully, "A really good life."

Derrick squirmed in his seat, his face grimacing as he fought against a torrent of emotions. *Stay in the present,* he coached himself. He tried to respond in a meaningful way. All he could manage was a monotone, "That's great, Parker. I'm happy for you."

"So," Parker continued, "that's why I called. I want to ask your forgiveness. I want to ask you to forgive me for not loving you well as a big brother. And I want a reset, brother."

Derrick's throat tightened as he pulled into his driveway. He hoped to use his arrival as an excuse to end the conversation.

"I . . ." Derrick cleared his throat. ". . . I don't know what to say, Parker. . . yeah I forgive you, but I don't know about . . . well, I just . . ."

As the car stopped short of the garage, his heart connected to his words like a sudden crack of lightning. He gritted his teeth and clenched his hands into fists. Derrick swallowed hard.

Parker broke the silence. "I understand, Derrick. And we can talk more, face to face. In fact, Becky and I were hoping you would come out and join our family this summer for vacation. Maybe then we can talk some more and try to figure it out—together."

Shielding Parker from his emotions, Derrick replied, "Yeah, well, okay." Derrick recognized a perfect exit point. "Look, I appreciate the call, but as you know, we've got a lot going on here and I just got home, so . . ."

Parker interrupted apologetically. "Sure, I know. And, Derrick, I probably should have waited until we're face to face to spring all of this on you. I don't know, I just felt like you should know that your big brother really wants to be a real brother."

"Of course, yeah. No worries. I am glad you called, Parker, and I . . ." The shield covering Derrick's emotions dropped. Slightly. "Parker, if you are serious, this is going to take time, man. A lot of time," Gaining strength, Derrick continued, "You do remember how you treated me growing up, right?"

"Yeah, I remember," Parker replied in a barely audible voice.

"Do you remember what you said to me, all the time? Every time you blocked my shot or dunked over me or stole the ball from me? Every time I failed to live up to your expectations." Derrick's voice raised in anger. "Do you remember, Parker?" Derrick's confrontation was not rhetorical.

After a long pause, Parker said, "Yes, Derrick. I do, and I'm sorry."

"Well, what was it, Parker? What were the words you drilled into my head over and over? Words that I still can't shake today?"

"I used to taunt you. I used to say," Parker paused. Derrick could hear Parker's breath growing heavy on the other end of the call. Parker continued, "I said, 'Is that all you got, little D? Is that all you got?' Derrick, I know, man. I was merciless. I put you down, way down. I'm sorry, Derrick. I am so sorry. I hate thinking about what a crapload of a big brother I was to you."

"At least I can say that you came by it honestly," Derrick said. "Carl left us one helluva legacy."

"That's no excuse, though," Parker stated firmly. "I wasn't there when you needed me. Especially after Dad's death and the whole mess when Mom—" Parker's voice halted.

Derrick's gut tightened. He felt like an NFL linebacker had hit him helmet first in the midsection. He wanted to end this conversation now.

"So," Derrick deflected, "I'm not sure I know what else to say right now. Maybe when this season's over we can get together."

Derrick pressed the button on the garage door opener, and pulled his truck into the empty garage as he listened to Parker's parting comments. "I would like that, Derrick. I have no idea where to start, but I would like that. Can I call you once a month, you know, just to check in? No pressure."

Derrick opened the service door to the kitchen and tossed his keys on the kitchen counter. Coming to a stop, he chose the path of least resistance toward ending the conversation, "Sure. Yeah, that's fine."

"So, one more thing," Parker added. "Would you and Nikki consider coming out to see me and Becky this summer? We're planning a special event and we want you both to join us."

"Yes, but with Nikki, that's . . . well, let's just say it's complicated." Derrick began walking toward his bedroom, and away from the extension Parker had added to the conversation. "There's no time to go into it right now, but . . . it's a very long story, but I'm not sure we will still be together by then." Derrick stopped short of the bedroom. He leaned his forearm against the wall and rested his head on it.

"I'm sorry to hear that, Derrick. I know how much you love each other," Parker said.

Derrick had no response. And no interest in continuing the conversation.

"Okay, I know you've got to go, but really quickly," Parker spoke at a rapid-fire pace.

Derrick rolled his eyes.

"Becky and I have been talking for a while with Nora and Spencer and, well, I am going to be adopting them! I am going to move from being a stepfather to being a legal, adoptive dad. And the kids, it was their idea and they are really excited about it—that's the best part."

"That is really good news, Parker. For real, I'm excited for you," Derrick replied with sincerity as he began moving toward the master bedroom.

"Thanks, bro. I know you need to go. I'll get back to you soon. Thanks for listening, Derrick."

"Sure, Parker. See you, man," Derrick's words took a hard turn toward exiting the conversation.

"Tell Coach Mac, 'Hey' for me. Coach Mac's the best. And now he's got you by his side. You're an unbeatable combination. Talk to you soon and . . . I love you, Derrick."

Derrick absorbed these words as he fell backward, collapsing on the bed. It had been twelve years since their dad's funeral, the last time Derrick had heard the words, "I love you" from Parker—except for a couple of times when Parker was on a bender, crying and verbally spewing nonsensical sentences about how much he loved his whole family. Those moments didn't count.

Struggling to respond, Derrick stared at the ceiling. All he could manage was, "Thanks, Parker, for your support." The words, the tone, the delivery—it couldn't have been a more thoroughly lame response.

After hanging up, Derrick threw his phone high into the air towards layers of square and round pillows stacked at the headboard of the bed. He thought back across the long arc of the day. Except for time with Coach Mac, the whole day had been a surreal mess. First, Mr. Clarke, then classes, then Nikki, then Parker. *I'm over it!* Derrick thought as he began to drift into a thin nap.

Before his sleep could thicken, Derrick heard the unmistakable sound of the garage door opening.

CHAPTER 15

The service door in the kitchen slammed shut. Keys jangled onto the counter. Footsteps moved away toward the living area of the condo. The next sound Derrick heard was the faint "whoosh" of someone collapsing into a heap on the sofa.

Derrick paused. He was torn. Should he wait? Should he move toward Nikki? *Dear God,* he prayed to no one in particular. *What am I supposed to do now?*

Derrick walked toward the door of the bedroom, halting at the doorway to reconsider his options. Then he strode toward the living room as casually as his emotional self-control would allow.

Nikki sat slumped on the coach. Her piercing green eyes looked up at Derrick, made even more stunningly beautiful as red lines and soft tears surrounded each emerald green iris. Derrick moved close, but not too close. He wasn't sure how to approach her.

"Nikki, what's wrong?" he asked.

"Do you love me, D?" Her question had no tone of anger or sarcasm. She was, however, distant and guarded.

"Nikki, I . . . I do. I mean, not as well or in the ways I want to . . ." he turned away for a moment before stumbling along. "What I mean is, yes, I *do* love you but, honestly, I'm not sure I know how to love you, in the way you want me to. I know that sounds like a stupid movie cliché, sorry." Derrick immediately felt annoyed by the words spewing thoughtlessly out of his mouth. Still, he stumbled on.

"Nik, when I look at my life right now, I am one hundred percent confused." Derrick stood motionless, the words hanging in the air, like a three-quarter court shot thrown in desperation toward the basket at the final buzzer. He reckoned his words had a lesser chance of success than a three-quarter court heave to win a game.

"D . . ." Nikki hesitated, "I have lived with you for half a year and not once have you spoken to me that honestly." Nikki paused. She intensified her scrutiny. "So, which are you, D? The defensive ranting guy I left earlier tonight or the open, honest guy I just met?"

"Well," Derrick started as he moved to the sofa, still maintaining his distance. "Coach and I had a conversation tonight, and . . ." Derrick scrambled for words like diving for a loose ball on the floor. "The truth is, Nikki, there's a part of me that's still that ranting guy. In fact, honestly, I'm probably mostly that ranting guy—for now. But I don't want to be 'that guy', Nikki. I wanted to say something like that so badly this afternoon, but then I completely blew the whole thing." Derrick stood up stiffly. His feet felt glued to the floor. Otherwise, he would have followed his default instincts and run out of the room. "Look, Nikki, I really do want to live with you and, of course, I love you. But not in the right way, not in the strong, courageous way I want to love you."

Derrick searched Nikki's eyes for any indication of what she was feeling. Seeing no signal he could interpret, Derrick added desperately, "Nikki, the only way that is going to happen is if I become a better man. I want to be that better man for you, Nikki."

"Do you really want that? To be with me? Be honest with yourself, D." Nikki couldn't read Derrick's face. Did she see hesitation? Hurt? Confusion? Wanting a sincere response she added, "Are you in love with me as a person or are you just in love with the idea of having a fun, live-in girlfriend—one who gives you sex and cheers for you at basketball games?" Nikki placed both hands on her chest, pointing her fingers toward her heart. "Honestly, D, do you really love me?"

Derrick looked directly into Nikki's eyes, then away. Then back again. This time Nikki knew what she saw on Derrick's face. Deep lines of sadness punctuated his watery eyes.

"Nikki," Derrick continued cautiously, "I do love you. I promise I do. But, if you're asking me to be honest . . ." Derrick paused again. He sat back down, this time much closer to Nikki.

Nikki nodded, turning her head to one side, and raising her eyebrows.

"Well, here's the truth," Derrick began, "I'm starting to think that I'm totally screwed up when it comes to relationships—like all of them. So, I don't really know what to think . . . about us, long term." Derrick leaned toward Nikki, adding, "I do know this: I've loved you, Nikki Coles, for a very long time. But I've not loved you *well* for a long time . . . if ever."

Nikki eyes narrowed. Her lips pursed together. She rose up straight to speak, then with a sigh slumped back down. She spoke softly, "D, I . . . I don't know what to say."

Derrick opened his mouth to clarify, but Nikki cut him off with her own words. "Derrick," Nikki added somberly, "to be, as Coach Mac always says, 'brutally honest,' I have to say that I have never felt more alone in my life than I have with you these past few months."

Nikki's words penetrated Derrick's chest like a jagged, rusty dagger. It was a fierce blow, mostly because Derrick knew it was true. Moving from the far end of the sofa, drawing himself close to Nikki, face to face, Derrick's voice quivered. He spoke directly into the green eyes that had captured his heart four years ago, eyes that he longed to see looking back at him with true respect, passion, and, above all, love. "Nikki, I am asking you to just give me a chance, just one more chance. If after these next few months—I don't know six months or whatever . . . if after that time I cannot commit my heart to you, to be your lover and, yes, your husband . . . if that's not in my heart or if I just can't man up to it . . . I will move out of this condo and away from you."

Derrick ceased his rambling. Nikki stared back at him blankly. Breaking the agonizing silence, Derrick pleaded, "Would you give me that chance?"

Nikki felt a violent struggle in her heart. She wanted to melt under Derrick's piercing blue eyes, the way he looked so handsome and sexy when he smiled at her, the way his words could make her feel warm and wonderful and beautiful all at once. It all made her want to say, "Yes."

Nikki pulled back, however, creating more distance between them. "Derrick, I used to dream that I would be the one to finally break down the thick walls you use to protect yourself." Nikki stood up, walking deliberately across the room. Leaning back on the wall, she added sorrowfully, "But, let's be honest," she continued firmly as her emotions began to regroup, "I'm not changing you, Derrick. You're changing me. And now I'm building my own walls—to protect me from you and your disinterest in me and my world. I don't want to live that way, Derrick. And I don't have to."

Her resolve having been restored, Nikki spoke compassionately. "I know you don't want to hear this. I know that you think my parents are just old-fashioned, unsophisticated, and way too religious country folk. And you think that way, because, well, they are," Nikki added with a half-smile. Then she continued, "But my mom told me, repeatedly, 'Nik, Derrick's not ready for the relationship you want. Your father and I are right about this boy—he can't love you the way you want him to love you. Maybe someday, but not right now."

Nikki wiped away a flood of tears that had begun pouring down both sides of her face. Her nose reddened to match her eyes as she struggled to overcome massive waves of grief. Having been damned up for a week, her tears ran like a torrent. She crossed her arms and looked down at the floor. Sniffling, she grabbed a nearby tissue and wiped her nose. Then she stood up straight, tossed her hair back, and directed her eyes back toward Derrick.

"But I love you, Nikki," Derrick replied, standing to move toward her. "I mean, I don't disagree with what you are saying, but don't give up on me—on us—yet."

"Stop." Nikki pleaded, stretching out her right hand to boundary Derrick's approach. "Just stop. I am kind of in shock right now."

After several uneven breaths and a loud sniffle, Nikki resumed eye contact with Derrick. As their eyes met, both trembled. Nikki pressed into Derrick's words angrily. "You gave up on me, first! Months ago." You traded me in for another life," Nikki cried. Tears of anger, sorrow, and relief flowed unrestrained as she confronted Derrick's abandonment of her heart.

"I get it, Nikki," Derrick affirmed sincerely. "There's no excuse for the man I've been in this relationship. But there is an explanation," Derrick added confidently. "The explanation is that your mom was right. I am not ready to be the man you need—the man you deserve. But if you would just give me a little more time, and a lot of grace . . ." Derrick's voice trailed off as he walked toward her cautiously. As he moved close enough to touch her, he pleaded, "I don't deserve you, Nikki. But I want you."

Nikki pulled away. "I don't know, D. I just . . ." Exasperated, Nikki added, "I planned to tell you tonight that it's over. That I'm leaving and going back to Iowa. But . . ."

"But?" Derrick asked, maintaining the personal space Nikki's movement had demanded. Nikki remained silent as she slumped back onto the sofa. "The 'but' is good, right?" Derrick said hopefully.

Nikki looked up at Derrick, responding with a sarcastic smirk. Her face melted into a slight smile. "But," Nikki said firmly as her smile receded, "I need time to think about it now. I am not going back to where things were, D. I don't know what I'm going to do, but I'm not going to do that."

"I understand. And you're right." Derrick sat in the chair directly across from Nikki's slouched body on the sofa. "We can't go back. I don't want that either."

Both stared straight ahead. After a few moments of silence, Derrick moved his hand within a few inches of Nikki's knee. Sighing a long, heavy sigh, Nikki lay her hand on Derrick's and squeezed gently. Then she rose, informing him, "I am going to get ready for bed. I am exhausted and I have to get some sleep. I'm going to sleep in the guest room tonight."

Derrick couldn't hide his disappointment, "Sure. I get it," Derrick said with sorrowful resignation. "But I should be the one to go into the guest room. It'll be easier for me to make the move." Nikki did not protest. Instead, she began making her way out of the living area toward the hallway.

Recovering a more positive tone, Derrick said, "Hey, Nikki, I'm going to stay up for a while longer anyway. I asked Coach Mac to coach me about life and relationships. He agreed but told me I had to start writing in a journal. So . . ." Derrick moved toward the counter where a blue spiral notebook lay. Picking up the notebook, he observed sheepishly, ". . . I need to get writing. And this has certainly given me something to write about."

Nikki laughed out loud. "What? A journal—like one you actually write in? Are you serious? Do I even know you anymore, Derrick Walker?" Her shoulders relaxed as her face broke into a light-hearted smile.

"I am not sure either of us knows me anymore, Nikki. By the way, please don't tell anyone I have a journal. Especially Parker!"

"Okay, sure, sure . . . you're right he would be merciless . . . And, just so you know, girls think guys with journals are sexy," Nikki teased Derrick. Her guard having slipped momentarily, she added severely, "I shouldn't have said that."

"That's okay. But don't be surprised if I buy two journals now," Derrick responded playfully.

Nikki rolled her eyes, then added, "Goodnight, D."

"Goodnight, Nikki. Oh, wait," Derrick questioned. "Are you still coming to the game Thursday night?'

"Yes, remember, I'm bringing Mrs. Gracie."

"Will you talk to her about this?" Derrick asked nervously.

"Do you not want me to?"

"No . . . I mean, yes, it's okay if you want to. I trust her as much as I trust Coach Mac." Then Derrick added weakly, "Maybe you should. It might help."

"Yeah," Nikki replied. "Maybe she can help us make sense of this whole mess."

"Coach Mac calls her a 'grace-giver.' I don't know what that means, but I think it's in my favor."

"This isn't a competition, Derrick. It's not about winning or losing," Nikki responded critically.

"Nikki, I didn't . . ." Derrick started then stopped. Walking toward her, he continued tenderly, "I'm sorry. You're right. Like I said, I'm pretty screwed when it comes to relationships."

Nikki stood motionless. "Well, I suppose we both are, right? Otherwise we wouldn't have gotten each other into this mess. Goodnight, D." Nikki turned quickly, removing herself from the moment as quickly as possible.

Once Nikki had left the room, Derrick made his way to the kitchen counter. Grabbing a pen from a faded blue and gold Northfield cup next to the refrigerator, he sat down at the kitchen table. To write. In a journal. Only because he had no idea what else to do at this point.

Opening to page one, he wrote:

Derrick Walker's Journal

DAY 1

Maxim 1 : PURPOSE

"My first commitment will be to a purpose greater than myself."

WHY DO I LIVE MY LIFE THE WAY I DO?

Derrick paused. He knew the answer. He had always known the answer. Derrick felt a small tremor in his body as he came face to face with the mirror of his truth. He knew instinctively that, once he wrote this truth down, there was no turning back.

WHY DO I LIVE MY LIFE THE WAY I DO?

Because I am afraid. I am afraid of not being enough, of losing Nikki, of being Northfield's biggest screw up AGAIN, of turning into Carl Walker.

Derrick stared at the hastily scribbled, barely legible words on the first page of his flimsy spiral notebook. His body, suddenly chilled from the inside out, shook with a rolling wave of small tremors. Clasping his hands behind his head, Derrick closed his eyes as he tilted his head backwards.

"Derrick?" Nikki startled Derrick as she leaned around the corner of the doorway. "I want you to know that I know this isn't just about you . . ." Nikki hesitated. Her eyes fell as she picked at the end of her sweater sleeve pulled over her left hand. Looking back toward Derrick's eyes, she continued, "I also want you to know, if the man I talked with tonight is the beginning of the man you are going to be . . . Well, don't hold me to this, but, you know," Nikki chewed on her inner lower lip, then continued, "maybe that's the guy I'm already in love with." Nikki shrugged her shoulders, then used both hands to pull her hair back in an unsecured ponytail.

The tension in Derrick's face morphed into a pleasing smile. "I don't think that guy has any idea what he's missing, Nikki—but I'm going to coach him up." Derrick swallowed hard, pressing his emotions back down into his chest. Clearing his throat, Derrick looked away momentarily. Gathering himself he added, "Because you're the one thing that guy—me—needs most."

Nikki's mouth turned upward slightly. She began to turn back toward the bedroom, then paused. Nikki glanced back over her right shoulder, her auburn ponytail swaying back and forth. Nikki studied Derrick, her right eyebrow raised with curiosity. She opened her mouth, hesitated, then turned. Silently she slipped away.

In the silence of the room, Derrick rehearsed Nikki's words over and over in his mind. *If the man I talked with tonight is the beginning of the man you are going to be . . . Maybe that's the guy I'm already in love with.*

Derrick turned back to his journal. Opening to page two, Derrick looked upward. He imagined the expansive starlit winter sky that lay on the other side of the roof. For the first time in his life, Derrick Walker wrote a prayer.

God, HELP! Please let me be that guy for Nikki.

CHAPTER 16

amarcus, I am turning the rest over to you." Coach Mac stepped to the side. At the edge of a moment that could define their Northfield legacy, all eyes turned to Jamarcus.

Jamarcus stood tall. He began a soft, slow cadence that gradually gained speed and volume as he spoke. "Since I could walk, all I ever wanted to be was a Northfield basketball player. Since I came to the first 'Little Norsemen' Kids Camp, the only coach I ever wanted to play for was Coach Mac. Since I was in middle school, the only point guard I've ever wanted running my team was Zeke. Since I was in ninth grade, when we lost the state championship to West Chamberlain, a team we should've beaten by 20, all I ever wanted was to reclaim our rightful place as number one.

"Since we repeated as state champions last year, all I ever wanted was to be was the first team in Northfield history to be back-to-back-to-back state champions. Tonight, we take the next step toward that dream coming true. And tonight, on this court, there is only one thing that can prevent us from taking that step."

The players and the coaches hung on every carefully chosen, passionate word.

"Do you hear me, men?" Jamarcus' voice rose. "Only ONE THING can prevent us from taking our rightful place as the number one team— in this region and the state!" He lowered his voice, almost down to a whisper. "And, brothers, that one thing . . ." The players held their collective breath. Then Jamarcus added sternly, "That one thing is not the West Chamberlain Bulldogs."

Like a revival preacher, Jamarcus paused to let his words capture the moment. With a long, sweeping motion, Jamarcus waved his left arm dramatically. He pointed toward the door that led to the Bulldogs' home court. He then pointed to himself before pointing at each player who sat before him.

"WE are the one thing that can lead us to defeat."

His cadence locked in at full speed, Jamarcus championed his conviction. "We are the only ones who can lead us to victory. Now," raising both hands to signal his congregation's movement, "Stand with me, men, as we recite the Northfield Way Maxims, loud and proud!"

Following Jamarcus' cadence, the team spoke in unison their shared vision:

PURPOSE
"My first commitment will be to a purpose greater than myself."

PASSION
"My first response to pressure will be passion."

LOVE
"My first priority will be love."

RESPONSIBILITY
"My first responsibility will be to lead myself."

HUMILITY
"My first ambition will be to serve with strength, courage, and humility."

Like a wildfire driven by huge gusts of wind, the energy in the room surged with each consecutive maxim. Then, without prompting, each player and their coaches placed a hand into the team's impromptu huddle. Jamarcus' voice ascended to the top once more as the team repeated the prayer of the Northfield Way, "Lord, make us strong, make us courageous, make us leaders. Amen!"

The team exploded out of the locker room and into their pre-game warm-up routine. The Warrior squad resembled nothing of the weak-willed, weak-minded team the Northfield Nation had witnessed in Monday night's loss. The Warriors were back, with a vengeance. The crowd knew it. The coaches knew it. The Northfield players knew it—and so did the West Chamberlain Bulldogs.

By some reports, ninety percent of the population of Northfield was jammed into the visitors' section of the expansive West Chamberlain Bulldog Arena. The standing-room-only crowd had amassed a full thirty minutes prior to tipoff. At midcourt, two rows off the floor, sat Nikki and Mrs. Gracie. Shoved tightly against one another, both were well adorned in Northfield navy and gold. Mrs. Gracie wore a cotton surgical mask to shield her vulnerable immune system from possible threats in the crowded air space around her. Nikki grinned nervously as the starting players shook hands around the center circle.

The game began with the Bulldogs controlling the opening tip. Methodically, they worked the ball inside to "Big Jim" Jenkins. The powerful Jenkins banked a turn-around jump shot from the right-hand short corner.

"If we are going to give them that shot, it's going to be a long night," Derrick shouted toward Coach Mac as the home crowd screamed its approval.

As soon as the ball had passed through the net, Marcus Litchfield snatched it in mid-air and headed to the baseline. Rushing to inbound, he lofted the ball to Zeke who caught the ball in stride at about one-fourth court. Zeke took two dribbles and lobbed the ball ahead to Jamarcus who slammed the ball into the basket with two hands. The whistle blew and Kevin Bolton of the Bulldogs had his first foul. Jamarcus calmly sank the free throw.

The successful free throw triggered the frenzied Fury press defense. By the time a loud whistle blew, followed by the PA announcer's words, "Timeout, Bulldogs," the lead had swelled to 8-2, Northfield.

The five starting Warriors danced their way toward their bench. High fives, fist bumps, and chest bumps punctuated their arrival.

"Congratulations, men, you just won two minutes of a basketball game. That's all," Coach Mac said flatly. "They're going to counterpunch and you need to be ready," he continued. "Coach D, how do you want to respond defensively?"

"Let's stay with our trapping full court man-to-man Fury press. Guards, stay right in their faces, force the inbounding player to make a hard pass and risk the steal. If he gets the ball in, defend the middle against the pass. Big men, do not let your man behind you. Be smart— but above all, be aggressive! Don't let up—we have a long way to go!" Derrick asserted, his voice brimming with confidence.

The rest of the quarter saw the Bulldogs struggle to advance the ball against the attacking Warrior defense. When they did manage to get the ball into their frontcourt, their half-court offense had only limited success. The Bulldogs' big men managed only a couple of put backs following offensive rebounds.

At the other end, the Bulldogs' 2-3 zone gradually put up a stiff fight against the hard driving Northfield offense. The Warriors were called for two offensive charges, one by Jamarcus and the other by Rico. Trying to shoot the Bulldogs out of their zone, the Warrior guards were a poor 1-4 from behind the three-point line. Zeke finally hit his second three as the first quarter buzzer sounded. The score was Northfield 15, West Chamberlain 8.

At the start of the second quarter, Derrick continued to step confidently into his role as defensive coordinator. To disrupt the Bulldogs, Derrick switched the team into its 1-3-1 trapping half-court defense. The 1-3-1 was risky against the Bulldogs' huge frontcourt, but carried the advantage of the element of surprise. Unfortunately, the team played the 1-3-1 with an alarming lack of urgency. The momentum quickly shifted to West Chamberlain. Coach Mac, shaking his head with disgust, yelled, "Timeout!"

Coach Mac stepped aside, taking Derrick with him for a quick coaching sidebar. In the meantime, the players angrily grumbled about their failure to hold the Bulldogs down.

Coach Mac and Derrick returned to the bench. "Coach Walker and I agree on what needs to be done next. You and you and you," Coach

Mac shouted as he pointed to Zeke, Jamarcus, and Marcus, "are rotating too slowly on the 1-3-1. Your lack of pressure is putting the weak side at risk. And all of you, get your doggone hands up before I lose my mind! You're all passive!"

Coach Mac pounded his right fist up and down as he yelled over the noise of the crowd, "You've gone soft because you have a lead. Now, take personal responsibility to play the zone the way we practiced it. Or, I *will* find players who want to play our way, the Northfield Way!"

"Coach is right." Jamarcus spoke directly to his teammates. "We didn't do our jobs. We let up on 'em! LET'S STEP IT UP NOW!"

Coach Derrick leaned in to challenge the players, "PRESSURE. PRESSURE. PRESSURE the man with the ball. Trap at the foul line extended and the corners. Thor, you stay in front of Jenkins! Wings, get weak side rebounding position. Overplay the passing lanes! Now let's get this thing done!"

The hyped Warriors quickly regained control of the game, stretching their lead to an impressive 25-12 margin. The run set fire to the anger of the Bulldogs' coach, Rod Baker. Following a blistering tirade by Coach Baker during a timeout, the West Chamberlain five began to execute with more patience and determination. However, they managed to regain only a small bit of ground. The teams jogged off the court at halftime with the score Northfield 33, West Chamberlain 23.

During halftime, both teams' coaches addressed improving the execution of their original game plans. Coach Mac stressed how, in spite of a solid lead, the Warriors were lacking a sufficient killer instinct. He waved his long pointing finger towards his starting five, challenging them to "start the second half as if you are ten points behind, not ten points ahead."

The Northfield coaches agreed to begin the second half in the same manner they had begun the game, utilizing the Fury press. Though the results were not as exceptional as the game's first two minutes, the Warriors ultimately extended their lead to 43-30. Given this success, Coach Mac's sudden timeout shocked the five players on the court.

The players looked at one another with uncertainty as they made their way toward the bench. Coach Mac awaited them, arms crossed, eyes staring without blinking. The starters took their place on the bench. Looking up, they held their breath. They waited, all the while wiping sweat off their faces and arms. For several seconds, he said nothing. Then, Coach Mac broke the silence with a soft-spoken question, "Men, do you want Jamarcus Denton's dreams to come true?"

"If you mean the basketball ones, then yeah," Rico said with a big grin.

"Thanks for clarifying, Rico," Coach Mac responded with a roll of his eyes. Contagious laughter released the team's pent-up tension. Coach Mac smiled momentarily, then returned to the severe look that had welcomed them to the bench.

"Men, do not let up! Give me five more minutes of your highest passion," Coach Mac continued in his deepest, loudest voice, "Put this team away now. Don't leave them an opening. If you do, I guarantee you they will take it. If you want to be champions, you have to finish off teams like this. Leave nothing to chance."

Coach Mac's words were forceful. They were inspiring. And, for reasons yet unknown to the Warriors, they would prove to be extraordinarily memorable.

Jamarcus held out his hands, awaiting the handoff from the ref. Zeke stood poised to receive the inbounds pass. The remaining Warriors faced in Jamarcus' direction as well. That placed the Northfield bench somewhere behind their line of sight.

As the referee turned toward Jamarcus to hand him the ball, the roaring crowd suddenly fell silent. Someone directly behind the Northfield bench began shrieking wildly, "Oh my god!! Oh my god!! Oh my god!!"

The Northfield players instantly pivoted. Their eyes locked on a small area near their bench. The space was being hastily filled by two referees along with Derrick and the Bulldogs' Coach Baker. All four were bent over the floor, hovering over whatever or whomever lay below them.

"Coach Mac!!!" Zeke yelled. Then he and Jamarcus rushed in a full sprint to the crowded circle near the scorer's table. As soon as they arrived, the reality of the moment struck the young captains. Coach John McKissack lay motionless on the floor.

Frightened and disoriented, the players pleaded for an explanation. Distraught, Zeke and Jamarcus yanked Derrick aside. As they did so, two doctors arrived from the stands to attend to Coach Mac.

Zeke and Jamarcus hurled rapid-fire questions toward Derrick.

"Is he breathing?"

"For real, what happened?"

"C'mon, man, why can't we see our coach!"

"This is so wrong, nobody's talking to us!!"

Jamarcus, seeing his beloved Coach lying motionless, yelled,

"C'mon, Coach—you're gonna be all right!! You gotta be!!"

Derrick motioned the two captains and the rest of the team toward the bench. As paramedics arrived, Derrick directed the players, in spite of their resistance, farther away from the alarming scene.

Nikki passed by, walking arm in arm with Gracie McKissack toward the scorer's table. Her eyes caught Derrick's. She immediately looked away, shielding herself from bursting into tears.

Passing the players, Gracie reassured the team, "It's going to be okay, boys. I promise you, it's going to be okay."

"Guys, stay here." Derrick instructed. "I am going to see if I can find out what's going on."

Jamarcus Denton grabbed the guys by their jerseys, drew them close in a circle. Taking turns around the circle, the players began pleading with God on behalf of their coach and leader. Half of the team had never uttered an actual prayer, except for the ritual of reciting the team prayer. In this moment, however, no one could doubt that their frantic prayers were an authentic search for divine help. A similar scene could be observed on the Bulldogs' end of the court, as their Assistant Coach Wes Harriman led his team in prayer.

Drawing close, Derrick saw Coach Mac lying immobilized on his back. Thankfully, he had regained consciousness.

"Thank you, Jesus!" Derrick shouted reflexively, not religiously.

"I'm fine, I just passed out. I'm fine. Just let me get back to coaching." Coach Mac began to argue intensely with the young paramedic. He treated the EMT like she was a referee who had just made a bad call on his Warrior team.

On the Northfield bench, players applauded, yelled, and collapsed with exhausted relief onto the floor. On both sides of the arena, a collective sigh of relief filled the stands. Celebrative hugs among Bulldog fans were no less in number than those among the Northfield Nation section.

As Gracie made her way to his side, a large male paramedic slowly assisted Coach Mac in sitting up. Coach Mac reached out to receive Gracie's worried embrace. "My Gracie, I am so sorry to worry you. But I am fine."

Gracie smiled broadly. As she relaxed, tears streamed down her face in rapid succession.

"Okay, okay, enough of this nonsense. I need to get back to coaching my team. Coach Walker, call a timeout and let's get regrouped," Coach Mac barked.

"I am sorry, sir." The female paramedic's tone was respectful, yet resolute. "We need to take you to the hospital for observation. They will need to run some tests."

"Tests? What kind of tests? I just passed out. Probably too little sleep last night. I'm fine. Tests? You've got to be kidding me," Coach Mac argued.

"Sir," she responded firmly, "you may have experienced any number of medical episodes. Returning to the game without being checked . . . well, let me blunt, sir, that could be potentially life threatening." The stretcher arrived. The young attendant continued, "I know you want to be here—everyone wants you here, even the other team's fans want you here!" She smiled, placing her left hand gently on his shoulder. "Look around you—it's crazy," she added. She motioned with her hand sweeping towards both sides of the gym. "But it's our job to get you onto this stretcher, into the ambulance, and to the hospital as soon as possible. Please, sir, for your sake, for your wife, for everyone, let us help you onto the stretcher."

Coach Mac silently relented. As the paramedics transferred Coach Mac onto the stretcher, he motioned Derrick to come toward him.

"D . . . Derrick?" Coach Mac called out.

"Coach, you had us scared, man. We are so glad to see you're going to be okay." Derrick's voice sounded giddy, almost childlike.

"D, bring the team over here. I need a minute with them before they cart me off on this dang thing."

"Sir, we really need to get moving," the paramedic interrupted. Agitated, she reminded Coach Mac, "We need to get you to the hospital."

"Look, I'm going to go," Coach Mac said in a huff. "But I insist on one minute with my team."

"You're a hard man to say no to, sir," she said with resignation. Sighing deeply, she held up her right index finger, pressing it toward Coach Mac adamantly, "Okay, one minute—and I mean *one* minute."

"You'd make a great coach," Coach Mac teased.

"One minute," the paramedic said, ignoring Coach Mac's charm.

Derrick brought the whole team to the stretcher. Arms around each other in a tight circle, joined by Gracie and Nikki, the players alternately wiped wet eyes on their shoulders and jerseys. Each spoke words of encouragement to Coach Mac.

Coach Mac called out, "Men, recite Maxim 2 to me loud and proud,"

They spoke as one, nearly screaming the words,

PASSION. *"My first response to pressure will be passion."*

"I am going to be okay—and so are you," Coach Mac added. "You've stepped up tonight, *everyone of you*, for the first 20 minutes of the game. Now you have to put this whole episode out of your minds. Focus only on playing with passion for the last twelve minutes. Trust Coach Walker. He's ready to step up and be your point leader. Men, you step and lead, too. Understood?"

Every player nodded vigorously. Each added his own enthusiastic, unique version of, "Don't worry, Coach, we've got this!"

Nikki, standing at Derrick's side, squeezed his arm and pulled herself close.

"Sir, your minute is up!" the young paramedic demanded.

"Okay, okay. Fellas, I'll see you tomorrow at practice."

"Don't worry, Coach Mac. We're going to win this game for you," Rico said, his voice quivering slightly.

"No, no you're not," Coach Mac replied firmly. "You're going to win this game for all of us, every player and fan and member of the Northfield community. This is our win, not mine."

A chorus of, "Yes sir," rang out in unison.

As the stretcher was hurriedly wheeled out the door, fans from every row and corner of the gym clapped, stomped, and shouted their respect for Coach Mac. For his part, Coach Mac gave a reassuring two-thumbs-up signal all the way out the door.

Stunned, the Northfield faithful struggled to come to terms with their new reality. If Coach Mac was indeed to win game number 679 tonight, if he was to become the state's winningest coach in history, the job would have to be finished by his assistant, Derrick "D" Walker, the same D Walker who, just eight years earlier, had completely destroyed all hopes of the state's number one team winning a state championship.

West Chamberlain's Coach Baker huddled briefly with the officials, the principals of the two schools, the two athletic directors, and the newly appointed Northfield Interim Head Coach Walker. After a few moments of dialogue, Coach Baker took the PA announcer's cordless microphone.

"Ladies and gentlemen, we are going to continue the game. We are thankful that Coach Mac is doing well. We will continue to keep him in our thoughts and prayers. We know that finishing the game is what Coach Mac would want us to do—especially since his team has a 13-point lead!" Laughter rippled through both teams' fan bases, lessening the heaviness that had settled into the stands. Coach Baker continued, "We will take a short three minutes to warm up. Then we will continue. Before we do so, however, I would like to ask you to join me in a moment of silence. Please either think positive thoughts for or pray for Coach Mac. He is currently headed to Bellmire Hospital for observation and testing."

After a brief period of silence and the abbreviated warm-ups, the teams took the court again. For the first time in almost four decades, the Northfield men's basketball team would face an opponent without the powerful presence of Coach John McKissack. It was a moment no one in Lewis County could have been prepared to for, least of all Interim Head Coach Derrick Walker.

CHAPTER 17

Rico inbounded the ball to Zeke to resume the game. The play unfolded precisely the way Derrick had designed it during the time-out, and Zeke quickly swung the ball to Marcus Litchfield on the left wing. Thor Thornton rotated from the short block on the left side up to the high post. As he did, he drew the attention of the long, tall Bulldog frontcourt. At that exact moment, Jamarcus peeled off his position on the lower wing, and headed to the basket on the baseline. Marcus' lob pass was perfectly timed and perfectly placed.

Jamarcus approached the rim, and the Northfield Nation faithful rose to their feet in anticipation of the monster slam dunk. Jamarcus hammered the ball into the net with powerful authority and a fierce primal scream.

Responding as if they were one being, the crowd released the tension that had been building since Coach Mac collapsed. The arena practically shook under their feet. The cheerleaders ratcheted up the emotion, stirring the Northfield Nation into a frenzy. "WE ARE!" the cheerleaders screamed. The Nation responded rowdily, "NORTHFIELD!"

Less than three more minutes of game time passed before West Chamberlain called a timeout. In that short span, the Northfield lead had widened from 43-30 to 51-34.

As the ambulance turned hurriedly onto Bellmire Hospital Drive, Gracie saw the red neon lights that said "EMERGENCY ROOM." At that very moment, her cell phone vibrated. She ignored the text until Coach Mac said, "Maybe it's about the game—you better take it."

Gracie glanced at the screen and read the sender's name: Nikki C. Her text read:

Up 51-34, 1:44 to go in the third quarter. Coach Mac would be so proud!! Northfield looks unbeatable.

Gracie read most of the text to Coach Mac, carefully editing out the final sentence. Sixty-two years of living and thirty-six years of being a coach's wife had taught her, if nothing else, that no one and no team should ever be described with the word, "unbeatable."

The Bulldog squad had returned four of their five starters from last season. Alton Evers, the lone exception, was having a miserable night shooting the ball, going 0-6. In his place, Coach Baker inserted a pale-skinned, thin-as-a-rail #13 who possessed arms and legs far too long for his body. Alongside the large, man-sized Bulldog front-court, #13 looked like an awkward seventh-grader at best.

With Jamarcus and Zeke having three fouls each, Derrick called off the full-court pressure. "Lay off the press, but keep them away from the basket. Don't trap unless the ball gets into the corner. But DON'T BE PASSIVE!" Derrick had barked just before the players returned to battle.

West Chamberlain hurried the ball up court. As the ball passed the half-court line, "Big Jim" Jenkins sat a crushing screen on Rico, freeing #13 for a pass from Datavius Johnson. The kid caught the pass and, almost simultaneously, he released a 21-foot three-pointer that was nothing but net.

Before inbounding the ball, the ref stopped play. Rico was bent over, rubbing his jaw, his face wincing in sharp pain. Derrick summoned TJ Moore into the game for Jensen.

"For the love of . . . men, call out the screens!" he yelled angrily. "You could have gotten Rico killed!" Derrick's anxiety spiked.

A medical team took Rico to the locker room for concussion protocol. Then play resumed. The shaken Warriors responded with a lob pass to Thor. Standing only five feet from the basket, the hulking forward shot softly toward the backboard. The Bulldogs' Jenkins elevated quickly and achieved his fourth block of the game. The gangly #13 picked up the ball at full speed, heading toward the basket with Moore in hot pursuit. This time the kid pulled up at 20 feet. Whether it was his pump fake or the fact that Moore had just entered the game. Moore fouled him in the act of shooting. The foul had knocked #13 off balance, but just enough to cause the ball to bank in for a three.

"Where did this kid come from?" Derrick called out rhetorically.

Bam Bam Wells, not catching that the question was rhetorical, called out, "He's a new transfer from somewhere out east, Coach Walker. My dad told me about him. His dad was a big-time D1 player—Syracuse, I think. Just became eligible this semester, I heard."

Derrick looked at Wells, blinked a couple of times, then returned his focus to the game.

"The kid," as he would be known for the rest of the game, calmly sank his free throw to complete the four-point play. Forty-five seconds remained in the third quarter. The lead had shrunk, from 51-31 to 51-38, in less than thirty seconds.

Derrick held up one fist to instruct Styles to run a motion play against the Bulldogs' 2-3 zone. The play included setting screens against their top two defenders to free up three-point shooters. "We'll fight fire with hotter fire," Derrick confidently announced to his bench.

The "downtown" play, as it was called, included three well executed passes and an outstanding screen by Marcus. Catching the ball with no one to pressure him, Zeke lifted high off the court, lofting a soft three-point shot. The ball initiated a circular movement as soon as it touched the rim. At one point, the orange sphere dipped below the top edge of the rim, but it ultimately rimmed out. Leaping from his wing position,

Jamarcus exploded above the huge Bulldog defenders. He grabbed the ball violently with his massive, powerful right hand pulling it into his chest with a sweeping, ripping motion. Rising above his equally large opponents, Jamarcus' superior athleticism was on full display. There were oohs and aahs from both sides of the gym as Jamarcus returned to the ground.

On landing, he immediately let out an agonizing scream, crashing into a heap on the ground with a loud thud. The massive power forward sat up immediately, pounding his right fist to the floor in thunderous blows accentuated by loud wails of, "NO! NO!"

Racing toward the writhing Jamarcus, an official immediately whistled the play dead. The Bulldogs' Jenkins and Bolton were the first on the scene. Concerned, they knelt beside their wounded opponent and motioned rapidly for a trainer to come onto the court.

The first Northfield player to come to Jacmarcus' aid was his closest friend of seven years, Isaiah "Zeke" Styles. Before the trainer and Derrick could get to the fallen player's side, Zeke had already begun helping Jamarcus to his feet. The self-proclaimed brothers, both unwilling to accept the reality of the situation, began to walk together. But after two agonizing steps, the pain of Jamarcus' injured ankle put him back on his knees.

"Just wait, Jamarcus, just wait. Help's coming," Zeke reassured him with a calm voice. He pressed his eyes shut in a desperate attempt to block out the reality of the situation.

The Northfield faithful once again stood in stunned silence. Some prayed. Others held hands. Still others sat motionlessly, their faces void of expression. The two greatest and most beloved Fighting Warriors ever known to the Northfield Nation, Coach Mac and Jamarcus Denton, had been sent helplessly to the floor in a span of less than fifteen minutes. The hearts of the Northfield faithful had plummeted with them.

"Coach Mac, I am Dr. Sam Barone. My nephew, Brent Barone, played for you a few years ago. It's truly a pleasure to meet you personally—though I do wish it were under better circumstances."

Coach Mac extended his large hand and, gripping Dr. Barone's hand with vise-like strength, replied, "Glad to meet you as well. Brent is a fine young man, with great character. I am proud to have been his coach. . . So, how long until I can be back with my team, doc? It's already late in the third quarter."

"Well, sir, I'm afraid you won't make it back tonight," Dr. Barone's voice was warm and patient, but also very serious.

"What's wrong with Coach, Dr. Barone?" Gracie inquired with a shallow, quivering voice.

"We don't know. The most likely diagnosis, given the preliminary readings from the monitors in the ambulance, is that is that it's not immediately life-threatening. But we have to rule out, conclusively, all potentially serious diagnoses, Coach Mac." Dr. Barone moved closer to both Gracie and Coach Mac as he delivered the news. He placed his right hand reassuringly on Coach Mac's broad shoulder, rubbing his back with small, comforting circles. Dr. Barone smiled warmly, then continued, "Losing consciousness is a significant event, at any age. At your age, we have to treat this as a potentially serious matter. But let's remain optimistic and not worry about what we don't know."

"So, Dr. Barone. There's no bad news so far, right?" Gracie asked.

"Correct—and for that we can be thankful. But I don't want to make a premature diagnosis. Sit tight, try to relax, and we'll get this underway. By the way, I heard on the radio your team had the game well in hand. I know that's really good news for you, Coach."

"Hasn't Nikki texted any more updates?" Coach Mac pressed Gracie impatiently, ignoring the doctor's comments. "She was supposed to keep you posted."

"Don't worry. D has it well in hand and I'm sure Nikki will text us a final score," Gracie responded. Moving to his side, Gracie brushed aside the various wires and tubes attached to the beloved Coach's suddenly vulnerable body. Kissing him gently on the lips, she then drew back ever so slightly. "It's just you and me, right now, Johnny. That's what it always comes down to in the end. Just you and me. And," she added tenderly, "We always make it, don't we, Coach?"

"Yes, we do," Coach Mac replied with a wink. "Love always creates a way, Gracie. And I sure love you."

Gracie Mac laid her head on her husband's chest. For a moment, she lay there lost in the memories of all they had been through over the decades. Then, raising her head off her husband's rising and falling chest, Gracie asked sweetly, "What are you thinking about, Johnny?"

"I sure hope D keeps the pressure on their guards. That Bulldog squad is dangerous if they get the ball inside, Gracie."

"You're such a hopeless romantic, Johnny Mac," Gracie Mac replied, softly slapping his massive chest with her tiny hand.

Coach Mac reached out, swallowing her hand into his. Gracie climbed into the bed, nestling her small frame alongside his wide, long body. In the silence that followed, four decades of relationship enveloped them in the security of a love that was deep and fierce.

The Northfield crowd, dazed and disheartened, applauded nervously as Marcus and Thor helped Jamarcus to the bench. Arms around their shoulders, Jamarcus hobbled off the court on his remaining good leg and ankle.

As they headed toward the bench, Derrick pressed the Northfield trainer for information. "What do you think, Sara? Can you tell what happened?"

"We won't know until we have an x-ray. Maybe an MRI. It could be that we are just looking at a painful sprain. In that case, he could be back in a week or so with an aggressive treatment plan. But, worse-case scenario, he has either a broken bone or torn ligaments." As they reached the bench, Sara turned to face Derrick. Making eye direct eye contact, he informed the anxious young coach, "If either of those is true, that's it for the season."

"Can you take him to the hospital now, to get an x-ray?" Derrick pleaded.

"Already on it. Jamarcus' dad, Martin, is out of town. But Mrs. Denton said she and his grandmother would pull up to the back door of the gym. We'll take him through the training room and out the back. You can check in on him after the game."

"Along with Coach Mac," Derrick couldn't hide his frustration, or his disappointment.

Over the roar of the night's second standing ovation for a wounded Warrior, Derrick yelled "TIMEOUT!"

Pulling the huddle into tight formation, Derrick took charge of the moment. "Men, I want each of you to look me right in the eye. I need your undivided attention." Derrick pointed two fingers towards his eyes. "We have been presented with a severe test. But our "WHY" is big enough for us to pass this test. If we can't play the game with Jamarcus and Coach Mac, then let's play the game for them! Remember, WE ARE . . ."

"Northfield!" the team replied with restrained enthusiasm.

Derrick prayed for the third time in the last two days. All three prayers formed around one simple word: "Help."

CHAPTER 18

Slowly, steadily the lead slipped away. The Warriors played like a muscle-fatigued climber who, having accidentally slipped off the ledge of a 100-foot cliff, now clung wearily to a single branch. Fatigued by the disheartening losses of their key leaders, the Northfield Warriors were losing their collective grip.

Rico had returned early in the fourth quarter after testing negative for concussion symptoms. His speed and aggressiveness had given the Warriors a desperately needed energy boost. Still, even with the ball in their hands, they were clearly not on the offensive. To a man, they were playing not to lose. Derrick could hear Coach Mac's words in his mind as clearly as if his mentor were standing right next to him, *"Winners play to win, losers play not to lose."* On the clock, 3:22 remained. Something had to be done.

"TIMEOUT!" Derrick screamed as a well-executed Bulldog trap in the corner put the Warriors' control of the ball at great risk. The Northfield five shuffled to the bench, heads down and hands on their hips. Zeke looked positively dazed.

"Look over at your opponents. Seriously, look at them," Derrick demanded as the players huddled listlessly around him. The team all turned in the direction of the Bulldog bench. Their compliant glances lasted less than three seconds each. The players had no idea and, therefore, no interest in what their coach wanted them to see.

"Now, look at the 2000 Bulldog fans—go on, look at them." Derrick was adamant. The players turned awkwardly toward the home stands, compelled only by Derrick's forceful tone. "You know what they are saying to you? Do you know?" Derrick demanded.

"You suck?" Rico blurted. To his credit, that was literally what the Bulldog student section was chanting. Ignoring Rico, Coach Derrick continued, "They're looking at you and saying to you, *Is that all you got? You don't have Coach Mac. You don't have Jamarcus. You don't have what it takes to beat us!*"

Moments earlier, the players had stood with arms crossed. Disengaged and distancing themselves from their coach, they appeared passive. On Zeke's lead, however, they now leaned in with arms uncrossed.

"Men, you know how Coach Mac always says it, 'Attack or be attacked'? Which one is happening right now?"

"We're being attacked—and we're playing scared," Thor exploded.

Zeke spewed. "Man, we got what it takes! I'm talking about all of us, Coach Walker, me, you, all of us—WE GOT WHAT IT TAKES!"

"Zeke," Derrick's eyes widened as he looked into the eyes of the Warrior senior point guard. "Coming out of the timeout, I want you to hit a three. Which side?"

"The left, Coach."

"Okay, run downtown with Thor setting the high ball screen on the guard on Zeke's left side of the zone. As soon as Zeke hits the three, we get after them with our man-to-man trapping press.

The players looked at Coach Walker; they were beginning to feed on their energy, but were still hesitant. "What if Zeke misses?" Marcus asked aloud the question they were all thinking in silence.

Derrick turned to Zeke. His stare placed the leadership mantle squarely on Zeke's young shoulders. "I got you, coach. I won't miss."

"Remember, man-to-man trap," Derrick added hurriedly as the buzzer sounded. "Everybody, take chances on the inbounds—Marcus you make sure they can't make the home run pass to one of their big men. All right, let's get the win!"

The play call worked perfectly. Zeke hit a 21-foot three that was perfectly dropped into the middle of the basket, making a popping sound as it exited the net. The entire Northfield section erupted with clapping, screaming, and dancing. The scoreboard read 60-54 Northfield with 3:05 left in the game. Unprepared for the pressure and the intensity of the Northfield man-to-man press, the Bulldogs' Johnson dribbled the ball off his foot on the ensuing inbounds play.

"Attack or be attacked," Derrick smiled to himself.

"TIMEOUT!!" Coach Baker yelled with transparent disgust.

"Perfect!! We ambushed them! Now remember, we're in the Fury press with Ty on the inbounds. Marcus, nothing deep. Rico, Zeke, Thor, TJ, take chances on the inbound pass. Any questions?"

"No, sir," every valiant Warrior shouted in unison.

Rico added, "We can do this, men. We *have* to do this. RIGHT NOW."

The inspired Warriors executed the Fury press perfectly. Rico stole the ball on the inbounds, passing to TJ Moore, who cut across the middle of the lane. TJ lofted a short jumper. To TJ's surprise, the Bulldogs' six-foot-seven-inch Billy Hayes, who had made the errant inbounds pass, reached out to make contact with the ascending ball. Hayes' swat sent the ball like a cannon back to half court, where Bolton picked it up. Passing ahead, Bolton hit to the streaking Johnson for an other-worldly slam dunk. The Bulldogs served notice that the last 2:49 were going to be a dog fight to the finish.

With the lead whittled down to 60-56, Rico missed the next Warriors' shot. The ball careened sharply out of bounds, last touched by TJ. On the ensuing inbounds play against the Warriorss Fury press, Zeke intercepted a pass aimed for #13. He would have had a wide-open lay up, had he not been immediately fouled by the desperate freshman. The Bulldogs' coach threw his arms up in despair as the referee signaled a one plus one bonus for Zeke.

Stakes were high and emotions even higher as Zeke stepped to the line. He shot the first free throw like a sniper—calm, focused, and completely confident. 61-56. He lined up for the second with the same form and poise. Falling short, the shot glanced the front of the rim, bouncing just hard enough to hit the back of the rim and then back to the front. Several young men converged toward the basket for the all-important rebound. Multiple hands touched the ball, but it was Zeke who ultimately took possession. In a split second, Zeke gained possession of the ball and shot it gently back into the basket as the whistle blew.

The Bulldog fans reached a near riot level frenzy immediately; until, the referee made the call. "#1 blue, over the back. #34 white, shooting 1 and 1."

Zeke unraveled. Pounding his thighs with his fist, he lifted his head toward the sky and screamed, "You're crazy!! That's bullsh—!!"

No one heard the last syllable of Zeke's rant. A long, loud whistle drowned out the expletive. The seasoned referee blew his whistle sharply as he strode angrily to the scorer's table. Dramatically, he placed one hand horizontally, then raised the other hand vertically to form an exaggerated "T."

Derrick frantically signaled Zeke to the bench. On the way, Zeke ripped off his jersey, waving it and slamming it on the floor. Another technical foul initiated Zeke's automatic ejection. Security guards moved in front of the Northfield fan section that had likewise began to unravel.

Zeke, coming to terms with what had just happened, stopped abruptly, frozen in shame and tears. Derrick approached his young leader even as he worked to gather his own emotions. Empathizing with Zeke and all that had led up to the moment of his meltdown, Derrick comforted him, "It's okay, Zeke. It's okay. It's been a long night for all of us." Zeke blew a large burst of air out of his cheeks and through his lips. Looking back over his shoulder at the scene unfolding behind him, Zeke spoke sharply through his tears, "Dammit, Coach. It's just not fair. It's wrong man, it's all so wrong."

Derrick surveyed the brokenness on Zeke's face. Turning toward the remaining players he saw teenage boys collapsing under the weight of a moment. Derrick looked past the distraught players and into the seething mob of Northfield fans. Derrick lowered his head. He inhaled a long, hard breath. It was too much for him to bear as well.

———————————

At 9:17 p.m. on this frigid, snowy January night, Coach Mac wanted two things. First, as he declared repeatedly, he wanted to "get this whole thing over with." Second, he was on a mission to know the score of the game.

"Coach, I really agree with Mrs. McKissack on this one," Dr. Barone stated with an unwavering voice. "I don't want you giving any attention or energy to the game right now. Once the game is over, I promise, I will get you the score. So, let's get these tests completed as soon as possible."

Coach Mac squirmed impatiently in his wheel chair. Reluctantly he yielded to the slow pace of the hospital attendant in blue scrubs wheeling him down the narrow hallway and around the corner toward the labs.

"Coach Mac," Jamarcus Denton shouted from a wheelchair just outside the x-ray lab.

"Jamarcus . . . Jamarcus? What are you . . . what in the world are you doing here, son?" Coach Mac held up his hand to signal the young attendant to halt.

"I always said, 'I want to be just like you, Coach.'" Jamarcus' attempted humor was sincere, but marked by an undeniable heaviness.

Gracie made her way quickly down the hall to hug Jamarcus. As she did, Coach Mac began barking directions to the mystified attendant, coaching him like a point guard running the offense. Arriving as he had instructed, Coach Mac requested "Jamarcus, son, tell me what happened?"

"I grabbed a defensive rebound . . . we were trying to stop their 7-0 run . . . I came down on one of their players. You know, it just twisted pretty bad. I'm sure it'll be okay." Jamarcus muddled through the details, his own mind still trying to grasp them. "So far, it looks like it's just a sprain, but they tell me I need x-rays. I tried to walk on it, Coach, I tried my best, but I just . . ."

"You did the best you could, Jamarcus," Coach Mac interrupted. "I have no doubt." As if a light just illuminated a dark spot in his mind, Coach Mac suddenly thought aloud. "A 7-0 run? Surely, they didn't get back in the game? We had 'em buried!"

"It was 51-38 after the 7-0 run. But, don't worry, coach, I'm sure the guys are taking care of business."

"Gracie, you have got to text Nikki or Principal Davis and get me a score!" Coach Mac demanded. "You have to get me a score!" Gracie ignored the demands even as she secretly checked for a text from Nikki.

"Jamarcus, I tell you what." Coach Mac's voice returned to a more hopeful tone. "Let's both get checked out and get the heck out of this place. I'll race you home, Jamarcus."

"All right, but if it's a race, we may have to do it in these legit four-wheelers. I don't think I will be walking or running anywhere tonight, Coach."

"Young man, let's get this thing done," Coach Mac instructed to the still confused attendant. "And Gracie," Coach Mac added as he whirled around looking for her, "What's the problem with getting a dang score? Why don't you step outside and try getting your messages in the lobby?"

Gracie smiled softly. "Okay, dear, you take care of the tests and I'll take care of the texts," she chuckled. "By the time they wheel you back to your room, I am sure I'll have the final score."

Gracie's promise was truthful. She was not, however, entirely forthcoming. She feared that reading Nikki's latest text would send her wounded Warrior over the edge.

MRS. GRACIE! Zeke got a double technical. He was ejected. They hit all four free throws. Then they scored. We're losing, 62-61! Two Northfield fans were just ejected. It's crazy!!!!!! Pray for safety. AND a win!

Then a final text just seconds later read:

It's over. We lost. 65-63. It's awful. I'm so sad. How is Coach Mac?

Upon returning to his room, Gracie initially avoided eye contact with her husband. Coach Mac then pressed her relentlessly. "Gracie, it has to be a final by now. We won, right? Right?"

"No," she relented, "we lost 65-63. It was just too much, Johnny. Too much. I'm so sorry." She leaned over, stroking his arm. "I'm so sorry for you, for the boys, and poor Derrick. He must be crushed."

Coach Mac sat silently. After a few moments of blankly staring at the seemingly colorless hospital walls, Coach Mac gazed upward into

Gracie's compassionate eyes. "I feel helpless, Gracie. The team, Derrick, the community. They needed me and I wasn't there for them. And, you. Gracie, you've got cancer and here I sit. I know I'm being a burden to you, too."

Staring downward at the wires and tubes surrounding him like tangled vines, Coach Mac added, "I don't know how to do this, Gracie. And I don't want to learn."

Derrick was the last person out of the visitors' locker room. He had given his best "we'll get 'em next time" speech laced with sports clichés even he didn't believe. As he finally exited the locker room, the arena was being cleaned by the custodial staff. Waiting at the exit door stood Nikki, her arms folded tightly across her chest. Her lips were pursed, her body swaying back and forth.

Covered in layers of melting thick white flakes, Jimmy Thompson approached Derrick cautiously. "Just a couple of comments, Coach?" Jimmy asked apologetically. "It's a mess out there. I know we both want to get home."

"Sure, Jimmy? Where do you want me to start? How about, 'We blew a 17-point lead in less than 10 minutes'? Or, 'We failed to finish Coach Mac's record-setting win?'" Derrick continued sarcastically. "Coach Mac's health is completely uncertain? Jamarcus' injury may cost us a state championship? More accurately, my coaching may have cost us our best chance at setting up a state championship?" Derrick's voice trailed off as he looked past Jimmy as Nikki turned to walk out the door.

Nikki had heard every harsh word Derrick delivered to Jimmy. It made the pain worse.

Jimmy stood frozen. Eventually he managed, "Yeah, I'm sorry, Coach. Obviously it's been a helluva night."

"You think?" Derrick's voice dripped with dejection. "Look, Jimmy. I know you're just trying to do your job. I get it. But," Derrick continued with less anger but equal force, "I wouldn't wish this on my worst enemy. . ." Derrick looked again over Jimmy's right shoulder. Seeing no sign of Nikki, he added quickly, "I've got to go, but here's your 'coach-speak' quote."

Jimmy pressed "record" for the first time since their contentious dialogue had begun.

"Coach Mac has coached up Northfield teams with the Northfield Way for longer than I've been alive. And that's what he, and I, will continue to do. Right now, our prayers and thoughts are with Coach Mac, Mrs. Gracie, Jamarcus, and the Denton family," Derrick recited flatly.

"Thanks, Coach. Is that all for tonight?" Jimmy inquired robotically.

"Yeah, Jimmy. That's all," Derrick replied dismissively. "Goodnight, Jimmy."

Derrick hurriedly passed through the large metal exit. As he transitioned into the wet, frigid night Nikki pulled up alongside the curb.

"Take me to the hospital, Nik," Derrick ordered.

"Coach Mac and Mrs. Gracie asked to be alone tonight. They want us to come in the morning to visit. The doctor highly recommended that too." Once Derrick was seated, Nikki moved the car forward, adding sympathetically, "I'm sorry, D—about everything,"

"What about Jamarcus?" Derrick shot back, ignoring Nikki's compassion.

"Good news! I just got the text. He's headed home. He has a pretty severe high ankle sprain. My oldest brother had that in high school, too. So, I'm pretty sure he should be back by the state tournament," Nikki encouraged, her voice rising optimistically as she turned left in the empty parking lot.

Derrick sat, slumped and silent.

"At least there's some good news, right?" Nikki reached out to squeeze Derrick's left arm.

Pulling away, Derrick shot back, "Yeah, well you're assuming that we make state without Jamarcus—and that Coach Mac comes back in time to save the season."

"Well, I for one believe Jamarcus can do it. And I think you can do it, D—no matter how long Coach Mac has to take off to recover." Nikki nodded confidently.

Derrick, his head rigidly facing forward, shot a sideward glance toward Nikki. "Really? Don't talk down to me, Nikki. I'm not an idiot. We're screwed without Coach Mac." Turning his head and eyes toward the passenger side window, Derrick shifted his body further away from Nikki. Leaning his elbow on the door, he placed his head into his right palm. Derrick then muttered the last words he would speak on the trip home, "I'm screwed without Coach Mac. I can see the headlines now, 'Derrick Walker: Northfield's Biggest Loser, the sequel.'"

Nikki opened her mouth to speak. No words formed. Through falling snow and falling tears, she aimed the car toward Northfield. Sobs heaved just below the surface. "It's been such a horrible night," she thought to herself, "I can't make it worse." She shook her head sadly. Tightening her grip on the steering wheel, she put her head down and pressed forward.

Arriving at their condo, Derrick threw his keys, clipboard, and jacket on the kitchen counter. The keys slid off, clanking on the tile floor. Derrick made no effort to pick them up.

"Guest room, right?" he asked, making no effort to look back toward Nikki.

"Derrick," Nikki said, catching her breath immediately afterward. "We need to talk."

Derrick instantly stopped walking. He turned slowly, deliberately taking his time in order to guard his words. *10, 9, 8 . . . ,* he recited in his head. By the time he made full eye contact with Nikki, he had repressed much of his aggressive anger. But not all.

Nikki, taken aback, retreated. "Maybe this isn't the best time . . . It's just, I don't know what to say, I . . ." Nikki's voice faltered. Sobs she had previously held back by sheer force of will now burst out uncontrollably, forcing her to lean on the counter to steady herself.

As waves of grief rolled over and over Nikki, Derrick's stare softened. "Nikki, what's wrong?" Finding himself swirling in a strange emotional brew of compassion and anger, Derrick moved uneasily toward Nikki. As he approached, she fell awkwardly toward his arms. Neither felt free to surrender fully to the other's embrace. But neither had any idea what else to do. So they stood, leaning against each other stiffly.

Gathering herself, Nikki gently pulled back. Grabbing a paper towel, she wiped her face. "Can we sit down for a minute, D?"

"Yes," Derrick responded nervously. The two made their way to the sofa, sitting at a distance that mirrored their uncertainty with one another in this moment. Nikki kicked off her shoes and sat crossed-legged. Her eyes faced downward. She nervously twisted the snotty paper towel she still held in her hands. She knotted it repeatedly, until the damp paper began to fall to pieces. Still trying to catch her breath fully, she managed a halting, "Okay, I know the timing is terrible."

Nikki glanced up at Derrick for reassurance. His face was expressionless.

"So, Derrick," Nikki breathed in deeply as her upper body shuttered. "I, uh . . ." Nikki's mouth opened, her breath released. But no words formed. She managed a quick, "I . . . honestly, D, I didn't know for sure until today," Nikki pleaded. "I'm sorry, really. I just kept thinking, 'this can't be happening.'" Nikki's face fell into her lap, her shoulders heaving with sobs.

Derrick placed his arm around Nikki's rapidly rising and falling shoulders. "Nikki," Derrick asked as his face began to mirror Nikki's frightened expression, "What's going on?"

"I am . . ." Nikki drew in a breath. With one word, buried in a sorrowful cry, Nikki bared her soul and her secret, ". . . pregnant."

CHAPTER 19

'm sorry, D. I'm so sorry to tell you this now." Nikki's words tumbled out so rapidly on top of one another that they were hard to understand. "On top of everything else going on with you and me, Coach Mac and Gracie, Jamarcus . . ." She choked back another sob as her words trailed off miserably.

Derrick stared at her in quiet shock, his mind racing. How could he accurately capture his swirling thoughts? He felt panic and elation competing for his emotions. He chose the latter.

"Nikki," Derrick said gently, cupping her cheek gently with his hand so he could look deeply and warmly into her eyes. "It's going to be okay." His serious gaze widened into a lengthy smile. "This is actually good news, right?" His eyes searched hers for some small glimpse of positivity.

Nikki's eyes blinked rapidly. She gritted her teeth and swallowed hard before opening her mouth to speak. Derrick interrupted again.

"You've wanted us to get married all along. Right?" Derrick's hands reached to grasp hers. "I've been showing you I'm willing to change. We can get married, have the baby, and be a family."

Nikki stared down at their clasped hands, including the damp fragments of shredded paper she had been clutching like a pitiful security blanket. Biting her lower lip, she responded cautiously, "That's one option, D." Nikki surveyed Derrick's face. She held her breath a long pause followed.

"What? What do you mean, one option?" Derrick stood, turning away and massaging the back of his neck with his right hand. Turning back, he asked pointedly, "What other options are you considering,

Nikki? What other options are there for us, Nikki?" Sensing for the first time just how wide the gap between them had grown, Derrick spoke somberly into the cavernous divide. "Nikki, it's my baby, too. You know that, right?"

"Of course, I know. And I'm not trying to leave you out." Nikki looked toward the ceiling as her mind searched like an internet search engine for the right response. She breathed deeply through her mouth, then steeled herself against the urge to run from the room. "That's why I chose to talk to you tonight, of all times," she explained, "because ultimately it is your baby, too." Sitting up straighter, she added firmly, "But the final decision begins with me, Derrick, not you."

"Okay . . . but what are the options?" Derrick plopped onto a chair, facing Nikki directly.

"One option, getting an abortion, is not on the table," Nikki said adamantly. "I don't believe it's right. Plus, in my family . . . well, there are secrets you don't know—nobody else knows. Let's just say, I've seen first hand the painful, lingering impact of abortion. I'm not going there."

Derrick dropped his head. "Well, okay. I kind of expected that—" Derrick said, then added, "not the part about your family, though."

"Yeah, I know." Nikki waved her hands back and forth. "Your family's not the only one that's got hidden secrets, D. Mine's just . . . okay, that's not the point." Nikki stood, pacing nervously as she continued. "But, here's the thing, D. I want to be clear . . . because it's important to me to say this."

Derrick sighed heavily, trying to find the emotional strength for this conversation.

Nikki ratcheted up the intensity in her delivery. "My decision not to abort is not just about the pain in my family. It's not right—and God knows, truly, God knows . . ." Nikki dropped her head, gathering composure. "I've run through the stop signs of my convictions over and over." Nikki's chest heaved again. Having nothing left to wipe her nose with, she used the sleeve of her sweater. She continued, "And I can't continue to live that way."

Where was Nikki going with this? Derrick felt they were on shaky ground here. Unsure of the best response, he tried to cut to the chase. "So, what's left? Besides us getting married?"

Nikki moved restlessly to an adjacent chair, looking for physical distance to express the emotional distance she was feeling. Her eyes were heavily swollen, her face covered with red splotches. The tip of her nose was bright red, irritated by the sobbing and paper towels. She felt and looked an absolute mess—an uncharacteristic quality in this surreal moment.

"Nikki, no matter what you are about to say," Derrick offered directly into her red-lined eyes, "I need you to know that I love you. I've already admitted that I haven't loved you the way you want me to . . . but," he pleaded, "I do love you."

Derrick struggled to keep his composure even. "Nikki, I lost tonight's game. If Coach Mac doesn't come back soon, I'll lose a lot more games. Then I'm likely going to lose my job." Derrick swallowed hard. The pitch of his voice rose in desperation. "And I can probably take all of that. Hell, Nikki, I've had a lot of practice losing. I'm pretty good at it," he chuckled sarcastically as he wiped his eyes with the thumb and forefinger of his left hand. "But I can't take losing you." Derrick paused, then added softly, "Or our baby." Taking both of her hands, Derrick passionately pleaded his case, "I can't lose us."

Filling her lungs and arching her shoulders back, Nikki retreated from Derrick's hands and his emotions. "D. You must know—surely you know me well enough to know—that a part of me wants to fall passionately into your arms, tell you I will marry you tomorrow, and live happily ever after—"

"I like that part of you." Derrick smiled wryly.

"No kidding, I know you do." Pausing with the slightest of smiles, Nikki continued, "So do I. But, D, that is not all of me." Nikki leaned back, awkwardly resting her head on the back of the chair. "The other parts know there's another problem here, a problem I've been afraid to admit for months. The problem is . . ." Nikki paused again. Placing both hands firmly on her chest, pointing her fingers back at herself, she released words she had relentlessly denied for months, "The problem is, I've lost myself, D. I don't even know which parts of me are real. I've completely lost any idea of who I am." Nikki threw up her hands before letting them fall gently back onto her lap.

Derrick stared at Nikki with a painfully puzzled face.

"I feel like I'm coming apart at the seams, D. I'm just lost." Nikki's head slumped into her hands as she sat forward. Without looking up, with her head shaking in her hands, she added, "Before I can consider whether I'm ready to marry you or whether I'm going to raise this child as a single mom—with you, of course, involved—or whether I want to proceed with an adoption—"

"What?" Derrick rose rapidly, as if shot out of his chair by force. He threw up his hands in disbelief. "Adoption? What the hell are you talking about, Nikki?" Derrick walked to the other side of the room, waving his right hand high in the air, as if releasing untamable energy through its rapid motion. Turning toward Nikki, Derrick slapped both of his hands forcefully onto his thighs. The impact made a loud smack that echoed throughout the room.

Nikki made her strongest appeal yet to Derrick, "We have to think about what's best for the child, D."

"You know what, Nikki. I am thinking about what's best for the child." Derrick's voice was firm, his body rigid as he pointed angrily at Nikki. Catching himself, he dropped his accusatory finger, quickly backing down his intensity. "I'm not losing my child, Nikki." He turned his back momentarily, then quickly turned back. "And my child's not losing me," Derrick added firmly.

"It's not like that, D. Remember that my oldest sister is adopted. I've told you that before. Adoption, even in my weird family, can be a cool thing."

"Your 'weird' family has nothing to do with this. And even less to do with us," Derrick added resentfully. He stormed into the kitchen, opened the refrigerator, and pulled out a tall Budweiser.

"D, don't you think it's a little late to be dri—" Nikki halted in mid-syllable. Derrick shot her an unmistakable *Don't even go there* look.

"D, I'm not saying we should definitely place our child with another family, but—"

Derrick interrupted again, "Well, Nikki, I am saying that we definitely should not. No more losses for me and my family, Nikki. No more."

Nikki responded softly, "I know how much you've been hurt in the past."

"No, Nikki. No, you don't." Derrick drew a huge gulp from the large red and white can, then returned to sit in the chair next to Nikki. "You can't begin to know what I've been through. And that matters, you know."

"Of course, it does," Nikki lifted her hands toward Derrick. He sat rigid, unresponsive, drinking another large gulp of the cold beer. She spoke compassionately, "You matter as much as I do. And you're right, I don't understand. Not really. I'm sorry for saying that."

Derrick sat the beer down on the floor next to his chair as he turned his body more directly toward hers. Derrick silently contemplated Nikki's apology. He looked toward her, then away. The fingers on his right hand rolled one after the other, cycling rhythmically on the chair's smooth armrest. The longer they sat in silence, the louder the distance between them grew.

"Derrick," Nikki began, "we're parents now. Tonight. Right now. And our baby needs us to choose what his best for him, or her." She offered the palms of her hands to Derrick once again.

Reluctantly, Derrick accepted the invitation, joining his palms to hers. At first, his grip was loose, almost passive. Soon, however, he grasped her hands tightly. The impact of Nikki's touch burrowed far beneath Derrick's skin. He began tenderly stroking the backs of her hands with his thumbs. He focused his eyes on their hands joined together, then turned toward her. "Nikki. I'm . . . I'm just . . ." Derrick's words stumbled, then stopped.

"Scared?" Nikki asked.

"Yes," Derrick admitted, looking back at their tightly clasped hands. "I'm scared. I can't keep losing, Nikki. At some point . . ." Derrick's eyes rose again to meet hers, mirroring the redness in the whites of Nikki's eyes. "At some point, I'm not going to have anything, or anybody, left."

"D, you have got to hear me on this," Nikki pleaded, shaking their hands up and down emphatically. "As of tonight, I am not choosing to leave you. As of tonight, I'm not choosing anything related to our baby's future. What I am choosing—and what you must also choose for the sake of our baby—is to find my 'why.' I've lost my 'why' along the way. I've lost myself."

"Have you been talking to Coach Mac about this?" Derrick pulled his hands away, feeling betrayed by the thought.

"No, of course I've not been talking to Coach Mac about this," Nikki defended. "But I've been listening to him. And to Mrs. Gracie. They've taught me that everything starts with the 'why.' And this baby," Nikki repeated herself to make her point, "this baby can't be our 'why' for getting married or even for staying together."

"What's wrong with that, Nikki?" Derrick implored. Their knees touched as Derrick leaned into toward Nikki. He reached out with his right hand to gently move tangled strands of auburn hair sticking to Nikki's tear-stained left cheek. Derrick bent his head slightly, raising his eyebrows to signal his question was not rhetorical.

"It's not a big enough 'why,' D," Nikki explained, leaning away. "Not big enough to get married." Nikki paused, considering her next words carefully. "Not a big enough 'why' for us to choose to raise this baby, either."

Derrick dropped back into his chair. He glanced down at his watch: 11:47 p.m. His body fell limp as he tilted his head back, staring blankly at the ceiling. He noted the small water stain in the near corner of the ceiling. The sight triggered a recent memory. Like so many other things in their lives, Derrick's failure to repair the water stain had instigated an argument. The squabble had been just another downward step in the long decline of their relationship.

"Okay, Nikki. It's your call," Derrick conceded, still staring at the ceiling. "What's next?" he asked with a sigh.

"I'm going to need some space to work this out, D. I'm going to move in with Michelle for a while," Nikki spoke hesitantly. "I'm also planning to go home to Iowa for a few days. You know, to get my head together."

Derrick slowly lifted his head off of the back of the chair. "How long are you going to be gone?" he asked sadly.

Pursing her lips, Nikki shrugged her shoulders and raised her palms upward in a gesture of uncertainty.

Derrick rubbed the back of his neck with his right hand. Exhausted, he joined his left hand to his right, his fingers intertwined behind his neck. Derrick then added, motionless and emotionless, "Well, I guess that's that."

"D, I'm not doing this to hurt you. You know that, right?"

"And yet, Nikki, here I am." Derrick's eyes opened widely, then narrowed again. "Coach Mac's in the hospital. You're out the door—with our baby. And, apparently, I'm headed toward becoming the biggest disappointment in Northfield history for the second time in my 26-year-old life." Derrick dropped his hands to his sides and stared at Nikki blankly.

After a tense, long pause, Derrick rocked his head up and down, speaking in barely a whisper, "I'm tired, Nikki. I am really, really tired."

"I know," Nikki comforted, "And I'm so sorry, D." Nikki scooted back toward Derrick, her knees coming into contact with his once more. "If it helps at all, I'm pulling for us to make it. I promise you, that's what I'm hoping for. I know that's hard to believe, but it's time." Nikki unconsciously rested her right hand on her heart as she spoke.

"Well, I think we finally agree on something," Derrick chuckled humorlessly.

"What's that?"

"We both think it's hard to believe your promise." Derrick's voice dripped in angry sarcasm.

Nikki's shoulders fell as if tethered to her sinking heart.

Derrick grabbed his beer and stood up. Silently, he headed toward the guest room. After passing through the kitchen, Derrick turned back toward Nikki. Looking back, he said sincerely, "That wasn't fair. I'm sorry, Nik."

Derrick looked down the hall, then at his tall Budweiser. He sat the can on the counter then turned back toward Nikki's crestfallen face. Looking back at the counter, Derrick picked up the flimsy blue spiral notebook lying next to the can of beer. Pulling it toward his chest, he purposed in his mind to send it flying as far across the kitchen as he could fling it. Stopping himself short, he tossed it lazily back on the counter. Derrick shook his head and let out a long, slow breath.

Turning once again toward Nikki's swollen, tear-stained face, Derrick shook his head side to side for a moment, then stood still and silent. He closed his eyes, listening to his own breathing. Opening his eyes, he looked down at his chest, watching it rhythmically rise and fall. Cautiously, Derrick's eyes rose toward Nikki. Four simple words escaped without forethought or filter. "I love you, Nikki."

Nikki had no words. She managed a weak smile, then breathed in a long, slow cleansing breath. She mouthed the words, "Thank you," but no sound followed.

Derrick turned, retreating toward the guest bedroom. Once there, he collapsed onto the bed fully clothed. Derrick stared at the ceiling, replaying the events of day in his mind. Then, as he had been learning to do lately—he prayed.

Derrick whispered a panicked prayer, pleading with God for Coach Mac to recover. For Nikki to come back to him. For something good to come out of this dreadful mess.

As he considered the alternative to God answering these prayers of desperation, Derrick's chest constricted so tightly he could hardly breathe.

MARCH

"A full life begins with an emptied self."

Coach John McKissack

CHAPTER 20

Jimmy Thompson rubbed his chilled palms against one another. He blew hot breath across his hands to increase the heating effect.

It was 6:20 a.m. on a damp, cold Saturday morning in Northfield. Jimmy sat in his regular spot in Thingstead Café. Near the kitchen, and by far the draftiest place in the building, all his spot afforded Jimmy was the assurance of privacy.

The Thingstead, named after the meeting place of Norse communities in the Middle Ages, was almost as central to life in Northfield as Coach John McKissack and his beloved basketball dynasty. Not surprisingly, each successive Northfield squad became the main topic of discussion on most mornings in the Thingstead.

The teams would always be Norsemen, not Warriors, to the café's aging patrons. Old Red, owner and primary cook, even refused to hang jerseys or banners on the walls that bore the word "Warriors." In the Thingstead, change didn't just happen slowly. It just didn't happen.

Next to Jimmy sat his favorite Saturday morning companion, a pot of Red's "Nordic Brew" coffee. He drank it black, as strong as Old Red could brew it, in his prized orange ceramic Clemson mug with a white tiger paw. Next to the mug he had his notebook and the empty plate from his "Big Thing" breakfast. Fueled and ready for work, Jimmy reached into his backpack for his headphones.

Before placing the headphones tightly on his ears, Jimmy paused to listen to the morning buzz. He laughed to himself as he listened to various personality types assess the current state of Northfield basketball.

There were the optimists: *Just one more win and it's on to state. Then we get back Jamarcus and Coach Mac—just in time for a three-peat!*

There were the pessimists: *We've already lost to West Chamberlain once. And we're only six and six since then. We're gonna get killed Monday night!*

There were the critics: *So we won a district championship? Against inferior opponents. So what? Come Monday night, Coach Walker will screw it up, just like he did the last time we played the Bulldogs.*

Then there were peacemakers: *I just hope the boys play well on Monday night.*

Jimmy marveled once again at the religious fervor of the Northfield Nation. The Nation's intensity was as high as ever. Their anxiety, however, was far greater than ever.

Donning his noise-cancelling headphones, Jimmy shut out the tiny world of Thingstead. His mind welcomed a flood of smooth jazz as his "Smooth Life" playlist pumped into his ears.

"Legacies can only be forged by exposing a leader's metal to the white-hot coals of adversity," Jimmy read as he dove into his final phase of editing. As a pre-cursor to March Madness, CBS Sports online was running a series of high school basketball stories. CBS pitched the concept to Jimmy as a shorter, lighter version of ESPN's 30 for 30 series. The network planned to post the article on Monday morning with a Tuesday morning follow-up. The Tuesday article would focus on the relationship between the outcome of the West Chamberlain rematch and Coach Mac's Northfield legacy. If Northfield somehow won, the dramatic return of Coach Mac promised to be great reading. Only a few people, excluding Jimmy, considered that an actual possibility. Still fewer, including Jimmy, expected the Warriors to win state—even if they miraculously escaped West Chamberlain with a win.

At 8:40 am, Jimmy hit "send." His first national exposure article entered cyberspace. Jimmy raised both fists into the air, pumping them wildly to the driving beat of a Boney James saxophone rift. He then unplugged his computer power cord as his head continued dance to the beat of the music, and closed his laptop. Before completing the process of packing up, he decided to text Tara.

It's done! I'm headed home. Just you and me and the kids for the rest of the day! Love you!

Jimmy pushed the send arrow. Immediately the screen lit up with an incoming text. The instantaneous response surprised Jimmy. But it wasn't from Tara. What he read next nearly sent him into shock.

"JT, they're putting up a website, 'nhsdarknation.org.' They're going to launch it Monday night, as soon as the Warriors lose. There's nothing I can do to stop it. It's not going to look good for Coach Mac. I'm afraid the comment section is going to get nasty. You HAVE to tell him! Man, you should have already!"

Another text quickly followed: *#nhsdarknation on Twitter Tuesday.*

Jimmy typed hurriedly, *Who are "they"?*

No reply. Jimmy's left leg rapidly bounced up and down. His body shook with nervous energy. Then the phone vibrated. *I can't tell you. I'm sorry.*

Jimmy's fingers angrily tapped out his reply. *Oh, yes you can—but you WON'T!*

The response was immediate. *No, I CAN'T!*

After a brief pause, the phone vibrated again. *But you can do something, JT. Tell Coach Mac—now!*

Jimmy stared at his phone for several minutes. His mind raced. Then it went numb. Then it raced again. In the moments it raced, his mind ran in several scary directions.

"You want some more coffee, Jimmy?" Old Red interrupted Jimmy's scattered thoughts in his distinct, raspy tone. Fifty years of smoking unfiltered Camel cigarettes had morphed Old Red's voice into a course, gravelly growl.

"No, Red. Not now," Jimmy mumbled. Anxiously, Jimmy leaned over his phone, shielding its screen from Old Red.

Old Red bent down to look Jimmy in the eye. "Are you okay? You don't look so good, JT, " he said.

"Yeah, yeah, I'm fine. Hey, I've got to go." Jimmy tossed a twenty-dollar bill onto the table. "Here's a twenty. Just keep the change," Jimmy said. Without making eye contact, Jimmy hastily brushed by Old Red toward the exit door.

Once inside his Forerunner, Jimmy called Tara. After explaining the whole story, he asked, "Tara, what am I supposed to do?"

"Just what you said. Go talk to Coach Mac," Tara said firmly. "And, honestly, Jimmy, you should've done this a long time ago."

Jimmy ran his fingers through the hair sticking out from under his beanie. Soon he was scratching his head. His whole body shivered. "I know, I know," Jimmy lamented to Tara, "I was going to talk to him—had it all set up. Then he passed out, went to the hospital, got confined to rest at home . . . I just . . . I was afraid the stress might, you know, push him over the edge . . ." Jimmy tugged anxiously at his hair.

"I know, Jimmy. And I'm not saying that you had any good choices then. But . . . now? Now you only have one choice."

Jimmy's heart beat rapidly. His breathing sped up as if he were climbing several flights of stairs two steps at a time.

"Pray for me, Tara," he gasped.

"Pray for you? What? Where did that come from?" Tara laughed.

"I don't know. I'm feeling pretty desperate here," Jimmy replied.

"Well, I'm on your side, just know that. But I don't think I'm quite ready to get religious over it." Tara paused. "Not yet, anyways," she chuckled. Switching her tone, she added, "Look, we don't really know anything. People slander each other all the time on social media. Don't panic. At least, not yet."

"Too late," Jimmy replied flatly. "I'm on my way to Coach Mac's right now," he said.

"You've already called?"

"No, but I'm going to text him and just show up. This can't wait," Jimmy said.

"You're doing the right thing," Tara encouraged.

When Jimmy arrived at the McKissacks', he had to force himself out of his SUV. "You can do this. You have to do this," Jimmy coaxed himself out loud.

Gracie Mac greeted Jimmy at the door. "Come in, JT," she invited warmly. "I've just made some blueberry muffins. They're Johnny's favorite. You have to try one," she said, motioning Jimmy toward the den.

Entering the room, Jimmy saw the furniture strewn with shoeboxes, paper clippings, and photos. Coach Mac sat among the piles wearing a pair of ancient Northfield Norsemen sweatpants and a much newer navy Warrior sweatshirt.

"Hey, JT. Glad to see you. Sorry for the mess, but you said it was urgent. I didn't have time to clean up," Coach Mac began to clear away several piles of boxes stacked high on a chair. "Here, have a seat. Looks like it's the only one we've got,' Coach Mac grinned.

"Thanks, Coach. What are you up to?"

"Trying to get organized," Coach Mac explained. "Principal Davis asked me to help put together an archive of my tenure as Northfield's head coach," He paused, then winked at Jimmy, "I hope he's not keeping something from me!" Coach Mac laughed.

Jimmy tried to laugh too. Instead, he made an anxious, grunting noise. Coach Mac's eyes squinted and blinked as if he were trying to bring something far away into focus.

Jimmy deflected Coach Mac's curiosity. "So, what are your favorite memories, Coach?"

"Well, I'm old, JT. So there's a lot to choose from," Coach Mac laughed again. "Here's a good one." He passed to Jimmy an old, low-resolution photo of a long, lanky player. The string bean of a young man wore a white Norsemen #51 home jersey. "Slammin' Sammy Johnson," Coach Mac said proudly. "Our first all-state player. Sammy's a good man. Coaches at a junior college in Florida. Been very successful. But, you know what?" Coach Mac asked.

Jimmy looked up from the photo to see Coach Mac's face lit up with a smile. "What's that, Coach?"

"He still calls me, at least once a month," Coach Mac said as he smiled broadly. "Can you believe that?"

"Well, actually, Coach, I can," Jimmy replied, matching Coach Mac's smile.

"Here's another one. Norman Harrison," Coach Mac said as he passed the newspaper clipping over to Jimmy. The ragged-edged, yellowing newsprint included a black and white photo of a small, slender player wearing a dark Northfield away jersey, #2.

"I've heard of him. Didn't he pass away recently?" Jimmy asked.

"Yeah. So sad. Brain tumor. Left behind a wonderful wife, Sally, and three teenagers. He was another good man, JT," Coach Mac reflected.

"How about just one more?" Jimmy asked. He welcomed the distraction. At the same time, he needed to get to the point of his visit soon. Otherwise, he might chicken out.

"Okay, but I don't mean to bore you," Coach Mac replied.

"I'm not bored, believe me," Jimmy said.

Coach Mac held up a high-resolution, professional photo for Jimmy to see. Jimmy emitted an impressed, "Wow!" as he observed the attractive couple. The man was sharply dressed in a formal tuxedo, the woman in an elegant black evening gown.

Coach Mac laughed a jolly laugh as he handed the glossy photo to Jimmy. "That's Hinton and LaKeisha Carson! They're a good-looking couple, aren't they?"

"Yes, sir. Isn't she a correspondent with CNN? I've heard her name, but I've never associated her with Northfield," Jimmy said admiringly.

"Yep. The very same. Hinton was—still is—the life of the party. He turned every post-game into a dance-off. LaKeisha Melton, though . . ." Coach stopped long enough to replay a memory, "She was as shy as deer in the woods. Kept her distance from everybody but Hinton."

Coach Mac leaned in, dropping his voice as if he were telling a secret. "I asked Hinton one time, 'Are you sure she can handle you, Hinton?' He told me, 'Trust me, Coach. I know what I'm doing here.'"

The two shared a laugh as Coach Mac took the picture from Jimmy's outstretched hand. Jimmy's hand trembled slightly as he returned the picture to Coach Mac. Trying to cover for himself, Jimmy fake laughed again, "I guess he did . . . that is, he knew what he was doing."

"Jimmy, what's wrong, son?" Coach asked. Coach Mac's wide smile instantly morphed into downturned lips, accompanied by a deeply furrowed brow.

Jimmy swallowed hard. He lowered his eyes, then turned to look out the window. "Is there any way out of this?" Jimmy thought to himself. He turned toward Coach Mac and, by sheer force of will, said, "I need to show you something. Can I come sit beside you?"

"Sure, JT." Coach Mac cleared a spot next to himself on the sofa. As he did, Gracie entered the room with muffins and juice. Silently, with a look, Coach Mac encouraged Gracie to retreat from the room.

"Coach Mac, would you please read this text thread on my phone?" Jimmy asked, his hands still shaky.

"Of course," Coach Mac said. "Let me get my reading glasses." Coach Mac reached behind onto the end table to retrieve his glasses off a scattered pile of clippings. "Okay, what do we have here?" he muttered curiously. Coach Mac leaned forward on the edge of the sofa and began reading. After less than a minute, he handed the phone back to Jimmy. Slowly, deliberately, he removed his reading glasses and carefully folded them in his lap. Then he scooted back on the sofa, sighing so forcefully that Jimmy could see his massive chest expand and retract. Turning toward the kitchen, he softly called, "Gracie, could you join us, please?"

Upon seeing Coach Mac's expression, Gracie's face dropped. She gently set the tray of muffins and juice on a stack of boxes on the coffee table. Without speaking a word, she moved into the chair Jimmy had just left open.

Jimmy watched Gracie's movements closely, especially her glances toward Coach Mac. Jimmy felt "something" in the room. It was invisible and unspoken; its presence, however, was undeniable.

"Gracie, you need to see something," Coach Mac said gravely. Jimmy handed his phone to Gracie. Coach Mac offered her his reading glasses. Drawing close to her side, he placed his hand on her knee.

As soon as the glasses brought the texts into view, Gracie gasped, "Oh, Johnny. Oh, no. Oh, dear God, no." Immediately, her shoulders began to heave as huge sobs moved like large waves through her body.

Gracie covered her mouth with her right hand. She then reached for Coach Mac's hand with her left.

Jimmy sat stiffly on the couch. He alternately stared into the McKissacks' grief, then looked away. He felt as if he were occupying a space where he didn't belong.

Coach Mac stood up, hugged his wife tightly, then sat back down next to Jimmy. "I'm sure you have some questions, Jimmy," he said kindly.

"Yes, I—" But before Jimmy could complete his sentence, a loud crash resounded from a room across the hall. Startled, Coach Mac moved quickly. Following him, Gracie and Jimmy arrived to see the McKissacks' front room strewn with shards of broken glass. The drapes flapped wildly as a blustery, frigid wind rose and fell in the room.

Coach Mac stepped carefully among the pieces of glass shrapnel. He bent over to pick up an object he had identified as foreign to the room. He studied it carefully, then walked back to Jimmy and Gracie.

"Brick," he said angrily, holding it up for both to see. Loosening a rubber band from around the brick, he unfolded the thick piece of beige construction paper that was wrapped around it. He read its contents, his face growing sterner with each passing second. Coach Mac held up the paper for Jimmy and Gracie to read. It said,

WE KNOW
SOON EVERYONE WILL KNOW
MURDERER + WIFE BEATER
+ RACIST = NORTHFIELD WAY
#NHSDarkNation

Gracie's sobs began again. Jimmy reached out to hold her hand as Coach Mac announced, "I've got to call Sherriff Cooley."

Cooley answered his cell phone immediately. Coach Mac began, "I think we need you over here, at our house, as soon as possible."

Gracie and Jimmy moved back into the den where they sat without speaking. As soon as Coach Mac concluded his call with Cooley, he dialed the cell number for Billy Anderson, Lars' son. Billy was the manager of the local hardware store and a former player for Coach Mac.

"Billy, I hate to bother you on a Saturday, but I've got freezing air blowing through my broken front window." After securing Billy's assistance, Coach Mac turned his attention toward Gracie.

"What are we going to do, Johnny?" Gracie asked. Her head remained down as her eyes continued to pour wide streams of tears.

"We're going to call together everyone who needs to know," Coach Mac instructed. "And we are going to do it immediately. We're going to address this head on. We've got to shut it down, Gracie."

Gracie patted her running nose with the tissue Jimmy had given her. After a deep breath, she looked toward Coach Mac with red, swollen eyes. "We should have done this years ago, Johnny," she demanded. "I knew this would happen."

Jimmy's head turned quickly toward Gracie. His eyes widened and his mouth lay open. "That's it," Jimmy said to himself. "There's the 'something.'"

"I've dealt with this responsibly, Gracie," Coach Mac defended. The veins in his neck bulged as he continued adamantly. "None of this is anyone else's business—except the few people who already know. I've done the right thing, Gracie," Coach Mac said in a voice sharpened to a fine, angry point. He protested harshly, "I make no apologies. No one in this town has ever walked in my shoes. No one!"

"Johnny," Gracie said as she moved next to Coach Mac's side. "You're right. No one has ever walked the path you've walked. But this is not the time to dig a trench and hunker down." As Gracie spoke, she gently stroked Coach Mac's left arm. Then taking his long, wide hand into both of her small, soft hands, she continued, "This is our community. They're our family. They've trusted you, Johnny. Now it's our turn."

Coach Mac bit his lower lip as he stared forward. After a few seconds, his shoulders and head drooped. He pulled Gracie's hands to his chest. "You're right, Gracie. But we don't know . . ." his voice trailed off.

"We don't know what?" Gracie asked gently.

"We don't know what they'll do. People, even good people, Gracie—they can be very cruel and unforgiving," Coach Mac said in a hushed voice.

Gracie turned fully toward her husband and placed her palms on both sides of his face. She kissed him sweetly on both cheeks. "We got this, Coach. With God's help, we got this."

Coach Mac placed a gentle kiss on Gracie's lips, then turned toward Jimmy. With clear eyes, a taught jaw, and a straightened posture, Coach Mac said, "Time to get this thing going, Jimmy. Let's get out ahead of whatever they're planning."

"Yes, sir. But what does that mean?" Jimmy asked. Before Coach Mac could answer, Jimmy continued, "Coach . . . uh, I think, and I believe you will agree that . . ." Jimmy stalled momentarily. Gathering his strength, he asserted, "If we are going to get through this, we can't keep secrets—from anyone."

"Yes, I agree." Coach Mac lovingly patted Gracie's hands before releasing them.

"Jimmy, for thirty-six years, I've informed the school administration and every Lewis County School Board Chair regarding my past. I can assure you," Coach Mac slapped his right palm against his chest as he leaned forward, "there are no secrets being kept from school officials."

"Then why keep it from everyone else, Coach?" Jimmy asked.

"I didn't think they needed to know," Coach Mac defended vigorously. "Some things are personal, especially when you're . . ." Coach Mac paused as he looked back at Gracie. Her soft eyes called him to a different place than his emotions were leading him. "I was wrong, Jimmy."

Mrs. Gracie smiled softly toward Coach Mac. He responded with a gentle nod. Turning back toward Jimmy, he lowered his head and paused. "I was wrong not to be more open," he sighed heavily.

Over the next fifteen minutes, Coach Mac provided a brief review of the true story behind the website's harsh accusations. Gracie offered her own commentary as needed to tell the story clearly.

At the end of the fifteen minutes, Jimmy collapsed onto the back cushions of the sofa. "Wow. I had no idea," he reflected as his head shook back and forth in an exaggerated motion.

"Now you know the real roots of the Northfield Way," Coach Mac remarked.

Jimmy sat up and leaned forward, his elbows resting on his knees. Nodding his head, he reached out to place his hand on Coach Mac's shoulder. "And now everyone will know, Coach." Jimmy paused in mid-thought. After a few seconds of silence, Jimmy took a sip of juice and concluded, "That's going to be a good thing, Coach."

"I hope so—but you never know, Jimmy. . . you never know." Coach Mac replied as he reached over to squeeze Gracie's knee. "Now, let's get on the phone and get this meeting arranged. Tonight. We can't afford to be chasing the story. We have to lead the story."

"The Northfield Way?" Jimmy asked.

"Yep. The Northfield Way," Coach Mac replied, "Grace under pressure."

CHAPTER 21

hortly after Jimmy left the McKissack home, there was yet another knock at the front door. Coach McKissack rose to answer the door, with a reassuring nod to his wife.

"D, come in, come in," Coach Mac encouraged. He hastily opened the door just wide enough to let Derrick into the house. Shielding himself from the gusty, wet winds of an incoming warm front, Coach Mac quickly closed the door.

"So glad you could stop by, D," Gracie said warmly, and with relief. She hugged Derrick and gave him a quick kiss on the cheek. "Let me take your coat and gloves."

"Thank you. It's great to see you both as well," Derrick said. "I can't wait to have you back next week, Coach."

"I hope I will be. I really do," Coach Mac replied as the trio made their way into the McKissacks' living room.

The room had been cleared of Coach Mac's piles of boxes, photos, and clippings. A vanilla scented candle filled the room with warmth, and a large bouquet of fresh spring flowers filled it with life. As they sat down, Derrick began to catch Coach Mac up on his world.

"Yes." He was still journaling, currently on round three of covering all five maxims.

"No." He and Nikki had still not decided on their future. The next day, Derrick explained, would be a very important conversation. Coach Mac and Gracie committed to be praying. "That," Derrick said wistfully, "would be very helpful."

"Yes." Practice was excellent yesterday. Everyone was in a positive frame of mind. "Lots of passion," Derrick reported. Then he added, "And a good bit of pressure, too. If you looked closely in their eyes, Coach, they're trying to believe, but . . ." Derrick held his hands open in front of his chest as he shrugged his shoulders. His eyebrows raised as he finished the thought, "You know, we've got a steep hill to climb Monday night."

Gracie cleared her throat, then shot a quick glance toward Coach Mac. She flashed a polite smile towards Derrick and redirected the conversation, "It's so good to catch up with you, D. We're so proud of the way you've led in Coach's absence."

"Yes, we are," Coach Mac added. "I knew you had it in you, D. But, still, very impressive." Coach Mac spoke cheerfully with a broad smile. His rapidly tapping foot and wringing hands spoke more loudly.

"I couldn't have done it without both of you," Derrick said. "I will always be grateful that you believed in me. I don't know why," Derrick said "But I'm so glad you did."

"D, we do care about you. That's the reason we asked you to come by. We wanted to meet with you before everyone else." Coach Mac was speaking in an oddly formal tone.

Coach Mac and Gracie sat forward, moving to the edges of their seats. Coach Mac clasped his hands together tightly and rested them on his knees. Grace's hands lay still and folded in her lap. To Derrick, the whole scene felt rigid and staged, like awkward actors in a B movie.

Coach Mac continued, "Once everyone gets here, in about an hour, Gracie and I will be telling a story. And, to be honest, it's likely going to be painful to hear." Coach Mac's forehead filled with sparsely dotted beads of sweat. "So, we wanted to give you a heads up," Coach Mac said.

"We also know you'll have questions, D," Mrs. Gracie chimed in. "We want you not only to hear our story, but to understand it as well."

"Yes, that's important to us," Coach Mac added as he reached out to hold Gracie's hand.

"Oh, my gracious," Gracie said suddenly with alarm. "I didn't even offer you anything to drink? We've got coffee, tea, Coke, and water."

"A glass of water would be nice—no ice, please," Derrick said.

While Gracie was in the kitchen, Coach Mac and Derrick engaged in shallow chatter about the upcoming March Madness tournament. Both agreed the Big Ten should have six teams in the tournament, but they disagreed on whether the sixth team should be Minnesota or Northwestern.

When Gracie returned, Derrick enthusiastically reached for the water. As he drank, Coach Mac and Mrs. Gracie silently exchanged nervous smiles.

"So, let's get started," Coach Mac said with a clap of his hands.

"Okay," Derrick responded weakly.

For the next forty-five minutes, the three of them walked together through multiple layers of Johnny and Gracie McKissack's past. Derrick repeatedly shook his head in disbelief. His mind became foggy as an overwhelming amount of information and emotion surrounded his thought processes.

Just when Coach Mac had brought Derrick up to speed, the doorbell rang. The opportunity for clarifying questions disappeared with the early arrival of a guest at the front door.

Coach Mac's face clearly displayed his frustration. "Gracie, will you answer that, please," Coach Mac asked impatiently as the doorbell rang a second time. "I want to talk to Derrick alone for a couple of minutes."

"Of course," Gracie responded. Before going to the door, however, she walked over to Derrick. Leaning down, she hugged him tightly. As the doorbell rang a third time, she hurriedly said, "We love you, D. I'm sorry we haven't told you all of this before." Leaning back, her hands still on his biceps, Gracie said, "I hope you will forgive us. It seems that all of us need a lot of grace these days."

"Yes, ma'am. I guess we do," Derrick responded with a forced smile.

As Gracie exited, Coach Mac leaned in. His elbows rested on his knees, his arms extended from his body, and his hands were once more clasped together. "Derrick," he began as he raised his clasped hands and rested his chin on them. "I know this is a lot to absorb. Just know, whatever you need, know that I'm here. Gracie is here, too. You don't have to deal with this alone."

Derrick couldn't string together enough coherent ideas to respond. All he could manage was an obligatory, "Thank you."

"The timing on this is awful, I know," Coach Mac continued as he leaned back on the sofa. "If it were not for this threat to my family and our community, I would never be bringing this up right now. I promise."

"Yeah, I know," Derrick replied just as Principal Davis entered the room.

"Frank," Coach Mac said as he shook Principal Davis' hand.

"John," Principal Davis responded in a much warmer tone than Derrick had ever associated with the reserved administrator.

"Principal Davis," Derrick said, extending his hand to shake.

"Coach Walker," Principal Davis replied with a firm handshake and his more typically stoic facial expression.

Derrick couldn't help but feel the awkwardness in the room.

Over the course of the next fifteen minutes, the room filled. AD Butler, school board chair Johnson. Women's basketball coach Carlene Dale and her husband, Steven. Sherriff Cooley and his deputy, Will Wiseman, Jimmy Thompson, and the head of the Northfield Nation Boosters, Jimbo Larsen.

Jimmy's trained journalist eye didn't fail to notice that Jimbo, who always looked put together, looked uncharacteristically unkempt. His eyes were puffy and swollen. The heavily wrinkled cotton fabric sported a small red stain underneath the shirt pocket, and one side of the button-down collar was unbuttoned. The collar itself was also unbuttoned around the neck and his tie hung loose. Everyone in the room immediately and silently formed an unspoken opinion about Jimbo's level of inebriation. What a contrast he looked to the fashion statement that was his wife, Carla Marie. She had not accompanied her husband to the meeting.

Once everyone had taken a seat, Principal Davis began with an introduction, delivered in a stiff, monotone voice. He informed the circle about the impending website, the brick through the window, and the mysterious texts Jimmy had received. At the conclusion of his remarks, he asked somberly, "Are each of you willing to commit to absolute confidentiality regarding what is said in this meeting?"

There was a quiet but unanimous, "Yes."

Then Coach Mac began, "Mrs. Gracie and I are honored that you have joined us. And by the way, isn't Gracie looking especially beautiful this evening?" Blushing like a school-girl, Gracie dismissively waved her hand. A nervous chuckle rippled through the group. They all knew Coach was trying to soften the moment.

"Let me begin by saying that nothing I am about to share has been hidden from Northfield's school administration or Lewis County's School Board at any time—ever," Coach Mac said emphatically.

A visible sigh of relief made its way around the tight circle. Like the wave in a sports stadium, a succession of shoulders and necks softened into relaxed angles. Reassuring smiles were exchanged as well. A wildfire of anxiety was slowly being extinguished.

"I am a man of faith." Coach Mac declared, "I base my entire life on God's gift of grace. You all know how firmly I hold to this conviction. I do not, however, take my past sins lightly. In the end, I am neither defined by or condemned by my past. Clearly, there are those who do not agree," Coach Mac said, his voice growing sharper, "The 'Dark Nation', whatever that is, clearly does not share my convictions. Nor do they share my commitment to this community. I believe they want to destroy me and the Northfield Nation we have built together." Coach Mac paused, making eye contact with everyone in the circle. He then said defiantly, "But they will have to deal with God on that. For my part, I'm standing on grace and truth."

Jimmy offered a vigorous nod of affirmation. Had he been a man of faith, Jimmy's response would have included a hearty, "Amen."

"In order to keep this brief yet thorough, I am going to read the rest from a prepared statement. Please bear with me." Coach Mac cleared his throat and took a sip of water. He then carefully lifted, from a side table, two pieces of paper that were attached by a paper clip. Gracie offered a pair of reading glasses, momentarily squeezing Coach Mac's hand before letting go of the glasses.

"There are three events for which I carry a deep sense of loss. All three events occurred between the ages of eighteen and twenty. Each is a very personal, private part of my story. Each event is also very painful for me to talk about." Coach Mac looked up, his eyes peering over the reading glasses at the end of his nose. Going off script, he added with an antagonistic edge to his voice, "I still believe that this is no one else's business, but for the good of our community . . . I'll continue."

Pushing the reading glasses back up his nose, he resumed reading. "Events two and three were triggered by the first event: the murder of my brother, Wesley McKissack. Wes was returning to Michigan State University after standing beside me, my sister, and my mom at my basketball senior night at Roosevelt High School. Wesley was an All-Big Ten tight end. He held aspirations of playing in the NFL. Ultimately, he planned to become an attorney who would serve as an advocate for the poor in our community." Looking up again, Coach Mac added, "Lord knows we needed the help."

"Wes was shot by a white police officer at 1 am at a convenience store outside of East Lansing. The officer later testified that Wes matched the description of a suspect being sought for a string of armed robberies. The officer also claimed that Wes was 'aggressive in his language and behavior' when they approached him. He claimed he had immediately suspected drugs to be involved."

Around the circle, each person's body absorbed and reflected the tension in the room. Fingers drummed, teeth ground, and lungs coughed sporadically as restlessness overtook the room. Several people shot sideways glances in the direction of Sherriff Cooley. These glances added to the considerable tension already present in the circle.

Coach Mac sighed heavily. He raised his head back, looked toward the sky, and whispered words no one else could hear. Then he resumed his reading.

"Both the officer and his partner testified that the officer drew his gun in self-defense. Wes, of course, was unarmed." Coach Mac stared silently at the paper.

"You need to understand," Coach Mac resumed, peering over his reading glasses. with eyes burning with passion. "My brother, Wesley, was the finest man I have ever known. He was a powerful, humble man of integrity. A man committed to his God and his family."

Coach Mac's hands began to shake. He laid the paper down, and attempted to restart, "Wesley bled . . ." After a few seconds, Coach Mac managed a strained, "I'm sorry," with a trembling voice. His increasingly reddened eyes communicated, without words, "Give me a minute."

Gracie handed Coach Mac a tissue. Then she offered to pass the box around the room. As Coach Mac attempted to catch his breath and find his voice, the blue tissue box was passed from person to person. Almost everyone took at least two tissues. Some took several.

Coach Mac then resumed reading slowly, "Wesley bled out in a filthy convenience store parking lot, fifteen minutes from his apartment." His voice deepened from anger. "The ambulance, according to witnesses, arrived twenty-five minutes after the deadly shot was fired. Had the paramedics arrived promptly, my brother's life would have been saved."

The circle took a collective deep breath as Coach Mac focused his eyes on the next paragraph. Stopping himself, he lowered the paper and took off his reading glasses again. His gaze turned toward Sherriff Cooley.

"Rod," Coach Mac said graciously, "You know that I have the utmost respect for you. You are a dear friend."

The Sherriff nodded. "Yes, John. I know." Cooley then circled the room with his eyes, adding, "It's okay. I hate this kind of thing as much as anyone."

"You're a good man, Rod," Coach Mac added as he looked again toward Cooley. "I wouldn't want anyone here to think I feel otherwise. You're a white cop. And a good man. I know . . ." Coach Mac paused, his voice shaking slightly, "I know what it's like to be labeled by stereotypes."

"John, as we often say to each other," Cooley said. "There's good and bad people of every color and in every profession."

"Yes. I believe it, Rod," Coach Mac replied. He placed the reading glasses back on his face and continued, "Over the next few months, I became hateful and bitter. I became filled with rage, especially toward white men. I was like a volcano just before it erupts. Eventually, I began hanging around on the fringe of a black militant gang. The gang gave me permission and justification for marinating in hatred."

Jimmy, Derrick, and Carlene exchanged brief glances with one another. Carlene shook her head slowly, her mouth suspended open. She let out a long, slow, measured breath. Jimmy and Derrick responded with expressions that silently screamed, "Can you believe this?"

This silent exchange repeated itself over and over around the circle of Northfield influencers. Each person struggled, in her or his own way, to process Coach Mac's startling revelations.

Only Jimbo Larsen opted out of the group's silent conversations. Jimbo sat alone, head down and arms crossed, looking directly at the floor.

CHAPTER 22

oach Mac drew another long breath, as if he were about to dive deep into a pool of water. "Eventually," Coach Mac read on, "I began to spew my rage on everyone and everything—including my girlfriend, Grace Martinez. That led to event number two," Coach Mac said sadly.

"Gracie, with whom I was living at the time, called the police on me one night. She was afraid I was about to harm her." Coach Mac's chest heaved and his voice trembled, but he continued, "I was drunk and I verbally threatened her." Coach Mac stopped. He lay the papers and his reading glasses in his lap and, with his used tissue, he wiped his eyes. At this point, everyone was wiping their eyes with whatever they could find, be it paper tissue or cloth sleeve.

Coach Mac, still looking down, said, "This is harder than I thought." Looking up, he smiled softly and added, "Thanks for bearing with me."

"We're here for you, Coach," Carlene said warmly, her eyes glistening with unshed tears.

"Take your time, John," Cooley said.

"No worries, Coach," Jimmy added. "We're here to support you." Around the room, quiet words of affirmation ranged from, "That's right," to "Absolutely, Coach," to "Amen."

"Okay, let's continue," Coach Mac replied as he returned his glasses to his face and lifted the papers from his lap. "I blasted Gracie with racial slurs. I ridiculed her mixed Latino and African-American heritage. I had a whiskey bottle in one hand and . . ." Coach Mac paused. His eyes squinted and his head shook side to side. He appeared to be having a hard time accepting the words he had written. "I was swinging the bottle wildly in Gracie's direction and screaming at her when the police arrived."

One face after another expressed astonishment. Even those who had previously heard parts of the story struggled to comprehend the picture Coach Mac painted. "Thank God, I never laid a hand on her. Thank you, Jesus," Coach Mac said as he closed his eyes and reached out to hold Gracie's hand.

At this point, no one moved. Not a finger. Not an eyelash. Then, without looking back down at the paper, Coach Mac added with a somber voice, "That night, I scared myself, too. Nothing like that ever—and I do mean ever—came close to happening again. I will, however, go to my grave with deep regret for how I treated my precious Gracie on that terrible night."

Gracie kissed Coach Mac's cheek and caressed his arm with her hands. Then she spoke, her voice soft yet resolute. "I have forgiven Johnny for that moment. In truth, I've had to forgive him for that whole season of our lives."

Gracie paused, her eyes turning to meet Coach Mac's before returning to the circle of dazed eyes staring back at her. "Johnny is not the same man he was back then," she continued. "But I did what I had to do at the time—I protected myself."

"It was the strong and courageous thing to do," Coach Mac added, his face wincing from the memory's sharp edges. He exhaled slowly with a trembling whisper. "Gracie, I'm so thankful I still have you." Reaching for her, Coach Mac's large hands gently engulfed Gracie's slender, clasped hands.

Gracie smiled warmly in response to Coach Mac's tender touch. Then she added, "Since that horrible night, I have never felt unsafe in Johnny's presence. Don't get me wrong, it took a while—but I've got more than three decades of evidence that tell me, and I hope you do as well, that John McKissack is a man who can be trusted. I trust him with my life and . . ." Gracie's eyes watered and her voice cracked as she completed her thought, "and with my heart."

Again ignoring his script, Coach Mac spoke to Gracie as if no one else were in the room, "To this day, you are the clearest picture of God's grace I've seen in this life. You are my grace, Gracie."

Coach Dale used her forefingers to wipe the smearing mascara from beneath her eyes. Principal Davis abandoned all attempts to hide the tears rolling over the edges of his eyelids. The room rippled with sniffles and sighs.

Suddenly Board Chair Johnson broke the silent stillness. "You know," he began, "I've read the original report handed down by Principal Pederson four, maybe five times. But I must say, Coach, hearing you talk about this is much more difficult than reading it on a piece of yellowed school board stationary. Much more."

All eyes turned nervously downward. Everyone froze when Dr. Johnson expressed his degree of shock. He looked down at his empty notepad while twirling a pen in his right hand. The room fell still. "I feel privileged to be here tonight with you Coach Mac, and with you, Gracie. I respect you both even more than before—I mean that, truly," Dr. Johnson said with a softness in his eyes.

"Thank you, Dr. Johnson. We appreciate that," Coach Mac replied.

"Yes, we do," Gracie added, her face widening into a deep smile of gratitude. Looking back at Coach Mac she said, "More than you know."

"So, now let's go to event number three," Coach Mac instructed.

"But first, a little background. Just before the incident with the whiskey bottle, I had been suspended from the University of Illinois at Chicago basketball team for disciplinary reasons. Later, when I turned my life around, Coach Norman reinstated me. His high expectations and deep grace were used by God to save my life, on many levels. Everything I teach in the Northfield Way I learned from the wisdom and strength of Coach Norman." Looking up, Coach Mac added, "Coach Norman and Wesley are my spiritual fathers."

Coach Mac turned his whole body in the direction of Derrick sitting three seats to his left. "That makes them the spiritual grandfathers of all my players, doesn't it, Coach D?"

All Derrick could manage in response was a weak, "I believe so, Coach." For more than an hour, Derrick had been trying to plug gaping holes in his mental imagery of Coach Mac. With each new revelation, another breach opened. Flooded by emotions, Derrick had finally lost all capacity for coherent thought.

Coach Mac paused. He studied Derrick intently. Derrick stared back with an empty expression. Coach Mac nodded to Derrick, then continued reading his prepared script.

"The third event occurred between being suspended at UIC and being reinstated. It was a huge crossroad in my life," Coach Mac said haltingly as his voice lowered and his face grimaced. "I was present at an incident that almost led to someone's death. The young man was white and the brother of a known white supremacy leader in northern Indiana. I don't know whether or not he was actually a white supremacist. At the time, it didn't matter to me."

Coach Mac shook his head, then turned toward Gracie. She smiled reassuringly.

"I did not inflict any injuries on the young man. But I was there. He was beaten mercilessly and left lying in an alley gasping for breath. That night," Coach Mac continued with conviction, "I walked away from the path that led me to that place. I turned and walked away," Coach Mac said, nodding his head. "Not just from the gang, but from hate, from prejudice, from violence. I walked away, forever."

"Thank God." Dr. Johnson spoke on behalf of the group.

Coach Mac, still holding the papers in his right hand, raised both hands toward the sky. In a worshipful gesture, Coach Mac said, "Yes, thank you, Jesus."

Coach Mac began reading again. "I learned later that the man lived and eventually recovered fully—at least physically. The crime was never reported. He was likely too frightened to implicate gang members. I tried to reach out to him years later, but understandably he just wanted to put it all behind him. I was left, therefore, to find my grace in God alone."

Coach Mac surveyed the whole room, which now sat in motionless silence. Coach Mac broke the silence. "Okay, home stretch. Thanks for your patience."

"Thank you, Coach Mac," Jimmy responded. "Yes, thank you," echoed others throughout the room. Only Derrick failed to speak.

"As you now know," Coach Mac began again, "Years eighteen to twenty were dark years for me. Only by the grace of God, His grace in my Gracie, and His grace in Coach Norman am I even alive today." Coach Mac's mouth expanded into a gently sloping smile. "I am fundamentally undeserving of all the good things I have experienced at Northfield High School and all the good people with whom we have shared life for the last thirty-six years. My life with you has been a great gift. I hope that, somehow, my sharing these broken parts of my life will be a gift to you."

Coach Mac slowly folded the pages of paper into increasingly smaller rectangles. Then he closed with, "We love you all."

Everyone leaned back in their chairs. Brief glances and slight smiles slowly passed back and forth across the room. The tissues made their rounds again as small pockets of hushed conversations sprang up around the circle.

The doorbell rang, interrupting all of the side conversations in the room. Gracie made her way to the door. As she left, Principal Davis put his arm around Coach Mac's broad shoulders. "Are you okay, friend?" Principal Davis asked.

Coach Mac hesitated. "I think so . . ." he said unconvincingly. Then, in a more confident tone, "Yes, actually, I'm good."

Deputy Taylor entered the room with Gracie. She offered him the only remaining unoccupied chair. The officer offered an anxious, "Thank you. All of you, thanks." He sat rigidly in his chair. His head barely moved, but his eyes roamed the circle. Deputy Taylor, sensing the moment, searched for clues to identify what kind of surreal world he had just entered.

Sherriff Cooley called out to Taylor from across the circle, "Andrew, I'll catch you up later." The words helped set Deputy Taylor at ease.

Principal Davis unwrapped his arm from around Coach Mac and stood beside him. Commanding the room, he announced, "So, friends, now we prepare to enter the next chapter of Coach Mac's story and of his storied career." Turning first toward Gracie and then toward Coach Mac, Principal Davis smiled at them both with great affection. As if giving a toast at joyous event, he said with a huge smile, "May the next chapters of your lives be as filled with the same measure of strength and courage as all the ones before."

"Now," Principal Davis said, returning to his typical formal self, "Let's discuss how we are going to inform the public. These are very private and sensitive issues for Coach Mac and Gracie. However, I fully concur with Coach Mac and Jimmy. We must get ahead of the social media release of the Dark Nation's devastating lies."

Everyone in the room had a piece of advice or word of encouragement to offer. Everyone, that is, except Derrick and Jimbo. Derrick, with the exception of an occasional strained smile, remained unresponsive. His mind wasn't just stunned. It was blown. All he could think was, *I've got to get out of here.* As the other guests began to make their departure, he rose to his feet and quietly slipped out of the house along with them, without a word to Coach Mac and Gracie.

By contrast, Jimbo Larsen remained in his seat. He made no movement toward anyone, until the last guest had departed. Once he was certain that he was alone with Coach Mac and Gracie, Jimbo began to sob uncontrollably.

"I'll get you some water, Jim," Gracie offered as she headed toward the kitchen.

Coach Mac sat down next to Jimbo. He placed his left arm around the top of Jimbo's heaving shoulders. Jimbo buried his head deeper into his chest.

Without looking up, Jimbo began to speak. He stopped and started as he fought for the breath necessary to form his words.

"I'm so sorry, Coach . . . I'm just . . . so . . . very, very . . . sorry."

Coach Mac reached with his right hand to steady Jimbo as he appeared to be on the verge of collapsing into the floor.

"I knew . . . I . . . ," Jimbo once again gave way to a wave of overwhelming sorrow.

Gracie returned and offered Jimbo a glass of ice water. He did not respond. She silently sat the glass on an end table next to him. Gracie then made her way to a seat across from the two men. Her eyes met Coach Mac's with a glance of caution and concern.

"What are you trying to say?" Coach Mac asked firmly.

"I'm the one who sent the texts," Jimbo said in a rush of words and breath. He looked up for the first time, though not directly towards either of the McKissacks. "I wanted to tell you, but I just . . ." Jimbo's head dropped as he rocked back and forth. "But I was too afraid."

Coach Mac's voice grew stern. "You knew about this?" His thoughts were beginning to piece together this new data. Coach Mac quickly added, "And you knew who's been doing this—and you never told us?"

"I couldn't . . . I mean . . . I know I was wrong . . . It's just. . ." Jimbo's words trailed off and he wiped his nose with one sleeve of his disheveled dress shirt. With the other sleeve, he wiped his sweaty forehead.

"There's no excuse for this, Jim," Coach Mac said sternly.

"Yes, sir. I know." Jimbo heaved a deep sigh, then drew two long breaths. "No excuse. That's what you taught me," Jimbo said as his voiced cracked. Breathing another heavy sigh, he continued. "It's Rolf, Carla Marie's older brother. He's a mean SOB, Coach. He's just so filled with hate."

"Is he the one they call 'Wolf?'" Coach Mac inquired roughly. *Racist piece of . . .* John McKissack struggled to suppress his thoughts. "Go on, Jimbo."

"Yes, sir. The same. He moved here about 18 months ago, trying to find work. I tried to help him, but he's a worse drunk than me." Jimbo's head dropped again as his shoulders slumped as far forward as possible without leading him to the floor. "He's gotten into a crowd that blames everybody else for their problems, especially . . ." Here he paused again, avoiding the Coach's eyes, "people who look like you. I'm pretty sure he's tied in with those Bedford County Wilson boys. I tell you, Coach, Wolf is just about the worst of all of them."

Coach Mac began to open his mouth, but stopped to filter his next words carefully. Slowly he started again, "Why didn't you just come to us, Jimbo? Why have you let this go on so long?"

"I thought, maybe if JT would investigate it or try to stop the whole thing, then maybe—I don't know, Coach. I just needed it to go away. I never wanted it to become public. And, I thought . . . I was stupid." Jimbo reached for the glass of water beside him. He looked toward Gracie. "Thank you," he said as he began to drink rapidly. Seeing Gracie's wounded expression, however, Jimbo choked on his drink. He put the glass down, coughed three times, and continued. "Carla Marie grew up in the coal mining hills of West Virginia, and . . . well, folks don't know this, but it was pretty bad. The kids in school always made fun of her and her family. 'White trash'—that's what they called them. I knew how much it would hurt her if this became public. With Wolf and his cronies at the center of the scandal, she—and me—would become 'those people' everybody talks about in a small town like Northfield."

"So, you allowed this to build up and build up, never telling me, never stepping up to deal with this, because you were trying to protect Carla Marie? And your reputation!" Coach Mac asked angrily.

"Well, it's what I thought was right. But it wasn't. So I just sent texts to Jimmy. And I drank . . . Coach, I've made a helluva mess," Jimbo lamented.

"Yes, son. Yes, you have," Coach Mac said, his voice rising. "You threw me and Gracie, this community, and even Carla Marie under the bus because you were afraid to do the right thing! And you used a bottle to drown your shame!"

"Johnny," Gracie said cautiously. "There's a lot . . ."

"Mrs. Gracie," Jimbo interrupted. "He's right. I make no excuses. And I'm ready to deal with the consequences, whatever they are."

"Are you?" Coach Mac snapped back. Coach Mac then stood and stared out the window. The three sat in silence for a long, tense minute. Coach Mac then turned toward Jimbo. "Jim, I'm exhausted. And I'm angry. And I'm certainly not confident that I can talk to you further without saying things I will later regret."

"Yes, sir," Jimbo said, raising his eyes to look Coach Mac in the face for the first time in the evening. "I deserve all of that—and worse."

"I want you to know that I choose to forgive because of all that God has forgiven me. But, Jim, you need to leave—now," Coach Mac said as he rose from his chair.

Jimbo stood and began to walk towards Coach Mac. The expression on Coach Mac's face convinced him otherwise. Stopping several feet from him, Jimbo said, "I know this isn't what you taught me. I know I've failed badly. But, Coach, if you won't give up on me, I'll do whatever it takes to make this right."

Coach Mac shook his head. "I'm not sure you can make this right, Jimbo."

Jimbo's chin dropped to his chest.

"Jim," Coach Mac said sternly.

Jimbo's eyes raised respectfully.

"Do what's right going forward. Maybe one day you and I can be fully reconciled. But not tonight, Jim. Not tonight."

"Yes, sir. Thank you, sir. I understand." Jimbo turned to leave, then glancing over his shoulder, he said, "I want to make you proud, Coach."

"I know, Jim. We're both going to need a lot of grace to get to that point. Thankfully, God has a lot of grace to give."

"Thank God," Jimbo sighed.

CHAPTER 23

Derrick stared into the full-length mirror on the bathroom door. Staring back at him was a man dressed in slim blue jeans and an untucked white shirt. On his feet, he wore a pair of gray casual dress shoes. Over his shirt and shoulders, he wore a thin-cut blue blazer. "Do I look religious enough?" he questioned himself in the mirror.

As he ran his fingers through his hair, Derrick recalled his conversation with Mrs. Gracie. "Sure, I'll go to church with you one Sunday," Derrick had replied to her soft invitation.

"How about the first Sunday in March?" she suggested.

"Sure, why not?" he'd said.

"My timing is terrible," he muttered to himself as he walked toward the kitchen. The second to last thing Derrick wanted to do was to go to church this morning. The last thing he wanted to do was go to church with Coach Mac and Mrs. Gracie.

After last night's revelations, Derrick couldn't pretend everything was normal. He had questions. Lots of them. Besides that, it had been five weeks since Nikki had announced her pregnancy and moved out. Besides a few emotionally complicated phone conversations, they'd had no communication. *This sucks,* he thought bitterly. *My whole life sucks.*

Derrick grabbed his keys from the counter. The page he had written in his journal last night caught his attention. Derrick paused to read it once more.

MAXIM 3
LOVE
My first priority will be love.

I CANNOT believe what I just heard! He's the one who always told me, "Love fiercely," and, "Speak the truth. Press into the hard things. Don't run away from conflict." Well, Coach, here we go. Risking it all. I HATE this.
Things to do on Sunday:

1. *Talk to Coach Mac and Gracie after church. Say the hard things. Don't run!*
2. *Talk to Nikki. Listen first. Tell the truth. Love fiercely.*
3. *Call Carlene. Ask her to help with coaching.*
4. *Prepare final game plan.*
5. *Pick up the pieces of whatever's left of my life.*
6. *Sleep—if I can.*

"The stronger person in the room is the one least afraid of conflict." Coach Mac says. Then, why?? Why?? WHY didn't you talk to me about all of this before last night?? Nothing makes sense anymore.

Derrick picked up his journal and gently slapped the counter with it, forcing himself out of his pity party. "Here we go," he said to the empty room as he flicked the journal across the countertop.

———

Following church, Derrick drove to the McKissacks' home for Sunday lunch. Normally, a Sunday afternoon at the McKissacks' would have been Derrick's idea of heaven. Gracie was a legendary cook who loved to lavish on Derrick.

"I'm afraid you don't get enough good food, Derrick," she would say in her perfectly crafted doting mother voice.

"Truth is," Derrick would tell her every time, "There's no way I could ever get enough of your cooking, Mrs. Gracie."

Gracie's bright smiles suggested that she enjoyed his compliments as much as he enjoyed her food.

A match made in heaven, for sure, Derrick regularly thought to himself.

On this day, however, after church Derrick asked if it would be possible to talk for few minutes, before the meal. "And, I apologize," Derrick added, "I will need to leave a little early. I'm meeting Nikki at the Echo Lake Forrest Preserve at 2:30."

"Of course," Mrs. Gracie responded as she motioned Derrick toward the living room.

Settling into his favorite chair, Coach Mac said, "We've invited Nikki to come over later tonight, D. We're going to tell her our story in person. We thought that would be better."

"Yeah, she told me. I think that's a very good idea," Derrick said in a serious tone.

Gracie sat down and smoothed out her skirt. She sat facing Derrick in a polite, proper position. Coach Mac leaned forward, his elbows resting on the arms of his chair.

"So . . . well, Coach, Mrs. Gracie," Derrick said by way of introduction. "I was journaling about maxim three last and I . . ." Derrick shifted in his seat and breathed in nervously. He then made a second attempt to get to the point. "When the preacher said what he said this morning about 'speaking the truth in love,' I was surprised . . . I thought that was an original quote from you." Derrick smiled thinly.

"Derrick, I doubt I've had an original quote in my life!" Coach Mac chuckled.

"You don't give yourself enough credit, Coach." Derrick smiled weakly again. He crossed his legs and slid a few inches lower in his seat. His voice, and his courage, stalled.

"Derrick," Mrs. Gracie said as her eyes connected with his. "I would imagine you've got some things you need to say to us."

"Yes, ma'am. I do." Derrick uncrossed his legs. He sat up straight. "Coach Mac," Derrick started, "I don't understand." Derrick turned his eyes downward. He clasped his fingers together, rubbing the palm of his left hand with the thumb of his right hand. The motion was a calming distraction for his frayed nerves.

"What don't you understand, D? Say what you need to say," Coach Mac encouraged.

"I don't understand." Derrick breathed a deep breath, unlocked his fingers, and pressed into the conversation. "I don't understand how you can tell me year after year, 'You can talk to me, D. Don't close yourself off, D. Love fiercely, D. Speak the truth, D.' But you . . ." Derrick placed his elbows onto his thighs. He tapped his fingers against one another as if he were playing the piano on a mirror. Derrick swallowed hard, then began again, "But—"

"But I don't do the same with you?" Coach Mac interrupted.

Derrick's fingers ceased tapping. "Yes," he said with a voice steeled by a fierce determination to speak his truth.

"That's fair, D. But you also need to understand a couple of things," Coach Mac responded. "I came here as a young black man with a questionable past. Coach Norman knew Principal Pederson from their military service together in Korea. That's the only reason I got the job—that and the fact that Northfield was desperate."

"Yeah, I get that," Derrick said as he leaned back and crossed his legs again. "But, Coach, that was thirty-seven years ago. Why wouldn't you trust us now? Why did you hide all this from us? From me? I'm on your side—haven't I proven that?"

Coach Mac stared back unblinking. He opened his mouth to speak, then closed it again. His head moved slowly up and down as he measured his words. "You may be right, D. I'm not saying you're wrong," Coach Mac said softly. "But, D, until you've been in my place, until you've been shitted on over and over and over because your skin is black, until you've had to be better than everyone else—just so you can gain their respect— only to have them say, 'He's such a gifted leader *for a black man*,'—until you've been in that position, Derrick," Coach Mac's eyes flared and his right index pointed angrily at Derrick, "Don't assume you know what I should or shouldn't do."

"Johnny," Gracie said softly, her hand resting on his.

"I get it, Coach. Maybe I should've just kept my mouth shut," Derrick said as he squirmed. He looked like a man sitting in a pile of ants nipping at his backside. Derrick began to rise out of his seat, turning himself toward the door.

"Derrick," Coach Mac spoke firmly.

Derrick returned his eyes to Coach Mac's face. He recognized that look immediately. It was the same look Derrick had first seen at his father's funeral a dozen years ago.

A lot of first-time events had suddenly occurred in a very short amount of time. Derrick had confronted Coach Mac. Coach Mac had spoken to Derrick in an angry, defensive tone. Derrick had heard Coach Mac swear. And now, peering back at Coach Mac's sad, yet compassionate eyes, Derrick added another first.

"I love you, Coach Mac," Derrick said for the first time ever. Derrick's eyes and nose began to sting from moisture rising in both. "I'm not trying to judge you. I'm just trying to understand," he said as his head sank in despair.

"Of course you are, son." Coach Mac rose from his seat. Coach Mac's arms reached out to embrace Derrick. Welcoming the moment, Derrick wrapped his arms tightly around Coach Mac.

After pounding each other on the back with loud slaps of their palms, the two released their embrace. Pulling back, each offered a supportive smile and nod. No words were spoken as they gathered their emotions and returned to their seats. Just before Derrick sat down, Gracie walked over to his side.

"Johnny was right about you," she said softly as she reached out to hug him. "I love you, D."

"I love you too, Mrs. Gracie," Derrick replied, adding another first to his list of new experiences.

Coach Mac took a long drink of water as Gracie returned to her seat and Derrick plopped back onto the sofa. "D," he began, "It's been a long weekend." He paused and looked out the window at white wisps of clouds streaking across a bright, blue sky. "But a good one," he added, still looking out the window.

"Coach, the people of Northfield love you. They're not going to turn on you," Derrick said confidently.

"I hope not," Coach Mac sighed, clearly unconvinced.

"They won't, Johnny," Gracie spoke with confidence, "Derrick's right. They love you. You've been there for them for 37 years." Gracie placed her hand gently behind Coach Mac's neck. Her smile widened and her eyes softened. "They'll be there for you."

"Gracie, you of all people should know by now," Coach Mac challenged, "it's not a level playing field for a black man with a past."

"Coach." Derrick hesitated. His eyes dropped, then he said without looking up, "If I could . . . say something about that."

Derrick's hands balled into fists as he pulled them close into his stomach. His lips pursed together as Coach Mac replied, "Of course, D."

"I want to be very careful here, so please forgive me if I say this wrong," Derrick spoke haltingly.

"Go on," Coach Mac spoke, his curiosity raised.

"I could never speak to what it is like to be a black man in this community—especially 30 years ago. So, believe me, I am not trying to say that I do . . . that is, that I know what you've been through." Derrick paused to gauge Coach Mac's response.

Coach Mac nodded, so Derrick continued. "But I do know a little bit about having a past . . ." Derrick checked in once more. Coach Mac nodded again. "And I know what it's like to be ashamed of stupid decisions in my teenage years. And, Coach, I also know what it's like," Derrick continued, his words and his tone gaining strength, "To have people judge you when they have no idea of the demons you've had to fight or the things you've been through. I know that much, Coach. I know that for damn sure."

"Yes, you're right, D. You know a lot about dealing with the shame of a dark past. More than I probably realize." Coach Mac said, his facial expression morphing into an intense stare. "But, you're also right. You don't know what it's like to be a black man—especially from my generation. You can never know or assume you know what it's been like for me. You have to keep that in mind, no matter what you've been through."

"Yes, sir. I will," Derrick responded.

"I trust that you will," Coach said sincerely. "And, I understand your point as well. I can't let the past wounds of people's hate and prejudice become an excuse for walling off people who want to love me well. That's not the Northfield Way. It's not the way of Jesus, either."

Derrick looked down at his hands. He loosened his tightly clenched fists. "Coach, I have received so much love, from both of you—and from others in the community, too. And . . ." Derrick dropped his hands. His face tensed as he searched for the right words. His hands, still in his lap, he opened them, palms up again. "Look, you've taught me that it's worth letting people in—even if only it's only a very few people who choose to give you grace and to love you well."

Sensing Coach Mac was tracking with him, Derrick continued enthusiastically, "You've taught me so much—but especially this one thing: people can't offer you their grace and love if you shut them out."

A slight smile unfolded across Coach Mac's face. With a wink, he said, "You know, Coach Walker, the greatest compliment a teacher can receive is being taught by his student."

Derrick sat quietly, looking first at Coach Mac, then back at Gracie. He had no words left.

"Thank you, D," Coach Mac added, "For reminding me that I'm never too old to keep learning."

Derrick finally broke his silence. "I learned it from the best, Coach." Derrick smiled, then added cautiously, "And that brings me to one more thing I need to say." He paused, tilting his head to the side, his eyes moving downward. "Something I should have told you long before now,"

Gracie glanced apprehensively toward Coach Mac. Clasping his hands together, Coach Mac slowly leaned forward. With his elbows pressing at a severe angle against each arm of his chair, Coach Mac's chin came to rest on his interlocking fingers. His voice deepened in tone and slowed in cadence. "And what would that be, D?"

"Nikki's pregnant. I'm going to be a dad," Derrick said with muted enthusiasm.

"D, that's wonderful!" Gracie exclaimed as she rushed toward Derrick, arms outstretched. "How far along is she?"

"About sixteen weeks . . . I think that's right," Derrick replied.

Coach Mac rose as quickly as his knees could straighten into an upright position. In disbelief, he said, "Derrick, I have never been happier for you—but why have you waited so long to tell us?" As he spoke, Coach Mac embraced Derrick with a signature John McKissack bear hug, accented by several strong thumps on the back.

Derrick stepped back. Sighing deeply, he said, "I know. I should have told you. I'm sorry, but it's just . . . well," Derrick hesitated. "It's just so complicated. And, after she and I talk this afternoon, it may be even more complicated. I just don't know . . ." Derrick dropped his chin. Closing his eyes, he paused. As he opened then raised his eyes, Derrick's attention was arrested by a ticking clock hanging on the wall just behind Coach Mac. Startled, he looked at his watch. "Good grief, it's 1:15 already!"

"Then, let's eat, shall we?" Gracie replied enthusiastically. Then she gushed, "And I want more details on this precious child about to be born into the world!"

"Yes, ma'am." As they began to move toward the dining room Derrick added, "Hey, Coach, I was wondering if, over lunch, I could also ask you for some more details—especially about Wesley and Coach Norman—if that's okay?"

"Of course. There have never been two finer men on God's green earth, D." Coach Mac sighed, then continued with a distant longing in his voice, "I just wish you had met them."

"Me, too. But it's not too late for you to introduce them to me," Derrick replied.

Coach Mac affectionately slapped Derrick on the back once more. He squeezed his shoulder tightly. "No, D. It seems like it's not too late for any of us to benefit from the grace of God in my past."

Derrick ate faster and lighter than usual. His stomach continued to churn with anxiety. The conversation with Coach Mac had gone better than he had feared. Still, there was much yet to be worked through in their relationship. And, of course, the day of hard conversations was only half over.

As Derrick stepped off the McKissacks' porch, he was greeted soberly by Jimbo and Carla Marie Larsen.

"Good day, Derrick," Jimbo said.

"Yeah, good day, Mr. Larsen, Mrs. Larsen," Derrick replied with a nod of the head. Looking back over his shoulder he wondered how many more conversations the McKissacks had planned for their day.

Once inside, the Larsens perched anxiously on the McKissacks' large sofa. "Thank you, Coach, and you, too, Mrs. Gracie, for giving us your time this afternoon," Jimbo began.

"I'm trying to do what's right, Jim. I'm not sure this is a good idea, but my Gracie said it was the right thing to do. I trust her," Coach Mac responded politely.

"Thank you, so much," Carla Marie nodded. As always, she was well dressed, though not in as flashy a manner as usual. Today she appeared frail, in body and in spirit. She scooted closer to Jimbo, as if she required his strength just to stay upright. He responded by holding her hand.

"We don't want take up too much of your time—just a few minutes in fact," Jimbo said.

Coach Mac and Gracie nodded.

"I want to communicate three things to you both. At some point, I . . ." Jimbo looked at Carla Marie for a moment, smiled nervously, then continued, "At some point, *we* will tell our story and ask forgiveness from all those we have hurt by our silence."

Coach Mac's broad shoulders softened ever so slightly. His jaw, however, remained clenched, as were his fists.

"So, I've written these down. I would like to read them to you," Jimbo said. Clearing his throat, he put on his reading glasses and began reading. "First, I want to ask your forgiveness for my silence. I failed you. I had so many opportunities to act with strength and courage. Instead,

I gave in . . ." Jimbo cleared his throat again. He sat back to breathe in a deep breath and pressed forward, "I gave in to weakness and fear. I was a coward, Coach Mac.

Second, I want to ask your forgiveness for not living by the principles of the Northfield Way. You taught me Purpose, Passion, Love, Responsibility, and Humility. I have dishonored your impact in my life. My heart is . . ." Jimbo fought off the emotions welling up in his throat. After a brief pause, he managed, "my heart is absolutely broken over this."

Carla Marie wiped the tears from her eyes with her hands. Gracie carried a box of tissues to Carla Marie's lap. "Here, dear," Gracie offered compassionately. The kindness, in word and action, launched an even larger stream of tears.

"And, third, we want to confess something to you. This is the hardest part, Coach. I make no excuses, but I am telling you the truth. Only now do Carla Marie and I realize how much we have failed you as friends." Jimbo looked toward Carla Marie for reassurance. She nodded vigorously as she moved her gaze away from Jimbo and toward the McKissack's.

Sorrowful words staggered and stuttered out of Carla Marie's mouth. "Coach, Gracie, I . . . we. . . . Oh, Lord, I am so, so sorry . . . We just . . . I got scared and, like Jimbo said I don't want to make excuses . . ." Carla Marie drew a deep breath, regaining her composure. Wiping her eyes once more with an already soaked wad of tissues, she spoke more clearly, "I have failed you as a friend. And even though I don't deserve it—at all," Carla Marie shifted forward as she pleaded, "I do pray that you will find a way, in your hearts, somehow, to forgive us."

Carla Marie paused, then looked back at Jimbo. "Okay, honey, you can go on now. I just needed to say that." Then she added quickly, "Jimbo's truly reading this for both of us. Coach, Mrs. Gracie, we both mean every word."

As Jimbo returned to his notes, he tagged Carla Marie's closing thought with a firm, "Yes, we do." His voice rose in conviction. "We have been at every Northfield Warrior basketball game for decades. We've been the lead boosters for most of that time. We've been in your home and had you in our home. Dang it, Coach, we've been in church with you for at least fifteen of those years." Jimbo shook his head in disbelief as the words on the paper struck him hard once gain. "And, yet, we have failed to speak up against the racism that continues in our community. We've not stood with you, not like real friends do. We've not said what should have been said. Too often, when racist comments were made, in the stands, at work, and, in our home, we've remained silent. Passive. We are accomplices to racism, Coach. And, honestly . . ."

Jimbo laid down the paper on the table. After a long pause, Jimbo looked Coach Mac directly in the eye for the first time. Jimbo spoke with a tremor in his voice. "Coach, it means that in a very real way, I've been living as a racist. If I were truly a man who condemned racism for the evil it is, I would not have tolerated all the things I let go. And for that, I beg your forgiveness—" Jimbo looked away from Coach Mac. His head shook up and down. His jaws clenched. He forced himself to breathe slowly, then reconnected his eyes to Coach Mac, "Just like Carla Marie said, I beg your forgiveness, even though I don't deserve it."

"That was very powerful, Jimbo, Carla Marie," Gracie said warmly. "I think that is a good start."

"Yes," Coach Mac added flatly as he nodded toward Gracie, "It's a good start. I'm certainly not ready to talk any more today. However, this at least turns us toward a day when I will be ready."

"Well, we won't take more of your time," Jimbo said, as he and Carla Marie rose to their feet. "Thank you," he added.

Coach Mac extended his hand to shake Jimbo's. "Jim. Carla Marie," Coach Mac said with a slight softening of his face, "As I said before, I choose to forgive you. It will, however, be a long while—if ever—before I decide to trust you."

"That's all I could ask, Coach," Jimbo replied, fighting back a rising tide of emotion.

"Yes, that in itself is such a gift," Carla Marie said as she moved forward to hug Coach Mac.

Coach Mac pulled back, offering his hand. Carla Marie quickly transitioned into a handshake. "I understand," she said.

"Thank you," Coach Mac said.

"Yes, thank you," Gracie added as she leaned in to hug Carla Marie.

Turning toward the door, Jimbo said, "Coach, I won't be talking to anyone about this without talking to you first."

"That sounds right, Jim. But I challenge you to go directly to Jimmy and, with confidentiality, tell him the truth as well. You owe that to him."

"Yes, sir, I do. I owe him that." Jimbo paused, then added, "I'm going to talk to Sheriff Cooley tonight as well. I . . . we want him to get on this as soon as possible." Jimbo moved his right hand through his hair as he spoke. "And, one more thing, Coach. I'm going to go to a residential rehab program later this month. I'm ready to admit that I have a problem."

"Excellent, Jim. I'm proud of that choice."

For the first time in months, Carla Marie watched a natural smile unfold across her husband's weary, swollen face.

CHAPTER 24

errick arrived at Echo Lake Forest Preserve just before 2:30 p.m. His stomach was still filled with Gracie McKissack's ham, sweet potato casserole, green beans, buttered rolls, and coconut cake. His mind was likewise full. Highlights from Coach Mac's stirring revelations about Wesley McKissack, Coach Norman, and Coach's own misdeeds replayed over and over in his thoughts.

Derrick walked toward a wide gravel path that wound itself like a loose ribbon around Echo Lake. He sat down on a wooden bench, spreading his arms and legs to soak in the warm sun. To his left, he saw the marshy eastern edge of the lake. Glancing to his right, he recognized Nikki's black Mini Cooper snaking its way along the flat, winding road leading to the Preserve. The car swiftly navigated the curves. It was sporty, aggressive, and cute, all at the same time.

"Just like its owner," Derrick observed.

Nikki stepped out of the car with a wave and a smile. Not having seen her in person in the past five weeks, Derrick had no idea what to expect. Nikki met him with a hug, an affectionate kiss on the cheek, and a sincere, "I'm glad to see you, D."

"I've missed you, Nik. More than you know," Derrick said thickly as he stepped back, fully appreciating Nikki's presence with him. "A lot's been happening—and I mean it when I say mean 'a lot.'" Derrick replied earnestly.

"Same here," Nikki replied. "Except, maybe not as much?" she added, curious. She had been taken aback by Derrick's unusually high emotional energy.

"I don't know where to start," Derrick began.

"Well, it's a beautiful day. I'm in no hurry. So, let's start with a walk. We can catch up along the way," Nikki suggested.

"Sounds great!" Derrick responded. He reached out to hold Nikki's hand, then caught himself. His eyes met hers anxiously. With a gentle smile, she wrapped her wrist around his elbow and began walking closely alongside him.

Derrick breathed a sigh of relief, followed by a deep breath to calm his nerves. Nikki's touch felt like an electric current on his skin. His palms were sweating and his throat ran dry. He felt like a thirteen-year-old on his first date at a middle school dance.

After a few moments of trivial chit chat, Derrick stopped walking. He allowed Nikki's arm to drop so that he could stand facing her. "Nikki, how are you doing? For real?"

Nikki stared back thoughtfully, one eyebrow raised. She carefully studied Derrick's eyes. She read the curve of his mouth. Nikki's head tilted slighted as she strained to interpreted Derrick's expression.

Nikki placed a hand on Derrick's arm. She gently brushed it up and down. "That's sweet of you to ask, D," she said. She dropped her hand to meet his, giving it a gentle squeeze, then returned her wrist to his arm. The two resumed strolling, but at a much slower pace.

"Since you asked," Nikki began. Nikki reviewed her last three weeks. The highlights included several hard conversations with her parents.

"Last Wednesday night," she said, "My dad came home from church. Honestly, I was just avoiding him. I'm tired of his vibe about how disappointed he is in me." Nikki watched her feet move sluggishly along, dispersing loose rocks with each step forward. "It's not like I'm super proud of where I am in life, right now, you know," Nikki said, still staring downward.

Nikki raised her eyes to Derrick's. "D, I'm really trying to get this right." She paused. "The truth is my dad always gets stuck in his own crap. He never sees me or understands what I'm going through. But," Nikki's eyes widened to match the smile spreading across her face, "Last

Wednesday, Dad came over to where I was sitting. He knelt down beside my chair and said, 'Nikki, I need you to know I'm very proud of you.'"

Derrick could only mutter a quiet, "Wow," in response. Then he reached across his body with his left hand to hold the hand Nikki had wrapped around his right elbow.

Nikki used the fingers on her other hand to pull away several strands of hair covering her eyes. She tucked the hair behind her ears and continued. "D, then—for the first time in years—my dad actually said, 'I'm sorry.' Then he said, 'I love you, Nikki. And I know you're going to be okay.'"

"That's great, Nik." Derrick was genuinely glad. He knew how much she craved affirmation from her parents.

"I know," Nikki replied, her head nodding up and down enthusiastically. "That's not all," Nikki said as she once again took his arm and began to walk by his side. "Dad talked about how, in his words, he's been in similar situations. He told me, 'I've needed God's grace so many times, Nikki. But for some reason I've completely forgotten how to give it.' He started talking about grace, D!"

"That's so weird," Derrick said.

"Yeah, right?" Nikki responded, her voice rising in amazement. "Grace. My dad and I were talking about grace—the same way I've been talking with Mrs. Gracie and Coach Mac about grace. So crazy . . ."

Derrick turned his head toward the noise of a large bird taking flight in the distance. Still looking away, he said, "Well, it's about to get weirder, a lot weirder." Derrick shuddered as he turned back to look at Nikki.

"What do you mean?" Nikki asked.

"Oh, I . . ." Derrick retreated from the topic. "Look, let's not go there now," Derrick said, deflecting. "It's just a lot's going on in Northfield. You'll know soon enough." He squeezed Nikki's hand.

He wanted to get back on track, and quickly. "Let's get back to us," Derrick said as he stopped and turned his attention to Nikki's eyes dancing in the sunlight. He quickly turned away, fighting a growing urge to kiss her passionately on the lips.

Nikki pulled Derrick nearer. "Yeah, I'd like to get back to us."

Derrick suggested they walk over to the dock. On the way, Derrick recounted the morning of what should have been his graduation day. He had never told anyone about the despair of that day. It was time she knew the shame that drove him. It was time that he, like Coach Mac, made full disclosure.

As they arrived at the dock, they both lowered themselves into a cross-legged sitting position.

"That story is so sad, D. It makes me wish I had been here for you."

"Oh, no . . . no, no, no," Derrick laughed, raising his hand in protest. "No way! I'm so glad you never knew that version of me." Derrick peered over the edge of the dock. Sparkling ripples streaked across Echo Lake's surface as spring breezes rose and fell across the water's surface. "I've got a lot of big dreams buried down there, Nikki." Reaching his hand to hold hers, Derrick turned toward Nikki and smiled. "But not all of them."

"Speaking of," Nikki began, her face growing serious. "I know it's our decision to make together, but I want to tell you where I am in regards to our baby. I—"

"Wait," Derrick interrupted. The hand holding Nikki's began shaking. The words that came next were sincere but unsteady. "Whatever you say—and I mean this. Thank you for including me. Honestly, Nik, thank you."

"Of course, D. It's the right thing to do," Nikki said, squeezing Derrick's hand as she released it, "And, like I said, I'm really trying to do the right thing." Leaning back on her elbows, Nikki began again. "D, I don't want us to place our baby with an adoptive family."

Derrick's head dropped in relief. He placed a hand on Nikki's arm and patted it. He turned his whole body towards hers, gazing directly into her eyes and said, "I'm here for you. And for our baby, Nikki."

"I believe that Derrick. Honestly, if I didn't, I'd probably consider adoption. But I do believe you. And I want to partner with you."

"What does that mean?" Derrick inquired hesitantly.

"I'm not sure. It depends on what happens next . . . in our relationship, I mean."

"And what do you want, Nikki?" Derrick asked.

"Well, I know what I want. I want what God wants for us. Both of us. So, as Coach Mac says, 'If you want to find God and His will, then you have to live in reality. That's where He lives.' So, D, I guess we need to dive into the deep end of reality. So . . ." Nikki shrugged her shoulders and pursed her lips. She paused, waiting for him to catch up with her thoughts.

"Let me make sure I understand," Derrick began cautiously. "One way or the other, we're going to share parenting. Either as a married couple and family or you will be a single mom, at least for now."

"That's how I see it," Nikki said.

"Well, that's how I see it, too, Ms. Coles or, maybe, Mrs. Walker," Derrick said playfully.

A smirk crossed Nikki's face as she rolled her eyes. "Yes, either way, Mr. Walker." Nikki said. "So, your move," she said, joining his playful manner as she pointed her finger gently into his chest. "What do you want, Mr. Walker? What's your reality?"

"My reality is: I've got three huge challenges in front of me."

Counting off on his fingers, Derrick said, "One, I've got to coach the Northfield Warriors against the number two team in the state—in their home gym, without Coach Mac or Jamarcus. Two, I've got to deal with the fallout of all that's going on in Northfield—more about that later."

He paused when he got to the ring finger on his left hand. "And, three, I've got to be here for you."

With each successive finger, Nikki's shoulders slumped. The thought of competing against Northfield basketball as priority number one in Derrick's heart was disheartening.

Derrick reached out both hands to take Nikki's left hand. Tapping her left ring finger, Derrick said, "And *this* is by far the most important of the three. I can lose the regionals, I can lose my job at Northfield. Heck, I can lose all respect from the people in my hometown—" He then added, "for a second time." Pulling Nikki's left hand into toward his chest, "But I can't lose you. So, whatever it takes, know this: my number one priority is you."

Derrick scooted himself close enough for their knees to touch. Both became keenly aware of an invisible energy passing between them.

Derrick's voice raised in excitement, "Nikki Coles, if God gives me the grace I need to make it happen, I plan to put a ring on this finger. And I will wait," Derrick slowed the cadence of his words, "for as long as it takes to become the man you want to marry. That's my reality."

Derrick leaned in closer, his eyes fixed on Nikki's. Without speaking a word, Derrick's face managed to say, "Is it okay?" Nikki's eyes, silently yet eloquently replied, "Yes," as she pulled his face to hers for a long, lingering kiss.

After a minute or two, Nikki gently moved away, allowing her lips to very slowly release contact with Derrick's. Nikki touched her right index finger softly on Derrick's lips. Then, with the back of her hand she grazed Derrick cheek as she reached toward his hair. She tenderly ran her fingers through his hair. Her eyes followed the path of her hand as it returned to Derrick's face. Nikki searched deeper and deeper into his eyes.

"D," Nikki said, "It's a boy."

CHAPTER 25

"West Chamberlain 13, Northfield 12."

The scoreboard mirrored precisely the competitive battle being waged in front of a packed house of crazed fans.

Huddled in a tight circle near their bench, the Northfield players focused intently on the words of their 26-year-old interim head coach.

"Our defensive effort is outstanding. Great passion. Great energy. Zeke, keep making Browning work for every touch. He's hit some shots. He'll hit some more. But if we just keep them playing our game, we'll go home with the win."

On the first possession of the second quarter, the Bulldogs ran a baseline screen off their post player. That was followed by a down screen. Both were designed to free Browning for an open three. Zeke fought through both screens as he gave chase. Still, the Bulldogs' sharp shooter launched his fade away three-pointer before Zeke could close the gap.

The ball went into the net, followed immediately by the shrill whistle of a referee.

"Foul, number one, blue. Basket is good. Shooting one," the referee yelled, pointing toward Zeke.

The Warrior point guard instinctively ran toward the ref, shouting, "What the?! What are you talking about?" He stopped within inches of the ref's stoic face. Zeke clamped both hands on his head. Bending down in a pleading position, he continued angrily, "I didn't touch him, man! And you know it! What the hell's wrong with you?"

Another shrill whistle, accompanied by a furious stare from the ref. "Technical foul, number one, blue," the ref deadpanned as he looked angrily toward the despondent Zeke. It was Zeke's third foul.

Derrick slammed his towel on the scorer's table. He yelled and motioned to the offending ref, George Wilmot, "Come over here! I want to talk to you! I need an explanation!"

One of the other referees, Sam Hanson, warned Derrick, "Sit down, Coach! Sit down, *now!*"

Hanson, as well as half the people in the stands knew the history of bad blood between Wilmot and Derrick. Wilmot still saw Derrick as the cocky, disrespectful superstar he had teed up more than a dozen times during Derrick's playing career. Derrick still regarded Wilmot as an arrogant old man on a striped-shirt power trip.

"I've put up with his ego for years!" Derrick complained to Hanson. "And you know what I'm talking about."

Hanson, playing the role of peacemaker, tried to ease Derrick back toward his seat. Derrick began retreating toward the bench, then screamed loud enough for everyone to hear, "That was a horrible call and you know it!"

As he neared his seat, Derrick yelled back over his shoulder, "Get your head out of your ass, Wilmot!"

"Technical foul on Northfield's bench," Hanson announced to the scorer's table. Derrick wheeled around, ready to take him on as well.

Coach Dale, however, rushed to Derrick's side. She positioned herself between Derrick and Hanson, urging Derrick to sit back down. Coach Dale knew a second technical meant automatic ejection.

"Sit down," Coach Dale said in a steady, firm voice. "You don't want this to get worse, Coach." By the time Coach Dale's voice of reason connected to Derrick's sense of reason, his knees felt weak. He sat down with fists shut tightly and his face growing bright red.

Derrick immediately looked for Nikki in the stands. She had one hand wrapped across her waist, tucked in behind her back. With her other hand she covered her mouth. The look on Nikki's face mirrored the tightness rising in Derrick's chest.

"It's okay," Nikki mouthed silently as she brought both hands into her lap. Placing her palms downward she raised and lowered them in a short, gentle motion.

Derrick nodded. "I'm okay, Coach," he said as he looked up to see Carlene. She was still standing between him and the court when he added, "Thanks for saving my behind."

By the time the dust settled, Browning had hit all five free throws. That made eight points on one play so far, with a new offensive possession to follow. The inbounds pass led to a short baseline jumper that brought the single possession's point total to a staggering ten points.

Derrick called a timeout. He drew the team in close. "Men—and Coach Dale—I apologize. I was right about the call. It was terrible. But the way I blew up was wrong. That's on me. And you, too, Zeke. That cost us. Bad. And I'm sorry."

"I'm sorry, guys," Zeke said with his hands resting on top of his head. "I'm sorry, Coach—Jamarcus, everybody." Zeke's head dropped as he pulled his jersey over his face.

Jamarcus, still sidelined from his injury yet fully engaged in the game from the sidelines, pressed his way into the huddle. "This is not over—we are not losing this game! We are NORTHFIELD—WE ARE WARRIORS!" Jamarcus' voice carried to the very top row of the Northfield Bezerkers' section.

The Bezerkers followed suit, rallying the Northfield Nation with several "WE ARE! NORTHFIELD! WE ARE! NORTHFIELD!" chants. The Bezerkers then screamed, "Skol! Skol! Skol!" as the Viking Warrior mascot was passed up and down successive waves of students' hands.

Derrick concluded the huddle, yelling over the noise of the crowd, "Let's win this thing, for each other, for the Nation," he shouted, pointing toward the Bezerkers, "and for Coach Mac."

The Warriors regained enough composure to play the Bulldogs evenly the rest of the half. Given the enormity of their early second quarter implosion, being down only ten points at halftime felt like a small victory.

As the team entered the locker room at halftime, Jamarcus asked Derrick if he could speak first. "Brothers," he began, "you know how much it means to me to win state this year. Winning back-to-back-to-back championships is something I—we—have fought hard to achieve. But, listen to me," Jamarcus pounded his right index finger into his chest, "there is something bigger than winning state."

As Jamarcus' emotions rose, the rhythm and tone of his voice, even the timing of his movements, closely mirrored the commanding presence of Coach Mac. "The most important thing for me, and for us, today and every day, is living and leading the Northfield Way."

Jamarcus walked over to Zeke, whose face remained downcast after sitting out the rest of the second quarter. Placing his hand on his best friend's shoulder, Jamarcus aimed his words directly toward Zeke's heart. "Zeke, I love you, man, and I'm proud of you. But, bro, you still got your head down. Let it go. We forgive you. Put it in the past, man."

Zeke looked up at Jamarcus and nodded with a half-smile. "Lead us, Zeke," Jamarcus exhorted with spiritual fervor, "Lead us to the promised land. We can win this thing!"

"And, Coach Walker," Jamarcus continued, as the players began to sit up straighter, "You did go a little crazy." Everyone laughed nervously as they awaited Derrick's reaction.

Derrick smiled. Jamarcus smiled back and said, "Okay, you went a lot crazy!" More laughter, but less nervousness followed.

"But, Coach, you had my man's back. You had all our backs." Jamarcus extended his hand for handshake. "And we've got yours, Coach. So, tell these guys what to do and, I promise you . . ." Jamarcus looked back at his Warrior family, "Whatever it takes, they're going to get it done. That's the Northfield Way."

Derrick shook Jamarcus' hand vigorously. He then hugged the young man who dwarfed him in size. As if he were on the verge of sharing a very sacred prophecy, Derrick began addressing his team in near whisper, "Here's what we're going to do."

Like an actor delivering the most crucial lines of his performance, Derrick used his voice and his eyes to draw the team into his passionate vision for the second half. "We're going to love each other like never before, because," Derrick paused, "that's all we have. Each other. And it's enough."

Each player's body shifted forward toward Derrick and his words. Derrick's eyes widened, and the pace of his words accelerated. "Each of us is going to take responsibility for our part. That starts with me." Coach Walker glanced toward Coach Dale, who had likewise leaned in toward his voice. "Then Coach Dale, then the seniors, and the rest of you. Every minute. Every possession. Our game, the Northfield Way."

Derrick motioned for everyone to join him as he spread his arms and waved his hands toward himself. "Stand with me. Let's stand together. What are our maxims?"

In unison, the players shouted, "Purpose. Passion. Love. Responsibility. Humility."

"What are those maxims?" Derrick shouted.

"THE NORTHFIELD WAY!" the players screamed.

"And we play the Northfield Way because WE ARE," Derrick preached.

"WARRIORS!!" the players added with applause, shouts, and high fives.

In that moment, just before the second half tipoff, the emotional winds that would soon propel the game forward suddenly shifted dramatically. The Northfield Warriors' will to win became the most powerful force in the building.

Making his way out of the locker room, Derrick walked directly toward the referees gathered near half court. Seeing Derrick, all three stiffened into defensive postures.

The impending encounter did not go unnoticed by the crowd. Waves of nervous chatter circulated throughout the arena. One by one, fans called the scene to one another's attention. When Derrick reached the huddle, he extended his hand to Wilmot for a handshake. Reluctantly Wilmot accepted Derrick's offer.

"I apologize, men, for my behavior—and especially for my words," Derrick said as he made his way around their huddle. "There's no excuse."

Wilmot stood with his arms crossed after the handshake. Hanson and the other ref relaxed their postures and even smiled briefly.

"The truth is, gentlemen, whatever harm the foul call on number one could have caused was nothing compared to how much my actions hurt my team." Derrick turned to walk away, then turned back toward Wilmot, "And, by the way," Derrick said, "Number one deserved the technical call. I support you on that." Turning to Hanson, Derrick added, "And so did I."

Derrick jogged back to the Warrior bench. The Bulldog fans booed Derrick mercilessly. The Bezerkers chanted, "Skol! Skol! Skol!" Derrick smiled at both sections of the stands.

"What did you say, Coach?" Rico asked.

"I told them I was wrong because I was," Derrick responded.

"Responsibility. Humility," Carlene said.

"That's the Northfield Way!" Jamarcus yelled out. "It's on!"

From the opening tip, the Warriors played like untamed tigers released from their cages. Zeke harassed Browning into consistently poor shot selections. When Browning finally hit an off-balance three pointer over Zeke's outstretched hand, Zeke remained undaunted.

A local sports writer covering West Chamberlain basketball would write, "Northfield's third quarter was like a powerful tropical storm." He would, however, refer to the fourth quarter as a "Cat-5 hurricane." What had been a ten-point halftime lead for West Chamberlain became an eleven-point deficit midway through the fourth quarter.

Browning, the Bulldogs' all-region wing player, fouled out with two minutes to go in the game. He had scored only five points in the second half. Browning retreated slowly back to his bench, his head bowed and shoulders slumped under the weight of his final moments in a Bulldog uniform. In short order, the Northfield fans joined the Bulldog faithful in giving him a standing ovation.

Derrick was the first one on the Northfield bench to stand, moving quickly past the scorer's table to shake hands with Browning. Derrick praised his effort, adding, "I am one of your biggest fans, young man. I can't wait to see you play at the next level."

Moments later, the final buzzer sounded mercifully for West Chamberlain. The Bezerkers stormed the court. They swarmed the players, who had formed an impromptu mosh pit just in front of the Warriors' bench. The Northfield pep band cranked out the Northfield fight song. "Fight on, ye Fighting Norsemen! Fight on to victory!"

Once inside the locker room, Derrick's first order of business was to FaceTime Coach Mac. The entire team huddled around the phone.

"Coach! They did it!" Derrick shouted over the cheers and screams of the players.

"I am so proud of you." Coach Mac shouted back. "In all my years of coaching I've never seen a ten-point possession in a game. To tell you the truth, I hope I never see one again, unless it's on our side," Coach Mac laughed. "Men," he continued joyfully, "That may be the most impressive win in Northfield history."

The players responded with more cheers as they broke out in the "Skol! Skol! Skol!" chant.

"Coach," Derrick said, "I'm sorry about the technical and all . . . I just . . . look, there is no excuse. I embarrassed myself and the whole community."

"In the heat of battle, a lot can happen. It's happened to me—more than once. There's grace for that, Coach. But—"

"I'm sorry, too, Coach," Zeke interrupted with a shout.

"I'm proud of you, Zeke. I'm proud of all of you. But I challenge you all, coaches and players, to learn from tonight. Keep growing. Keep improving. You've got a state championship to win!"

"Yes, sir!" Derrick yelled back. "Hey, Coach, before you go," Derrick said as he pointed toward Zeke. "Zeke, come over here, closer to the phone."

Zeke began to maneuver his way through the large, smelly mass of bodies between him and Derrick. Numerous pats landed affectionately on his back a he cleared a path to the center. As Zeke neared Derrick and the phone, Thor shoved Zeke playfully forward.

"Coach, I know you listened to the game, but I wish you could have seen it with your own eyes. Zeke led the way for all of us in the second half!" Speaking toward his cell phone, but turning his eyes toward Zeke, Derrick continued, "Zeke, you stepped up and you grew up tonight."

Jamarcus grabbed his best friend, squeezing him into a tight bear hug. Jamarcus lifted him off the ground as the team shouted, "Zeke! Zeke! Zeke!"

Coach Mac smiled and nodded. He added a salute just before he shouted, "I miss you all. And I love you, men!"

Several versions of, "Love you, Coach Mac," were expressed before Derrick stepped away for a more private conversation.

Standing in the corner, away from the melee, Derrick listened as Coach Mac coached him up. "There are much bigger challenges ahead for you, D, and I need you—we all need you—to keep stepping up as a leader."

"I will, Coach. But, honestly, it's going to be a lot easier for me with you coming back," Derrick said cheerfully.

"We'll talk about that later," Coach Mac said, cutting off the conversation. "Now, go celebrate! And give Nikki a big hug for me, too!"

"Gladly! That's something I can do for sure," Derrick laughed. He ended the call with his second ever, "I love you, Coach."

Twenty minutes later, the victorious Northfield interim head coach Derrick Walker emerged from the visitors' locker room. A barrage of handshakes, hugs, words of affirmation, and affection awaited him. Once Derrick arrived on the bus, last and late, he engaged in another round of reveling with his team.

As the bus lunged into first gear, Derrick checked his cell phone There were multiple texts expressing several variations on the theme, "Congratulations on a great job, Coach!"

One was from his brother Parker. *Derrick—you've got what it takes!! We all listened to the game online. I AM SO PROUD OF YOU. I kept yelling to the kids, "That's your uncle! That's your uncle!" Love you, P.*

Derrick read the text again, laughing aloud. *Could my life get any more bizarre? You can't make this stuff up,* he thought to himself. He immediately responded to Parker, *Thanks, bro.*

The next text, from Coach Mac, read, *Derrick, you did a GREAT job tonight. Please call me ASAP. I have some new info I need to share.*

Derrick turned his face toward the cold, drafty window of the bus as he dialed Coach Mac's number. He used his jacket to shield the phone from the players' rowdy voices as he waited for Coach Mac to answer.

Coach Mac answered with, "Hey, D, thanks for calling."

"Hey, Coach Mac, what's up?" Derrick tried to sound more casual than concerned.

"Well, I hate to talk about this over the phone—but you need to know sooner than later. My doctor's appointment did not go as well as I hoped. My heart's still not performing up to the doc's standards, apparently. It's just tired, I guess." Coach chuckled, then continued, "Makes me think of the Indiana Jones line, 'It's not the age, it's the mileage.'" He laughed and then sighed. "Well, in my case, I guess it's both. Bottom line: I can't coach this weekend."

Coach Mac paused. Derrick said nothing in response. Coach Mac pressed forward, "You know how hard this is for me to ask, but I need to. Would you and Coach Dale be willing to finish the season for me? I'll try to attend the championship game—I'll probably have to sneak out of the house to do so, but I plan to at least be there!"

Derrick remained speechless. Thoughts fell and bounced inside his head like tiny pieces of hail landing on the sidewalk. How would he deal with the pressure of the finals? What if Jamarcus didn't make it back? Or what if Jamarcus wasn't ready to play at his highest level? What if he blew up in the finals the way he exploded tonight? How could he ever keep coaching and living in Northfield if he failed—again?

Collecting himself, Derrick finally replied, "Coach, your health is the most important thing. And, I, I mean we, the guys and me and, of course, Carlene, we'll give it our best shot." Trying to convince himself more than Coach Mac, Derrick continued to ramble. "And, of course, Jamarcus will be back—so that will help . . ."

"You'll be fine, D. I've been watching you closely. You've got this. And God's got you—don't forget that," Coach Mac said.

"We won't let you down . . . somehow, we will find a way . . . you know, the Northfield Way . . ." Derrick said, trying to force a cheerfulness he didn't feel as his voice trailed off.

"You couldn't possibly let me down, D. Not with the heart and effort you're giving."

Checking to be sure no one was listening in, Derrick lowered his voice to a near whisper. "Are you going to release your statement tonight, Coach?"

"Tomorrow morning. Principal Davis and I just got off the phone. We decided to let the team and the community revel in the moment." Coach Mac paused, then added, "You know it's going to be an emotional week—for everyone."

"I know," Derrick said with a sigh.

"You do know there's no way I would do this, to you or the team, if it weren't necessary. Right?" Coach Mac questioned.

"Yes. Of course," Derrick said quietly into the phone. "You're doing the right thing. It's hard and the timing sucks, but, like you say, 'It's always the right time to do the right thing the right way.'"

"Let's talk more in the morning, after the statement is released," Coach Mac suggested.

"Sounds good. Goodnight, Coach," Derrick said.

"Goodnight, Coach Walker. And, again, congratulations," Coach Mac said.

Derrick turned and looked slowly around the bus. Players laughed with each other as well as at each other. Rico, as always, was the center of the party being held in the back of the bus. Jamarcus, by contrast, sat quietly in the front of the bus discussing his future plans as a Marquette Golden Eagle. Carlene, a former DePaul University player, shared her experiences as a player in the Big East.

Derrick eavesdropped briefly. "We had to play UConn every year. You know how good they were then? They had winning streaks that went on for multiple seasons!" Carlene said with excitement as she reminisced. "Every basket we scored against UConn was like a mini victory."

The two laughed and joked about what it felt like to play a team that dominant. Jamarcus leaned forward in his seat and said, "Coach Dale, if

I hadn't gotten hurt and if Coach Mac hadn't gotten sick, I think . . . no, I know we would have been the UConn of our state. "

"Jamarcus," she replied, "A win is a win. A championship is a championship. You may not have been the UConn of the state this year, but believe me, you and Coach Walker and Zeke—the whole team—have gained the respect of every coach and player in the state. Trust me. I hear the word on the street."

"It's been a wild ride, for sure. Coach, I can't wait to get back on the court." Jamarcus mimicked shooting a jump shot with his arms and hands. "This weekend, I'll be playing again! It's a dream come true for me—especially if we win state!"

Derrick felt like he was strapped into an emotional rollercoaster that kept looping and looping. One moment, he felt proud of what he had accomplished. Then he felt terrified at what was coming next. One moment, he was filled with gratitude because of the restoration of his relationship with Nikki. That thought opened his eyes to dreams of the son he would soon meet. Just as quickly, he would recall how easily he had lost control tonight. The memory would spiral him downward into the darkness of shame. Asking himself, *What kind of father will I be?* was the scariest moment of all. The emotional lows and highs continued as Derrick entertained thoughts of Parker, Coach Mac and Mrs. Gracie, the anticipation of the community's response to Coach Mac's revelation, and Collierville's impressive unbeaten season.

Soon the gears on the bus ground slowly as it jerked and swayed its way into the bumpy Northfield parking lot. Derrick helped unload the bus. Then he reminded the players and waiting parents of the practice and travel schedule for the week. Attending to these details were a welcomed distraction for Derrick's emotions.

On the way home, he called Nikki. "Just need to hear your voice, Nik."

"It's good to hear yours, babe. I still can't believe what a great game that was tonight. We destroyed them!" Nikki said, her voice still riding the adrenaline tidal wave of the second half.

"Nikki," Derrick said seriously, "Coach Mac can't coach this week. He's out until after state."

"Oh, no! That means . . ." Nikki cut herself off. Restarting her response, she spoke convincingly and excitedly, "D, that means you're about to win your first state championship as a coach! How exciting!"

Derrick laughed. "Well, I'm glad one of us is excited. You know, there's a little problem called Collierville standing in the way."

"I know, but—" Nikki began before Derrick interrupted.

"And Coach Mac is releasing his statement in the morning. Who knows what the community and the 'DarkNation' will do after that?"

"So, what you're telling me, Coach Walker, is that not only are you going to win a state championship, but you're going to do it with all the odds stacked against you?" Nikki asked confidently.

"Is that what I'm telling you?" Derrick laughed. "Because if that's what I'm telling you, then I'm also telling you that I've lost my mind!"

"You see, Derrick Walker," Nikki said softly. "That's your problem. You always think you're losing something."

Derrick sat silently as Nikki's words fell heavily on his chest.

"The fact is," Nikki said, "You're a winner, Derrick Walker. You've just got to start looking at the right scoreboard."

CHAPTER 26

uesday morning unleashed a maelstrom of activity in Northfield. The first order of business was the reading of Coach Mac's statement, which was to take place at a Northfield High School student body assembly. Without being told the full content of the statement, local media outlets were invited to attend. Judging rightly that the statement would address a significant mystery surrounding the legendary Coach John McKissack, reporters and cameramen drove from as far as three hours away.

As soon as Principal Davis concluded the reading of an abbreviated version of the statement, the full statement was released on social media and posted on the Northfield High School website. The city of Northfield also posted the full statement on its website.

An "NHS Dark Nation" website did indeed go live within minutes of the assembly's conclusion. The true meaning of the organization's name, DarkNation, was unmistakable. The mocking term referred explicitly to the skin color of the Northfield Nation's patriarch, John McKissack. Sheriff Cooley left the assembly immediately to bring Rolf Henderson in for questioning.

The national media quickly grabbed the story and ran with it. The articles Jimmy Thompson submitted to cbssports.com quickly became primary sources for reports on the alleged scandal. By noon on Tuesday, Jimmy found himself representing the community through interviews with CNN, Fox News, ESPN, and the CBS *Evening News*. The story also captured the attention of rogue conspiracy theorists on numerous websites, and there was no limit to the irrationality of their tales of small-town shame. Jimmy later referenced this phenomenon in an online article for the Lewis County Gazette's website, *"Northfield has become the focal point for a scandal that is as unwelcomed as it is untrue."*

All day and into the next, the whole county seemed blanketed by a dark, gloomy cloud of anxiety. The attention from outside the community felt intrusive, like the whole world was secretly listening in on what should have been private matters and conversations. The safety and security of Northfield Nation's small corner of the world appeared to be threatened on every front.

For the Northfield Warriors, the angst was inescapable. During Tuesday's practice, the players' effort was scattered, uneven, and highly emotional. Uncertain where to turn, Derrick called Principal Davis on his cell phone.

"Sir," Derrick pleaded desperately once Davis was on the line, "We have to do something. My players are like zombies. Even Zeke and Jamarcus are struggling to maintain focus. This whole mess is a kick in the balls for them," Derrick said, then added quickly, "I apologize for the analogy, sir."

"No apologies needed, D," Principal Davis responded after a long pause. "I think you've got it about right. What do you suggest?"

Derrick looked around at the walls surrounding him in Coach Mac's office. He sat in one of the folding chairs, where he always sat. Since becoming the interim head coach, Derrick had only sat in Coach Mac's desk chair one time. For him, the whole experience somehow violated the natural order of things.

"I don't know . . . I just don't know," Derrick replied to Principal Davis. "But I do know this," he said, raising himself up in his seat, "We've got to get people into a room and talk to them. And our team needs to be there."

"We should hold a town meeting, tomorrow night, in the arena," Principal Davis suggested.

"Do you think we could get Coach Mac there? He needs to be there." Derrick said.

"I'll get to work on it right away," Principal Davis said. "Would you call Jimmy Thompson and get his input? Especially about how we handle the media attention."

"Sure," Derrick replied hesitantly. "But you do know that I don't know what I'm doing?"

"Welcome to the club, Derrick. There's no script for this. We just dive in and ride the wave," Principal Davis said reassuringly. "I appreciate you taking the initiative to move us forward."

Derrick ended the call, then laid his phone on the desk. He slumped down in his chair. Without moving his head, he retraced the timeline from Coach Mac's first team photo to the present. As his eyes traveled to his senior year, he gazed more intently than ever at his face. "If you only knew," he said to the younger version of himself.

Sparked by the thought, Derrick hastily pulled his journal out of his backpack. He turned to the first open page and began to write. Like a runaway train, thoughts began surging through his brain at an overwhelming rate.

> *To the younger D Walker,*
>
> *Man, you just don't know. You don't know that your selfish attitude is about to destroy everything you care about. You don't know how far down you are about to sink. And you don't know how far up you're going to rise one day. You don't really know the Northfield Way or how it will change your life or how Coach Mac will be there or that you will meet this beautiful, amazing, spiritual woman named Nikki. You don't know someone's looking out for you. You don't know God has grace to save your screwed-up life and give you a new one. You don't know how to say, "I love you," and mean it. You don't know that you don't have to be alone. You don't know that a basketball scoreboard is not the scoreboard you should be looking at.*

The last sentence stopped Derrick in his mental tracks. *You don't know that a basketball scoreboard is not the scoreboard you should be looking at.*

Derrick picked up his phone and said, "Siri, call Jimmy Thompson." Derrick stood up and began to pace the room.

"Hey, Coach Walker, what's going on?" Jimmy asked.

"I need your help, Jimmy. I need to write something—and it needs to be really good," Derrick hurriedly explained. "So, I want you to help me."

"Of course, whatever you need help with, I'm here," Jimmy replied.

"Well, JT, I need help with everything," Derrick said as he breathed in and released a shallow laugh, "But for the moment, I just need help writing this one thing."

On the following night, a full hour before the appointed 7:30 meeting, the arena was flooded by an anxious crowd hoping to secure a seat at the meeting. Store owners had closed their businesses, pastors had either canceled or shortened mid-week church prayer meetings, and families with young children had scrambled relatives and friends from other counties to babysit in order to make their attendance possible. It would be the most well attended town meeting in Northfield history.

Nervous energy hummed in the room like the sound of electricity traveling across the large overhead power lines dotting the Midwestern landscape. Unlike the Northfield Nation Nights each November, worry was being worn like a tight-fitting mask on everyone's faces.

Principal Davis brought the meeting to attention with a moment of silence "for prayer and positive thoughts." Thirty seconds later, he began. "The purpose of this gathering," he declared in his most formal voice, "is to bring understanding and unity to our community. This, of course, is in direct response to Coach Mac's statement released yesterday morning."

He went on, "Please hold all applause and response for the next several minutes. I think it would be most appropriate for us to listen before responding." Principal Davis then said, "Okay?" The crowd indicated its approval and Principal Davis moved on to the next phase of the gathering.

"We will hear from Coach Mac and Mrs. Gracie momentarily, as they will be arriving soon. But first, we thought it best, in keeping with

Northfield Nation tradition, to have an introducer speak before Coach Mac and Mrs. Gracie. So, please welcome the interim head coach of the Northfield Warriors, Derrick "D" Walker."

A handful of folks offered polite, sporadic applause, in spite of Principal Davis' instructions otherwise. Derrick squeezed Nikki's hand just before he rose from his seat. She leaned over and gave him a kiss on the cheek.

Derrick looked down at the players seated with him on the first row. Rico blew a mocking kiss in his direction. The rest of the players fell out in laughter, sharing a private moment no one else in the auditorium understood. Nikki blushed. Unconsciously she began to rub her abdomen as she said a silent prayer for Derrick.

Derrick unfolded his introduction. He took a deep breath. He had already read his script no less than twenty-five times. But reading it aloud, in front of over 1500 members of the Northfield Nation was different. Way different. His hands rattled the paper as his anxiety worked out its energy through his body.

"Principal Davis, Mayor Collins, members of the Northfield Nation, including our Northfield High School students, especially the Bezerkers—"

The Bezerkers' favorite chant, "Skol! Skol! Skol!" briefly interrupted Derrick's introductory remarks. Principal Davis stood and faced the disruptive students, giving them his infamous "evil eye," and adding a pointing index finger to reinforce his authority. The Bezerkers returned quietly to their seats.

"I can only imagine," Derrick continued with a smile, "what it's like for most of you to see me standing here. Especially on such an important night in the history of our school and community. I know many of you remember me as a cocky, disrespectful, selfish . . ." Derrick paused, "I've tried to find the right word here without being inappropriate to the occasion. I was such a—"

"Dumbass!" a familiar voice yelled from the far right.

The Bezerkers gasped, then broke into unhinged laughter. Parents with young children present covered the children's ears. As they did so, they searched, faces aghast, in the direction of the voice.

Rico said, loud enough for several rows to hear, "Oh, no, he didn't!!" A stare from Principal Davis persuaded everyone to dial it back immediately.

"Thank you, Zeb, for that accurate, though questionable description," Derrick replied as he nodded his recognition of Zeb Sweeting. Zeb had been a classmate of Derrick's. Together they had shared a passionate love for beer and an equally passionate distaste for homework.

Zeb's wife, Lizzie, punched him hard in the ribs and buried her head in her hands as all eyes turned toward their way. Red faced and a bit too jovial, Zeb appeared to be at least two beers beyond caring.

"So, Zeb having clarified that for us," Derrick continued to low rumbles of laughter, "let's get back to what I think would be your first question: Why is Derrick Walker even at this school, much less talking to us in this very important moment in our community?"

Derrick raised his eyes to survey the room. He saw a sea of former teammates, classmates, teachers, neighbors, and fans, each face with multiple memories attached to it. Most were happy but, in several cases, the memories were terribly sad. Derrick began to feel all those feelings at once. Overwhelmed, he turned toward Nikki. The way she looked at him, hopeful and compassionate, steadied him.

"For three and half years, I recited the five maxims of the Northfield Way. Purpose. Passion. Love. Responsibility. Humility. I probably had more than a hundred Coach Mac quotes in my head. You know them. 'Life expands to the size of your "WHY"?' 'No one lives well who lives alone.' 'The strongest person in the room is the person least afraid of conflict.' But for some reason . . ." Derrick sighed, then began again, "No, for lots of reasons, none of it made its way to my heart."

Five minutes earlier, the faces in the room had been dominated by skepticism. Gradually, the leading expression became intense curiosity. The name "Derrick Walker" had been attached more to a symbol than an individual for the majority of the Northfield Nation. Now, they were faced with Derrick Walker as a person. Suddenly it occurred to the crowd that they didn't really know him.

"So, I screwed up. I failed. Horribly. Shamefully. I was, you know, what Zeb said earlier,'" Derrick said as muffled laughter rippled through the crowd once again. "Then my life began to change. Why? The easy answer is Coach John McKissack. And, for that reason, I have been trying for months to be just like him. I've tried to talk like he talks. I've tried to act like he acts. And, of course, I've tried to coach like he coaches." Derrick took several seconds to look at each section of the stands before continuing. Then he lowered his head. In a very low volume, Derrick said, "But, the truth is, I can't." A few pockets of hushed murmurs opened up, then quickly closed down.

"As I finally figured out this last week, I can't because . . . ," Derrick stopped and made eye contact with each section, ". . . that's not the point. The point is not Coach Mac," Derrick declared like a coach redirecting his team's focus. "It's really not even the Northfield Way."

Derrick let his words come to rest fully in his listeners' minds and hearts. He could see the unease in the room; several in the audience wore disapproving faces. He understood their response. To the majority, Derrick's words were the equivalent of heretical Northfield blasphemy.

"The point," Derrick continued as he leaned his face close into the microphone, "is the grace and love at the root of the Northfield Way." Sheila Jordan called out in her Sunday morning voice, "That's right! C'mon."

"Coach Mac," Derrick continued, "learned grace and love from his brother, Wesley, and from his mentor, Coach Norman at UIC. I learned grace from Coach Mac and from my wonderful . . . my beautiful . . ." Derrick searched for the word. He was off script on this sentence. ". . . my best friend, Nikki Coles," he said as he threw a quick smile in Nikki's direction.

Returning to his script, Derrick then said, "You see, I began learning—really learning—to live for a purpose greater than myself, to overcome pressure with passion, to choose love as my first priority, to take responsibility to lead myself, to live with humility in service only after I began to understand grace the way Coach Mac understands it. Grace, in its purest form, is a gift from God. A gift to be given away over and over again in families, among friends, and throughout a community."

The room fell into a silent hush. Derrick paused again. Unhooking the microphone, he unwrapped the cord from its metal stand and moved toward the audience. Standing beside Nikki while facing the crowd, he resumed his speech from memory. "I know I personally have so far to go on the journey of the Northfield Way. But, I'm going to get there the same way I got here. By grace, with love." Derrick paused as his voice became quiet and reflective, "And I hope one day that will include your love." Derrick breathed deeply, swallowing the emotion welling up just below the surface of his throat.

"Coach Mac has another quote that I'm just starting to understand. He says, 'Basketball is about performance, but life is about grace.'" Derrick turned his eyes towards Nikki. As their eyes met, he spoke directly to her. "I plan to be the kind of teacher, coach, friend, and father who passes along the Northfield Way. I want the question, 'How am I doing when it comes to grace?' to be more important than, 'How am I doing on the basketball scoreboard?' I hope you will join me in that same commitment."

Holding the microphone in one hand and gesturing adamantly with the other, Derrick transitioned into his leadership voice, "And the only reason I have any hope of living in this way, the only reason I even know the Northfield Way of grace under pressure, is because God, by His grace, placed Coach John McKissack in our community, in our school, and in my life."

"Amen!" Jamarcus yelled from the end of the first row. The applause that followed was deafening. But different. The Bezerkers didn't go unleash their typical chaos. No one started chanting, "Skol!" There were no screams or yells at all. Instead, a long, thunderous, sustained applause filled the room.

Derrick motioned for everyone to sit down. He rewrapped the microphone around the stand's metal attachment. "In closing, I will quote Coach Mac one more time: 'It's never just about basketball.'" Once again, applause broke out, first in sporadic pockets then across the entire crowd. Derrick waited a few seconds, then continued, "And tonight should not be just about basketball or even the fact that Coach John McKissack is our basketball coach. Tonight should be about how we all got here—and where we are all going from here. Tonight should be about extending grace and love to a man who needs it just as much as we do," Derrick said with the fervor of religious conviction as he spoke his closing words. "So, please join me as we welcome the leader of our Nation and my spiritual father, Coach John McKissack, and his beautiful wife, Gracie.

Coach Mac and Gracie entered the court from the doorway of the home locker room. The moment the crowd saw them, they burst into a standing ovation that doubled the volume of their previous applause. By the time Coach Mac finally convinced the room to sit quietly, the standing ovation had lasted well over three minutes.

During the lengthy ovation, Coach Mac had lowered his head and closed his eyes several times. Each time his lips moved silently and he pointed his long right index finger toward the sky. Gracie, by the end of the ovation, appeared to be about halfway through the box of tissues that had been provided for her on the podium.

Coach Mac appeared to have lost several pounds since his collapse two months ago. His gait was slower, his limbs were stiffer. Folks would later observe, "He looks like he's aged five years in the last two months." His presence, however, had not diminished.

"We have no words with which to thank you. All of you," Coach Mac began. "These have been difficult days."

"Amen!" Sheila Jordan cried out along with several others.

"We love you, Coach Mac!" a young woman in the Bezerker section cried out to the laughter and approval of the crowd.

Gracie placed her arm around Coach Mac's waist. Coach pulled her closer to his side as he began again in his typical fatherly tone, "But these have also been good days, too."

Coach Mac brought his elbows onto the podium as he leaned forward. He rested his long arms and clasped his hands as if he were about to pray. "For thirty-six years I have been privileged to serve this community. As Coach Walker said, it's never been just about basketball. It's always been about my purpose. My 'why.'"

Coach Mac paused as he reached into his pants pocket and pulled out a small, blue Bible. He slowly began to turn the book's thin, delicate pages. Then, as he placed his reading glasses onto the bridge of his nose, he said, "I want to read two passages from the Bible that have shaped my life for more than four decades. From the prophet Micah, chapter six, verse eight." The tone and cadence of his voice now captivated the room as if he were a Broadway actor delivering a poignant soliloquy. He read solemnly, "'He has told you, O man, what is good; and what does the Lord require of you but to do justice, and to love kindness, and to walk humbly with your God?'"

Coach Mac paused briefly, thumbed through more pages in his Bible, then continued, "And, from the Apostle Paul, Ephesians chapter two, verses four and five: 'But God, being rich in mercy, because of the great love with which he loved us, even when we were dead in our trespasses, made us alive together with Christ—by grace you have been saved . . .'"

Coach Mac closed his Bible, reverently and slowly. He laid the Bible and his glasses down on the podium beside one another, and addressed the group again. "When I was a young man, I was a man of injustice. I was a man filled with anger and rage, and with arrogance and violence." Coach Mac breathed deeply. A shiver convulsed through his body. He instinctively reached to his side and pulled Gracie close under his arm. "But God . . ." Coach Mac's voice trailed off into a whisper as he repeated softly, "But God."

A broad smile gradually began to spread across the full width of Coach Mac's face. His voice then rose in triumph, "But God, by His grace, brought light into my darkness. He showed me justice, He offered me kindness, and He loved me with a love I did not deserve—a love I could never have earned. He did all of this through Jesus Christ, who became my salvation, my redemption, my life. Then He gave me a wife. And a daughter. And as if that were not enough, by His grace He blessed me with generations of young men to lead on the path of the Northfield Way." Coach Mac wiped tears from both eyes. He added tenderly and slowly, "All of this because of His great love."

Derrick felt his heart beating faster. As he looked around the room, he could sense he was not alone. Derrick reached over to take Nikki's hand. She smiled, keeping her gaze on Coach Mac, and at the same time tenderly pulling Derrick's hands up close to her belly.

"And my soul purpose in coaching," Coach Mac continued forcefully, "in leading the Northfield Way—my 'why'—has always been to invite others to join me in humbly learning how to live by His grace and to walk in His love." Taking a deep breath, he added solemnly, "However, over these past few days, it's come to my attention, that I have, in significant ways, fallen short. Because of pride. Because of fear. Because of past injustices and injuries."

Coach Mac's barrel chest expanded widely as gathered sufficient breath for his next comment. "God forced my hand this past week. At first, I felt threatened by the lies and the attacks of people who wanted to destroy what we've built. But then I realized something." Coach Mac leaned forward once again. His right hand gestured dramatically as his voice lowered and deepened. "We didn't build the Northfield Nation on shame and fear. We didn't build this Northfield Nation on injustices and prejudices. In fact, *we* didn't even build it. All of this has been a gift."

"So, now I'm asking for your forgiveness—because I need grace and love to help me get me past my anger. Because, the truth is, I've always thought about how much I wanted to be there for all of you. But now I'm realizing how much I need all of you to be there for me." Coach Mac once again put his arm around Gracie and pulled her into his side. He smiled at her and she smiled back, leaning her head into his chest. "So, I ask you please forgive me for holding back the most important parts of my story, for not trusting you in the ways that I've asked you to trust me. I'm deeply sorry. Gracie and I ask for your grace and your love to help us learn more, with you, about how to live the Northfield Way."

As applause began to cascade down the row after row of bleachers, Coach Mac looked back toward the stands. "We love you. Thank you and," Coach Mac nodded toward Gracie. Together they leaned into the microphone, then shouted in their loudest voices, "GO WARRIORS!"

Immediately the crowd leapt to its feet and began clapping and yelling "We love you!" and "We forgive you!" and, of course, "Go Warriors!" The building shook as if the earth had just tremored beneath it. Coach Mac and Gracie waved good-bye and began to make their way off the court. There were brief hugs along the way from Derrick and Nikki, Principal Davis, AD Butler, Coach Dale, and Jimmy Thompson. As they neared the exit door, the McKissacks repeatedly turned back to wave to the roaring crowd.

Once the McKissacks had exited, the crowd sat back down. The room was still filled with loud conversations and boisterous activity when Principal Davis returned to the microphone. After quieting the crowd, Principal Davis offered specific instructions on how to email their questions to Coach Mac. He assured them that that everyone would receive some form of response.

Principal Davis then invited Jimmy Thompson to the podium. Jimmy explained in detail how the community would be informed of further developments through *The Gazette* website. He also described how he would work with Coach Mac, Principal Davis, and Mayor Collins to keep building a page of FAQ's and answers.

Principal Davis rose to conclude the evening. "Well," he began, "whatever your religious persuasion, including none, we all have to admit that we are blessed."

Principal Davis moved out from behind the podium. His face dropped its rigid lines of formality. Raising both arms high into the air, he looked up and down the front row of Warrior players. "And I know," he began shouting at the top of his lungs, "You will all join me," Principal Davis paused for effect, "tomorrow night . . ." He paused again as the energy began to build toward a crescendo, the continued, ". . . at the Sequoia Coliseum where the Northfield Warriors . . ." The crowd rose to its feet. The Bezerkers began stomping their feet. ". . . will bring home a third straight state championship!"

The crowd dug deep for one more ecstatic moment as Principal Davis began wildly pumping his left fist into the air, then screamed, "WE ARE!"

"WARRIORS!" the crowd roared back.

Principal Davis repeated the chant several times, until his voice was hoarse and his shirt soaked. Interim head coach Derrick Walker had never felt more like a welcomed member of the Northfield Nation family.

Ironically, as the crowd began chanting, "Three-peat! Three-peat!" he also felt very much alone.

CHAPTER 27

Once the Northfield Warriors arrived at Sequoia Coliseum, the team jumped into action in top form. Rejuvenated by Jamarcus' return, the Warriors dominated the quarterfinals and semifinals with impressive blowouts. The Warriors romped to an 87-59 win in the first game. In the second game, the Northfield team led by twenty-five early in the second half. The wide margin allowed Northfield's top six players to rest most of the third and fourth quarters.

Everything fell into place for the long-expected, long-awaited showdown between former #1 Northfield and the current #1 Colliersville. Both teams' rosters were filled with outstanding talent. Both schools were rich in basketball tradition. The game promised to be, as one local reporter wrote, ". . . all that is excellent in high school athletics."

Back in Northfield, Coach Mac had continued to press his doctor for permission to attend the championship game. On Friday afternoon, the doctor pressed back, saying, "While I don't approve, I can't stop you from going as a fan. However, I will not clear you to be present in any official capacity. Without my clearance, the school has no choice but to restrict your access to the team. I'm very sorry, Coach Mac, but I would be violating my professional integrity otherwise."

Coach Mac called Derrick early Saturday morning. "Can't wait to see you tonight, D. I finally get to watch you coach!" he exclaimed in a giddy voice. "I just wish I could be on the bench or at least in the locker room with you."

"Just having you in the building will be a huge lift to our team," Derrick said. "And to me."

"Derrick, I have one suggestion, if you don't mind," Coach said cautiously.

"Are you kidding? I'll take anything you can give," Derrick replied.

"I've coached in sixteen state championship games and won eleven of them. Still, nothing makes me more nervous than walking into a gym with a state championship on the line," Coach Mac shared.

"Is that supposed to make me feel better?" Derrick chuckled.

"No, I guess not," Coach Mac laughed. "But here is my suggestion. Before you go to the coliseum this afternoon, take fifteen minutes to yourself. Once you're in the gym, things will start happening really quickly."

"Thanks, Coach. That makes a lot of sense. I'll do that between the pre-game meal at the hotel and the bus trip over to the coliseum," Derrick said.

"Perfect," Coach Mac encouraged.

"Thanks, Coach. See you tonight," Derrick said.

"Yes, sir. I'll see you on the court during the victory celebration—the doctor didn't say anything about keeping me away from the post-game celebration!" Coach Mac laughed.

After the pre-game meal, Derrick gave the players thirty minutes to be dressed and ready to load onto the bus. As the players dispersed to their hotel rooms, Derrick took a comfortable seat in the hotel lobby to wait. His respite was almost immediately interrupted by Jimmy Thompson coming around the corner.

"Derrick, you got a minute?" Jimmy asked.

"I've got about five, JT. What's going on, man?" Derrick asked with peaked curiosity.

"Have you checked your email in the last ten minutes?"

"Uh, no. I've been kind of busy here," Derrick replied.

"Yeah, I know. Dumb question from the reporter." Jimmy smiled as he dropped into the seat beside Derrick. Then he instantly transitioned into a more serious tone. "It's a highly confidential email from Jimbo Larsen. He sent it to the people who were at the McKissacks' the night Coach told his story."

"What does it say?" Derrick asked.

"Here, look at it on my phone," Jimmy replied as he turned his screen toward Derrick and handed him his phone.

"What the . . . !" Derrick mouthed quietly.

Jimmy took back his phone and explained the email. "It's basically a summary of what Jimbo read to Coach Mac and Gracie on Sunday afternoon. Of course, there's the added apology to the community and, specifically, to the Northfield Nation."

"So, you knew about this?" Derrick whispered.

"Yes. Jimbo came to me on Sunday night. He was a broken man."

"I guess so." Derrick pondered the meaning of what he had just read. "This makes so much sense now. The strange moment I had on the sidewalk when I saw them Sunday. Their absence at the state tournament. Wow." Derrick paused again. "Just, wow."

"Yeah, it's going to be—"

Derrick interrupted. "Wait, so Jimbo was the anonymous texter?" Derrick's words rapidly accelerated. "And Jimbo knows the source of all that DarkNation crap? And Coach Mac knows it was Jimbo?" Derrick's mind raced faster than his words.

"Yes, to all of that," Jimmy said.

"So, who was it?"

"I'm not sure I can say yet," Jimmy replied, his head shaking side to side.

"Well, that's a switch—the reporter replying with 'no comment.' "

"Something like that," Jimmy chuckled. "But, honestly, this is going to be pretty hard on our community. I think a lot of us thought racism was a thing of the past, something only perpetuated by the fringes of our community. But if anything, Jimbo's letter has made me realize that this is an ongoing battle, one we all must fight. Hopefully, this will be the beginning of a hard conversation and active change. Right now, though, you've got to go out there and give us something to feel good about as we head into a very long off season."

"We'll do our best, JT. I can promise you that." Derrick looked at his watch. In less than twenty minutes, he had to be ready to load the bus. "Look, Jimmy, I've got to get my head in the game. We'll have to talk later," Derrick said hurriedly. "But, hey, thanks for the update. I needed to know."

"That's what I thought, too." Jimmy then added, "Hate is a tough opponent, D. It just keeps attacking our community, wave after wave."

"JT, I think that's the battle Coach Mac has been fighting all his life," Derrick said as he pulled his journal out of his backpack.

Jimmy concluded, "When you think of it that way, the whole Northfield Way thing has a lot more meaning, doesn't it?"

"That's what I'm learning, Jimmy," Derrick said as he took out his journal and pen, signaling the end of the conversation. "Lately, that's what I'm learning every day."

"Good luck tonight, Coach," Jimmy said.

"Thanks, I'm sure I'll need it—lots of it," Derrick replied.

Derrick set a ten-minute timer on his phone, then opened his journal to its next blank page. Derrick's mind churned. He reflected on the information Jimmy had just shared. He rehearsed several specific challenges the Warriors would soon face against the 33-0 Colliersville Spartans. And he considered once more how surreal his life had become. In a very short window of time, 26-year-old Derrick Walker had become a father-to-be as well as the interim head coach of the Northfield Warriors.

Derrick began writing furiously. His thoughts tumbled out on top of one another.

MAXIM 4
RESPONSIBILITY
My first responsibility will be to lead myself.

I have one job. ONE JOB. DO MY PART. Keep my emotions under control. Lead myself. Keep my thoughts focused. Lead myself. Keep my passion strong. Lead myself.

BE THE LEADER on the sideline I want our players to be on the court.

LEAD MYSELF, no matter what happens. Take responsibility if I make a mistake. Hold players accountable only after I've done the same.

If I don't like something, change it. Make no excuses.
BE STRONG. BE COURAGEOUS. BE THE LEADER.

Derrick checked the timer. 2:01, 2:00, 1:59. After quickly reviewing his jumbled journal entry, he wrote a brief prayer. *God, for one night, for just three hours, please show me how to lead with strength and courage, to do my part—no matter what happens.*

Derrick closed up his journal, grabbed his backpack, and stopped the timer at :26. Stepping back into the crowded area of the hotel lobby, Derrick chuckled to himself, "Maybe I should've just prayed for an easy win."

———————

"I've never seen anything like this, Coach!" Derrick shouted in Carlene's ear.

Carlene heard him, but only barely. She shouted back, "It's like a rock concert in here!"

The clock continued counting down to tipoff, with just over eight minutes to go. The Northfield Nation, led by hundreds of Bezerkers, suddenly took the decibels to an almost unbearable level.

Derrick and Coach Dale searched the coliseum for the source of the Bezerkers heightened enthusiasm. Their eyes landed on Coach Mac. On his left arm, Gracie beamed as if she were the homecoming queen being escorted onto the court.

As Coach Mac and Gracie made their way up the coliseum steps, several posters were raised across the seething sea of navy and gold. The posters included:

→   ONE NATION, UNDER MAC
     #NORTHFIELDNATION

→   Seasons   **36**
     State Championships   **11 (so far)**
     Coach John McKissack   **1**
     Being in the Northfield Nation   **Priceless**

To everyone's surprise, Colliersville's coaches and players made their way across the floor to greet Coach Mac. Soon they were joined by the referees. Media cameras, as well as cell phones scattered all over the coliseum, scrambled to capture the moment.

The Northfield players waited until the crowd thinned around Coach Mac. As one unit, the Warriors jogged to Coach Mac's side. Each player took a turn hugging both Coach Mac and Gracie.

With 3:35 left on the pregame countdown, Derrick called his players back into their warm-up routine. "Three minutes! Game speed. Let's go! Don't wait 'til tip-off. The Northfield Way starts now!"

Exactly 2:04 remained in the pre-game warm-ups when Principal Davis, accompanied by AD Baker tapped Derrick on the shoulder. Derrick's first thought was, *Something's happened to Coach Mac again.* He immediately searched for Coach Mac in the stands. He was nowhere to be seen.

Principal Davis motioned for Derrick to follow him, which Derrick did, joining Davis and AD Baker at a spot near the Warriors' locker room door. As the trio arrived, Principal Davis began. "Coach, it's Jamarcus' dad." Principal Davis' face was pale from worry. "We've been on the phone with his mom. Evidently Mr. Denton had a heart attack at the hotel. Paramedics saved his life. What should we—"

"We've got to tell him," Derrick interrupted.

"Before or after the game?" Butler asked.

"Before." Derrick responded without hesitation. "This is just a basketball game. We're talking about a kid and his dad."

Principal Davis voiced his agreement. Reluctantly, AD Butler did the same.

"Coach Mac should be the one to break the news, though," Derrick added. Looking at the pre-game clock ticking down to 1:04, 1:03, Derrick said, "I've got an idea. It will require you two to explain the situation to Coach Mac."

"Will do, Coach," Principal Davis said.

Derrick looked back at the clock . . . :50, :49 . . . "Men, we came here to win a state championship," Derrick declared to the Northfield administrators as they prepared to end their brief conversation. "Nothing's changed. Same goal. Same heart. Same Northfield Way. Just bigger mountain to climb." With murmurs of agreement and reassurance, the trio dispersed.

Just before the buzzer sounded, Derrick gathered Coach Dale, the referees, Coach Cohen of the Colliersville Spartans and the Spartans' assistant, Dewayne Mayberry. Standing near the scorer's table at half court, Derrick briefed everyone on the situation.

Coach Cohen spoke first, "I am so sorry to hear this, Coach." Placing his hand on Derrick's shoulder, Coach Cohen inquired sincerely, "How can we help?"

The coliseum crowd stared at the unusual pre-game huddle, curiously questioning its purpose. The stadium's loudspeakers then blared, "Three minutes have been added to the pre-game warm-up."

A tidal wave of "Boo!" swept the room from the fans.

"Coach Cohen and his Spartans are a class act," Derrick remarked to Carlene as they returned to the bench. "If this thing goes off the rails, at least it will be against a solid program."

As soon as the warm-ups restarted, Derrick asked Jamarcus to join him for a moment. As they walked toward Coach Mac and Principal Davis, Derrick said to the puzzled superstar, "God's got you, Jamarcus. I know that for sure. And, he's got us, too," Derrick said as he looked upward into Jamarcus' concerned eyes, "So, I want you to trust Him on this." Derrick silently added, *I think that's what Coach Mac would say.*

Coach Mac pulled Jamarcus into the hallway just outside the court and calmly explained the situation. Initially, Jamarcus stood paralyzed and silent. Coach Mac placed his arm around Jamarcus' wide shoulders and said, "There's every reason to believe that your dad will be okay. He's a tough son of a gun." Coach Mac smiled kindly. "But this is serious, so I'm going to drive you to the hospital."

Jamarcus said, "Let's go! I need to see my pops."

Derrick hustled back to his bewildered troops. Dazed by Jamarcus' departure, the players circled around Derrick. "First, there's good news," Derrick began. "Jamarcus' dad is recovering. That's what matters most."

The players' faces twisted with confusion. Derrick immediately realized that, in his anxiety and haste, he had failed to communicate clearly. Backing up to the beginning, Derrick said, "Mr. Denton suffered a heart attack at the team hotel. Miraculously, he is now resting at a local hospital," Derrick spoke calmly. He reached out and grabbed Zeke's arm, gently pulling him to his side. "Now, Zeke, I know how much you love Mr. Denton and, when this game is over, I will make sure that you're the first person to go see him." Derrick put his hand on Zeke's shoulder and held it firmly. "But for now, I need you to lead us, to not let us give up, to not let us lose heart."

Zeke wiped his face with the top of his jersey. "Yes, sir," Zeke replied with restrained enthusiasm.

Facing the rest of the team, Derrick said "No matter what, we've got to play our game, our way. We've got to give our whole hearts to this game—" The buzzer sounded. Derrick placed his hand in the middle of the circle. His hand was joined by the players, Coach Carlene, and even Joey, the manager. Derrick shouted, "For Jamarcus, for Mr. Denton, for Coach Mac, for our Northfield Nation, for each other! WE ARE!"

"WARRIORS!" the team screamed.

Zeke wiped his face and hands on a towel just before stepping onto the court, remarking to Derrick, "Coach, God either hates or loves us."

Derrick leaned over and said quietly to Zeke, "You know, Zeke, it's only recently that I've actually started to believe in God,"

"Yeah me, too," Zeke said. Handing his towel to Derrick, Zeke looked up at him and added, "I just hope God still believes in us."

CHAPTER 28

T he opening tipoff flew in the direction of the Spartans' point guard, Oliver. Zeke cut in front of him to take possession of the ball. From that moment forward, Zeke continued to be brilliant on both ends of the court. By the end of the first quarter, he already had seven points, three assists, two rebounds, and two steals—with no turnovers. It was as close to perfect as a high school point guard could be expected to play. Largely because of that stellar effort, the outmanned Northfield squad fought their way to a 16-10 lead.

As Derrick and Coach Dale huddled their inspired Warriors, Coach Cohen delivered a blistering tirade to his Colliersville Spartans, who had been caught off guard by the depleted Warriors. Derrick knew the second quarter would be a very different story.

To maximize Zeke's energy, Derrick decided to sit him for two minutes. Given the time between quarters this nearly doubled the time Zeke would have to catch his breath.

Zeke protested. Derrick insisted. Zeke sat down.

"Hydrate and be ready to roll," Derrick shouted to Zeke.

As play resumed, Derrick watched his five Warriors match up defensively with the five Spartans on the court. As the Spartans set up their inbounds play, Derrick spoke wearily to his assistant. "Coach, we're playing that team." Derrick pointed toward the Spartans' five starters. "We are without Coach Mac, Jamarcus, and, for the moment, without Zeke. If this is a nightmare, please feel free—at any moment—to wake me up," he said sarcastically.

A well-designed play led to a Spartan alley-oop dunk off the baseline. Immediately, the game's energy and momentum dramatically swung in the direction of the Spartans. Ninety seconds into the second quarter, the Spartans led 19-16.

"Get back in there, Zeke," Derrick yelled. "Straighten this thing out," he ordered.

"Yes, sir, Coach," Zeke replied. "We got this."

With the offense struggling, Coach Walker decided to bring the freshman, Billy Connors, off the bench. The strategy paid off instantly. Billy went two of three from the three-point line and provided adequate defense against the Spartans' outstanding shooting guard.

As the second quarter wound down, two things were evident. First of all, the Warriors were not going to collapse, mentally or emotionally, under the weight of the Spartans' onslaught. Equally obvious, however, was the fact that the Spartans were steadily, incrementally burying the Warriors. They led first by three, then five, then back to two, then by five, then eleven. Northfield kept fighting back, but Colliersville was winning a war of attrition. With Jamarcus out of the picture, the Spartans' superior talent simply overwhelmed the valiant Warriors.

Zeke put up a short jumper as the half-time buzzer sounded. The referee signaled to count the basket as well as calling a foul against the Spartans. Zeke hit the free throw, narrowing the score to a respectable 33-25.

Stepping into the locker room, Derrick encountered a sea of weary faces. He recognized the expression immediately, as if he were looking in a mirror.

––––––––––

The ride to Lincolnwood Mercy Hospital took less than ten minutes. Jamarcus and Coach Mac listened intently to every second of the game on Coach Mac's car radio.

With each made basket, Jamarcus' and Coach Mac's spirits rose. Each missed shot, failed defensive stand, and turnover, however, brought them low again.

By the time Coach Mac angled his well-worn "green machine" into the emergency room parking lot, the game neared the end of the first quarter. Just before coming to a complete stop, Coach Mac and Jamarcus heard the Spartan radio announcer remark, "I've got to tell you, folks. There's no quit in this Northfield squad. The Spartans have a real battle on their hands tonight." Coach Mac and Jamarcus smiled at one another as Coach Mac's car pulled into an emergency room parking space.

As soon as Jamarcus stepped out of the car, the game became irrelevant. He sprinted through the extensive hospital corridor toward the emergency bay where his father, Martin Denton, lay. By the time he reached a small circle of Denton family and friends, Jamarcus had worked up a sweat.

The hallway gathering welcomed Jamarcus with hugs and tears. Jamarcus' brother, Chris, emerged from behind a near-by curtain and motioned Jamarcus inside. Chris smiled. "He's going to be okay, J-mar."

D'Lane, Jamarcus' mother, immediately arose from her seat next to Martin. She pulled Jamarcus into the tight space she had occupied since Martin's arrival in the ER. D'Lane's eyes were reddened and swollen. Her face wore deep lines of anxiety. "I love you, Jamarcus," she said softly as her son engulfed her with his arms.

Jamarcus moved from his D'Lane to Martin. "Hey, Pops," Jamarcus said enthusiastically through his tears.

Tubes ran in and out of Martin's body, crisscrossing his torso in multiple places. Wires ran next to and around every side of his upper body. A steady rhythm of beeps and humming sounds echoed from several brightly lit monitors stationed at the top of his bed. The scene nearly took Jamarcus' breath away.

"Hey, son. What are you doing here?" Martin asked. "You should be with your teammates."

"What are you doing here, Pops? You aren't exactly the hospital type, you know," Jamarcus joked. Jamarcus leaned over the bed rail and kissed his number one hero on the top of the head. At that moment, Jamarcus' number two hero squeezed himself into the tight cubicle-sized bay.

"Coach Mac? What's going on? Jamarcus has a state championship to win!" Martin voiced in frustration.

"You're my dad," Jamarcus said. "I had to be here . . . and Coach Mac agreed. So, he came with me."

"Martin, are you trying to be like me? Again?" Coach Mac joked as he leaned down to hug his dear friend. Martin pulled Coach Mac firmly into an extra-large sized embrace.

"Coach Mac, I can't believe you left the game. It's the state championship! I don't even know what to say . . ." Martin sat up as much as his confines and strength would allow. He adamantly added, "I do know one thing I need to say—thank you . . . for bringing my son. That means a lot. But now, Coach," Martin instructed, "I need you to do something else for me."

"Whatever it is, I am here for you and your family, Martin. What do you need?" Coach Mac replied.

"I need you to take Jamarcus back to the game." Reaching out to hold Jamarcus by the arm, Martin said, "I needed to see you. I love you, son. So much . . ." Martin's emotions welled up strongly, and he paused for a moment to reset himself.

"Dad, I'm not leaving you, or Mom, or our family. You are more important to me than any game—" Jamarcus protested.

"Jamarcus, you have two families," Martin Denton interrupted. "We are your first family—you proved that by leaving your team to come here. But your other family needs you more than we do right now—and they need Coach Mac to be there, too. I am really okay. And I'll be okay when you get back as a three-time state champion." Martin winked at his son as a mischievous smile covered his face, "Besides, Coach Walker's going to wind up in a hospital bed right next to me if he has to try to win without you."

Martin looked toward Coach Mac, "That kid's been through a lot. The Northfield Nation doesn't need two heart attacks in one night. Jamarcus needs to go back."

"Mom?" Jamarcus pleaded.

"Go, Jarmarcus," she implored. "We're fine."

"Yeah, you've got to go, Jamarcus," Chris offered. "And I want to go with you. Coach Mac, let me drive all of us back in my car." Chris hesitated, then said, "Nothing personal, but I'll get us there faster."

Jamarcus remained unconvinced. "I don't know, Pops. . . I don't know if I can leave you right now."

"Son, you're not really leaving me. You're just temporarily out of my sight. Now, go take care of your other family," Martin said. "GO, son!" he demanded as he nodded his head toward the door.

Jamarcus looked upward and prayed. He looked toward his dad and smiled. He looked toward Coach Mac and exclaimed, "Let's go get us a championship!"

They hustled downstairs, ran quickly through the parking lot to their car and jumped in, and headed toward the coliseum. "Hurry up, bro. Halftime's almost over," Jamarcus urged. As they approached a yellow light about two hundred yards away, Jamarcus yelled, "You can beat it!" Chris gunned the accelerator. He entered the intersection a full two seconds after the light had already turned red. Several cars honked angrily as Jamarcus frantically scanned behind them for any sign of police lights.

"Whatever the outcome of this game, Jamarcus," Coach Mac said as Chris turned his Nissan into the Sequoia Coliseum parking lot. "Enjoy the moment. Play with passion, trust the process, and lead with humility. Jamarcus, these are your last moments on the court as a Warrior—lead them like a warrior."

A handful of basketball junkies and old-timers in the coliseum were old enough to recall Willis Reed's dramatic return to Madison Square Garden in game seven of the 1970 NBA finals. Northfield Nation fans would each later swear that Jamarcus Denton's re-entry was as just as magical as Reed's historical moment.

As Northfield warmed up for the second half, Jamarcus entered through the fan entrance of the coliseum. Blowing past security, he sprinted full speed until he reached his teammates.

Northfield players instantly mobbed him. Zeke grabbed Jamarcus around the neck with his left hand, rubbing him comically and affectionately on the head with the knuckles of his right. "Man, am I glad to see you. How's Pops? Is he okay? Is he really okay?" Derrick allowed the chaos to work its way out for a moment.

Jamarcus finally made his way out of the mosh pit of players, cheerleaders, and over-zealous Northfield students. Without saying a word, Jamarcus winked at Coach Walker. In his typical "all business" approach, Jamarcus quickly busied himself with stretching and warming up. He had less than three minutes.

Derrick had gotten down to business as well. He and Coach Dale quickly adjusted their second half strategy to include Jamarcus. Having concluded their plans, Derrick surveyed the scene unfolding before him. He watched Coach Cohen of Colliersville come over to shake Jamarcus' hand. He watched Chris Denton settle into his seat, next to Coach Mac, Gracie Mac, and Nikki.

"Wow," he said to no one in particular. Then he turned toward Carlene who stood next to him. With a huge smile, he said, "Let's win a state championship, Coach Dale."

Derrick gathered the revitalized Warriors for a quick huddle. "Listen closely." Derrick spoke with carefully chosen words. "We've got a lot of work to do. And a very short time to do it in." Derrick circled the huddle with his eyes. "Every possession matters. I need you to play with a sense of urgency—because every play is urgent."

Derrick rose up from the huddle to see the clock, *:30, :29.* Dropping back into the huddle, he also dropped his emotional guard. "Having Jamarcus with us for the second half means a lot of things," he said as he patted Jamarcus on the shoulder. With a large smile, he added, "But it's definitely proof that God answers prayers!"

"Can I get a witness?" Rico chimed in.

Derrick downshifted into a more business-like voice, "Okay, team, we're down eight. And Jamarcus hasn't even warmed up—"

"I'm ready, Coach Walker—don't worry about me!" Jamarcus interrupted.

"Are you stretched out enough?" Derrick asked.

"Yes, sir! Ready to get the W!" Jamarcus proclaimed.

Derrick stared back at Jamarcus. He sincerely doubted that Jamarcus was actually ready to go. Derrick closed his eyes. Opening them, Derrick told Jamarcus, "You're in."

As soon as the team ended their "WE ARE! NORTHFIELD!" chant, the buzzer sounded. The players began to break the huddle. "One more thing—quickly!" Derrick motioned them back.

"All of you, right now, look to the Northfield Nation." Everyone knew where to focus their attention. "Let's send Coach Mac a message. I want you to take your right fist, all together, and pound it on your chest twice, then point to Coach Mac. Ready? 1, 2, 3, Go!"

Immediately Coach Mac responded with the same motion. A referee blew his whistle, then ordered Derrick, "Let's play, Coach!"

Jamarcus' return to the Northfield lineup was everything Derrick had expected, both good and bad. His athleticism and leadership gave an immediate boost of confidence to the team. At the same time, Jamarcus' timing, and his shot, were just off. The lack of flow, combined with his amped-up energy level, also contributed to two quick fouls. As a result, five minutes into the third quarter, Colliersville had stretched its lead back to eleven.

With 2:47 to go in the quarter, however, Thor scored a tip in after an impressive offensive rebound. Zeke made a brilliant steal on the ensuing end bounds pass, giving him an easy lay-up.

The whole building felt the moment shift. A missed shot by the Spartans set up the Warriors for the last shot of the third quarter. Patiently, the Warriors ran their motion offense for almost one minute of clock time. Sensing the loss of momentum, the Spartans' defense ramped up their intensity to a whole new level.

Jamarcus called for the ball from Zeke. The clock wound down to :12. Taking a page from the LeBron James playbook. Jamarcus rocked his defender back and forth with wide crossover dribbles. He took a jab step to the right, then hesitated. As the defender leaned back on his heels, Jamarcus exploded to the left, and in two steps he dropped a soft finger roll over the front of the rim.

The Bezerkers, the cheerleaders, and the entire Northfield Nation unleashed the full fury of their Warrior passion. Coach Mac hugged and kissed Gracie. Gracie then high fived Nikki who was wildly chanting, "Skol! Skol! Skol!"

The scoreboard read: *Colliersville 48, Northfield 43.*

"Right where we want them, men. Right where we want them!" Derrick shouted as he fist-bumped his players returning to the bench.

"Any thoughts, Coach Dale?" Derrick asked as the players settled into the huddle.

"Defense. It's all about defensive effort. You defend well; they don't recover the momentum. You defend well, our offense will take care of itself." Coach Dale smiled as she increased her tempo and volume. "You defend well for eight minutes and you go home three-peat state champions."

"That's right!" Jamarcus said as he furiously clapped his hands.

"We got this! This game is ours!" Zeke yelled as he pumped his clenched fists.

"We shouldn't be here, men," Derrick said, his voice layered with gratitude and love for his players. Derrick wrapped his arms around Rico and Thor, who were leaned over next to him. Each player, as well as Carlene and Joey, wrapped their arms around each other in the circle. "There's no way a team overcomes what we've overcome, unless . . . Unless . . ." he repeated, "they do it the Northfield Way."

CHAPTER 29

alling the Warriors to one more seemingly impossible uphill battle, Derrick yelled, "Like Coach Mac says, 'Love creates a way.' Using all the love that we have in this circle and in those stands," Derrick motioned his head back toward the shrieking Northfield Nation, "let's create a way. WE ARE!"

"WARRIORS!"

Beginning with Thor's inbound pass to Zeke at the start of the fourth quarter, the Northfield Warriors took the floor like a category-five hurricane. By the time the clock read 3:00 left in the game, the Warriors were up by two—and threatening to pull away.

Coach Cohen called a 30-second timeout to refocus his reeling Spartans. The Colliersville five walked toward their bench dejectedly, with heads down and shoulders slumped. The Northfield five sprinted to the sidelines, waving their arms to pump up the crowd.

Derrick stepped into the frenzied huddle and channeled his inner Coach Mac. "This game is not over!" he yelled sternly. The players settled down and locked their focus on Derrick.

"Those Spartans are champions, just like you. And they are hungry, just like you. They're not going down without a fight," Derrick challenged. Keeping his instructions simple, he added, "Defend. Rebound. Take care of the ball. Every possession is your next step toward the championship. Three minutes—we need three minutes from everyone, including the support of the bench. WE ARE!"

"NORTHFIELD!!"

Both Derrick and Carlene had played in meaningful NCAA tournament games. Each had also attended significant rivalry games among national powers like Duke and North Carolina on the men's side and UConn and Notre Dame on the women's side. Both, however, shook their heads in disbelief as the decibel level in the gym raised well above jet engine level.

Derrick used a rotation of Thor Thornton defensively and Billy Connors offensively on alternating possessions. Rightly executed, the strategy promised a high degree of potential success. In the real world, in real-time, however, anything could happen.

With just over a minute to go, the Spartans went on a 5-1 run to take a 62-60 lead. Coach Walker called a timeout, both to slow the Spartans and to prep his team for the final minute.

The Warriors final approach would be simple. They would work the ball inside out, looking for exactly the right opportunity to make an easy two. However, he instructed the young warriors, "If they give one of our guards a wide open three, as long as you are shooting in rhythm, you have the green light." Derrick's final commands were, "If you get into trouble or get caught in a battle for a loose ball, use a timeout—we have two left."

As the players left the huddle, Derrick yelled anxiously, "Whatever, you do, take care of the ball!" Derrick's eyes met Carlene's.

"You, okay? Derrick asked.

"I can't breathe," Carlene said jokingly.

"I'm not sure I want to," Derrick said as he glanced at the scoreboard.

The Spartans' inspired defense exerted constant, smothering pressure on the Warriors. With 31 seconds left on the game clock, the Spartans deflected a pass from Zeke to Billy. The ball bounced off Billy's foot, careening toward the foul lane. Rico rushed to the ball. He instinctively tossed it in the direction of Jamarcus, four feet away. Jamarcus barely outmuscled two large Spartan defenders, who were actually in a better position to capture the loose ball.

Jamarcus spun to his left to find the lane wide open. Even before he exploded for a thunderous tomahawk dunk, the Northfield Nation erupted with euphoric anticipation. Like a volcano blowing off its lid, the Bezerkers reached an even higher level of explosive celebration.

Coach Cohen called a timeout with 23 seconds to go, shaking his head with a disgusted, "I can't believe this" look. The Spartans appeared momentarily staggered by a lost opportunity, a gym-rattling dunk, and a tie score.

The Warriors' bench players stormed onto the court, greeting their teammates with high-fives, dance moves, chest-bumps and yells.

Derrick was still shaken. Watching Rico do exactly the opposite of what he had instructed sent him into an anxious tailspin. Jamarcus' fierce dunk, however, had immediately catapulted his emotions to heights of ecstasy. Derrick felt dizzy.

To the best of his ability, Derrick refocused himself on the moment at hand. The Warriors had to defend for 23 more seconds just to get to overtime. Derrick substituted Thor once again for Billy, and instructed his guards to battle against the Spartans' guards with aggressive on-ball pressure. He stressed defending the open shot. He also reminded them to communicate, to avoid fouls, and to rebound "at all costs."

"Overtime," Derrick concluded, "is a much better option than a foul or an offensive rebound. WE ARE!"

"NORTHFIELD!"

What happened next could never be fully explained by Derrick. As soon as Derrick saw both teams' players on the court, he suddenly realized his lineup was all wrong.

Even though they only need a two-point basket to win, Coach Cohen had chosen to go with a much, much smaller line-up. At no point in the season had the Spartans used this smaller line-up when tied or ahead at the end of a game. Coach Cohen was playing chess. Derrick had been caught playing checkers.

Impulsively, Derrick screamed, "Billy!" as he looked toward the bench. Derrick grabbed Billy by the jersey. With the ball on the verge of being inbounded, he thrust Billy toward half court, shouting, "Get in there for Thor."

Standing on the other end of the court, Thor was far away from the inbounds. Caught up in the frenzy of the moment, Billy bypassed the scorer's table. Running as fast as he could, Billy repeatedly yelled, "Thor, Thor!"

No ref motioned Billy into the game. No buzzer sounded for the substitution.

At that precise moment, the ref handed the ball to the Spartan ready to make the inbound pass. Coach Dale instantly recognized what was happening. She jumped out of her seat, screaming, "Billy, get back, get back!"

Derrick raced toward the ref, motioning wildly for a timeout, while screaming at the top of his lungs, "Timeout, timeout!" He was too late. The ball had been inbounded.

The entire Spartan bench immediately leapt to their feet. "Six men! Six men!" they shrieked repeatedly.

With 21 seconds left on the clock, tied with the powerhouse Colliersville Spartans in the state championship game, the Northfield bench was called for a technical foul.

"Illegal substitution. Six men on the court," the ref declared. Two free throw shots were awarded to the Spartans. To make matters worse, they would also retain possession of the ball.

Pandemonium broke on both sides of the coliseum. The Spartan faithful roared their approval, both with cheers and jeers. The Warrior fans booed, irrationally but incessantly.

Derrick collapsed into his chair. He held his head in his hands, muttering over and over, "This can't be happening!"

Coach Dale, acting more like a big sister than an assistant coach, placed her arm around Derrick's shoulders. Very briefly, she sat in complete silence.

Derrick's eyes raised to find Coach Mac in the stands. Coach Mac was hugging Gracie. She seemed distraught. Coach Mac, however, appeared to be at peace. When his gaze met Derrick's, Coach Mac simply nodded and smiled. As he pointed upward with his right index finger, his eyes followed the path of his hand.

Five despondent players shuffled back to the Warrior bench. Their presence startled Derrick back into his present reality.

Instinctively, Derrick wanted to scream at Billy, "What were you thinking? Why didn't you check in at the scorer's table?" But he knew better. It wasn't the fifteen-year old's fault. He was to blame.

Derrick gathered the disheartened Northfield squad around him. "Everybody lock arms. Come in close." The team locked their arms. Derrick pulled the circle in tight. Even so, with heads down and eyes empty, the players' hearts seemed far away.

"I get it," Derrick began. "After all we have been through. The loss of Coach Mac. The loss of Jamarcus for half a season—and the first half of this game. Martin Denton's heart attack. The way you've fought and fought. And now I've let you down."

"It's okay, Coach," Jamarcus said half-heartedly. "It happens."

"Well, it happened. That's for sure," Derrick spoke with a deep sigh. "I made a stupid, serious, bone-headed mistake."

Derrick turned to Billy whose eyes were swollen with tears, "Billy, you didn't fail this team. I did. And I'm sorry."

Derrick shifted gears. The players' heads lifted slightly. One by one, their body language lifted as well.

As Derrick set the strategy for the next 23 seconds, Lewis Oliver hit the first technical foul shot. The players winced as they heard the Spartan cheering section break into a full-blown party.

"The game is still within our reach," Derrick pleaded. "But we have to get the ball back within the first ten seconds. We have to get a turnover or force a bad shot. If not, we foul and take our chances. Understood?"

Everyone nodded. Still, any rise in hope was tempered immediately by the sound of the second free throw swishing gently through the net.

"64-62 Colliersville. Spartans' ball following the technical."

As Derrick expected, Coach Cohen called a full timeout to prepare his team for the final seconds. Confidently, the Spartans leaned in as their coach shouted his final instructions above the noise of the crowd.

Derrick huddled his beleaguered team as well. Just as he began to speak, however, the Bezerkers and the entire Northfield Nation exploded into absolute bedlam. The entire huddle, including Derrick and Carlene, turned their heads in the direction of the Northfield Nation. All eyes eventually landed on Coach Mac and Mrs. Gracie. Standing together at the foot of the stands, they were waving their arms up and down. Surrounded by the Warrior cheerleaders, the Viking Warrior mascot, and a Warrior football linebacker waving an enormous Northfield flag, the McKissacks chanted, "Skol! Skol! Skol!"

"I have no idea what to say to that!" Derrick laughed as he drew his players back in. Smiles spread quickly around the huddle. The mood changed in an instant. Derrick's tone reflected the change.

"A few moments ago I was thinking, *How could this be happening to us?* Now," Derrick grinned, "I'm thinking, *Let's make something happen!*"

Derrick explained, in great detail, a well-rehearsed defensive strategy. The team had practiced this exact scenario dozens of times. At any point, from the 21 second mark to the 15 second mark, every player would do whatever was necessary to create a turnover. Those six seconds would be considered "high risk, high reward" moments. If, after 15 seconds, they had failed to create a turnover, then the task would switch to fouling a Colliersville player.

"The next foul," Derrick reminded his team, "puts them on the line with a one and one. And," Derrick pleaded, "If at all possible, get the ball out of Oliver's hands."

The buzzer sounded. "Coach, you've got to get your players on the court," the ref warned.

Derrick hurriedly explained his vision for their last possession. "If they get to the free throw line, grab the rebound! Attack, attack, attack! Put the ball in Zeke's or Jamarcus' hands," Derrick implored as he pounded his right fist up and down on the palm of his left hand. "Be quick, but don't rush. We take a solid two to tie or a wide open three to win."

The huddle broke just as the ref said, "You don't want another technical, Coach." Derrick nodded apologetically.

"When I grow up, I want to be just like you, Coach," Coach Dale said with a smirk as the players took their places on the court.

"You need to aim higher, Coach," was Derrick's deadpan response.

On the Spartans' initial inbounds pass to Oliver, Rico got a hand on the ball, deflecting it out of bounds. Derrick and his players argued that the ball had been deflected off Oliver's hands, but to no avail.

On the next inbounds play, Zeke forced the inbounds pass away from Oliver. The inbounds passer made a sharp pass to the only open Spartan player, Adrian Lane. As Lane, a sophomore, dribbled toward Oliver to make a handoff, Billy reached across Lane's body. The whistle stopped the game clock at 00:17.

Derrick loudly applauded Billy's improvisational play. While the foul occurred earlier than Derrick had instructed, it also put the Spartans' least experienced starter on the line at the most crucial moment of the game.

Just as the young Spartan stepped to the line, Derrick started the motion of calling his last timeout. Instead, Derrick lowered his hands and closed his mouth. In a split second, he had weighed trying to "ice" the shooter against saving the timeout. Carlene's observation, "That kid looks scared to death," had tipped the scales. Derrick decided to keep the timeout in case of an emergency.

Lane received the ball from the ref, took three hard dribbles, then took a deep breath. He bent his knees and launched the most important shot of his young life. The ball bounced hard off the rim, ricocheting sharply to the right.

Jamarcus Denton swept in like a hawk sinking its talons into its prey. He grabbed the ball with his massive hands and immediately looked for Zeke on the fast break. By the time the ball was forwarded on the break to Zeke, there were fourteen seconds to go. Zeke pulled up at the three-point line. He turned to look for Jamarcus, whom he knew would be trailing the break in a full-speed sprint.

00:13, 00:12.

The Spartan defense eliminated the pass to Jamarcus, so Zeke looked back door to Rico. As the pass left Zeke's hands, Oliver stepped in front, deflecting the ball with his fingertips.

00:11, 00:10.

Once again, with everything at stake, the ball was on the floor.

Jamarcus lunged for the ball. He secured it to his chest. Before any Spartan had gotten near him, Jamarcus' hands had formed a "T" around the ball. As he did so, Jamarcus screamed, "TIMEOUT!" three times. With the possession arrow in favor of the Spartans, Jamarcus took no chances on the Spartans getting their hands on the ball.

The ref's whistle stopped the clock at 00:08.

"Nice!" Carlene exclaimed.

The only remaining timeout for Northfield was a thirty-second timeout—too little time to improvise. So, Derrick chose "Viking Express Option 2." Viking Express was a play Northfield had run for years. The play utilized misdirection to get the ball to a shooting guard coming off a screen in the corner. Option 2, however, had been created and practiced for a situation just like the one the Warriors were facing. Down two, only a few seconds left in the game—a game they had to win.

Viking Express Option 2 featured Rico as a decoy, with the real plan to result in either Zeke shooting a three off the wing or Zeke feeding the ball to Jamarcus for a shot in the lane. In practice, the play took exactly five seconds to execute. Given that the shot would take a good second or two to release, the eight seconds would be pretty much gone by the end of the play.

Neither team had any timeouts left. Eight seconds, one play, and a state championship on the line. Derrick hoped for overtime. He prayed for a win.

As the huddle broke, Derrick spoke as softly as the background noise would allow. Smiling he said, "You've worked hard for this. Your hearts are so strong, courageous, passionate. So, go have fun! It doesn't get any better than this! WE ARE!"

"NORTHFIELD!"

As the players broke the huddle, Carlene leaned over to Derrick. "Are you having fun, Coach?"

"Uhh, that would be a 'no,'" Derrick replied dryly. "You?"

"Ask me in eight seconds," Carlene said through clenched teeth.

"Here we go," Derrick announced as the ball inbounded toward Zeke. Once Zeke had the ball in hands, Derrick shifted from his seat to kneeling on the floor. Behind him, the whole bench sat locked arm in arm, leaning forward. As Zeke took possession on the inbounds play, Derrick lost awareness of anything but the movement of the basketball. The play unfolded across eight long, slow seconds. Derrick felt more like he was watching a movie than playing an active part in the game's outcome.

00:07.

Gesturing unconsciously as if he were a puppeteer pulling strings on a cast of marionettes, Derrick's arms mimicked the motion of Zeke feeding the ball to Jamarcus at the high post. Jamarcus took one dribble as he spun to draw the double team. He pushed a bullet of a chest pass toward Rico who had positioned himself in the corner off of a screen by Thor. At that very moment, Zeke brushed by Jamarcus' wide body. He raced to the wing to receive a touch pass already on the way from Rico. Jamarcus rolled to the basket.

00:04

Not expecting Rico to pass to Zeke for the three, the defense completely sold out on keeping the ball out of Jamarcus' hands.

00:02

Zeke released a three pointer just above Oliver's outstretched hand as the clock hit 00:01.

A deafening hush came over the Sequoia Coliseum. All eyes focused on a 29.5-inch-circumference leather ball as it floated nineteen feet, nine inches toward an orange metal circle attached to a clear piece of thick Plexiglas.

CHAPTER 30

n the hushed silence of the last second on the clock, the entire coliseum heard the distinct "swoosh" of the basketball through the net. Northfield players screamed to the rooftops then collapsed into a mountainous pile on the Sequoia Coliseum floor. Bezerkers rained down on the court like a summer thunderstorm unleashing its full fury. Older fans remained in the stands. Everyone in the Northfield Nation, young and old, celebrated with equal abandon. They hugged, danced, and shouted "Skol! Skol! Skol!" to the tops of their lungs.

Derrick Walker collapsed onto his knees. He sat motionless as the world swirled and danced around him. Suddenly, Derrick shot up like a rocket and yelled, "Coach Cohen!" Desperately hoping it wasn't too late, Derrick pushed his way toward the Spartans' bench.

Derrick had to press through layer after layer of crazed fans running in every direction. Much to his surprise, and joy, Coach Cohen still stood near the Spartan bench. "I don't know what to say, Coach," Derrick said with disbelief. "There's no way you deserved to lose this game."

Coach Cohen responded, "Well, honestly, I feel the same way. But, at the same time, you deserved to win. Make no mistake, Coach Walker, you've done a heckuva job holding this thing together." Coach Cohen then instructed his much younger counterpart, "Right now, you need to go celebrate with your team. We'll talk soon."

The two embraced, then Derrick walked past Coach Cohen toward the dejected Spartan bench. Derrick said to the players, "Keep your heads up. You're all winners in my book." A few players attempted half-hearted smiles. Two players, including the superstar, Lewis Oliver, managed a weak, but sincere, "Thanks, Coach. Congratulations."

As Derrick turned back toward his players, Nikki blindsided him. She jumped into his arms, kissing him square on the lips. Standing back on the ground, Nikki poured out an adrenaline-fueled stream of words. "You did it! You did it! I am so proud of you! You're a state champion, Derrick Walker. Can you believe it?"

Derrick leaned over to kiss Nikki again. This one lingered much longer than the first. As soon as their lips parted, Derrick shouted, "I love you, Nikki Coles!"

Derrick grabbed Nikki's hand and began weaving his way toward the players at center court. Just as they arrived, Coach Mac came alongside Derrick. Grabbing him from the side, Coach Mac pulled Derrick into his chest. "I am so proud of you, Derrick Walker. I knew you would do it!"

Taking Gracie's hand, Coach Mac said, "I told you, didn't I, Gracie!"

Gracie nodded in Derrick's direction, "He did, Derrick. He told me, right after that last timeout, 'We're going to win this game. Just watch.'"

Turning back to Derrick, Coach Mac spoke, "I never doubted it, D. I never doubted you. From the day I collapsed to Zeke's last second shot. I knew your love would create a way."

Derrick stood speechless. Before he could recover enough to find words to thank Coach Mac, the players converged upon them.

Rico and Zeke began to hoist Coach Mac onto their shoulders. Gracie thwarted the plan. She was adamant, "Put him down, boys."

"Okay," Rico said. Turning to Derrick, Rico enthusiastically suggested, "We'll carry Coach D!" Soon Derrick was awkwardly escorted across the floor on the players' unsteady shoulders.

Once they returned Derrick to the floor, he began to high-five each player. Halfway through the team, Derrick found himself wrapped up from behind. A pair of long arms lifted Derrick more than a foot off the ground.

"All right, all right, guys," Derrick protested. "That's enough for one night. Put me down, Thor."

Derrick turned to harass Thor. As he turned around, Derrick's eyes widened. "Parker? What the . . . ?" Slapping his palms on top of his head, he quizzed Parker, "For real. What are you doing here? What's going on?"

"I had to be here. I'm your brother, man." Parker wrapped his arms around Derrick's. He squeezed him so hard he could barely breathe. "I love you, Derrick. And I'm going to be here for you."

"I love you, too, Parker," Derrick replied. The moment added one more surreal experience to the most surreal week of his life.

"Well, hey, we can talk more tomorrow. I've already arranged with Nikki to see you both. Right now, you need to go join your team," Parker said with an affectionate slap on Derrick's back. As Derrick headed off to join the team still huddled around Coach Mac, Parker yelled, "And you've got to tell me all about you and Nikki. I need to catch up on all the good news!"

By the time all the celebrations and ceremonies were completed, it was nearly 9:45 p.m. Derrick decided to walk one last time back through the heavy wooden door leading back into the victors' locker room. Staring into its empty stillness, Derrick reflected on the week, the win, and the celebration. He felt true joy, deep relief, and almost total exhaustion.

A voice from the far corner of the barely lit room startled him. "Hey, State Champion Coach."

"Coach Mac? Is that you?" Derrick asked. He squinted to recognize the shadowy form coming towards him.

"Yes, sir!" Coach Mac exclaimed. Moving out of the shadows he engulfed Derrick in a bear hug. "You did it, Coach Walker."

"No, sir," Derrick corrected as they released their embrace. "Actually, they did it, Coach. And you did it. I just tried not to mess it up—and I actually I did mess it up! But we won anyway!" Derrick laughed.

Coach Mac joined the laughter. "Well, son, I have to admit you made it harder than it had to be!" Coach Mac's tone and facial expression quickly turned more serious. "D, don't miss what happened here tonight. And this week. This whole season. You lived and you led the Northfield Way. The way Coach Norman taught me. The way I passed it on to you. The way you passed it on to this team in the worst of circumstances." Coach Mac then spoke slowly, placing heavy emphasis on every word, "Your leadership has been exceptional."

"Well, that's definitely a gift of God's grace," Derrick smiled.

"Of course it is, D. It's all a gift," Coach Mac affirmed. Intentionally shifting the conversation, he said, "It's getting late, Coach. I think it's time for me to go home."

As the two turned to exit, Derrick said wistfully, "Well, at least the worst is behind me. It can't get any harder than that."

"You keep telling yourself that, Coach Walker," Coach Mac chuckled as he slapped Derrick on the back playfully. "You just keep telling yourself that."

Derrick opened his mouth to speak, then swallowed his words. He knew Coach Mac's jovial, casual comments were layered with wisdom far deeper than he could grasp tonight.

"I've got a long way to go," Derrick reasoned to himself. Then he looked up to Coach Mac. Seeing a face full of joyous satisfaction, Derrick thought, "But I'm on the right path. And I'm definitely following the right person. That's the greatest gift of all."

"You've got be kidding! It's 5:40 in the morning?"

After less than four hours of restless sleep, Derrick sat up in his bed. Adrenaline still coursed through body like water pounding its way through a fireman's hose.

Derrick decided to give in to the restlessness. He turned on the lamp next to his hotel room bed. Reaching into this backpack lying in the floor beside the nightstand, Derrick pulled out his journal and a pen.

"Maxim 5," he said aloud. "Time to finish this round and start over."

Fueled by a rush of frenetic energy, Derrick wrote his reflections rapidly.

MAXIM 5
HUMILITY

My first ambition will be to serve with strength, courage, and humility.

"My life is best lived in the service of others," Coach Mac says.
Humility. That's some crazy stuff.
The more I serve Nikki, the more she loves me.
The more honest I am about my weaknesses, the more courage I have. The more love I give, the stronger a leader I become.
The more I humble myself, the more the players respect my authority. Seems so backwards. But, like Coach Mac keeps telling me, "That's how God's grace works. We empty. God fills."

My prayer tonight: Help me to be humble, like Jesus. Like you. To create a way for those who come after me. Like Coach Mac did for me. Like Coach Norman did for Coach Mac.

Derrick re-read his journal entry. He clarified his prayer.

But not all at once. Please! I think you've humbled me enough lately. We're good, right? Let's take a break on that for a while— like a year. Or two?

Derrick put down his journal and pen. He went to the bathroom and brushed his teeth. It was 6:04 a.m. The Starbucks across the street would be open by now. He didn't need the caffeine, but a grande cappuccino just sounded good at the moment.

Derrick picked up his hotel room key card, his wallet, and his phone. As he stuck his phone in his pocket, it vibrated to signal an incoming call. Checking the screen, Derrick didn't recognize the number.

"Derrick, this is Amanda McKissack." Derrick immediately identified a shallow, strained tone in her voice. He knew Coach Mac's daughter wouldn't be calling him unless it was something urgent. His chest tightened and his stomach turned as he heard Amanda sniffle quietly on the other end of the phone.

"Yes, Amanda, what's wrong?" Derrick asked in a panic.

"My dad is gone, Derrick . . . he's gone. He fell asleep last night and never woke up." Choking back a wave of grieving sobs, Amanda added, "You're the first person Mom asked me to call. He loved you like a son, Derrick."

The phone dropped from Derrick's hands as his knees gave way. He crumpled onto the hotel bed, barely able to sit up. Several seconds passed before Derrick regained enough composure to retrieve his phone.

Derrick said numbly, "I'm sorry, Amanda. I . . . don't know what to say."

"For now," Amanda shifted into a more monotone, business-like tone, "Could you please call Nikki?"

"Of course, and. . ." Derrick's voice was as dazed as the glassy-eyed look on his face. "Should we come over or . . . what should I do? Do you need us there?"

"Not yet. I'll call when Mom's ready," Amanda replied, her voice beginning to tremble again. "For now, just let Nikki know." Then, rising to the occasion in a voice that echoed her father, Amanda coached Derrick, "Now's the time for you and Nikki to be together, Derrick. You need to be with her—and she's going to need you, too. Neither of you need to be alone with this."

"Yeah. Right. Okay," Derrick stammered. "I'll call her right away." As he began to put the phone down, Derrick quickly brought it back to his face and added, "He was like my dad, Amanda."

"I know." Amanda spoke softly as her grief once again rose to the surface. Inhaling deeply, she continued, "You know, Derrick, last night, Mom told Dad, 'D is the future of the Northfield Way, Johnny.'" A sob momentarily overcame her, but she kept pressing through to finish her thought. "But Dad—always the coach—said, in his typical way, 'No, Gracie, Derrick Walker is the present *and* the future of the Northfield Way." Amanda's voice cracked, then recovered. "Somehow, I think he knew."

Derrick thought back to Coach Mac's comments in the empty locker room. "I think so, too." As the weight of the moment begin to press into his chest, Derrick said tearfully, "Amanda, I really don't know how I'm going to get through all of this."

"By grace. And with love," Amanda said comfortingly. "The Northfield Way."

EPILOGUE

MAY

"Only the well-loved love well."

Coach John McKissack

errick spread a small Northfield Warrior blanket near the end of the dock. He settled onto the blanket first, then motioned Nikki to join him.

Nikki wrapped her sweater tightly around her chest. The sweater provided an extra layer of protection against the cold spring breezes blowing gustily across Echo Lake.

Sitting down in front of Derrick, Nikki leaned back against his chest. "Put your arms around me," Nikki pleaded with a shiver in her voice. "I'm cold."

Derrick happily obliged her request, wrapping his arms cozily around hers.

"D, what was this morning like for you? Being at your first graduation as a Northfield teacher and as the new Warriors head coach?" Nikki leaned her head back to see Derrick's face. Then she asked tenderly, "And being there without Coach Mac?"

Derrick squeezed Nikki tighter. He gazed thoughtfully over her shoulder into the distance. Derrick circled his lips and blew away strands of auburn hair blowing in wisps across his mouth. Then he replied, "Sad. It felt sad."

"Because of Coach Mac," she asked?

"Yes, and . . ." Derrick tilted further back, allowing Nikki to fall deeper into his lap. Leaning to one side, he looked into her eyes. "Do you remember me telling you about the dreams I buried beneath these waters?" Derrick raised his eyes toward the lake's choppy dark surface.

"Of course, I remember," Nikki said softly. She untucked her hands and rested them tenderly on Derrick's arms.

"Well, I thought a lot about those old dreams today. I always feel sad when I think about those wasted years." Derrick sighed deeply, then slowly raised Nikki off his chest. He repositioned himself so he could sit face to face. Smiling happily, he said, "But that's not all I thought about."

"Really? What else did you think about during graduation, Mr. Walker?" Nikki teased.

"About my new dreams," Derrick said.

"What new dreams?" Nikki quizzed.

"The ones I buried in the lake yesterday." Derrick offered a coy smile then turned his eyes towards a post at the end of the dock.

"You buried your dreams? Again? Yesterday?" Nikki asked, looking at Derrick with complete puzzlement.

"Yes. And I'm going to need you to resurrect them from their watery grave," Derrick said with the dramatic flair.

"And how am I supposed to do that?" Nikki questioned.

Derrick remained silent. He turned and stared at Nikki with a peaceful expression of deep contentment.

"Well, are you going to tell me?" Nikki asked, her curiosity growing by the minute.

"Yes, I am." Derrick pointed toward the post. "See the rope around that post?"

Nikki nodded, "Yes."

"Pull it up until it's all the way out of the water," Derrick instructed.

"I don't know what you're up to, Coach Walker," Nikki said. She then scooted over to the post and pulled the wet rope up several inches at a time. At the end of the rope, she found a small black bag made of thick waterproof fabric.

"What's this?" Nikki asked.

"It's a dry sack, to keep things from getting wet," Derrick replied.

Nikki sighed. "I know that, D," she said as she shook her head side to side. "You borrowed this dry sack from me last spring when you went camping,"

"Oh, you're right, Nik. Sorry about that," Derrick apologized.

Nikki rolled her eyes playfully, then questioned, "Okay, but what's in it?"

"Open it. You'll see," Derrick said.

Nikki carefully opened the dry sack, then pulled out a small blue spiral notebook. "Is this. . . ?"

"Yes," Derrick interrupted. "My journal. I told you when I started writing in a journal that there would be a day when I would want you to read it. Today's the day."

"D, that's so sweet. I'll start with day one," Nikki said.

"Wait!" Derrick interrupted again. "Day one is actually for later. First, I need you to help me resurrect the dreams I buried in my journal yesterday. You're the only one who can do it, Nikki."

"How?" Nikki asked, her voice edging toward impatience.

"By turning to the three marked pages," Derrick said. He pointed to three yellow sticky notes protruding unevenly from the journal's side.

Nikki sat up on her knees and turned to the first marked page. It read, *"I dream of being a great coach. Nikki, will you help me learn to be a better leader?"* Nikki smiled at Derrick, then turned to the second marked page.

"Wait," Derrick said, "Will you?"

Nikki tilted her head and looked skyward, pretending to be pondering her answer. "Yes, I will, Coach," she said with an exaggerated nod.

"Next." Nikki read, *"I dream of being a great dad. Nikki, will you help me learn to love and guide our son well?"*

"I don't have to think about that one. Absolutely, yes!" Nikki answered.
"Last one," Derrick said.

A strong gust sent a chill across the dock. The force of the wind nearly blew the journal out of Nikki's hands. She sat further back on her legs, pulling her sweater close once more. Nikki flattened the journal onto her lap to secure it, then turned to the third marked page. It read, *"I dream of being a great husband. Nikki Coles, will you marry me?"*

Nikki gasped. She covered her mouth with one hand and clutched the journal with the other. Her chest heaved. With eyes swimming in tears, she looked up to see Derrick bent down on one knee. She shook her head back and forth in disbelief, even as she kept reassuring herself the moment was indeed real.

"Nikki Coles, will you marry me?" Derrick said longingly.

"Yes, Derrick Walker! Yes! A thousand times, yes!" Nikki said joyfully.

Derrick moved toward Nikki to take her into his arms. As the two embraced, Derrick said, "I love you so much, Nikki."

With tears falling down onto Derrick's shoulder, Nikki said, "I love you, D. I can't wait to be your wife."

Derrick placed the engagement ring on Nikki's fingers as she gasped, "Oh, Derrick, it's so beautiful." Extending her arm and holding her hand in front of her face, Nikki repeated, "It's so beautiful."

Derrick squeezed Nikki as tightly as he could.

"Ohhh," Nikki said, pulling away and gasping for breath. She then said, "Whew!" as she inhaled a deep breath.

"Nikki, are you okay?" Derrick moved to her side to support her.

"I'm fine, but your son just gave me a sharp kick, right in the ribs. I don't think he likes you squeezing me so tight," Nikki replied as she massaged the muscles around her wounded rib.

"Or maybe he's just working on his vertical leap. He'll need that for rebounding," Derrick said with a sly grin.

"He's still in the womb, Coach. Isn't it just a bit too early to be working on basketball skills?" Nikki laughed.

"Nikki, this is Northfield! First grade. Toddler years. Second trimester. It's never too early. That's how just what we do it around here. It's the Northfield way."

Nikki playfully smacked Derrick on the head with his blue spiral journal. She took his hand and placed it with her hand on her belly.

"You feel him moving?" Nikki giggled. "That's your son, D. That's John McKissack Walker squirming around in there." Nikki raised herself up, holding her head high to mimic the posture of a proud member of a royal family. "And I'm going to be," she said with a mock British accent, emphasizing every word separately, "Mrs. Derrick Walker."

Derrick patted the place where Mac's head rested against Nikki's belly. "Nik, you know what's been my favorite part of learning to live the Northfield Way?"

"No, what?" Nikki asked as she stroked Derrick's hair gently.

"It led me back to you."

The meaning of life. The wasted years of life. The poor choices of life. God answers the mess of life with one word: GRACE.
Max Lucado

ABOUT THE AUTHOR

Rick Dunn is first and foremost a husband, father, and grandfather. His varied leadership roles throughout his life have included coach, mentor, pastor, teacher, non-profit organizational leader, and university professor. Currently, Rick serves as the Lead Pastor of Fellowship Church, a high school AAU basketball coach with teams based in East Tennessee, and a founding partner in Sequoia Leadership Concepts.

For over thirty-five years Rick and his wife, Teresa—a licensed professional counselor—have invested deeply in the lives of students and young adults. They have three children and two children-in-law (Jessica/Stephen, Zach, Ben/Katie) and two beloved grandsons, James and Abraham. Rick and Teresa make their home in Knoxville, Tennessee.

www.northfieldway.com

ACKNOWLEDGMENTS

I experience the creative process as inherently communal. Even as I sit alone at my computer, I am immersed in the presence of so many lives that have profoundly shaped me and the stories I tell. While I could never capture the depths of their invisible influence in a short paragraph, this is my attempt to say, "I see your impact," and, "Thank you," for your role in the telling of this story. I want to especially mention:

My parents for instilling in me a love of learning. My thirst for learning has unlocked countless doorways to imagination and creation.

The teachers who engaged my mind and my heart: Mr. Harris, Mrs. Blevins, Mr. Stein, Captain McGuire, Mrs. Scroback, Craig Williford, Perry Downs, Mark Senter, Linda Cannell, Ted Ward. You taught me to see the world in the context of a glorious meta-narrative, a story worth learning and telling.

My partners in leadership, Jana, Kevin, Greg, Michael C., Steve, Mike, Kyle, JC, and all the Fellowship elders, pastors, and staff. Your grace and love are woven into the fabric of every leadership story I tell and write.

My writing coach, Arlyn Lawrence, whose gifting and commitment to excellence transformed me as a storyteller. You, Kerry, and the Inspira team "coached me up" into an actual author of a novel!

My numerous "first readers": Jana, Atlee, Shane, Buddy, Carol, Steven, Mike, Barb, Brad, Joe, William, Tomi, Kevin, Keith, John, Doug, Steve, Guille, Angie, Russell, Natalie, and Teresa. Thank you for not telling me, "Stick to your day job," after reading those very rough first drafts.

My executive coach and leadership journey mentor, Dr. Harv Powers. Thank you for inviting me to live in fierce reality. Your truth soaked in grace reframed my story and, therefore, the meaning of this story.

My children, who lived in the story that lies underneath this story. Thank you for engaging your mom and me with the grace and love that keeps our family growing together on this redemptive journey.

My wife, Teresa, who sees me more clearly, loves me more passionately, and supports me more fiercely than I could have ever have imagined possible. Your grace made the writing of this story possible and, more importantly, the living of this story redemptive.

CPSIA information can be obtained
at www.ICGtesting.com
Printed in the USA
LVHW052219021219
639233LV00017B/541/P